William Dillon

Life of John Mitchel

Part 2

William Dillon

Life of John Mitchel
Part 2

ISBN/EAN: 9783337057879

Printed in Europe, USA, Canada, Australia, Japan

Cover: Foto ©Raphael Reischuk / pixelio.de

More available books at **www.hansebooks.com**

LIFE OF JOHN MITCHEL

II.   *a*

LIFE OF JOHN MITCHEL

BY

WILLIAM DILLON

IN TWO VOLUMES
VOL. II.

LONDON
KEGAN PAUL, TRENCH & CO., 1, PATERNOSTER SQUARE
1888

CONTENTS OF VOL. II.

———

CHAPTER I.

CONVICT LIFE (*continued*)—VAN DIEMEN'S LAND—ESCAPE—SAN FRANCISCO
—NEW YORK.

1853.

PAGE

Lotus-eating—An unnatural state for him—Tennyson's " Ulysses "—
Letter from Devin Reilly—Envies Reilly "for being alive"—A
chance of escape offers—Arrival of Smyth—Meeting with Smyth—
O'Brien decides to leave this chance to Mitchel—Buying a horse
from the enemy—First attempt a failure—Illness of Smyth—Another
attempt resolved on—Ride to the police-office, Bothwell—Met by
news that the ship had sailed—No matter; attempt must be made—
Scene in the police-office—Surrendering ticket-of-leave—Mounting
in haste—Charge of breaking his parole—An unfounded charge—A
ride through the woods—A winter night in the mountains—Friendly
settlers—Miller—Baffled attempt to embark—Letter to his mother—
Disguises and adventures—Sails at last—The *Emma*—His family
on board—Sydney—Sails for Tahiti—Joined by his family there—
Under the Stars and Stripes—San Francisco—Banquet, his speech
—Leaves for New York—The Nicaragua route—Havana—Bermuda
on the starboard beam—Reflections—Arrival at New York—End of
" Jail Journal "   I

CHAPTER II.

NEW YORK—TUCALEECHEE COVE.

1853—1856.

His reception at New York—Impressions—Banquet—Reminiscence by
Dr. Thomas Hunter—Prospectus of the *Citizen*—The Know-Nothings
—The slavery question—Mr. Haughton's letter—Controversy with
Beecher—Rage of the abolitionists—Rapid success of the *Citizen*—

PAGE

Controversy with Archbishop Hughes about the temporal power—
Injures the circulation of the paper—Eagerly watching the progress
of the war in Europe—Interview with the Russian Minister—The
Know-Nothing movement—Accepts a banquet at Richmond—Journey
thither, and to Charlottesville and Monticello—Sees that "there
are two nations in the United States"—The University of Virginia
—Oration at Charlottesville—At a New England watering-place—
Release of O'Brien and the other prisoners—Meeting in New York
—Tired of editing, gives up the *Citizen*—Migration to the South—
Knoxville, East Tennessee—Exploring the country—Tucaleechee
Cove—A mountain farm—Letters—How we live "up in here"—A
lecturing tour—The Jesuits in Tucaleechee—Decides on removing to
Knoxville—Building a house, but feeling that he "shan't live long in
it"—Society at Knoxville—Visit to Montvale—"Escaping from the
delightful vale of Tucaleechee"   35

CHAPTER III.

KNOXVILLE—THE "SOUTHERN CITIZEN."

1856—1858.

At Knoxville—Plans for the future—Second lecturing tour—Lecture at
Washington—Shall he resume his profession?—Letter to Dillon—
Mr. Swan—The South needs an organ—The *Southern Citizen*—
Surprise of many of his friends at the line taken by him on slavery—
Letter to Father Kenyon—*Apologia pro vita suâ*—Letter to a lady;
why he prefers the South—His position with regard to slavery, on
what he grounded it—Slavery *versus* free competition—Cash payment
sole nexus—Social organization still a difficulty—Winter of '57 and
'58, lecturing in the southern cities—Letters to Hon. A. H. Stephens
("Last Conquest")—Visit of James Stephens—Autumn of 1858,
Southern Citizen transplanted to Washington—Adieu to Knoxville
friends—Mr. McAdoo—A recitation in the rain 91

CHAPTER IV.

WASHINGTON—PARIS.

1858—1862.

Southern Citizen at Washington—Friends and society there—Visit of
O'Brien—His distinguished reception—His tour in the South and
departure for Europe—Letter to an Irish friend—The true method of
working in Irish politics—His edition of Mangan's poems—1859:
European affairs growing interesting again—Will England be involved
in the war?—The *Southern Citizen* wound up—Sails for France—
Paris—Visits of friends—Despondent about public affairs—Col. Byrne
—M. Marie Martin—Articles in the *Constitutionnel*—Letters—Cannot

PAGE

afford to stay in Paris, "looking out for squalls"—January, 1860: back to New York—A lecturing tour—Brings his family north—A holiday at the seaside—Returns to France, this time with his family —Paris, Rue de l'Est—As a newspaper correspondent—Letter to Mr. and Mrs. Dillon—An exile's Declaration of Rights—His eldest daughter a Catholic—Outbreak of war in America—His sons in the Confederate army—Choisy-le-roi—Visit of O'Brien, last meeting with him—Abortive projects in Ireland—George H. Moore, the O'Donoghue—French neighbours—A walking tour in Normandy— Another in the South—Correspondence with *Charleston Mercury* cannot get through—Anxiety about his sons—Determines to join them, Mrs. Mitchel going to Ireland—September, 1862: Southampton, New York 124

CHAPTER V.

IN THE CONFEDERATE STATES.

1862—1865.

Washington in war-time—Crossing the lines—All but captured—On Confederate ground—Richmond—Editing the *Enquirer*—The *Examiner*, John M. Daniel—Visit to his sons in camp—On the Ambulance Committee—Death of his daughter—Gettysburg, death of Willy— Captain Mitchel at Charleston, earning honours—Mrs. Mitchel in Ireland—Summer of 1863, war going badly—Leaves the *Enquirer* for the *Examiner*—Mrs. Mitchel resolves to join her husband and sons—Running the blockade—Reaches Richmond with loss of everything—A weak spot in the harness of the Confederacy—Mitchel in Richmond society—A lady's idea of him—Keeping the people "up to the fighting point"—General Grant's "simple arithmetical problem" —His manner of fighting—Exhaustion of the South—General Lee— Ambulance duty—The enemy "making furious rushes to get in upon us"—"A people stripped for battle"—Captain Mitchel in command of Fort Sumter—His death—Richmond no longer tenable—Mitchel goes with the Government to Danville—Surrender of Lee—Richmond half in ruins—The war at an end   165

CHAPTER VI.

NEW YORK—FORTRESS MONROE—PARIS.

1865, 1866.

Mitchel in New York, editor of *Daily News*—Justifies the South, while accepting her defeat—Warned that he had better take care—Pays no attention, there being no charge against him—Arrest by military order —Sent to Fortress Monroe—Life in a casemate—Mike Sullivan, from

PAGE

Fethard—Effect of hard usage upon his health—Refuses to complain
—The doctor's representations procure a mitigation—Fellow-prisoners,
Mr. Davis, Senator Clay—Memorial for his release, the Fenians—
Release—Joins his family in Richmond—No redress—An offer from
the Fenians—Goes to France as their financial agent—Paris, Rue
Richer—No hope from the French Government—Sees reason to doubt
the preparedness of the Fenians—Split in their ranks—Thinks he
cannot continue to be their agent—Pleasant visitors—Letters—
Warning off *mouchards*—Interview with M. Pietri—A lonely exile—
Gives up his agency for the Fenians—Visit of Martin and Kenyon—
A scene in the Irish College—Death of John B. Dillon—Return to
America—Farewell to France !   213

CHAPTER VII.

CLOSING YEARS AND DEATH.

1866—1875.

At Richmond—Broken by imprisonment—The "History of Ireland"—
Declines the headship of the Fenians—Letters on Fenianism—
Marriage of his daughter Minnie—Removal to New York—The *Irish
Citizen*—Not equal to his earlier newspapers—A grandfather—Visit
of the Martins—Letters—Answer to Mr. Froude—Fall of 1873, declining health—A testimonial to him—Lectures a little now and
then—A severe illness—Spring of 1874, a longing for home—Visit
to Ireland—Amidst old scenes, old friends—Return to Brooklyn
in October—A vacancy in Tipperary—Offers himself, and sails
February 6—Address—Speech on his election—Lecture in Cork;
too weak to deliver it—To Newry—Life ebbing away—Death—A
peaceful end—His character 252

LIFE OF JOHN MITCHEL.

CHAPTER I.

CONVICT LIFE (*continued*)—VAN DIEMEN'S LAND—ESCAPE
—SAN FRANCISCO—NEW YORK.

1853.

THE first entry made in the "Jail Journal," after the account
of the visit to O'Brien, is dated January 1, 1853. There are
passages in this entry to the same effect as in the letters
quoted at the end of the last chapter. These passages
allow us to see very clearly the direction in which Mitchel's
thoughts were now tending, and the feelings with which he
was coming to regard his Tasmanian life :—

It is long since I have made an entry in my log-book. Of
literature I am almost sick, and prefer farming, and making market
of my wool. There is somewhat stupefying to the brain, as well
as invigorating to the frame in this genial clime and aromatic air.
A phenomenon for which I strive to account in various modes.

  * * * * * * *

We, also, John Knox and I, have eaten narcotic lotos here ;
and if it has not removed, it has surely softened the sting, even of
our *nostalgia*. We, too, have quaffed in these gardens the cup of
lazy enchantment, mingled for us by the hands of Fata Morgana
the Witch ; and if we have not forgotten the outer busy world, at

least the sound of its loud, passionate working, comes to our ear from afar off, deadened, softened, almost harmonized, like the roar of ocean waves heard in a dream, or murmuring through the spiral chamber of a sea-shell.

Surely it is not good for us to be here.

The truth is, he was far from content with his life at Nant Cottage. Many people will perhaps think that he was hard to please, and that he was as well off at Nant Cottage as he was likely to be anywhere else. He was living in what he admits to have been a splendid climate; he had better health than he had known for years; his farm yielded enough to supply the wants of himself and his family, and he had plenty of time to devote to the education of his children. Well, I do not hesitate to admit that he was hard to please. Most men who have any innate nobility of character are hard to please with the conditions of life in this world; and especially in early life, the nobler kind of men, when they feel the *taedium vitae*, are apt to suppose that it is due in a great degree to the particular kind of life they are leading, and to long for a change. This kind of feeling had no doubt a good deal to say to Mitchel's discontent in Tasmania, as it had also a good deal to say to his discontent in after years, with other ways of life very different from that which he was then leading. But there was a special cause for his discontent at Nant Cottage which is hinted at in the passage last quoted from the "Journal," and which some men at least will find it easy to understand. Mitchel was a man by nature keen, eager, ardent, impetuous. He had been leading a life of constant and passionate activity. We have seen how, during the years preceding his transportation, his surroundings were such as to arouse his best passions and to call all his energies into play. From this state of excitement and keen human interest, he found himself

translated for the first time into a sort of lotus-eating existence. Of physical activity and of incentives to physical
activity he had enough ; but of incentives to mental and
spiritual activity he had none. Now, few men who have
not experienced it can understand how intolerable it is for
a man of Mitchel's nature, and who has lived as Mitchel
had lived, to find himself coerced by a force outside of his
own will to lead a life of spiritual lethargy, a life in which
circumstances force him to allow the better part of his
nature "to rust unburnished, not to shine in use." And
this quotation from Tennyson's " Ulysses " reminds me of
a conversation which I had with John Mitchel shortly
before his death, and which well illustrates what I am now
trying to explain. We were talking about Tennyson. He
said he could imagine that for some people Tennyson's
poetry might be more suitable, but, for himself, he did not as
a rule care much for it. " Yet," he added with emphasis, " he
certainly has written some fine things ; take, for example,
his ' Ulysses.' " The wandering instinct, the vague longing
for change, and still more, the eager desire for intense and
passionate life as distinguished from calm existence—these
feelings, so beautifully expressed in the " Ulysses," were
but too familiar to John Mitchel—

> " I cannot rest from travel ; I will drink
> Life to the lees."

So says Ulysses in the poem, and so said John Mitchel
in his heart. He, like Ulysses, spurned the suggestion
that mere existence without noble passion was a state to
be desired, with an indignant " as if to breathe were life."
Both extremes have been painted for us by Mr. Tennyson
and with almost equal power. In the " Ulysses " we see
the eager, restless heart for which calm and peaceful
existence means stagnation and death. In the " Lotus
Eaters," the cry is not for action, but for rest ; not for

passion, but for calm. Mitchel conformed to the type of
" Ulysses." With him, to live was to act ; and when he was
called on to lead the lotus-eating existence, he found it
intolerable ; all the more so because it was forced upon
him by a power he detested. A long letter which he
received from his friend Devin Reilly, then at New York,
early in 1853, stimulated his longing to get away. Reilly's
letter is a strange effusion, and is given at length in the
" Journal." He (Reilly) had been interviewing Kossuth,
and gives his impressions of the "intellectual Kalmuck," as
he calls him, and most vivid impressions they are. He
tells, too, how, with his wonted impetuosity, he had flung
himself into American politics, and was then engaged in
waging an implacable war against a political party whom
he denominated "the old Fogies." On the whole, the
letter, although it did not show that Reilly was happy
certainly did show that he was intensely alive. The reading of the letter over, a discussion upon its contents follows
between Mitchel and Martin. Martin maintains the thesis
that a gum-tree hut were better for Reilly than this life in
America, at least for the present. Mitchel goes strongly
the other way. Here is a portion of the conversation.
Martin has said of Reilly, " better a shepherd at the lakes
until better times," and Mitchel is anwering this. I may
here observe that the " Knox " of the following extract is
John Martin. Some one of the exiles had nicknamed him
John Knox, whether or not on the *lucus a non lucendo*
principle I cannot say.

" That may do well enough for you and me, Mr. Knox ; but
for Reilly, action is his life. In this same vehement action and
passion, in this grapple and struggle with fate and the busy world,
in exercising, and even wantonly wasting every faculty and energy
of mind and body, fitfully flashing out the rays of his intellect, be
it to illuminate or to set on fire—that restless spirit finds its only

joy, its only possibility of being. Bring him here, and he would
hang himself on a gum-tree. Rather let him expend himself there,
in fighting fogies, in crushing joyfully under his heel the head of
humbug and cant. He has, at all events, a noble aim, and he
will prosecute it nobly. Like Ram-Das, that Hindoo saint or
god, he feels that there is fire enough in his body to burn up all
the baseness and poltroonery in the world. Let him fire away."

"But he will perish."

" Let him perish. It will be in a great cause ;—and to *have*
an aim and a cause, is not this happiness? How many are there
of all the human race who have faith in anything, or aspiration
after anything, higher than their daily bread and beer, their influence, social position, respectability in the eyes of the un-
respectable world? Even in this very devout, almost despairing
loyalty to his discrowned queen and mother Ireland, is there not
a joy that colder, tamer spirits never know? Through his dreams
there shines in upon him the beautiful mournful face of his sad
Roisin dubh, the torn and crushed dark rose that he has worn in
his heart from a boy—thrilling him with an immortal passion, like
the passion that consumed the chieftain of Tir-conail.

*   *   *   *   *   *   *

—Happy, whose veins yet shoot and glow with red lightning
blood, instead of trickling white serum and Bothwell beer !"

" Don't the men," said Knox, " finish the hay to-night ? "

" Confound the hay ! I tell you that I envy Devin Reilly for
being alive—alive as you and I will never, never be alive again."

"And Nathan said unto David, 'Thou art the man.'"
If Martin had so said unto Mitchel as he sat there discussing of Reilly's need for vehement action and passion, he
would not, I think, have been very wide of the truth.

From what I have been saying the reader will easily
see that Mitchel's state of mind was such as to make it
certain that an opportunity of escape would be eagerly
welcomed by him ; that is, of course, provided the escape
could be effected honourably. The opportunity soon came.

About the middle of January, 1853, a week or so after
the talk over Reilly's letter, Mitchel had occasion to go to

Hobart Town. He went first to St. Mary's Hospital to see O'Doherty. O'Doherty at once drew him into a private room, making it evident by his manner that he had some important news to tell. The news was soon told. "Pat Smyth," * as O'Doherty called him, had arrived in Van Diemen's Land. He had been sent by a body known as the Irish Directory at New York, with instructions to bring about the escape of one or more of the principal Irish prisoners at Van Diemen's Land. Smyth was abundantly supplied with money, and O'Doherty expressed himself confident of success. Mitchel was not quite so confident, but he admitted that the matter looked serious. As he observes in his "Journal," Smyth was a cool-headed rebel, by no means likely to come so far without a plan, or to play at any child's game.

It was arranged that Smyth was to meet O'Brien at a place called Bridgewater, some ten miles from Hobart Town, on the evening of the day on which Mitchel arrived. O'Doherty and Mitchel at once provided themselves with horses and rode to the place of meeting. There they found O'Brien, but Smyth had not yet come. He was expected by the stage coach from Launceston; and the coach, though overdue, had not yet passed. Mitchel and O'Brien spent the afternoon in discussing various possible plans of escape; and O'Brien, at Mitchel's request, gave his view as to what it was incumbent upon them to do, before attempting to escape, in order to discharge themselves of their parole. The course which O'Brien prescribed as necessary to an honourable escape was that which Mitchel afterwards adopted.

At a certain hour in the evening O'Brien and O'Doherty were obliged to leave for their respective districts, the

---

* Well known as P. J. Smyth. He was afterwards Member of Parliament for Tipperary.

Launceston coach not yet having arrived. Mitchel remained at the Bridgewater Hotel for the night, waiting for the coach. The coach did at last arrive, and here is Mitchel's account of his meeting with Smyth :—

Amongst others, a young man stepped down from the coach, and entered. He looked me full in the face, and I him. It was Smyth; but neither of us, after four years knew the other. I listened, as he went to the office, and engaged a bed; yet I did not know his voice. He came out to get his portmanteau, and we passed each other again in the hall. " It must be Smyth," I said; " nobody else would be stopping short here, within ten miles of Hobart Town." So I followed him out, and went round after him to the outer side of the coach, where all was dark. " Is your name Smyth ?" He turned upon me suddenly; clearly he thought it was a detective—thought that he had been traced all the way to the very spot where he was to meet us—that he was a prisoner, and all was over. I hastened to undeceive him, for he looked strongly tempted to shoot me and bolt. " All right, Smyth. Silence ! follow me into the parlour."

The next day they went to see O'Brien. Smyth's instructions were to secure the escape of O'Brien and Mitchel, or of either of them, if both could not be got off. O'Brien declined to make the attempt. The reasons he alleged are given in the " Journal " :—

He had already had his chance, had made the attempt to escape from Maria Island—it had failed; and the expenses incurred by it had been defrayed by public money. *"This,"* he said, " is *your* chance. Besides, you have stronger motives to betake yourself to America than I have; and you will be more at home there. It may be," he continued, " that the British Government may find it, some time or other, their best policy to set me free, without making submission to them; in that case, I return to Ireland. If I break away against their will, Ireland is barred against me for ever."

O'Brien's. determination proved to be immovable. Mitchel and Smyth gave up the attempt to persuade him, and Mitchel declared to Smyth that he would make the attempt in the way recommended by O'Brien. Smyth then accompanied Mitchel to Bothwell, and after a few days' stay at Nant Cottage, left to make preparations for the intended escape.

While he was waiting for news of Smyth, Mitchel hit upon a happy idea. For the purposes of escape he needed a good horse in addition to those he already had. Now it so happened that Mr. Davis, the police magistrate of the district, was then the owner of the best saddle-horse in or about Bothwell. He was a white horse, half Arab, full of game, and of great endurance. Mitchel knew that this horse was for sale; and it struck him that to buy the horse would have the double advantage of strengthening him and weakening the enemy. Accordingly the bargain was made. The conversation between the police magistrate and Mitchel upon the delivery of the horse is amusing, viewed in the light of what afterwards happened :—

Mr. Davis, on delivering him, very conscientiously thought it his duty to give me a warning. "I must tell you, Mr. Mitchel," he said, "that if you attempt to put this horse into harness he will smash everything—he never was in harness but once, and it would be dangerous to try it again. I said, I was aware of that peculiarity in the horse. "It is right," he continued, "to mention the fact to you, as I do not know *the precise work* you want him to do." "Merely to carry me on his back, wherever I want to go —some time or other probably on a long journey." "Well," said Mr. Davis, "I know you ride a good deal; and you may depend upon Donald for that."

The first attempt to escape was a failure. Smyth made arrangements with the captain of a brigantine to take Mitchel off at a place called Spring Bay, on the eastern side of the island. But before the appointed day came, they were made aware, through a friendly resident at

Bothwell, that Smyth's whole plan had been intimately known to the governor for a fortnight. The thing had, therefore, to be given up for that time. Smyth went to Spring Bay to warn off the brigantine. There he found a force of constables waiting for him, and he was instantly arrested as John Mitchel. He was brought to Hobart Town, suffering a good deal of hardship on the way; and what between this and the excitement and disappointment he was seized immediately after his release with a severe attack of illness. Nearly two months passed before Smyth was sufficiently recovered to make possible a second attempt.

It is right to mention here that this first plan of escape was to have included John Martin. Mr. Martin had agreed to make the attempt along with his friend; and the method to be observed of surrendering the parole was the same as that afterwards adopted by Mitchel. But when this first attempt failed, and the authorities were known to be on the alert, it was thought better for Mr. Martin to abandon the idea for the present. Owing to a very marked peculiarity in his physical shape, effectual disguise would have been impossible in his case; and had he made the attempt after the authorities were put on their guard, his recapture would have been almost a certainty.

On June 8, 1853, the attempt, which eventually proved successful, was commenced. They had ascertained that a ship bound for Sydney was to sail from Hobart Town on the night of the 8th of June, and the agents of this ship were friendly to Mitchel, and might be relied on to put him on board after dark at the mouth of the river after all clearances by the police authorities. They had originally determined to make their visit to the police-office on the 8th, so as, if successful, to reach Hobart Town that night in

time for the ship's sailing. But on the 8th the town of
Bothwell happened to be full of police, and so the business
had to be deferred till the next day. Meantime Smyth
was not idle. By the prudent employment of some money
he secured that no more than the ordinary guard of constables would be present when the surrender of the parole
was to be made. Mitchel sent one of his boys down to
Hobart Town to see if the ship could be delayed for him.
But whatever the answer might be, they had made up their
minds that this time they would make the attempt.

On the morning of June 9, 1853, Mitchel and Smyth
rode together from Nant Cottage to Bothwell police-station.
Their object in visiting the police-station was to take the
step which, in the opinion of Mr. O'Brien, it was necessary
to take before an escape could be honourably effected.
Had Mitchel seen fit to dispense with this proceeding, he
could easily and without risk have escaped before this.
But he had given his promise not to escape so long as he
held the ticket-of-leave, and before he could regard himself
as released from the promise, the ticket-of-leave had to be
surrendered by him in person to the authorities.

Smyth was mounted on Donald, the horse Mitchel had
purchased from the police magistrate ; Mitchel himself on a
mare of his named Fleur-de-lis. On the way to town, they
overtook a neighbour and friend named Russell, and chatted
pleasantly about farming matters. Before they reached
Bothwell, they also met James—the boy who had been
sent to Hobart Town—returning at a gallop. He brought
a message from the shipping agents. The ship was gone ;
it was impossible to detain her without exciting suspicion.
As the thing then stood, therefore, they had absolutely no
plan for escaping from out of the island. If they went on,
and got clear of the police-office, they would simply have
to trust to hard riding, disguise, concealment, and good

luck.   But Mitchel was firmly determined that this time the attempt should be made, let the result be what it might.

Arrived at the police-office, they gave their horses in charge of one of Mitchel's sons, who was waiting there for that purpose.   They then went into the police-office, Mitchel leading the way.   The scene in the office is minutely and graphically described in the "Journal."   Several other accounts of the transaction have also come to my hands ; one by John Martin, and another by Mrs. Mitchel in letters written to friends.   They are all substantially in accord as regards the main features of the transaction ; but that in the "Journal" is the most vivid and altogether the most Homeric of the various accounts I have seen :—

We dismounted.   I walked in first, through the little gate leading into the court, through the door, which opened into a hall or passage, and thence into the court-room, where I found his worship sitting as usual.   Near him sat Robinson, the police-clerk. "Mr. Davis," I said, "here is a copy of a note which I have just despatched to the governor—I have thought it necessary to give you a copy."   The note was as follows :—

"*Bothwell, June* 8, 1853.
"To the Lieut-Gov., etc.
"Sir,—I hereby resign the 'ticket-of-leave,' and withdraw my parole.

"I shall forthwith present myself before the police-magistrate of Bothwell, at his office, show him a copy of this note, and offer myself to be taken into custody.

"Your obedient servant,
"John Mitchel."

Mr. Davis took the note.   It was open.   "Do you wish me," he said, "to read it?"   "Certainly.   It was for that I brought it."   He glanced over the note, and then looked at me.   That instant Nicaragua came in and planted himself at my side.   His worship and his clerk both seemed somewhat discomposed at this ; for they knew the "Correspondent of the New York

Tribune" very well, as also his errand from New York. I have no doubt that Mr. Davis thought I had a crowd outside ; there is no other way of accounting for his irresolution.

Then I said, " You see the purport of that note, sir; it is short and plain ; it resigns the thing called ' ticket-of-leave,' and revokes my promise which bound me so long as I held that thing."

Still he made no move, and gave no order. So I repeated my explanation : " You observe, sir, that my parole is at an end from this moment; and I came here to be taken into custody pursuant to that note."

All this while there was a constable in the adjoining room, besides the police clerk, and the guard at the door ; yet still his worship made no move. "Now, good morning, sir," I said, putting on my hat. The hand of Nicaragua was playing with the handle of the revolver in his coat. I had a ponderous riding-whip in my hand, besides pistols in my breast-pocket. The moment I said, "Good morning," Mr. Davis shouted, "No, no—stay here ! Rainsford ! Constables !" The police clerk sat at his desk looking into vacancy. We walked out together through the hall ; the constable in the district-constable's office, who generally acts as his clerk, now ran out, and on being desired to stop us, followed us through the court, and out into the street, but without coming very near. At the little gate leading out of the court into the street, we expected to find the man on guard on the alert between us and our horses. But this poor constable, though he heard the magistrate's orders and the commotion, did not move. He was holding two horses, one with each hand, and looked on in amazement while we passed him, and jumped into our saddles.

It has been said that the proceeding here described did not amount to such a surrender of the parole as to make Mitchel's escape honourable. That this should be said by English newspapers and English ministers at the time was to be expected. They were naturally exasperated at Mitchel's success in escaping, and at the reception which he subsequently had in America, and the charge of dishonourable conduct in the matter of the escape would certainly have been made by them under any circumstances.

If the matter stopped here, there would be no need to notice it further.

But the charge has since been renewed on different occasions by two prominent Irishmen. It was made by Mr. Duffy in 1854, shortly after the publication of the " Jail Journal." This charge was, however, obviously a part of Duffy's personal quarrel with Mitchel, and was made while Duffy was smarting under the attack made upon him in the " Jail Journal." If the matter had even stopped there, I should not have deemed it necessary to say much about it. But, strange to say, the charge has been renewed in more recent times by an Irishman who occupies a prominent position among his countrymen. I allude to the view regarding Mitchel's escape expressed by Mr. Justin McCarthy in his " History of our own Times." The passage occurs in the eighteenth chapter of the book. It dwells upon the fact that Mitchel carried arms when he went to the police-office, and states that Smith O'Brien disapproved of the plan of the escape.* Upon the whole case, Mr. McCarthy is of opinion that " it was a nice question of honour, which in the case of men of very delicate sense of honour could, one would think, hardly have arisen at all." A proposition which I would entirely indorse, but not quite in the sense in which it is here used.

Now, in the first place, we have upon the other side the opinion of the three leading prisoners themselves. Smith O'Brien, John Martin, John Mitchel—all of these were men in whom the sense of honour was exceptionally high

---

* The statement as to O'Brien is undoubtedly false. Mr. McCarthy's attention was called to this by Mr. Smyth, and in a subsequent edition he appended a note admitting his error so far as O'Brien was concerned. He had relied, he said, upon a statement of Lord Palmerston's which, so far as he knew, was uncontradicted. A statement of Lord Palmerston's, even if uncontradicted, would be hardly a safe authority upon which to base a charge against the honour of a distinguished Irishman.

and chivalrous, and all of these were of opinion that the plan of escape adopted by Mitchel was entirely honourable. Afterwards, when O'Brien was released, Lord Palmerston took occasion to compliment him on not having broken his parole, implying, of course, that Mitchel had done so. O'Brien indignantly repudiated the compliment. At a banquet given in his honour at Melbourne, shortly after his release, he spoke as follows :—" I refuse to accept a compliment of my Lord Palmerston accompanied by an insult to my friend, Mr. Mitchel. If he has violated parole, so have I, for the mode of his escape had my entire sanction and approval. I was not prepared myself to take a step which would have rendered it impossible for me to return to Ireland, and, therefore, I felt compelled to decline the services of my friend, Mr. Smyth. But the plan adopted in Mr. Mitchel's case is that which I would have approved of in my own."

But the matter does not stop here. O'Brien, Mitchel, and Martin were not the only Irishmen of distinction who expressed an unqualified approval of the mode of escape adopted. When Mr. Duffy, in 1854, charged Mitchel with having broken his parole, several leading Irishmen at once wrote letters—which were published in the *Citizen*, a paper then conducted by Mitchel—expressing in the most emphatic manner their view regarding the charge of parole-breaking. Amongst these were Richard O'Gorman, John B. Dillon, Rev. John Kenyon, Thomas Antisell, John Savage, Michael Doheny, and John O'Mahony. All of these gentlemen were perfectly familiar with the circumstances attending Mitchel's escape, and all of them were equally clear in the expression of the view that for the charge of parole-breaking there was no shadow of foundation.

In face of these facts no further defence is necessary. By most Irishmen, indeed, an elaborate defence of Mitchel's action in this matter would be regarded as an impertinence, because implying that such a defence was in some degree needed. Nor is the case one that admits of any long argument. The question must, in the main, be decided by each man for himself according to the dictates of his own sense of honour. When Mitchel landed in Van Diemen's Land, he was accorded a conditional liberty, called "a ticket-of-leave." The essence of the transaction was that he was allowed to go free, within certain limits, in the colony, upon the terms of his promising not to escape so long as he continued to avail himself of the "ticket-of-leave." If he desired at any time to resign his "ticket-of-leave," and return to his previous status, he was bound to present himself in person before the authorities, and to formally resign his parole under such circumstances as to afford to the officers a full opportunity of taking him back into custody, before making any attempt to escape.

Now, I so far agree with Mr. McCarthy as to wonder how any fair-minded judge can have serious doubt on the question whether Mitchel did all that his promise bound him to do. Did he or did he not give to the authorities a full and fair opportunity of taking him into custody after he had apprised them of the fact that his promise was withdrawn? This, after all, is the question upon which our judgment upon the point of honour must depend. It is true, as Mr. McCarthy takes care to observe, that Mitchel carried arms; but it is also true, as Mr. McCarthy does not observe, that Mitchel had no intention of using his arms in the police-office, and further, that he made it sufficiently clear to the officers that he had no such intention. He carried arms because, as he tells us, he had resolved that, if he once succeeded in leaving the police-office after discharging himself of his parole, he would never again be taken alive. But he took care to expressly tell Mr. Davis, during the

time he considered it necessary to remain in the office, that
he was there for the purpose of being taken into custody—
a statement hardly consistent with the supposition that he
meant to shoot down the first man who attempted to arrest
him. No doubt the mere sight of the arms may have
frightened Mr. Davis and his underlings. But I cannot
see that this has any bearing on the question, unless,
indeed, we are to hold that Mr. Mitchel was bound not
only to afford the authorities a fair opportunity of taking
him into custody, but also to provide them with officials of
sufficient promptitude and courage to avail themselves of
such opportunity.

Indeed, I can only explain the fact, if it be the fact,
that men not prejudiced against Mitchel have doubted the
honourableness of his escape upon one ground. Some
men are apt in certain cases to go astray in endeavouring
to apply the distinction between the letter and the spirit of
a promise. Mr. McCarthy, in what he has written on the
subject, seems to imply the opinion that, even although
Mitchel may have complied with the letter, he certainly
did not comply with the spirit of his promise. The answer
to this seems to me sufficiently obvious. The interpretation
which we put upon a promise, not absolutely precise in its
terms, may rightly vary widely according to our relations
to the party to whom the promise is made. If we give a
promise to one from whom we have never received anything
but generosity, and if the precise interpretation of the
promise be in any respect open to doubt, we shall ask
ourselves—in what sense may our benefactor be fairly
presumed to have understood the promise, and we will act
accordingly. If we give a promise to a highwayman who
has robbed and all but murdered us, and who holds out
the loss of liberty as the alternative, we will be entirely
within our right in adopting a very different principle of

construction. If there be any respects in which the line of action sought to be enforced is not precisely defined, we will ask ourselves—not what the highwayman may have intended—but what is the least that, putting a reasonable construction upon the language used, the promise binds us in honour to do. Mitchel's position, in relation to the British Government, belongs to the second of the two classes just indicated; and, when this is kept clearly in view, I am, I repeat, at a loss to understand how any one, not influenced by personal dislike or national prejudice, can really believe that John Mitchel's course in relation to his escape was censurable. If it be further said that the authorities would never have allowed Mitchel the "comparative liberty" if they had supposed for a moment that he would act as he did, the answer is still the same. There was nothing to prevent their making the terms of the promise more precise. No one who knows anything of Mitchel's character will have a doubt but that he would have surrendered himself alone and unarmed, and have remained an hour in the office after withdrawing his word, had the terms of his promise bound him to do so. The British Government had no right—no shadow of right—to expect that John Mitchel would put a chivalrous and quixotic construction upon a promise given to *them*, in order to carry out the object they had in view. If they were foolish enough to expect anything of the kind, they cannot reasonably complain of the consequences.

I do not know that I can better close these remarks upon the parole question than by quoting a passage from the letter written by John Dillon to the *Citizen*, in answer to Mr. Duffy's charge of parole-breaking. It is right to state that Mr. Dillon begins his letter by expressing a strong disapproval of Mitchel's attack on Duffy in the "Jail Journal;" a circumstance which, in my opinion, gives

all the more force to what Mr. Dillon has to say upon the
parole question.   Mr. Duffy had spoken of Mitchel's friends
as "hanging their heads when his name was mentioned"
by reason of his breach of parole.   Mr. Dillon writes :—

The passage in Mr. Duffy's letter, from which I would record
my dispute, is that in which he accuses you of having broken your
parole in escaping from Van Diemen's Land.   I have, I believe,
a pretty accurate knowledge of the facts connected with your
escape, and I am at a loss to find in those facts any foundation
for the accusation in question ; unless there be some code of
honour, yet unheard of by me, which makes a prisoner responsible
for the cowardice or disaffection, or venality, of his jailors.

I was one among many thousands in this city, who celebrated
your escape by public rejoicings, and since then no new fact has
come to my knowledge which causes me to regret the part which
I took in those rejoicings.   It seems superfluous to add that there
is one of your friends at least, who—not agreeing in all your
opinions—does *not* "hang his head when your name is mentioned ; " but who, on the contrary, is proud of your friendship,
and would freely stake his life on your honour.

Having now said all I deem it needful to say upon the
parole question (and perhaps I might have done better to
treat the charge with silent contempt), I return to my
narrative.

When Mitchel and Smyth left the police-office, there
was absolutely no preparation of any kind made for getting
off the island.   They had to trust entirely to their horses,
to the friendly feeling of the settlers, and to good fortune.

Here is Mitchel's account of his last sight of Bothwell :—

Mr. Davis and two constables rushing against one another,
with bare heads, and loud outcries ; grinning residents of Bothwell on the pathway, who knew the meaning of the performance
in a moment—and who, being commanded to stop us in the
Queen's name, aggravated the grin into a laugh ; some small
boys at a corner, staring at our horses as they galloped by, and
offering "three to one on the white 'un ; "—this is my last impression, of Bothwell on the banks of the Tasmanian Clyde.

After leaving Bothwell behind them, Mitchel and Smyth continued to ride at full speed until they reached a spot in the forest about a mile to the south-west of the town. There they stopped, exchanged horses and coats, and parted. Smyth rode to Nant Cottage, intending to call there a moment to report progress, and then go on to Oatlands to take the Launceston coach. At Nant Cottage, Smyth found the following note which Mitchel had left for him :—

MY DEAR SMYTH,
        As we are to part to-day to pursue our several roads, and to encounter our respective adventures, and as we may never meet again in this world, I cannot go without leaving this hurried note to convey to you my most fervent gratitude for the zealous friendship you have shown me in your operations for securing my escape. This enterprise, indeed, may fail, as the previous one two months ago failed ; but assuredly it is not your fault in either case. If I happily escape to America, I have no doubt of being able in time to save you harmless at least from pecuniary loss, though it would be hard indeed to compensate you for your five months incessant toil and privation, accompanied with insult and outrage such as a gentleman could not, I believe, be subjected to in any country on earth but this detestable den of devils.

Meantime, Mitchel rode to a place in the woods, half a mile further on, where he met, by appointment, a young man, called in the "Journal" J. Howells, who was to be his guide at the outset of his perilous journey. This J. Howells was the son of an English settler, and I find a good description of him in a letter written by John Martin shortly after Mitchel's escape. Mr. Martin describes him as "a youth six feet in height, sixteen stone in weight, a bold and excellent horseman, a most experienced and almost unrivalled bushman, as generous and good-natured as he is big, and altogether a right good fellow, and right proud of his office."

After a brief consultation, they decided to strike northwards, making for the district of Westburg, which was chiefly inhabited by Irish immigrants, and where they would be within a day's ride of Bass's Straits. They rode all day through a country wild, mountainous, and wooded. When night fell they were upon a mountain ridge somewhere in the district of Lake Sorel. They had still the most steep and difficult part of the journey to do in order to make the hut of the shepherd where they proposed to spend the night, and it was "dark as Erebus." The place they were making for and where they proposed to spend the night was the hut of one Job Sims, a shepherd of Mr. Russell's. Like the father of Mitchel's guide, this Job was an Englishman; yet the following day Mitchel intrusted him with a note to Nant Cottage, knowing, as he states in the "Journal," that Job "would not sell that note to the enemy for a thousand pounds." But when last we left Mitchel and his guide they had not yet arrived at Job's, though now and then they could hear far below them the dogs at the hut barking. They were going down a steep descent covered with large rocks, brush, and trunks of gum-trees. In the black darkness they could see nothing; and both they and the horses they were leading frequently stumbled or fell. At last, although both men and horses were worn out for want of food and water, and although the guide, who even then knew pretty well where he was, asserted that they had only three miles further to go, Mitchel decided to pass the night where they were. It was the middle of the Tasmanian winter, and the weather was extremely cold. The night bivouac is thus described :—

We lighted a fire with some dead branches (for no true bushman goes without matches); tied our poor horses to a honeysuckle-tree; looked at our pistols; picked the least polygonal stones to sit down upon; lighted our pipes, and prepared to spend eight hours as jovially as possible. Soon, sleep overtook us, from utter exhaustion, and we would lie a few minutes on the sharp stones by the fire until awakened by the scorching of our knees, while our spinal marrow was frozen into a solid icicle. Then we would turn our backs to the fire, and sleep again ; but, in five minutes, our knees and toes were frozen, our moustaches stiff with ice—our spinal marrow dissolving away in the heat. Then up again—another smoke, another talk.

From the scene at the police-office in Bothwell until Mitchel's final escape from Van Diemen's Land, there elapsed just one month and ten days. His adventures during this period are minutely narrated in the " Journal," and they are sufficiently exciting. Sometimes we find him hiding at the house of some friendly settler. Then again we meet him, disguised as a priest, travelling in broad daylight upon the stage coach from Launceston to Hobart Town with the last attorney-general for the colony, who was personally acquainted with Mr. John Mitchel, seated opposite to him. I have already noted the fact that his first guide was the son of an Englishman, and that his first place of shelter after he left Bothwell was the hut of an English shepherd. In reading the account of his adventures from the time he surrendered his parole to the time of his escape from the island, nothing strikes one more than the zealous and constant aid he received from Englishmen and the descendants of Englishmen. It is hardly necessary to say that whenever and wherever he met with Irish settlers, he was enthusiastically received, and aided in every possible way. This is only what we would expect ; but although his English friends were not so enthusiastic, in effective help they were in no way behind. Once he stayed for more than a week at the house of an Englishman named Miller, who is thus described :—

Miller is an Englishman, long resident in London ; but, like all the other honest people in this country, he cordially abhors Sir William Denison and his government, and will go any length in my service ; not, perhaps, that he loves me more, but that he loves Sir William less.

Miller's friendship was certainly not wanting in thoroughness. Witness the following conversation :—

" All special messengers," said he, " bearing despatches from Launceston, must come to me, and request me to put them across the water in my boat, which is the only boat on this side. So, you see, it is all right ; you can stay here in perfect safety."

O'K—— declared he could not see how *this* made all right ; for said he, " if our journey in this direction comes to be known, as it must be in a few days, your *next* visitor will be another express constable."

" The very thing," said Miller, " that we want. The fellow can't go over without my help. I can make him drunk here, and take the despatch from him, or bribe him to return and say he delivered it ; or drown him, if you like, in the passage."

Miller had a plan of effecting Mitchel's escape from the island which was certainly bold, and in the way he proposed to utilize the service of the chief-constable of police, highly amusing. The police-office of the district was within a mile of Miller's house, and from the shelter of a natural shrubbery which was near the house, Mitchel used to watch the constables sauntering about the sleepy-looking village with their belts and jingling handcuffs. Miller learned one day that there was a vessel in the mouth of one of the rivers, fourteen miles west, about to sail with a cargo of timber for Melbourne. He immediately formed a plan, the details of which can be gathered from the following conversation :—

" I also mentioned you to the chief of police, telling him, that, although you have been so short a time here, you are tired of the country (which is true) and want to go to Melbourne

again. I told him you did not much like the idea of travelling
back to Launceston to take your passage in one of the steamers,
and asked him if there were not a good vessel shortly to sail from
some of these rivers. ' There is the *Wave*,' said he; ' the very
thing for your brother.' "

" Well," I asked, " what more ? "

" Why," said Miller, " he is going over to the Forth to-morrow,
will go on board the ship, and will bring us back full particulars
as to the accommodations, fare, etc. Then you and I are to dine
with the police-magistrate on our way; and the clearing officer
will have an interview with you in the police-office, and will
make all smooth for my brother. This thing will do. You must
come."

" I agree to everything but the dinner-party at the police
magistrate's. I will not sit down at any man's table under a
feigned name; but let us impose on him otherwise, if you like."

" You agree, then, to go as my brother ? "

" Certainly. I am tired of skulking about; though your
society and conversation, my dear fellow, are—— "

" Hurrah !" said Miller, running to tell his wife of our plan.

But the plan was not fated to be carried out. Before
the time arrived, special messengers came to bring Mitchel
to Launceston, where another plan had been devised by his
friends. This plan also proved a failure. They had a night
voyage of some fifty miles down the Tamar in an open
boat. It was a dreadful night, wet and stormy, and
Mitchel was soaked through even before the voyage commenced, having ridden fifty miles during the day through
rain, rivers, and morasses. The attempt had to be made,
however; and they arrived at the mouth of the river just
in time to see the vessel that was to have taken Mitchel on
board moving from her anchorage and steaming off to
Melbourne. Speaking metaphorically, and by no means
climatically, the place had become too hot for her.

At one time he lay concealed at the house of an Irish
settler named Burke for some ten days. During this time

he wrote letters to his wife, his mother, and others. The following extracts are taken from a letter written to his mother :—

Your most welcome letter arrived last Thursday, just as I was about to make an almost desperate attempt to regain my liberty. My letter to William will explain all the particulars. And as I am now forced to lie still in concealment for a little, I use my leisure to write to you. I am sorry to have to write in a state of such suspense, but perhaps an appendix to my letter may contain better news.

*   *   *   *   *   *   *

I may never see my poor Jenny again. I may never live to give her a peaceful home in America, and it is a horrible thought to me to think of this, for she has been a good and brave and affectionate wife to me.

Do not let any of my sisters suppose that I have ever abated in my regard for them. You may well conceive how fondly a captive in a distant land turns back to the home of his youth, and the scenes of his father's fireside. Do not, my dearest mother, think that I forget them. I often look back with remorse on the grief and anxiety I caused to you, and to my father, and on the almost incredible forbearance and indulgence you both showed me—forbearance that I believe I would not show to a son of mine who should act with such reckless disobedience. The feeling that these are perhaps the last words I shall ever address to you by tongue or pen forces me to say all this. And I entreat you to forgive my many faults and to bless me.

At last, after various adventures and various escapes, we find him, on the 12th of July, at the headquarters of the enemy—Hobart Town—disguised as a priest. Here he again met Smyth for the first time since they had parted near Bothwell on the 9th of June. Smyth speedily arranged a plan of escape. The *Emma*, a regular passenger brig, was to sail for Sydney in about a week. The plan formed was again a bold one, but this time it illustrated the truth that the boldest plan is often the wisest. It was decided that Mitchel should go to Sydney by the *Emma*, and that his wife and children should sail by the same vessel. This last part of the plan may seem of doubtful wisdom ; yet perhaps it was in truth the wisest course they could have devised. The authorities would of course be aware of the fact that Mrs. Mitchel and her children were leaving by the *Emma;* but it would hardly occur to them that Mr. Mitchel would sail by the same ship. They would be rather led to infer that he had already escaped from the island, and that Mrs. Mitchel was going to join him. On the day appointed, Mrs. Mitchel and the children embarked. They went on board the *Emma* at the wharf in regular form, before the vessel was cleared by the authorities. As for Mitchel, the friend at whose house he was concealed undertook to take him down the bay in a boat, and put him on board the *Emma* after dark, and after all searching by the authorities was over. Captain Brown, the captain of the *Emma*, was taken into their confidence, and proved himself entirely trustworthy. Mitchel of course preserved his incognito, and went by the name of Wright. The plan was entirely successful. Mitchel was put on board the *Emma* in the bay by moonlight. Captain Brown received him as a passenger he had been expecting, merely observing quietly, "You were almost too late, Mr. Wright." Mrs. Mitchel was sitting on the poop with the children. As may be supposed, she watched the process with anxiety but did not give her husband the least sign of recognition.

On July 20, 1853, John Mitchel took his last look of Van Diemen's Land :—

This evening we are fast shutting down the coast of Van Diemen's Land below the red horizon, and about to stretch across the stormy Bass's Straits. The last of my island prison visible to me is a broken line of blue peaks over the Bay of Fires. Adieu, then, beauteous island, full of sorrow and gnashing of teeth ;

island of fragrant forests, and bright rivers, and fair women ; island of chains and scourges, and blind, brutal rage and passion ! Behind those far blue peaks, in many a green valley known to me, dwell some of the best and warmest-hearted of God's creatures ; and the cheerful talk of their genial firesides will blend for ever in my memory with the eloquent song of the dashing Derwent and deep-eddying Shannon.

During the voyage an incident occurred which very nearly betrayed the secret of Mitchel's identity. The two eldest boys knew who Mr. Wright was, but the younger children knew nothing about their father being on board. One evening the gentlemen were talking in the main cabin and the children had gone to their berths for the night. Mr. P. J. Smyth was sitting close to the door of the room in which the Mitchel boys slept. He suddenly heard little Willie Mitchel, then about eight years old, exclaim, " As sure as I am living, it was my papa said that." Mr. Smyth rose quietly and went into the boy's room. He managed to make the little fellow understand that he must not mention his father at all during the rest of the voyage. The boy observed this rule strictly, but he followed Mr. Wright about on the deck until that gentleman turned and asked him, was he not one of Mrs. Mitchel's little boys ? This puzzled the little fellow, and he did not pursue his investigations any further.

On the 23rd of July they arrived off the bay of Sydney. Here again there was risk of discovery. The *Emma* had to be searched by the police authorities, who no doubt had a description of " the man of five feet ten, with dark hair," etc. However, Captain Brown, who was an old friend of the chief officer's, took him down to the cabin, produced brandy and water, detained the official with some jocose conversation, and so got rid of him. Then the captain got ready his own boat and took Mr. Wright ashore before the

other passengers. Mr. Wright was in search of a gentleman named McNamara, the owner of the *Emma*, to whom
he had been recommended to go by friends in Hobart
Town. Captain Brown did not leave him until he had
conducted him safely to Mr. McNamara's house. Of a
truth, John Mitchel, wherever and under whatever circumstances he found himself, had the faculty of making zealous
and faithful friends.

Mitchel remained at Sydney a little over a week.
During this time he stayed at Mr. McNamara's house;
and deeming it advisable to again change his name, he
went by the name of Warren. Mrs. Mitchel had lodgings
for herself and the children at a place called Wooloomooloo,
a suburb of Sydney. After a few days, Mr. McNamara
ascertained that a barque named the *Orkney Lass* was
about to sail for Honolulu, in the Sandwich Islands, and
that she had just room for one passenger. It was deemed
desirable to get Mr. Warren out of Sydney as soon as
possible. It was therefore decided that he should go by
the *Orkney Lass* to Honolulu, whence it would be easy to
get transit to San Francisco. A few days after the day
fixed for sailing of the *Orkney Lass*, an American ship, the
Julia Ann, was expected to call at Sydney on her way
from Melbourne to San Francisco. The family were to
come on by this ship if there was room.

There was some little delay about the sailing of the
Orkney Lass. Some of the sailors left the ship, announcing
their intention to go to the "diggings." Legal proceedings
of some kind had to be taken, and the ship was for a few
days infested with officials known as "water-police"—a
class of men whose presence was not entirely agreeable to
Mr. Warren. At last they got off. Under date of
August 2, 1853, the "Journal" has this entry :—

On board. The complement of our crew is made up. We

·lifted our anchor at eleven o'clock. Very faint breeze, and that
rather against us. The ship was to be searched at the Heads—
the *last* searching.

It is over. The man five feet ten in stature, with dark hair,
was recognized by no enemy; and we cleared the Heads about
four o'clock; and a fresh breeze sprung up from the north; and
now the sun is setting beyond the Blue Mountains; and the coast
of New South Wales, a hazy line upon the purple sea, is fading
into a dream. Whether I was ever truly in Australia at all; or
whether in the body or out of the body—I cannot tell; but I have
had bad dreams.

After three weeks of quiet sailing over the Pacific
Ocean, which on this occasion showed itself worthy of its
name, they reached Tahiti. There the *Orkney Lass* stayed
nearly three weeks discharging cargo. The " Journal" has
an amusing description of the social condition of Tahiti,
the Cyprus of Polynesia. The ladies of Tahiti, said not to
be over-strict in their morals, are thus described :—

The women have great black eyes; long, smooth, black hair;
and on every glossy head a wreath of fresh flowers. They wear
nothing but the *parieu*, a long robe of some bright-coloured fabric
(made for them in world-clothing Manchester), gathered close
round the neck, and hanging loose to the feet, without even a
girdle. I am not reconciled to this dress, though they generally
have forms that no barbarity of drapery can disguise—nor to their
wide mouths, though their teeth are orient pearls.

And again, a page or two further on :—

Sunday Evening.—Strolled up with Bonnefin to Queen
Pomaré's palace or cottage. It has been a gala evening. The
admiral and governor are in the queen's verandah ; the delightful
band of the frigate playing polkas and schottisches. The maids of
honour (of whom there are six or eight, all in pure white *parieus*,
with flowers radiant in their dark hair), and scores of other
Tahitian maidens, some of them splendidly dressed, were dancing
on the lawn in front with the young French officers. Mr. Warren
is pained to say that the feet of the girls are broad ; figures other-

wise faultless, eyes supernatural, and the carriage of the head and neck, of that proud and fierce beauty that you see in the bearing of the desert panther.

On the 13th of September, just as the *Orkney Lass* was getting ready to leave Tahiti, a barque was reported in sight off the reefs. She proved to be the *Julia Ann* with Mitchel's family on board. She did not enter the harbour, but sent a boat ashore expressly to see if Mr. Warren was there. In an hour or so, Mr. Warren was on board the *Julia Ann*, and became once more John Mitchel. The wish he had so often expressed in Van Diemen's Land was accomplished at last. He had got from under the shadow of the British flag, and he took off his hat in homage to the stars and stripes.

On October 9, 1853, nearly a month after they left Tahiti, they arrived at the Golden Gate. The next three weeks were spent in California ; partly at San Francisco, partly at San José, and partly in the country. Mitchel was prepared to meet a warm welcome from the Irish in America, but his reception at San Francisco was a surprise to him. The enthusiasm with which he was received was not confined to the Irish ; it was largely shared by the American population. There were various honours and festivities, and finally, shortly before Mitchel's departure for the east, there was a grand reception banquet, by much the greatest thing of the kind which had as yet taken place at San Francisco. In a copy of the San Francisco *Herald* for November 1, 1853, I find a very glowing description of the dinner, and, what is more important, a full report of Mitchel's speech thereat. The governor of the state presided, and the mayor of San Francisco assisted him as vice-president. Covers were laid for four hundred persons ; and nearly all the leading citizens of San Francisco were present, as well as not a few leading men from the neighbouring territories. As a matter of course, Mitchel's reception was enthusiastic. His speech was characteristic; plain and terse in language—and in this respect a decided contrast to some of the other speeches delivered—but evidently animated throughout by intense though suppressed feeling. The concluding sentences may be given here as suggesting the nature of the feeling which animated him, and the view which he took of his duty as an intending American citizen :—

What I have said to-night is no more than what I said in the criminal's dock before the false judge—no more than what I have printed again and again in the public newspapers of Van Diemen's Land. Thank Heaven, my head has been always high, my heart has been always free, and I wore my fetters lightly as wreaths of roses. When my enemies sought to kill me by long and rigorous confinement in an unwholesome den, what, think you, sustained me and kept life in me?—rage and scorn, and a firm reliance on God's justice and the immortal thirst of vengeance. I thank my enemies now that they refused to release me ; I am glad they waited for contrition ; I am proud that I was liberated, not by their Queen's pardon, but by the disloyal aid of some of her Majesty's subjects in Australia, and by the daring and energy of my brave confederate and brother-rebel who sits at this table. Enough, then, of the past. I fling it behind me from this night, and look forward, forward. I have commenced in your state my novitiate in order to become an American citizen. Before Heaven, I declare that I will be a true and thorough American, as my naturalized countrymen generally are. But I believe America will not hold it disloyal to her if we Irish-Americans look anxiously out for an opportunity, and if we one day dash at the opportunity, to wipe off the dishonour of the old mother-land, and to dry her tears, and staunch her wounds, and make her a participator in that noble republican freedom that your fathers have shown all the world the way to win.

Mitchel was strongly pressed by his friends in California to stay in that state. They wanted him to settle at San

Francisco, and to resume the practice of his profession. They assured him that he might be confident of making a large income from the very start. But New York was Mitchel's objective point. New York was the great world-city of America, and moreover (and this was its chief attraction to Mitchel), it was within reasonable distance of Ireland. Mitchel had not yet by any means abandoned hope of effecting something in that country ; and in those days there were no railroads across the Rocky Mountains, and the journey from San Francisco to Ireland took a much longer time than it does now.

On the 1st of November, Mitchel and his family left San Francisco by the steamship *Cortez*, bound for New York, by the Nicaragua route. It took them some ten days to reach the place of disembarkation in Nicaragua. Thence the whole party had to travel on mules to the lake. They crossed Lake Nicaragua in a steamer, and then floated down the San Juan to Greytown. At Greytown they were delayed four days, waiting for the steamer which was to take them to New York. Here the first news reached them of that invasion of Turkey by the Czar, which eventually led to the Crimean war. This was what Mitchel called "portentous and thundering news." Several pages of the "Journal" are devoted to speculation as to what the outcome of this portentous news might be. Mitchel foresaw clearly enough that this move of the Czar's must lead to a great European war ; and he had vague hopes that in the general *melée* something good might turn up for Ireland. His thoughts were not of a kind likely to prove edifying to the members of the Peace Preservation Society. Here is a specimen :—

I dwell to-night on the hopes and fears of these foreign lands, and am afraid to breathe the name of Ireland, or to write it down, even in my secret tablets, as the name of *one* of the nations that have a destiny to achieve, and wrongs (how matchless and how bitter !) to avenge.

*   *   *   *   *   *   *

The very nation that I knew in Ireland is broken and dis-troyed ; and the place that knew it shall know it no more.   To America has fled the half-starved remnant of it ; and the phrase that I have heard of late—"a new Ireland in America," conveys no meaning to my mind.   Ireland without the Irish—the Irish out of Ireland—neither of these can be *our country*.   Yet who can tell what the chances and changes of the blessed war may bring us ? I believe in moral and spiritual electricity ; I believe that a spark, caught at some happy moment, may give life to masses of coma-tose humanity ; that dry bones, as in Ezekiel's vision, may live ; that out of the "Exodus" of the Celts may be born a return of the Heraclidæ.

Czar, I bless thee.   I kiss the hem of thy garment.   I drink to thy health and longevity.   Give us war in our time, O Lord !

On the 19th of November, they left Greytown in the *Prometheus*, for Havana and New York.   They reached Havana on the 22nd, and stayed there a day.   Mitchel went to explore the city with Smyth and an American friend, whose acquaintance he had made on the steamer. Partly his own observation, partly the conversation of the American, who had a patriotic hatred of the Spanish government, induced Mitchel to conclude that Cuba was "another Ireland."   He contemplated the palace of the captain-general with feelings the reverse of friendly :—

Passed on to the palace of the captain-general, a very hand-some and massive-looking house, near the quay.   In front of it is a shady court, open on all sides to the streets.   There I stood awhile, and looked up at the palace with horror and hatred, as at another Dublin Castle.   Those two strongholds of hell !   When will they be razed and swept away, and the places where they stand sown with salt !

On the evening of the 23rd, they left Havana for New

York. Three days later they were off Cape Hatteras.
Mitchel thought of the Bermudas, lying on their starboard
beam, and at no very great distance ; and his mind
wandered back to the ten months he had spent there and
to the years that had since passed :—

I can fancy that I see the baleful cedar-groves blackening the
eastern horizon. What change has come for the better, since I
ruminated there, four years ago, in my cell of pain ? If I am to
consider myself a "martyr," has my martyrdom done any service
to my cause ? or the reverse ? If I regard myself as a mere
prisoner, fraudulently seized upon, and cruelly used, what chance
have I ever for justice in my own person, to say nothing of
justice for my country ? Here I am now, with all dungeons behind
me, and a wide world just opening before—that is to say, the
time of irresponsible idleness and midsummer nights' dreams is
past ; the time of responsible action in broad day is upon me.
Shall I do good, or evil in my generation ? Or would it be
better that I had died amongst those black cedars there, and had
been buried in that foul cemetery, where all the dust is dust of
demons !

A gloomy question to press itself upon me now, just as I am
about to tread the land of Washington ! I am going to be a
demigod for two or three weeks—so my American friends warn
me, with many a prudent caution—going to have a reception, and
dinners, and shall be material for paragraphs in the morning
papers. If I were a fool, I would be happy.

He was neither very happy nor very sanguine. He did
not indeed despair of the cause which he believed to be
just ; but I find in the " Journal," shortly after the passage
last quoted, a slightly modified version of a famous Latin
proverb, which probably represented with approximate
accuracy his view regarding the future of the human race
in general, and of the Irish part of it in particular, " Magna
est veritas, et *non* praevalebit."

On November 29, 1853, John Mitchel with his wife and

family landed at New York. His brother William and
T. F. Meagher stepped on board to welcome them. They
were conducted direct to Brooklyn, where Mitchel's mother
and sisters, and Mrs. John Dillon, were waiting to receive
him ; and—here ends the " Jail Journal."

CHAPTER II.

NEW YORK—TUCALEECHEE COVE.

1853—1856.

THE story of John Mitchel's life during the thirteen years which succeeded his landing in New York has been written by himself in what he called a continuation of the " Jail Journal." This supplemental journal, however, was in strictness not a journal at all. It was not written during the period covered by it, but afterwards. Some admirers of the " Jail Journal " suggested to Mitchel, at a late period of his life, that a continuation of the "Journal" would be welcomed by his friends. In compliance with this request, he undertook to write the continuation. It was published in weekly parts in the *Irish Citizen*, during the years 1869 and 1870; but it has never appeared in book form. In point of literary power, the continuation is very decidedly inferior to the original " Journal." Still, it is John Mitchel's own account of his life during the period covered by it; and while I deem it best to make this life of Mitchel complete in itself, I would here remind the reader of the advice offered at page 253 of Volume I. From 1848 to 1866 the best life of John Mitchel is that to be found in his " Jail Journal," and in the continuation thereof.

Upon his arrival at New York, in November, 1853, Mitchel went direct to his mother's house at Brooklyn. During the period of his captivity, his mother, brother, and sisters—indeed, the whole Mitchel family—had emigrated to America. Mrs. Mitchel had heard of her son's escape, and had made her preparations to receive him. When he walked up to the door of the house in which his mother lived, he was surprised to see his own name upon the door-plate. His mother had furnished the house nicely, and had fitted up one room expressly for P. J. Smyth. The house was situated on Union Street, near the corner of Hicks Street, and in this house Mitchel continued to reside until he removed to East Tennessee. Of course, there was great excitement over his arrival, no end of deputations, addresses, processions, freedoms of cities, and hand-shaking. After the first five days, his right hand was quite swollen and painful, and for one day he was obliged to wear his right hand in a sling and to offer his left. Of these deputations and hand-shakings he says :—

This sort of thing went on for three or four nights; there seemed no end to the societies, clubs, companies, that each made it a point to come and welcome me to their hospitable land. Now it would be a most formidable body of piratical-looking fellows with glittering axes—the ship-carpenters, at your service, bearded, brawny. And as to their hand-shake, one had better shake hands with a vice. Then would follow several delegations from benevolent societies, with ribbons in their button-holes; and multitudes of little speeches had to be made—nonsensical enough, to be sure, but reporters of the morning papers were at our elbows taking down every word.

New York seems to have been a surprise to Mitchel in many ways. In particular, he was struck with a pheno-menon which is to-day even more apparent and more wonderful than it was in 1853 :—

I am bound to say, also, that I find it, in other and more important respects, a very grand and wondrous city. Consider this one fact : Since I arrived here, only a few days ago, a great many thousands of Irish men and women (about eleven thousand per week) have been emptied out of emigrant ships upon these quays. This is not counting Germans. Now, what becomes of these people? They are not to be seen crowding the streets and making mobs; they do not organize themselves to rob houses and cut throats; in fact, they are not seen at all: the potent vital force of this mighty country somehow absorbs them at once; they permeate and percolate through the community, and find their place and find their work. They get into railroad cars on the very evening of their arrival, and are whirled away to where loving friends are awaiting them on the banks of the Wabash, or hard by some bright lake of Michigan; or else they get immediate occupation in this city itself, where there is always a fine demand for broad shoulders and willing hands. This phenomenon is, on the whole, the most wonderful and admirable thing I have seen in New York.

At New York, as at San Francisco, he had a public reception and a banquet. The reception was at the City Hall, the banquet at the Broadway Theatre. In an interesting "Reminiscence of John Mitchel," supplied to me by Dr. Thomas Hunter, the President of the Normal College of New York, I find a passage in which the reception banquet is referred to. The passage is further interesting as giving the general impression which Mitchel, at this time of his life, produced upon the writer :—

"The first time I saw Mr. Mitchel was at a banquet given in his honour soon after his arrival in New York from Australia. The great lawyer, Charles O'Connor—himself the son of a '98 rebel—very appropriately presided; and thus '48 and '98 clasped hands across the festive board. This was in the winter of 1853–54. John Mitchel was then in the prime of his manhood, a little above the middle height, with a frame compact and well-proportioned, and a finely formed head resting on a strong and graceful neck. His face was a clear pale; his eyes a grey-blue; his hair a dark brown; his features faultless, with that indescribable something in the expression which indicated the scholar and thinker, if not the man of genius. . . . When Mitchel spoke in reply to the toasting of his name, one could readily understand why the London *Times*, the bitter and implacable foe of the Irish race, should have exclaimed that, in transporting Mitchel, the head and shoulders were taken from the revolutionary movement. The man was terribly in earnest ; he meant every word he uttered. The very tone of his voice proclaimed his sincerity. Patriotism with him was a passion, not the craft of a politician. He might be mistaken in his opinions ; but as long as he had faith in them, no earthly power could prevent him from expressing them. He was an Irishman in whom there was no guile; he had an utter abhorrence for everything in the form of cant and hypocrisy.

" It struck me, as I listened to his speech that evening, that as an orator he had been underrated. True, he was inferior to Meagher in the eloquence of passion ; but in a clear, incisive, logical statement of facts, he was vastly his superior. Mitchel in his youth had been a student of Swift ; and he had all Swift's dislike of ornament. What he had to say he said in the fewest and simplest words ; so that his presentation of a subject was as conclusive as a geometrical demonstration."

Both the banquet and the public reception at the City Hall were striking demonstrations, attended by leading Americans as well as by Irishmen. At first Mitchel seems to have somewhat misunderstood the import of these honours. He attributed to them more meaning than they were intended to convey. In answering the mayor of New York at the City Hall, Mitchel took care to say that he accepted honours of that kind in America expressly as an insult to the British Government. The mayor did not exactly like this. A friend who was present on the occasion suggested to Mitchel that, inasmuch as his entertainers did not in truth intend any special insult to the British Government, it was hardly fair of him to put that construction upon their acts. Mitchel saw the force of this; and in his "Journal" he admits that he made a blunder; that he had no right to "thrust his construction in public down the throats of his hospitable entertainers." But, when once it was made clear to him that these demonstrations were intended merely as passing tributes of respect to him, he ceased to take much interest in them.

Events were then taking place which interested Mitchel much more than receptions or banquets. It was evident that war between England and Russia was near at hand. It was not yet certain what course France would take. Mitchel began again to have hope for Ireland. With him, the great object was to secure that, if the opportunity came, Irishmen would be in the proper temper to take advantage of it. He wished to do his part in bringing about that result; and the only way open to him was to resume that profession of a journalist which had already brought him into collision with the British Government.

The first journal that John Mitchel conducted in America was called the *Citizen*. He seems to have had a particular liking for this name. The two other papers which he subsequently conducted in America were also *Citizens*, though in each case with a qualifying adjective prefixed. The idea of the *Citizen*, he tells us, was conceived within two weeks of his arrival at New York. The first number appeared on January 7, 1854. The paper was announced as to be conducted by John Mitchel, assisted by Thomas Francis Meagher. Mr. Meagher had permitted his name to be used, and had promised his help. But other matters speedily engrossed his attention, and as a matter of fact he gave little, if any, assistance in the conduct of the paper.

The main work of the paper fell on Mitchel himself; but he received considerable help from John McClenahan and John Savage. The following passages from the prospectus will serve to indicate the tone of the paper, so far, at least, as concerns Irish matters :—

The principal conductors are, in the first place, Irishmen by birth. In the second place, they are men who have endured years of penal exile at the hands of the British Government for endeavouring to overthrow the dominion of that Government in their native country. In the third place, they are refugees on American soil, and aspirants to the privileges of American citizenship.

The principles and conduct of their new journal will be in accordance with their position, their memories, and their aspirations.

They refuse to believe that, prostrate and broken as the Irish nation is now, the cause of Irish independence is utterly lost.

They refuse to admit that any improvement in the material condition of those Irishmen who have survived the miseries of the last seven years (if any improvement there be) satisfies the honour, or fulfils the destiny, of an ancient and noble nation.

The *Citizen* continued to be conducted by Mitchel for just one year—the year 1854.

In American politics the paper was mainly distinguished for its opposition to the abolition movement and its fierce denunciations of the Know-Nothings. Of political writings, the best in the paper are the "Letters to the Rev. Henry Ward Beecher," hereinafter noticed, and the "Letters to a Know-Nothing Acquaintance," published towards the close of 1854. Of the latter, the following passage may be taken as a specimen :—

A Mr. G. W. Bryce has published a long Know-Nothing letter in reply to Mr. Wise, of Virginia, wherein we find such sentences as this :—

"There are no men more earnest advocates of religious freedom, or more decided opponents of party corruption, than those who belong to the organizations which you oppose. It is not the religion of the Catholic more than that of the Protestant to which they object, but it is freedom for all which they advocate—*freedom from the tyranny of priestcraft*, and freedom in our government from all religious interference. They are unwilling that any church shall hold spiritual supremacy in these United States."

Here is a choice sample of Know-Nothing cant. The Order, according to this exponent, are " earnest advocates of religious freedom," and all other freedom ; but they will require their fellow-citizens to be free from the religious influence of ministers of religion—provided those ministers be priests. Why not insist also upon freedom from the dictates of conscience ? freedom from the marriage tie ? freedom from the obligations of debt ? freedom from the restraints of law ? This man wants " freedom in our government from all religious interference "—that is, all Catholic religious interference ; but the Protestants being the stronger, he would leave Protestant religious interference to disfranchise the Catholics. " They are unwilling that any church shall hold spiritual supremacy in these United States." But the thing cannot be helped. So long as there are any Catholic citizens here, the Pope at Rome, with the bishops he appoints, will assuredly hold spiritual supremacy—just as they do over the Catholic Swiss cantons, which are Republics quite as democratic as these United States.

And how happens it, if your Order be indeed against foreigners, not against Catholics, how happens it that we see none of its animosities directed against the Germans ?

In short, I am ashamed to argue the point. I take it as admitted, and hold it to be proved, that the Order is nothing else than an arrangement made by one set of Christians for hunting another set, according to the ancient sporting traditions of true religion ; and that it is to be dealt with accordingly.

The literary page of the paper, during more than half of the year of Mitchel's editorship, was taken up by the publication of the " Jail Journal." After the " Journal " was finished, there were various literary papers and reviews. For example, I find a notice of Ruskin's " Lectures on Architecture and Painting," written in terms of warm appreciation ; a paper on Richard Dalton Williams ; a very amusing critique on Mackenzie's " Noctes Ambrosianæ ; " a notice of Schelling, written on the news of his death ; a review in two parts of Bryant's poems ; and, last though not least, a review of the " Life of P. T. Barnum, by Himself." This last-named paper is a curious specimen of John Mitchel's power of taking useful lessons from books of a very rubbishy kind—a power referred to, as we have seen, in the " Jail Journal." The mixture of seriousness and irony is so well sustained, that it is not easy to tell when the writer is in earnest and when he is joking. Take, as a specimen, the following passages :—

The great moral value of this book, then, we take to consist in that for the first time swindling is here placed in its true, that is, its economic light, wherein alone an enlightened and commercial public ought to regard it. Humbug is lifted out of the mire, where an ill-informed public sentiment had long looked down upon it, and elevated to its proud position as one of the humanizing arts of life—nay, almost one of the fine arts. To fix the tail of a fish to the *torso* of a monkey, to advertise this as a mermaid captured at the Feejee Islands, to induce men, women, and children, under that representation, to come and pay their money for permission to come and see the thing—this and similar operations, which would certainly have, even one generation back, brought the operator under the penalties of criminal law, are related by Mr. Barnum not with an apology, not with an unbecoming boast either, but with a modest and manly pride, an evident absence of self-reproach, and a transparently clear conscience, as humble efforts of his to supply his " dear public " with what the "public" really wanted and was content to receive. The public, he tells us, like to be humbugged, will pay money to be humbugged. That they always got the worth of their money he assures us distinctly ; for when they came to see a woolly horse captured by Fremont in the Rocky Mountains, or Washington's nurse, or a mermaid, or whatever else was the exhibition of the moment, if they did not see what they paid for seeing, yet they thought they did; and, besides, did they not see a happy family, and many curious objects of nature and art, which were not in the bill at all, and were in themselves worth more than twenty-five cents?

*   *   *   *   *   *   *

Barnum in heaven will feel at home.   Hallelujahs will strike his ear as a familiar sound, reminding him of his own aerial orchestra, which across the busy scene of Broadway, serenades St. Paul for ever and ever.   Possibly his disembodied spirit will still watch over the corner of Ann Street, and he will at times think with yearning regret of his "dear public," gaping there for the thrilling excitements which only he could supply.   At such times he will gaze, perhaps, with a covetous eye at the Four Beasts, or privately offer an engagement to the eldest of the Four and Twenty Elders.

So much for the general character of the political and literary writing done by Mitchel in the *Citizen*.   I regret that the necessity of keeping this book within certain limits prevents me from quoting more fully from the paper. There are, however, one or two matters connected with Mitchel's editorship of the *Citizen* which call for a some-what fuller notice.

Very shortly after the *Citizen* was started, Mitchel was drawn into a controversy, which excited much attention at the time, and which probably had a large influence in determining the subsequent course of his life. The abolition party was then rising to power in the Northern States, and the questions which afterwards divided the Union were being hotly discussed.   Now, there lived in Dublin at this time a very benevolent old gentleman named James Haughton.   Mr. Haughton had known most of the Young Irelanders during the '48 time; and now that several of them were rising to notice in America, he was anxious that they should be found upon what he regarded as the right side in the slavery question.

He, accordingly, wrote and published a letter, which he addressed to Thomas Francis Meagher. In this letter he appealed, not only to Meagher, but also to John Mitchel, John Dillon, and Richard O'Gorman, and he called on them to prove themselves true men by boldly taking sides with the abolitionists. John Mitchel thought right to notice this letter in his paper. He had known Mr. Haughton in Dublin, and had never concealed the opinions which he even then held upon the slavery question. In his notice of the letter, he first refers to the fact that his views on the slavery question had long since been stated to Mr. Haughton, and then proceeds :—

And here, now, after six years, we find Mr. Haughton as fresh as ever, saying the very same things that were then so tedious to us. Others may exert themselves to gain justice and freedom for Irish serfs; he, for his part, will stand by the negroes, and scathe the cradle-plunderers. But what *right* has this gentleman to expect Thomas Francis Meagher, or the others whom he has named, to take up his wearisome song—which they always refused to sing at home? Now, let us try to satisfy our pertinacious friend, if possible, by a little plain English. We are not abolitionists; no more abolitionists than Moses, or Socrates, or Jesus Christ. We deny that it is a crime, or a wrong, or even a peccadillo, to hold slaves, to buy slaves, to keep slaves to their work by flogging or other needful coercion. "By your silence," says Mr. Haughton, "you will become a participator in their wrongs." But we will not be silent, when occasion calls for speech; and as for being a participator in the wrongs, we, for our part, wish we had a good plantation, well-stocked with healthy negroes, in Alabama. There, now! Is Mr. Haughton content? What right has he to call upon Mr. Mitchel the moment he sets his foot in America to begin a crusade for a cause which, as Mr. Haughton knows, was always distasteful to him in Ireland?

This was certainly plain speaking enough; such speaking as was certain to excite the fierce animosity of a powerful section of the community in which Mitchel then

lived.   He was prepared for a fair share of abuse ; but he
was not, he tells us, prepared for what actually happened.
He was not then fully conscious of the intensity and bitterness of the anti-slavery sentiment ; and the tempest of
execration which greeted his answer to Mr. Haughton fairly
astonished him.   I cannot here stay to notice the abundant
abuse of the New York press, nor to determine which of
the various journals carried off the palm for hard language.
But amongst Mitchel's fiercest assailants was one whose
attack calls for a special notice.   This was the Rev. Henry
Ward Beecher.   Writing many years afterwards of his
controversy with Beecher, Mitchel says :—

The *Citizen* had not been two weeks in existence when I was
startled, if not confounded, by a furious assault upon me by the
Rev. Henry Ward Beecher, a very popular clergyman in Brooklyn,
of the sect of people called "Congregationalists ; " an eloquent,
powerful, and rowdy preacher, of no great cultivation, but of
intense energy, and an appearance of wonderful earnestness.   Of
course, he was a violent abolitionist, and chose to consider my
declaration of adverse opinion as a fatal stab to my own character.
In short, he pronounced me a dead man, and thereupon proceeded to mangle my corpse and suck my bones.   First in a
public lecture, and afterwards in a weekly newspaper called the
Independent, this reverend man minced me extremely small.

Mangled as he was, however, Mitchel was able to strike
back with effect.   I shall take occasion further on to say
what I deem it necessary to say regarding John Mitchel's
attitude on the slavery question.   For the present, I will
merely notice one charge much dwelt on by Beecher.   It
was inconsistent, he thought, of Mitchel, the champion of
freedom in Ireland, to champion slavery in America.
Mitchel had little difficulty in disposing of this charge.   If
it be inconsistent to champion the rights of a nation to
freedom from foreign rule, and at the same time to hold

slaves, then the charge of inconsistency holds good against
Leonidas and Themistocles, against Washington and Jefferson. Mitchel might well be content to stand or fall in such
company. The controversy with Beecher was, in more than
one respect, a remarkable event in Mitchel's life. In the
first place, the answer which Beecher's attack called forth
is, in a literary point of view, one of the very best things
Mitchel ever produced. In no other one of his writings
does his wonderful power over the English language as an
instrument of expression appear with more telling effect.
Whatever may be one's opinion upon the subject discussed,
it is impossible to read the controversy without feeling that
Mitchel showed himself far more than a match for his
opponent. There are passages in the letters in answer to
Beecher which for irony and cutting sarcasm are equal
to anything in Swift. But it was not only by reason of
the display of literary power which it called forth that
this controversy was a remarkable event in Mitchel's life.
It was, I think, the first link in a chain of causes which
ultimately led to Mitchel's throwing in his lot with the
Confederacy in the war of secession. Not that he would
not in any case have sympathized with slavery and with
the South; he had done so before he came to America.
But I doubt if he would have considered himself bound to
take active part in a cause which, after all, was not his
own, had he not been powerfully roused and incited in that
direction. From the time of this controversy forward there
is an element of ferocity in his advocacy of slavery and
denunciation of abolition. I believe we may trace the
origin of this ferocity in that hatred of cant and hypocrisy
which was the ruling passion of his nature. He saw, or
fancied he saw, a large element of cant in the abolition
movement, as represented by Mr. Beecher; and the least
suspicion of cant was always enough to set him up in arms.

It would not be possible to select a few quotations which would give an adequate idea of the literary power displayed in the letters to Beecher. But the reader may take the following passage as representing the average of the whole as well as any other I could select :—

I do not affect to be ignorant that your little school claim the Founder of the Christian religion as an abolitionist ; not by reason of any positive condemnation or prohibition of slavery or slave-holding, but by virtue of what you call the development of the religion, which you suppose to be growing and advancing, as man grows and advances. Especially you dwell upon the great precept, " Do unto others as ye would that others should do unto you "— and you say *here* is abolition in embryo. Though a laic, I shall venture to suggest to you, most learned clerk, a simple explanation of that text, which, perhaps, never occurred to you before. It means, do unto others as you would wish (if they were in your circumstances and you in theirs) that they should do unto you. If you are a creditor, treat your debtor with that forbearance and consideration which, if you were the debtor and he the creditor, you might reasonably wish and expect him to use towards you. This does not mean, Creditors, discharge your debtors free. Again, if you are a slaveholder, use your slave with gentleness, humanity, and kindness, rewarding him when he does well, never punishing him wantonly or oppressively—in short, just as you could reasonably wish, were you the slave and he the master, that he would behave towards you. Therefore, the in-junction of the New Testament is, not, Masters, discharge your slaves ; but, be merciful to your slaves ; slaves, be obedient to your masters.

But I said something of slaves being *lashed.* Yes ; the very idea of a slave includes the idea of coercion, but does not at all include the idea of cruelty ; and when I wished for a plantation of negroes, your reverence, and the *Tribune,* with great candour, proclaim that I want slaves in order to have the luxury of flogging them. Does any man marry a wife that he may have the pleasure of beating his children ? Yet he who spareth the rod, spoileth the child. Does any man buy a horse for the sake of whipping him ? Did Washington keep negroes merely that he might indulge himself in thrashing them? In fact, I wanted to set down the principle as nakedly as possible—that it is not wrong to hold a slave; from this principle it follows that it is not wrong to make a slave work; and there is no way of making him work (in the last resort) but dread of the lash.

This is an ungracious task I find myself forced to undertake. On my side, in this controversy, everything sounds harsh and looks repulsive. Your reverence has chosen, if not the better, at least, the balmier part. Yours is the privilege, dear to the enlightened modern heart, of uttering kind-looking sentences. It comes easy to you (for all the prevailing cants are with you) to assume for yourself and your followers, the credit of benevolence, and philanthropy, and enlightenment, and "progress," and all the rest of it; while I, to escape the charge of barbarous cruelty and bloodthirsty atrocity, am forced to shield myself under the authority of mere ancients, persons behind the century, persons who had not the advantage of hearing your lectures at the tabernacle, persons like the legislators of the Jews, and the wise men of the Greeks and the framers of the Declaration of Independence. It would be easy for me also, and it would be true, to assert that I am not cruel or tyrannical by nature—that I hate all oppression—that, if I had slaves, I would influence and govern uniformly by kindness instead of coercion; in short, that I would use them as humanely as Jefferson himself, whose enthusiastic reception by his attached negroes on his return to Monticello, forms so agreeable a picture in Tucker's life of that illustrious man. It would be easy; but I do 'not condescend to treat the question in this personal and restricted manner. My position was, and is, the naked assertion, " that slaveholding is not a crime;" and that nobody ever thought it a crime until some time towards the close of the last century.

Many of his friends were surprised and pained by this explicit declaration in favour of slavery; and many wrote to remonstrate with him. I cannot find, from his correspondence, that he took much pains to justify his view. But some letters he did answer. The following is taken from a letter written from New York, on April 24, 1854, to Miss

Thompson, the friend to whom he wrote the letter from Van Diemen's Land already quoted :—

. . . We were very glad, at all events, to see your letter. Write again, even, if you think it right to criticise me severely. I am glad you find anything to read with pleasure in my " Jail Journal," but it seems incomprehensible to me when you say you " find it hard to reconcile my sentiments." Does it not occur to you to inquire whether in other ages, and even so late as the age of our fathers, those two sets of sentiments, now called irreconcilable, were not in fact constantly reconciled, and whether people so much as suspected that there was any discrepancy to reconcile ? My dear lady, beware of the nineteenth century ; and when any of your taunting friends asks you again, " What do you think of Ireland's emancipator now? Would you like an Irish republic with an accompaniment of slave plantations ? "—answer quite simply, " Yes." At least, I would so answer ; and I never said or wrote anything in the least inconsistent with such a declaration. But enough of the blacks.

There can be no doubt but that, viewed from the standpoint of self-interest, Mitchel's declarations on the slavery question were highly imprudent. But whatever may have been his virtues, I fear it must be admitted that worldly prudence was not amongst them. Circumstances led him to conclude that it was " in some sort needful " for him to come out and define his position on the slavery question ; and straightway he " did it effectually and finally," without for one moment stopping to think what might be the effect upon his worldly prospects. Possibly some people may think that there was no duty cast upon him to make the declaration at all, and that he would have done better and more wisely to have kept his views upon the slavery question to himself. It is enough here to say that, if he had so acted, he would not have been the John Mitchel he was.

The success of the *Citizen* at its start was probably

without precedent in the history of American journalism. Within a few weeks of its commencement, the paper reached a circulation of fifty thousand. The paper would undoubtedly have proved a very valuable property, and have yielded its owner a large income, had he but been willing to be governed by maxims of prudence. But the policy of saying out just what one believes to be true, irrespective of consequences, is not the policy most likely to conduce to the financial success of a newspaper.

The outlook for the *Citizen* soon became clouded. The declarations on the slavery question above referred to prob-ably hurt the paper a good deal ; but more serious harm was done to it by another controversy in which Mitchel some months afterwards became involved. In this second controversy his antagonist was no less a person than Dr. Hughes, the then Roman Catholic Archbishop of New York. There was a good deal of controversy then going on regarding the temporal power of the Pope, who had recently been restored to his dominions by French aid. Mitchel, in the *Citizen*, opposed the temporal power on the ground that the Romans had as good a right as any other people to change their form of government, if they wished to do it. Writing an account of this controversy years afterwards, he says he has since had reason to believe that he then somewhat misunderstood the real feeling of the Romans ; and he adds :—

However, the doctrine of the *Citizen*, that the Romans had a right to change the government of Rome, scandalized a great many of the Catholic clergy of the United States ; and Archbishop Hughes came out and scathed us in the newspapers. I am not patient of ecclesiastical censure ; and replied, perhaps too bitterly, and more than once. It was an unfortunate controversy for me, and for the purposes and objects of the *Citizen*, inasmuch as most of the readers of that paper, those indeed, to whom it was mainly addressed, were just the flocks of this very prelate, and of the rest of the Catholic clergy. Independently, however, of the effect of the dispute upon the fortunes of the *Citizen,* I do admit, now, after fifteen years, that I would, if I could, erase from the page, and from all men's memory, about three-fourths of what I then wrote and published to the address of Archbishop Hughes. This I say, not by way of atonement to his memory—for he deserved harsh usage, and could stand it and repay it—but by way of justice to myself only.

The *Citizen* never quite recovered the effect of this controversy with the archbishop. Yet it continued to have a large circulation so long as Mitchel remained the editor.

Meantime there were matters going on in the old world which interested Mitchel more keenly than either the temporal power or the slavery question. The great struggle between the two great western powers and Russia had begun. Mitchel watched eagerly for some turn in the progress of affairs which might hold out hope for Ireland. At length he became impatient, and he bethought him of going to Washington, and calling on the Russian ambassador there. His account of the interview is amusing :—

Went to Washington, travelling through the great cities of Philadelphia and Baltimore, to see the Russian minister at this capital, the Baron Stoeckl. Found him residing in a house at a place called Georgetown Heights, and when he received my card he came instantly to greet me with much warmth. He was a subscriber, he said, to the *Citizen,* and a " constant reader ; " yet the baron surmised, not without some show of reason, that the part which I took in the pending war, endeavouring to turn away the sympathies of America from the allies, and engage them on the side of Russia, was instigated by my abhorrence of England only, not by any particular love of Russia. I admitted the impeachment.

He met Baron Stoeckl twice : once at Washington, and once, at the baron's own request, at New York. But nothing came of it. Neither the Russian minister nor Mr. Mitchel himself could see very well how Russia was to get at Ireland while the English and French were sweeping the sea. And Mitchel admitted, in answer to the baron's questions, that money would be of little use without a covering force.

Ireland was always first in Mitchel's thoughts; and, therefore, he generally took a keener interest in European politics than in American politics. But occasionally things occurred in home politics which roused him thoroughly. He was so roused during this year 1854 by the movement known as "Know-Nothingism." In the account which he gives of the rise of this movement, he begins by asserting that it was in truth the British press which suggested the idea of the crusade. The cry was the echo of a like cry previously raised in England. It would never do to give up American liberties to the Pope of Rome, the Jesuits, and the Dominicans of the Inquisition. This was the cry used to rouse the people. As regards the true motives of the leaders, Mitchel writes thus :—

To come down from those high considerations—which, in truth, nobody ever thought of for one moment—the case was this : One party, the Democrats, held power and enjoyed the emoluments of office too long; the Whigs, Federals, Massachusetts Protectionists felt that they should have their turn, so they raised a cry. They thought it would answer at least for a campaign; and it really did answer, to an extent I had never expected, amongst the uneducated people of this most noble country, a class of the people indeed which I find to be in very enormous proportion to the rest. No old story out of Fox's "Book of Martyrs" was too monstrous to be dwelt upon by the orators of this grand Protestant movement. The old women of all the three sexes, masculine, feminine, and neuter, were to be frightened and irritated, and this was easy enough.

An apostate Italian priest, named Gavazzi, had come but lately

to this country, and had gone round lecturing against the Pope
and the Irish servant girls.

*   *   *   *   *   *   *

On the whole, I think it would be hard to point out, in the
history of any civilized (or demi-civilized) country, so foolish, so
filthy, so imbecile a movement as this of the Know-Nothings, and
the "mystery of iniquity," in the densely peopled parts of the city
chiefly inhabited by Irish Catholics ; and these, though patient
and good-humoured, could not always endure the outrage.

There were many brutal outrages on "papists" and
"foreigners." Churches were wrecked ; and in one case a
priest, an old man, was beaten, stripped naked, and tarred
and feathered in a New England town. Of course, there
was resistance and retaliation, and in some cases serious
rioting. In the *Citizen*, Mitchel very pointedly said what he
thought about the Know-Nothings, as he did about most
other things that he dealt with.

What with abolitionists and Know-Nothings, Mitchel's
enthusiasm about his new country began sensibly to abate.
In the month of April or May he received an invitation
from the mayor and council of the city of Richmond, in
Virginia. The Virginians, it appears, had admired his
boldness in declaring for negro slavery, and they were
desirous to do him honour. The municipal authorities in
the capital of Virginia proposed to give a banquet in his
honour, and hence the invitation. In the mood he was
then, any excuse for quitting New York was welcome.
He at once decided to accept. He left New York towards
the end of May ; travelled by rail to Washington ; thence
along the Potomac by steamer to a place called Aquia
Creek ; and thence by rail to Richmond. Arrived at Richmond, he found that he had two or three days to spare
before the time fixed for the banquet. He determined to
utilize these days in visiting Charlottesville, the seat of the

University of Virginia, near to which was situated Monticello, the home of Jefferson. He had no letters of introduction to any one in that part of the country, and he was
confident that he could go around and look at things for
himself without having them *shown* to him. In this respect,
however, as the event showed, he was over-sanguine.

A detailed account of the visit to the university and to
Monticello, and of the impressions which Mitchel carried
away regarding Jefferson's taste in architecture, is given in
the " Journal Continuation." One result of the trip was
that Mitchel received and accepted an invitation from the
presidents of the literary societies of the University of
Virginia to attend their annual " commencements " in the
following month, and to deliver the oration customary on
such occasions.

On his return to Richmond, he found everything ready
for his reception. The banquet was quite a noteworthy
affair. It was attended by the leading citizens of Richmond,
and by not a few of the Virginian planters. Mitchel was
puzzled to know why Virginia should be so enthusiastic
about him :—

Again I applied to a friend about the meaning of this
enthusiastic Virginian hospitality to me. " Why, in New York,"
I said, " where I was received at first quite as illustriously as
here, yet, at this moment, when people speak of me at all, they
abuse me." " That," he answered, " is because you wished for a
plantation in Alabama, and vindicated slavery against Reverend
Beecher. Well, it is for these reasons that you are warmly welcomed
here." I began to understand fully now, what I had partly suspected before, that dwelling on this land of the United States
there are two nations, not one only ; and that the two are separated
not more sharply by a geographical line than by their institutions,
habits, industrial requirements, and political principles. There is
a northern nation and a southern ; and possibly it may come to
this, that they must either peaceably separate, dividing the continent

between them, or else the one must conquer the other. For so far I do hope that it will *not* come to this ; but, if it do, I think all my sympathies would be with the south.

Mitchel stayed in Richmond some three or four days after the banquet, and made many pleasant acquaintances. He then returned to New York, and resumed his work on the *Citizen.*

To get done with Virginia for the present, I may here mention that towards the end of June in this year, 1854, Mitchel once more visited Charlottesville, in fulfilment of his promise to deliver the annual oration in the University of Virginia.   The scene on this occasion afforded a marked contrast to certain other scenes which Mitchel recollected in his own university days :—

Entering the stately rotunda, under its colonnade of Corinthian pillars, and passing through a large octagonal hall, we enter the new and handsome building in the rear.   Its benches are already crowded, mostly with ladies in bright summer costumes ; the atmosphere is perfumed by a hundred bouquets and cooled by the fluttering of five hundred fans.   At the upper end is a handsome carpeted platform, already occupied by professors, by the state examiners, and other notabilities.   At the other end is a gallery accommodating a fine band, brought specially from Baltimore, which makes some music in the intervals of the business.

Very different, indeed, from the scene at Trinity College, Dublin, when Mitchel had his degree conferred upon him. "Which is the better system ?" he asks. " I mean better in the academic point of view, for which is the pleasanter no one need doubt ? "

After the degrees had been conferred, Mitchel's turn came :—

I was nervous, for I saw very well my audience was a critical one— some of the foremost Virginians were upon that platform—

and I knew that I was going to shock some of the current and accepted opinions of our times. The address was on " Progress in the Nineteenth Century," and the drift of it was to show that there is no *progress* at all; that is, no progress making men wiser, happier, or better than they were thirty centuries ago ; but admitting, also, that they are no worse, no foolisher, no more wretched than they were at that period and ever since. Of course, gas, steam, printing-press, upholstering, and magnetic telegraphs could not be denied, but they were put aside as altogether irrelevant to the inquiry. I could see that those around, how courteously soever they listened, and even sometimes applauded, did not in their own hearts assent to my conclusions.

I take the following passages from the address itself, as illustrating the drift of the whole, as well as any other isolated passages I could select :—

What if human progress, after all, be like the progress of the material globe in a cycloid; if the motion of every individual human society be a real wheel of fortune, whereupon it climbs, culminates, and falls ; if there be indeed an intellectual and moral summer for each region of the globe, warming men just then and there, with the vital fire of national spirit and individual intelligence, and giving social life its highest and grandest development, but followed, as surely and inevitably, by the withering winter? All the analogies of nature preach this to us aloud. History, so far as the glimmering lamp of history throws back a ray, tells the same tale.

  * * * * * * *

Thus, if this cyclical law be the true law, there is continual compensation to maintain equilibrium, one nation always sinking in exact proportion as another climbs. If our age credit itself with the life and action of Europe, let it debit itself with the death and burial of Asia.

  * * * * * * *

Are we going back, then? Going down? Grows the world worse instead of better? More wretched instead of more happy? God forbid ! Some nations indeed have gone back and gone down; and human nature and life have therein fallen into blank etiolation, darkness, and decay; but just in that exact proportion, other parts of the world have been emerging into the sunlight; and the life of man has quickened into intense vitality, and sprung into glory and power.   As twilight shadows have been creeping over western Europe, the rosy fingers of morning have been opening the gates of dawn upon America.   Perhaps the truth is, that while we know man, the individual, may and can advance, by high culture, by self-denial and heroic energy and faith, to the loftiest heights of human intellect and virtue; that while nations can grow great, free, and happy, each in its day, man, the family or *genus*, never stirs a step, either backward or forward.

Upon the whole, although he could not persuade his hearers to entirely accept his views regarding the nineteenth century, Mitchel seems to have been much pleased with his visit.   He thus sums up the impression made upon him :—

This visit to the Virginia University has been to me a very great pleasure, as well as a high honour.   The weather has been charming; the people all kind.   It forms a bright picture, which I hang up in the chambers of my memory, framed with gold and wreathed with flowers.

He returned by a different route from that by which he had come : over the Blue Ridge by railway to Staunton, and thence down the valley of the Shenandoah, by Winchester to Harper's Ferry.   He thus saw a very beautiful part of the country at the very time when it looked best.

When Mitchel again got back to New York and to the *Citizen* office, it was midsummer, and the heat in the city was intense.   Mitchel was feeling discouraged and out of sorts.   The Crimean War was not progressing exactly as he wished.   As it became more evident that the war was likely to be localized, and not to involve more parties than those already engaged, Mitchel's hopes for Ireland diminished.   Then, at home, the Know-Nothing cry was working to the entire satisfaction of those who started it.

Mitchel determined to get out of New York for a time, and to take his family to the sea. It was arranged between Mitchel and his friend, John Dillon, that the two families should go together to a place called Stonington, in Connecticut. This was one of the regular watering-places for New Yorkers, "occupied by vast hotels or public boarding-houses, where people live in crowds, as New Yorkers delight to live, and where the main occupation of the women is dressing, that of the men lounging and smoking, with their heels upon a balcony rail."

The society at Stonington was far too Puritanical for Mitchel ; yet some of the people there were disposed to be social and friendly after their fashion :—

It happened that there were two or three professors of what are called here "colleges" amongst the guests ; and these, when they found out who Mr. Dillon and I were, showed a disposition to enter into conversation with us. It appeared that they were particularly delighted with me on account of my letters to Archbishop Hughes. They praised my style of writing—had the kindness to bid me *stick to that*, and came out with a good deal of mere vulgar Protestantism on the occasion. This was highly offensive to me; and I opened upon their Protestantism in a manner which made Dillon laugh loud. My professors smiled also, in a dubious way. It was clear they thought they had lighted upon a very bright and intelligent maniac. They continued quite polite until we left Stonington; yet as they spoke to me the dubious smile was still there.

From Stonington he wrote to Miss Thompson on the 26th of August, a letter from which the following passage is extracted :—

. . . We live (as all people at American watering-places do) in a huge hotel with a public table, the guests almost all descendants of the Pilgrim Fathers, with a righteous horror of the South. They looked at me with a sort of obscure and grave horror at first, for I am a hissing to New England. Yet I have conciliated some of the dismal folk; and as for Jenny, she is a favourite. Amuse-ments—boating, driving in hired conveyances to the neighbouring Connecticut villages, all clean, prim, and wooden as Stonington, bathing, for which the beach is not very favourable, and, by way of variety, there was last night a "fair" in the school-house attached to one of the churches, the sort of thing which in Ireland is called a bazaar, for selling knick-knacks to raise money for some congregational purpose. On the whole, I like Virginia much better than this region; and if I had only "a good planta-tion" there—— But I will not shock you.

After a stay of a few weeks at the seaside, during which they "derived from Stonington all the health and amuse-ment it was calculated to afford," Mitchel and his family returned to New York.

During the remainder of the year 1854, and until Mitchel severed his connection with the *Citizen*, his outer life was uneventful. The course of his mental life, the subjects which mainly occupied his thoughts, can be traced in his writings in his paper. In the month of October he received the news of the unconditional release of Smith O'Brien and the other political prisoners in Van Diemen's Land. The fact of the pardon being unconditional was a surprise to the prisoners themselves; but Mitchel was not in a mood to allow much credit for this to her Majesty's ministers. A great meeting was convened at the Tabernacle in New York to adopt an address of sympathy with O'Brien. The requisition calling this meeting was signed by the mayor, the ex-mayor, and many of the leading citizens of New York. Mitchel had by this time learned to estimate these demonstrations at what they were worth. But, with all allowance for motives, he was much pleased with this O'Brien demonstration :—

On this occasion I am in high good-humour; forbear even to intimate that all the parade is only to make capital for certain politicians with the multitudes of Irish voters. What if it be so? Is it not gratifying that the said politicians know they can make their capital with our people only by sympathizing with rebels and affronting the English Government?

The meeting was a marked success. The Tabernacle was crowded to its utmost capacity; and although the great majority of the meeting were Irish, there were upon the platform quite a number of prominent Americans. Mitchel and several of his friends were present :—

Other associates of Mr. O'Brien were present—Meagher, O'Gorman, Doheny, Dillon, and the present writer. We were there to enjoy the scene, not to take part in it; but were all called upon imperatively by the audience; obliged, in short, to come to the front to say a few hearty words.

On the whole, I must admit, though hard to please, that the occasion was one of unmingled gratification. We knew well how these words of cheer, coming from the grand free city of New York, would soothe the spirit of the brave and impenitent rebel.

This was the last noteworthy public occasion in which Mitchel took part in New York for some considerable time. It was now near to the end of 1854, and Mitchel had been a year in America. He had learned a good deal during that time; and what he had learned had considerably chilled that enthusiasm for America and American institutions with which he had landed at San Francisco a year before. Above all, he had learned (what was new to him) that the United States was, in truth, inhabited by two distinct nations; and the whole bent of his nature led him to sympathize with the planters of the South rather than with the Puritans of New England. From the time of his first visit to Virginia he had wished for a residence in the south; and many motives now combined to make him anxious to leave New York. Amongst these motives was one not uncommonly found with men of genius. He expressed the feeling afterwards in a letter to a friend by saying that every place is detestable while you are there. He had a high ideal of what human nature ought to be, though not, strictly speaking, of what human nature might be, since he never had much faith in the perfectibility of the species. Still, when he found that the motives and desires of the crowd amongst which for the time being he moved were, as a rule, "pretty mean," he became impatient, and indulged a sort of vague hope that he might find things better somewhere else.

I have already tried to describe and account for that eager, restless tendency which was so marked during the life in Van Diemen's Land. This tendency was now asserting itself again. Indeed, from the time John Mitchel was carried off from Ireland, he seemed incapable of settling down finally in any one place. He had a sort of feeling that Ireland was his natural home, and that nowhere else could he have rest.

But, besides causes that formed a part of his character, there were special reasons which induced Mitchel to throw up the *Citizen* and leave New York. His eyes became affected, and he was advised that for a time, at all events, he must give up work at the *Citizen* office. But even this might have been got over. The motive which finally decided Mitchel was known to none except the members of his own family. He still continued to hope that affairs in Europe might take some sudden turn which would offer a chance for Ireland. He wished to be free to go over at once should the opportunity come. While his family were living in New York, and were depending on his pen for the means of living, he could not very well leave them. He wished to place them in such a way as would leave him free to go to Ireland in case the chance—so long wished for—were to come at last.

He turned his thoughts to the southern states. He had been told that the eastern part of Tennessee was a very beautiful country, and that land was to be had cheap there. He determined to move to East Tennessee, and to again try his hand at farming. It is true that his farming experiences in Van Diemen's Land had not been altogether pleasant. But he would never admit that this was a fair test. Any sort of life *there* would have been intolerable to him.

With the close of the year 1854, Mitchel ended his connection with the *Citizen.* The paper was made over to McClenahan. In a parting address published in the paper, Mitchel bade farewell to his readers. After giving some account of his experiences as editor, he proceeds :—

It is true that along with a great deal of sincere good-feeling, I have experienced a great deal of real, and much *more* fictitious, hostility. Probably I want prudence and "policy;" for on all sides I am credibly informed that I have made enemies. The "Alabama plantation" swept off ten thousand readers at one blow. Archbishop Philo-Veritas, with his pastoral crozier, drew away a few thousands more. The Rev. Mr. Beecher rushed upon me with his tomahawk at one side; some Catholic priests cursed me from their altars at the other. Now a zealous Irish Catholic wrote me an abusive letter; and now a true-blue Irish Orangeman sent me private intimation that he feared I would be assassinated. Yet the *Citizen* has survived. There has been proved to be enough of independent and honest feeling in the country to sustain such an organ as was needed. And I have some reason to believe that it may be still better sustained, and therefore more useful, when it is divested of that intense *personality* which, during my editorship, has attached to every article, every paragraph, almost every advertisement in the paper. It was all "John Mitchel," and therefore liable to all the disfavour and hatred which pursued that individual. Not so much the intrinsic truth or justice of what was said, but whether it became this John Mitchel to say it, was the thing generally considered.

Now, it would be affectation to pretend that these things seriously affect me. In fact, like Sir Fretful Plagiary, I rather like them. I have not been much alarmed by the tomahawk of Mr. Beecher, nor hurt by the crozier of Philo-Veritas. My friends, the Orangemen, have threatened me often before; and for altar-denunciations, Lord bless you! I was well cursed seven years ago.

Towards the close of 1854, Mitchel published the "Jail Journal" in book form. The "Journal" had, as already mentioned, been published in weekly parts in the *Citizen*. This was the second book that Mitchel published, "Hugh O'Neil" being the first. It had a large sale. In point of literary power, it is the best of his works. I have already quoted very fully from this book, and do not propose to make any further criticism of it here. Indeed, I may state here, once for all, that this "Life of Mitchel" will not contain any lengthy criticisms on his published works. These works have been before the Irish reading public for a number of years. In this book I have tried to compress a large mass of matter, strictly biographical, within reasonable limits. I could hardly find space for criticisms of books, even if I believed such criticisms to be needed. I shall, therefore, content myself with very briefly noticing Mitchel's books at the times of their respective publications.

Some months after its appearance, the "Jail Journal" was reviewed at length in the *Revue des Deux Mondes*. The writer of the review—M. Emile Montégut—did not at all share Mitchel's anti-English views; but he recognized the literary power of the book, and gave a careful analysis of it.

In the autumn of 1854, Mitchel also published an edition of Davis's poems, with an introductory memoir of the man whose friendship had so powerfully influenced the course of his own life.

Early in the spring of 1855, John Mitchel bid adieu to New York, and started with his family for Charleston.

This was then the best way of getting to Knoxville, the capital of East Tennessee. 'I have spoken of the motives which caused him to make this move. Here is his own account of the matter, so far as he deems it necessary to give any account of it :—

Why I should go to Knoxville, Tennessee, of all places in the whole world, and bring my wife and children with me ; especially as I had never seen Knoxville, and did not know one human being at Knoxville, might seem a question difficult to answer upon grounds which would be allowed as rational. There was not at that time so much as a railroad running from south-western Virginia through that great valley between the Alleghany and Cumberland, but lately the favoured hunting-ground of the Cherokees, which is termed East Tennessee ; and, on the whole, it was the most unfrequented, the most unknown and untrodden region in all the United States from the Mississippi to the Atlantic, and from the Lakes to the Gulf. What I knew of it was that in extent this valley was about equal to Ulster and Connaught together ; that it had but few towns, and those very small ; immense forests and mountains, with innumerable rivers ; deer, turkey, to say nothing of bears, wolves, and " painters." In short, I desired to fly from the turmoil of New York, and to try whether life might be possible for us amongst the woods. Other folks had found it so ; why not we ? Besides, ever since that banishment from my own country, and the sudden severing of all the roots that bound me to the soil, cutting of all the moorings that held me to the firm shore, I am conscious of a certain vagabond, or even half-savage propensity. But it is better not to investigate too closely : this introspection is not wholesome.

They remained a few days at Charleston, and saw the city and its environs. As they steamed into the inner bay, they gazed at the gloomy mass of Fort Sumter, little thinking what a fearful interest that same fort would one day have for them. The citizens of Charleston invited Mitchel to a public banquet, which, however, he respectfully declined. From Charleston they proceeded by railway through Georgia, and on to a place called Loudon, on the bank of the Tennessee river. Here the railway stopped, and the rest of the journey to Knoxville had to be made in a conveyance called a "carry-all." They arrived at Knoxville late at night, after a drive of thirteen hours.

It was in the month of March, 1855, that Mitchel and his family came to Knoxville. On the morning after his arrival, Mitchel was called upon by Mr. Swan, the mayor of the town, and a number of other gentlemen. Mr. William G. Swan and John Mitchel afterwards became and remained fast friends. This was their first meeting, and after some conversation they walked out to see the town. Mitchel has given us a brief description of Knoxville as it then was :—

Knoxville is built upon a hill rising somewhat steeply from the bank of the Holston River, a very large stream even here, though it has not received its greatest tributaries. On the opposite shore is a range of densely wooded hills ; and the forests are seen quite near on this side also, seeming to close in upon us at every side. The town has two or three decent streets, but not paved nor lighted with gas, although these defects are soon to be remedied.

Like every other town in the United States, it has a mighty future, and occupies itself much in contemplation of that good time. A railroad will in two or three years connect it with Virginia northwards and with Georgia southwards. A gas company has been formed to illuminate the place ; and if I doubted it, I had only to look at the bundles of main pipes laid down here and there upon the streets; a new market just finished; real estate enhancing ; lots rising ! Ah me ! give me a land where the lots don't rise.

He was somewhat disgusted to find the Know-Nothing craze in full possession of East Tennessee. It seems that the first Catholic church was then just about to be built in Knoxville. Mr. Swan told Mitchel, laughing, that as this little church was to be of solid stone, and as masons were already laying its foundations with massive blocks, the building was beginning to be an object of suspicion to the more vigilant of the Know-Nothings, who gave out, in fact, that there were to be vaults under the church for storing gunpowder to be ready for the use of the Jesuits when they should come to take the country, abolish its liberties, and set up the Inquisition in East Tennessee.

Mitchel had not been many days in Knoxville before he found that he was himself an object of curiosity and suspicion to the Know-Nothings. This fact he learned from his friend Mr. Swan :—

It appears that I have been the occasion of some know-nothing gossip here. Mr. Swan tells me that a day or two after my first arrival, a respectable stupid old Know-Nothing, who lives near the town, took occasion to warn him (Mr. Swan) against me and my designs. " You should not be seen so much with that papist Irishman," he said. "You are not aware, I am sure, of what his real business here is ; and the people are becoming excited about it." " And what," said Mr. Swan, " do you say *is* his real business?" "Why," said the profound Know-Nothing, "it is understood that he is the person who is at the bottom of this stone building here ; that he procured the ground for it, and is here to superintend its construction for the purposes it is designed for. You see the strong stone foundations ; they are intended to support vaults ; and—well, be warned in time."

If John Mitchel had any intention of settling at or near Knoxville when he first came there, he soon relinquished the idea. There was something about the tone of the place that did not suit him, and he resolved to fly still further from civilization and progress and Know-Nothingism. From some one of his new friends at Knoxville he heard of a beautiful valley called Tucaleechee Cove, situated high up in the Alleghanies, some thirty-five miles from Knoxville. He had already ridden a good deal round the country in the neighbourhood of Knoxville, but had not found any place to suit him. In some of these rides he was accompanied by a gentleman he had met for the first time at Knoxville, but who had already become a warm friend. This was Mr. W. G. McAdoo, then Attorney-General for the judicial district in which Knoxville was. Mr. McAdoo has furnished me with some reminiscences of his friend, from which I take the following passage :—

"I rode with him in search of his ideal. We went on horseback—he was a fine rider—to Clinton, Tennessee, twenty miles from Knoxville, and passed a night under the hospitable roof of my dear old mother. It was delightful to see how she was charmed with Mr. Mitchel's picturesque and brilliant conversation. The next day, we travelled along the eastern shore of the river some eight or ten miles, looking at the country ; but no locality satisfied him. The river Clinch—or, as he preferred to call it by the euphonious aboriginal name, the Pelissippi—was not abundant of the mountain trout ; nor were the wild deer plentiful.

"We dined at the country house of a substantial citizen, a fine old gentleman, a friend of my father's and mine own —Mr. Joseph Black. At the table, we were talking, or rather listening to Mr. Mitchel's answers to our inquiries. The old gentleman occupied the head of the table ; Mrs Black, a venerable, fine-looking old lady, with piercing black eyes, occupied the other end ; Mr. Mitchel and I occupied opposite seats midway between them. In the midst of our repast, Mrs. Black threw up her right hand, and uttered one piercing scream. We were startled ; our knives and forks were arrested for one instant ; then the lady went on calmly with her duties as if nothing had happened, while the old gentleman paid no attention to the incident whatever. No conversational allusion was made to the circumstance. We enjoyed the good dinner, and returned in the afternoon to Knoxville. Not long afterward, I made inquiry of a gentleman who had married a daughter, and he told me that the exhibition we witnessed was the sole remaining convulsive movement that the lady had contracted in those fervid camp-meeting scenes which gave many people in the pioneer days what was known as ' the jerks '—a sort of choreal malady springing from excessive excitement."

What these " camp meetings " were like, Mitchel had an opportunity of seeing later on.

I have said that Mitchel heard of a valley in the mountains called Tucaleechee Cove. The place, as described to him, promised to be lovely and secluded enough to satisfy his most misanthropic mood, and he accordingly determined to explore that part of the country.

For a few days after their arrival in Knoxville, Mitchel and his family had stayed at a hotel called the " Coleman House." Then they took lodgings at the house of a lady in the town, where they had neat and pleasant quarters. Having thus got his family comfortably housed, Mitchel felt more at liberty to proceed with his explorations in the surrounding country.

On the morning of April 1, 1855, John Mitchel and his son James started from Knoxville on foot, bound for Tucaleechee Cove. They walked all day, mostly through a thickly wooded country, but every now and then coming upon a clearing with its log house. At noon they stopped for dinner at one of the log houses, and then continued their walk till sundown, when they arrived at the entrance of the valley known as Tucaleechee Cove. Having rested for the night at a farmhouse, they started early on the following morning to explore the valley. Mitchel was much struck by the beauty of the place. As they neared the upper end of the valley, two men who were planting corn in a twenty-acre field observed them, and came over to speak to them. One of these men was the owner of the farm, and was anxious to sell out. Mitchel asked his price, and was answered—ten dollars an acre. The farm contained about one hundred and forty acres, of which some forty or fifty acres were in cultivation. The house was beautifully situated, but it was a somewhat sorry sort of dwelling for people who had been accustomed to live in comfortable houses in cities. It was a log house, with two rooms and a loft. The place was situated thirty-two miles from Knoxville, and twenty-two from the nearest village. As far as regarded solitude and retirement, the place was certainly all that could be desired. After a careful inspection of the farm and buildings, Mitchel and his son returned to Knoxville to hold a family council. The decision of the council was in favour of Tucaleechee. The farm was purchased, and they at once set about their preparations for this new migration.

I have said that the general tone of Knoxville did not suit Mitchel ; but I would not have the reader infer from this that all the society of Knoxville was distasteful to him. This was by no means the fact. Mitchel formed several friendships, even during his first short stay at Knoxville, which lasted his life. When the time for leaving came, he parted from those friends with regret :—

Knoxville begins to be pleasant to us in some degree. Several ladies have called on my wife ; and besides the native Tennesseean citizens, we find here a most agreeable colony of French-Swiss people from the Canton de Vaud. The head of one of these families is a clergyman of the Swiss national church, with the Puritan name of Esperendieu, a most excellent and accomplished gentleman, who has created for himself fruitful fields and a fine vineyard. For East Tennessee, amongst its other noble destinies, is to be a most abundant wine country. Everybody laughs when we name Tucaleechee Cove. Nobody of our acquaintance had ever penetrated to that valley ; some did not know that any such place existed. My friend, Mr. Swan, assured me that we would all soon tire of such an abode ; and that the people there were barbarians.   But I scorned his words ; told him I wanted to find barbarians to live amongst ; and that I intended to become a barbarian myself, and bring up my family in that line of life.

On the evening of May 1, 1855, Mitchel and his family reached their new habitation in Tucaleechee Cove.   The log-cabin looked dismal enough as they approached it. Two or three waggons came with them, bringing their furniture.   All the children were brought, excepting the eldest daughter, Henrietta, and the eldest son, John.   John was at this time studying the profession of an engineer upon a railroad in northern New York.   Henrietta, in order that she might continue her study of French and music, remained at Knoxville, at the house of a Swiss lady, who had become a friend of the family during their brief stay. The four others—James, Willie, Minnie, and Isabel—went with their parents to the farm.

For nearly a year and a half—that is, from the spring of 1855 to the fall of 1856, the Mitchels continued to reside at Tucaleechee Cove.   As was natural, and as might have been expected, Mrs. Mitchel never liked the life.   It was so entirely different from anything she had been accustomed to.   Life in log-cabins on the confines of civilization may be all very well in theory; but in practice it is not always so very pleasant.   Men can often stand it well enough ; but for a lady, who has been accustomed to the refinements and the social intercourse of cities, the sudden change to a life without society and without domestic help, is extremely trying.   Mrs. Mitchel stood it as long as she could, and tried to make the best of it for her husband's sake.   But at length her health began to give way, and, moreover, the life did not seem to agree well with her daughter Isabel.   This was the main reason why Mitchel, who was always most devoted to his family, finally decided to leave the Cove. But this came later.

During the years 1855 and 1856, and during the greater part of 1857, Mitchel did not have any newspaper work to do. In reading through his correspondence, it is easy to fix his periods of leisure. While he was engaged in journalistic work, he commonly wrote few letters. When he was free from the necessity of writing a certain amount each week, he seems to have enjoyed writing letters every now and then. The quality of his correspondence was always good, but the quantity varied much—mainly in the way just described. During the residence at Tucaleechee Cove, and the earlier part of the Knoxville period (previous to the starting of the *Southern Citizen*), the letters are abundant. They gave a full description of the farm at Tucaleechee and the life led there.

Believing that the letters themselves will be more interesting to the reader than a narrative grounded on them, I shall not hesitate to quote from them at some length. What I give, however, is only a small fraction of the whole. I would gladly quote more fully, but am re- strained by the desire to keep this book within certain bounds.

The following passage is taken from a letter written to John Dillon from Knoxville shortly after Mitchel's arrival there. The friendship between Mitchel and Dillon had ripened during the former's stay at New York. He now counted both Mr. and Mrs. Dillon as among the friends he would least like to lose :—

You would be amused at the press of Tennessee. The Boanerges of the profession is one Brownlow of this town, a Methodist preacher, who once preached with pistols and a bowie- knife on the Bible before him; who is systematically, *chronically* frantic in his personal abuse of all and sundry, and is generally understood to be perfectly ready to gouge any fellow-creature at a moment's notice. He is editor of the *Knoxville Whig*, a furious Know-Nothing organ; and as all the papers here were bound to have articles on me after my arrival, Mr. Brownlow had *his*—said the people of Tennessee were glad to see Mr. Mitchel; but would give him to understand from the start that he was welcome to live in Tennessee, but by no means to *dictate* to Tennessee. Further, that from his, Brownlow's, personal observation, he could say this, Mr. Mitchel was genteelly dressed, talked rather reasonably, and appeared to have been "well raised." Lastly, that the Tennesseeans were not the men to declare open war upon a stranger instanter, and would treat the distinguished stranger as a gentleman till he proved himself none. So this is the footing upon which I stand in the *Whig* office. No land taken yet. But we are very comfortably housed in a private family of this place; that is, my wife and children are comfortably housed; for I have little share in it as yet. I am always roving about the country, sleeping in farmers' houses, living on pig and corn bread. Soon, I think, I will have secured a small tract of barren mountain. . . . Give my warmest regards and my wife's to Mrs. Dillon. I wish you and she would think of settling in East Tennessee. You might live quietly here, but not presume to dictate.

A few days after the arrival of himself and family at Tucaleechee Cove, he writes to his brother William :—

We are here for six days, having arrived on Tuesday evening last in the midst of a thunderstorm. The valley looked grand enough, but the little log house excessively desolate. If we were even moderately comfortable here, it would be a delightful place to live; but being, in truth and in fact, immoderately uncomfortable, we have not so much leisure or disposition to enjoy the new state of existence. We have no help as yet, male or female. As to field work, I can get, and do get, such help as I want from the neighbouring "mean whites" of these parts; but James and I milk the cows, drive them out, drive them in, separate them twice a day from their calves, a task of much labour and sweat, feed horses, drive nails, light fires, make up fences; and I rode this day five miles down the valley on my horse bare-backed for a bag of flour, which I "toted" on the horse before me on my return.

The "mean whites" of these parts admire my conduct, costume, and manners much, and have hopes that I will become in time as good a citizen and as mean a white as any of themselves. . . . So far the dreary side of our story. *Per contra*, we are all in first-rate health. The weather, though now in June, is cool and delightful. The woods and hills are prime; the river, running before our door under the trees, is worth, say $40,000 per annum; and our frugal meals aforesaid, almost ever since we came, have been varied with venison killed "on the farm." I had left the two boys, James and Billy, up here for a week before we all moved; and by Tuesday last, when we came to our habitation, James had a quarter of venison for us. The deer had come down the river the evening before; and a man of the neighbourhood, happening to be here, borrowed James's rifle (your little one), which was luckily loaded, and killed the deer in the river. Four persons were concerned in the chase and capture of this deer; and James, being one, had his quarter. Again, three days ago, just as we jumped out of bed, at five o'clock in the morning, a deer was stalking about between the house and the river. Our dog, a kind of deer-hound, gave chase, as well as those of Cotter, our opposite neighbour, and we seized our guns and sallied out. After a while, the dogs came back, and the enemy seemed to have escaped; but yet an hour or two afterwards, either the same one or another was pulled down by the dogs close to our fence. James was in at the death again, and had his quarter. Therefore, you perceive manifestly that we are to have sport. In fact, I believe that it only needs that we go a very few miles up the river with a couple of dogs and guns, and we are certain of finding deer. I have a very fine horse; but as yet only one, though I want three or four. Do you think there is any chance of your coming out to see us in the fall? If you do, you must help in the harvest work, and sleep upon shucks with the boys in the loft. On these terms I would be glad to see you. Indeed, I cannot tell you how very glad.

Under date November 1, 1855, he writes to Miss Thompson. This letter contains a fuller description of the scenery of the Cove than any other letter I have seen :—

. . . . You and Mr. Pigot are the only two persons in all

Ireland who ever write to me (save a very rare note from one of my sisters), and I could by no means dispense with the letters of either. You have already some idea of our remote and solitary wigwam at the back of the Alleghanies, eleven hundred miles from New York; and, in the present state of communications, eight or ten days from that city, reckoning by the post-office, though only five of actual travelling.

And you wonder at my having taken my family to such a place. To some such place I was obliged to bring them, or else submit to a species of life in New York which (without some hope of a grand success) is to me the most wasting drudgery.

He then proceeds to comment upon the entire absence of any cultivated or refined society in the neighbourhood where they had settled, and proceeds :—

Yet I rather like all this. I have contracted (owing to an exaggerative habit) a diseased and monomaniacal hatred of "progress;" and would like rather to go back, and see people going back. Besides, I suppose the five years of my exile—most of that time passed in living among remote forests—have given me, if not a taste, at least a habit, and I feel at home in the woods. You see I do not altogether triumph in, or so much as entirely defend, this way of life. It is not natural. Society is natural to us, though this sort of thing was natural to the Cherokees. In fact, those red savages, as well as the tribe of white or sallow savages who have succeeded them, had society. Like sought and found like. Cherokee smoked the pipe with Cherokee, and Hoosier with Hoosier, enjoyed life at corn-schuck-ings and swap-horses, and exchanged ideas at camp meetings. Now, I don't pretend that we have exactly found our place; and when I resolved to leave New York, if I had possessed inde-pendent means, I should certainly have crossed the sea to *la belle France* with all my household. But what avails repining? Who does find his place? And being here among the Hoosiers, it remains to make the best of it. . . .

Reading over what I have written, I find it looks dreary, and will give you too dismal an impression of our lot, and of our endurance thereof; and there is also a bright side. Imagine a most lovely valley, five miles long, varying in breadth from a quarter of a mile to a mile and a half, and lying among the parallel folds of the great Alleghanies. Through it gushes and flashes one of the brightest and most crystalline of rivers—about half the size of the Bray river—whose banks are sometimes corn-fields fringed with trees, sometimes shelving beaches of sand, sometimes precipices twice the height of St. George's steeple, crowned and plumed with oaks and pines, and whose waters here dash and rave over broken rocks, there ripple gently over a pebbly bed, and there again lie in a still black pool, almost hidden from the sun by overarching boughs of great trees. Into or out of this valley you must go through a glen seven miles in length, where the river has cut its way through the Chilhowea mountains, travelling sometimes on one bank, sometimes on the other, and fording the river five times (for bridge there is none); and, in short, if you multiply and magnify the Dargle by about six in all its proportions, you will have some faint notion of the form of the glen. But, then, who is to give you a notion of its colours? Of course, all those mountains, and all the hills round about and far and near, are covered with unbroken forest of vast timber trees— oak, beech, maple, sycamore, chestnut, pine, cedar, poplar, hickory, and forty other sorts; and at the fall season, these trees robe the hills with a mantle of many colours. . . .

Now, young lady, at the very head of the above-mentioned valley, up in the nook where the river first bursts from its mountain solitudes, and its pine-shaded ravine expands into the vale of Tucaleechee—up so high that my only neighbours (going up the river) are the bears and deer, I have pitched my tent or wigwam. I am the highest man in the valley; so that your little French teacher truly said I was "très ambitieux;" and the Hoosiers can no more muddy the water flowing past my door than the lamb could disturb the wolf's drinking. Here we have a hundred and thirty-two acres of land, forty to fifty of those acres cleared and very fertile, a log house (which I am just about to enlarge by a good addition), and a good large barn, just now full of the fruits of the earth, two horses, three cows, and that indispensable part of a Tenesseean's stock—a multitude of pigs. Now, if we had our house once enlarged and made comfortable, and if we could but persuade even one family of our acquaintance to come and settle near us, don't you think life might be endured?

Having finished his description of the valley and the farm, he next proceeds to give some of his experiences and impressions of the people around. From this part of the letter I take the following :—

Indeed, this is an amusing people, or, as it frequently says itself, "a peculiar people." I will give you an anecdote quite characteristic. About sixteen miles from this place stands one of the great watering-places of the South, Montvale Springs, a vast wooden house, with accommodation for three or four hundred boarders, where many families from Georgia, Alabama, and Louisiana spend some time in summer, and drink the sulphurous water. About six weeks after I had come to Tucaleechee, a well-dressed stranger on horseback made his appearance. I was standing at my own gate. He looked curiously at me, and then at the wigwam, and said he guessed I must be the gentleman he was in search of. Thereupon, he pulled out of his pocket a packet of papers, whereby I learned that the inmates of Montvale—southern judges, members of the legislature, and no end of colonels—on hearing that I was near at hand, had convened a public meeting of the guests, male and female, appointed a chairman, named four secretaries, and, having read the requisition, proceeded to business. Five resolutions, previously prepared, were then moved and seconded with appropriate speeches, to the effect that, having heard I was settled in Tennessee, they welcomed me to the South ; that they sympathized with me as a patriot and martyr, and admired me as a scholar and a gentleman; that they warmly approved of my conservative principles (in the matter of slavery) ; finally, that, actuated by all these feelings, and having a strong desire to see me and make my acquaintance, they thereby invited me to go, together with my esteemed lady, and partake of the hospitalities of Montvale Springs at such time and for so long as might suit my convenience. That is to say, go and stop at that hotel at their expense. Then the chairman, having been moved from the chair, and thanked for his dignified conduct, the four secretaries despatched the courier to find me out at Tucaleechee.

I think you will laugh. We laughed; but not in the ambassador's face ; and I wrote a very curt answer, saying I was compelled by engagements at home to decline their more than polite invitation ; and, besides, that I was not a martyr, but a farmer.

To Mrs. Matilda Dickson, a married sister, who lived in the north of Ireland, he writes under date August 6, 1855 :—

. . . You ask a description of the farm, and of farming in these parts, and about markets, etc. Lord, bless you ! there is no market nearer than twenty-two miles—not such miles as you have on the road from Banbridge to Hilltown, but miles of wild mountain, forest, and the beds of foaming rivers. Commerce in this country ("up in here," as the natives say) is mostly carried on by barter, and the prices of produce are little affected by Sebastopol, or Mark Lane, or Wall Street; but mainly by a good or bad season. Some sending to market there is, however ; but the people have a saying that whatever they send to market must go on four legs ; that is, they must feed cattle and hogs with it, and then drive them down the glens to Knoxville or Maryville, or else over the mountains to North Carolina. I will add that they must not feed them too fat, or else they never could make the journey. A pig fed to the dimensions of one of your Tullycairn pigs is doomed to die and be devoured in the Cove. For my farm, I had on the ground when I took possession fifteen acres (English) of wheat, thirteen acres of oats, and twenty-five acres of corn—that is, maize, with a few drills of potatoes in a garden. The season, though very favourable to making a fine maize crop, has been so wet and stormy *up in here*, that my harvest has been very troublesome and precarious and expensive; wheat saved not in prime condition, and half the oats at least utterly lost Our corn harvest will not come on till the last of September. I forgot to mention that amongst our wealth we have a very good and large orchard, the best in the valley, with varieties of delicious apples, and a sufficiency of peaches. Along with the corn they sow beans, pumpkins, melons, and cucumbers, etc., of all of which we have plenty. ... . You will see from this sketch that my farming is not very likely to make me rich. In fact, I am a poor devil enough,

but I have done with paying rent. I am free ; and in quitting
New York, I have emancipated myself from much *blatherumskite*.

The " log house, with two rooms and a loft," was found
to be inadequate to the needs of the family. It was
decided to build a frame addition before winter came on.
But skilled work was scarce in Tucaleechee, and the progress of the building was slow. In a letter from Mitchel
to his sister Mary, dated November 1, 1855, I find the
following :—

As to the new house, it is as good as built; that is to say, I
have, somewhere in the woods hereabout, six thousand boards
split to roof it. I have the chimney built, the corner stones
squared, and have nothing to do but the main building. I am
like the author celebrated by Goldsmith, who had his valuable
work on the very point of publication, inasmuch as he had the
title-page, the dedication, the preface, the appendix, and the
index all quite ready, and had only to fill in the body of the book.
. . . We have three milch cows, and although the butter of these
southern states is not in general commendable, yet we have the
luck always to make delicious butter, which, I think, is a secret of
Jenny's. However, the butter produced by our three cows is not
as much as one decent Irish cow would give. An addition to our
stock lately consists of five goats, and that is all, I believe, we
have to boast of. . . .

On the whole, I am well pleased to hear that arming and
drilling are growing more active among the Irish in New York,
though they break into factions as usual. I am of none of their
factions. I have nothing to do with "Conventions," with
" Emmett Monuments," with " Emigrant Aid Associations," or
the rest, and especially nothing to do with the gathering of
money. Yet many worthy fellows are connected with all those,
and I would have no scruple in calling upon all for material aid
in money or in muscle upon a proper occasion. In the mean
time, I am obstinate in keeping out of all that for the present;
feeling that my infidelity, and still more my sneering disposition,
do more harm than good. John Martin writes to me that he
trusts living in the woods will make me genial again. Perhaps so.

During the summer of 1855, Mitchel made several trips
down to Knoxville to see his friends and learn the news.
He mentions that during the first three months of his life
at the Cove he made two such trips, and that upon each
occasion his first question was on meeting a friend, " Has
Sebastopol fallen ? "

It was during Mitchel's residence at Tucaleechee Cove
that he met with an accident which considerably altered
his personal appearance.   He was chopping a tree, when a
fragment of wood struck him on the face, laying him flat
on the ground, with his nose flat on his face.   When he
came to his senses, he straightened out the injured member
as well as he could.   He was for some weeks confined to
the house from the effects of the accident.   He came
all right again ; but the shape of his nose was considerably altered.   It had been quite straight before the
accident.

The society of the Cove was of such a kind as to render
an occasional trip even to Knoxville a very agreeable
variety.   The neighbours, as described by Mitchel, were
very simple and very primitive ; wonderfully so for America.
Indeed, I doubt much if it would be possible to find in the
United States now a community in which questions could
be seriously asked such as some of those put to Mitchel by
his neighbours.   For example :—

Sitting around our fire as we smoke, of course we talk ; and
my worthy friends of the " Cove " have many questions to ask.
" We're but ignorant fellers up in here," my next neighbour, Cotter,
would say ; " and you have seen a many countries, and they say
you have sailed over the sea."   This being a fact, and not denied,
curious interrogatories would follow.   Was it true, as we have
hearn, that the water of the sea is all salted ?   Yes, this was
actually true ; whereupon they exclaimed all around the fire,
" Wall, I do wonder ! " this being the usual remark elicited by any
singular intelligence.

Nothing has so powerful an influence in stimulating the mind to healthy action as intercourse with other minds like to itself. When I say, "like to itself," I mean that the minds in intercourse with one another must be each capable of at least taking an interest in the same subjects, otherwise the stimulating effect will not be produced. An assembly of farmers will talk about farming matters, and, so long as they are all interested in the subject, the conversation, although it may not be very intellectual, will exercise a distinctly stimulating effect upon their minds. But if there be a city man in the company who understands little or nothing about farming matters, and takes no interest in the same, the effect of the conversation upon him will be the opposite of stimulating. It will probably have the effect of putting him to sleep. Mitchel was now experiencing the effect upon the mind of being without congenial society. In this respect Tucaleechee was worse than Van Diemen's Land. There had been there a very fair share of cultivated society; but in the Cove there was practically none. In other respects, however, Tucaleechee had the advantage. He was there of his own free choice; and that counted for a good deal. Then, too, at Tucaleechee he was within such distance of his mother and her family as to make it possible for him to see them occasionally. This advantage is dwelt on in a letter to his sister Henrietta, written on December 19, 1855. He was just about to start on a lecture tour when he wrote :—

I am going to burst upon the astonished world like a thunder-bolt, or, in other words, I am coming down from my mountains in the winter like the wolves, and with the same object—prey. Do you remember Father Kenyon's interpretation of the O'Connell "nail our colours to the mast?" That's what I am going to do. If the weather were likely to continue so very fine as it has been the last six weeks, I should ride my horse to Charleston or else to

Richmond.   But the real winter is just coming on, and I fear the
rivers will be dangerous, and perhaps the tracks through the
woods blocked with snow.   By either of these roads I should
have six or eight mountain ranges to cross, and innumerable
rivers.   When I arrive, which will be quietly, and altogether
unannounced in the papers, I will go straight to Sackett Street,
and shave.   At present I have a monstrous beard, and shall wear
it and call myself Mr. Johnson upon my journey.   I have my
mother's letter, and defer answering it till I see her.   After all,
this is more convenient than Diemen's Land, seeing that I can at
least visit you all in New York once a year, provided I can only
vociferate enough to pay my expenses.   You may wonder that I
can leave Jenny and the children with no other man about the
place than James in this wild place.   But James is now very
nearly as tall as I, and as agriculture now stands still, and nothing
is to be done but feed the horses and cows, etc., and milk the last-
named useful quadrupeds, and as our neighbours are civil, and,
above all, as we have little to be robbed of, I am in no apprehension.   I have gone to the mill, twenty miles off, and got wheat
enough ground into flour to make bread until my return.   Beef,
venison, and hog are plentiful ; and on the whole they can await
my return with equanimity.   The heaviest work James will have
to do will be hewing logs for the fires.   We have sometimes very
cold nights now, but the days are still bright and warm.   All the
rest of my information, personal, meteorological, and philosophical,
I will keep till I see you.

The excursion referred to in this letter was, I believe,
Mitchel's second lecturing tour in the United States.   Lecturing was not an occupation at all to his taste ; but, then, he
found it a much more profitable occupation than farming.
Moreover, he had been often and earnestly invited by
friends and admirers in the various American cities to go
and lecture for them ; and now, at length, he decided to
accept.   The invitation which he first accepted came from
St. Louis ; but as he had previously received quite a
number of invitations from other cities, he was able without
difficulty to arrange a series of lectures, of which that at

St. Louis was to be the first. Upon this lecturing tour
he visited, amongst other cities, St. Louis, Chicago, and
Buffalo. At all these places he had public receptions, and
delivered lectures. From Buffalo he went to New York,
and spent a few very pleasant days with his mother,
brother, and sisters. I think it must be this visit that is
referred to in a reminiscence supplied to me by one of his
sisters :—

"He used to be so very fond of coming on to New
York, generally on a lecturing tour, and he made his
mother's house his head-quarters. Those were delightful
times for us all. He was so bright and genial, so affectionate
and sweet-natured ; and, though pleasant in society, it was
amongst his own people he shone particularly. He was so
courteous and thoughtful, and then he never was severe in
his remarks on other people. Quite quietly he could put
a stop to any of us who were prone to err in this way.
'How fortunate for you, ma'am, to have such a clever
family,' or some such remark. He was always very fond
of dancing even till those times, and he danced well, and
we sometimes had a party while he stayed with us. I
remember one large dancing-party we had on New Year's
night (of 1856, I think), at which Mr. and Mrs. Meagher
were present. John took such an interest in all the preparations, and in who had accepted the invitations, and he
danced away all night."

From New York he returned to Tucaleechee by the
same route he had taken when he first went there ; that is,
by Charleston, Atlanta, and Knoxville. At Knoxville, he
spent a part of the proceeds of his lectures in purchasing for
his wife a well-trained saddle mare and a side-saddle ; and,
there being no way of forwarding the side-saddle to
Tucaleechee, he was obliged to ride out upon it himself,
much to the amusement of those whom he passed on the

road. It is needless to say that the little crowd at the log house were glad to welcome him back again.

The following extract is taken from a letter to Miss Thompson, written during the summer following the lecturing tour just referred to :—

I am not sure whether I wrote to you since my lecturing tour of last winter. In the very depth of the severest winter which that old sinner, the oldest inhabitant, recollects, I travelled through ten of the United States, about four thousand miles, vociferating in various cities. The lectures were nothing, having both been written after I had arrived at New York to fulfil my engagement as per advertisement. The thing is, I fear, a sort of trade here. To be sure, I might sooth myself in the idea that I was doing some good, and at any rate no harm. At the very least, I was helping and spreading abroad the feeling of a determined abhorrence to the British Government, which is now pretty strong here, both amongst Irish and Americans. This I hold to be a religious mission and apostleship. Moreover, I was denying and setting at nought the " Know-Nothings," for whom I have no tolerance at all. Next winter, after I shall have settled them all comfortably in their new cottage, I am bound on another tour of the same sort—another stroke of trade. One thing I gain by it, an intimate acquaintance with the country. I am to go to New Orleans and St. Louis on the Mississippi, Chicago, Detroit, and Buffalo on the great lakes, besides the large cities of the east. Buffalo is one of the most beautiful and wealthy cities of America, and is within twenty-five miles of Niagara. I saw that marvel last winter, when all the world was covered with snow, and when the cataract, carrying along rolling, thundering blocks of ice, plunged in among cliffs and mountains of ice, for the spray had frozen in huge masses which clung to the cliffs at both sides, and to the base of Goat Island. It is dreary to see a mere summer resort in winter. Huge, empty hotels, the *Maid of the Mist* steamer, that dashes into the very smoke of the cataract all summer long with gaily dressed picnic parties, laid up now like a polar navigator's ship, between two icebergs ; and when I went into Goat Island, three feet deep in snow, I saw staring me in the face, a light and airy and gaily painted, but now empty and silent pavilion or pagoda, bearing on its architecture the legend " strawberries and cream." Next winter I don't know well what I shall vociferate about ; but vociferate I must, for I am already engaged in five or six places. I am in bad spirits about Irish affairs. This peace ruins my peace of mind ; and the British Government, I find, won't so much as dismiss Dallas. Everything points to peace for a while. Oh, the madness of sinful men to rush so blindly into the horrors of peace !

The life at Tucaleechee was monotonous enough ; but even there life was not entirely devoid of variety. In the late summer or early fall the inhabitants had their " camp-meetings." These came after the crops had been gathered in, and they seem to have been a curious combination of religion and festivity. Mitchel avoided them as much as possible, but on one occasion he was an involuntary spectator of a camp-meeting. He had stopped for the night at the house of a farmer about half-way between the Cove and Knoxville :—

After supper, my host, Goddard, told me he was going to camp-meeting, about two miles off, and invited me to accompany him. The night had fallen very dark ; and our way was a rough sort of track in the dense shade of the forest. At length the peculiar kind of outcry which characterizes such assemblages was audible ; and as we approached the spot the effect was very dreary and dispiriting. I felt inclined to turn back ; but knew I should never find the way.

The business resembled what is now known as a revival. There were hysterical women and penitent men in various stages of religious excitement. " Some were leaping and shouting inarticulately. Others were weeping and tearing their hair." On the whole, one experience was enough for Mitchel. He did not go again.

Mitchel's old enemy, Know-Nothingism, followed him even to Tucaleechee Cove. Like paganism of old (which,

however, was a much more respectable persuasion), after it
had spent its force in the cities, it lingered for a while in
the country.   Dreadful stories began to circulate at Tucaleechee about the Jesuits and their doings.   Mitchel himself
became an object of suspicion, as he had formerly been at
Knoxville.   The postmaster of the district intimated to
him, by way of friendly warning, that he was suspected in
the neighbourhood of being a Romanist.   Mitchel's account
of the Know-Nothing doings at Tucaleechee is good of its
kind :—

I hear that Know-Nothingism, which has in a great measure
died out in the civilized parts of the United States, begins to
possess the people's minds here in our valley ; and one day two
candidates for some county office in Blount County convened a
meeting of the citizens five miles from me at the lower opening of
the valley, and at the store of Snyder, the only storekeeper between
this and Maryville.   One of the candidates, a small attorney of
the county, being of the " Whig " party, horrified the Cove people
by his picture of a bloody conspiracy organized by the Pope and
Jesuits to take away from free and enlightened Americans the
liberty they had acquired by their revolution.   The prospect was a
pretty black one ; and the democratic candidate, for his part, not
being able to deny the fact of the conspiracy, could only protest
that he was not in it, and neither was old " Buckhannon," the
president.   It was all very well to say so ; but the Whigs carried
Blount County.

The winter of 1855–56 was severe ; but the Mitchel
family managed to get through it pretty well.   The addition
to the log house had not yet been built, though most of the
needful materials had been provided.   Mitchel began
seriously to question whether it was worth while to build
this addition at all.   His journal and his letters show clearly
enough that he had by this time fully realized that residence
at Tucaleechee Cove was for him little better than a kind
of vegetation.   He could eat, drink, and sleep there, and

II.

keep himself in good health physically; but his mental part was suffering for want of exercise.

Moreover—and it was this consideration which influenced him most—he began to seriously doubt whether he was justified in condemning his family to this kind of life. Know-Nothingism had exhausted its force in the centres of population and intelligence. The feeling of disgust at the motives and doings of his fellow-men which had grown upon Mitchel during his life at New York had had time to moderate during his residence at the Cove. As Mr. Martin put it, the life among the woods had made him genial again. Nature never intended Mitchel for a cynic or a misanthropist. The whole bent of his nature impelled him towards a life of action, such action as is only possible for one who is in constant contact with his fellow-men. He was in a state of reaction during the winter of 1855–56. His own inclination, as well as his feeling for his family, prompted him to return to a more social kind of life. And on every occasion that he rode down to Knoxville, which he did every now and then, his friends there urged him to bring down his family from "that hole in the mountains," and come to live in Knoxville. At length, in the early spring of 1856, Mitchel made up his mind to give up farming, and to bring his family down to Knoxville. But it was agreed that the move should not be made until the following fall, so that they might have another summer in Tucaleechee Cove.

The decision to move having once been made, Mitchel at once proceeded to prepare the way at Knoxville. He purchased a piece of ground—about twelve acres—within a mile or so of the town, and commenced to build a house upon it. In a letter written to Mr. John Dillon late in the spring of 1856, I find, mixed up with other matters, some description of the new location at Knoxville :—

Our house is to be among tall oak trees, close to a small stream, with a hill and a wood between us and the "city," so that while we are within fifteen minutes' walk of the said city, our immediate environs will be sylvan enough.   In fact, East Tennessee is a most beautiful country, but no doubt you think Ireland well enough.   There is nobody in Ireland with whom I should better like to spend an evening than Mr. O'Hara.   When I think of him, his grey head associates itself in my memory with one or other of these three circumstances: first, his bringing up to the poll at Galway the voter who expected to be bribed, and then ignominiously chasing him downstairs; second, his enthusiasm (in passing through the Curragh) to think what superb ground it would be for a cavalry charge; and third, the formula for avoiding all particular conversation with clergymen, which he has used with uniform success through a long and well-spent life.   Will you give him my warmest regards, and ask him if he remembers as many circumstances about me?

During the summer of 1856, Mitchel spent a good deal of his time at Knoxville, superintending the building of his house.   He had a presentiment already that he would not stay long at Knoxville.   He had before tried the place for a short time, and had not liked it.   Still, it was civilization itself as compared with Tucaleechee.   It might serve well enough as a temporary resting-place; and if after a time he found it intolerable, why there were plenty of other places to go to.   He was already getting habituated to the idea of wandering, and had begun to doubt whether he would ever have any permanent resting-place upon this earth.

In the month of July, 1856, Mitchel writes from Knoxville to Miss Thompson :—

Knoxville is the central point and chief town of the great valley of East Tennessee, a valley which is as large as two Irish provinces, and watered entirely by the river Tennessee and its numerous tributaries.   The town has about five thousand souls (if we may count a soul for every body), has gas, a railroad, river steamers, three newspapers—in short, has civilization and human progress. There are tolerable schools, and there is a post-office which actually transmits and receives letters by sure hands. For these reasons, looking both to educational and social advantages for the children, and to means of communicating more rapidly and certainly with the outer world, I am building myself a cottage in a pretty situation close to the town, amongst tall oaks, walnuts, and cedars, and on the banks of a little stream pretty enough, but yet far inferior to our more beautiful Cove. When I have my house built, I feel already that I shan't live long in it. I will make no permanent home in Knoxville, nor perhaps anywhere till I arrive at *Nox*-ville and Erebus-ville—if even there. Jenny might as well be married to a Tartar of the Oley or to a Bedouin Arab. You are to understand we came to Tennessee for a country and forest life. Now Knoxville is neither town nor country, and I calculate that in about one year and a half, I shall be in one of the large cities again. . . . There are in Knoxville some forty or fifty large and handsome private houses ; twenty lawyers, most of the said lawyers being majors and colonels ; a judge of the Supreme Court of the State and two judges of the circuit courts. The attorney-general also lives here. He is a great friend of mine, which you may think is somewhat like the lamb (that's me) lying down with the wolf or playing at the cockatrice's den. But never fear. In this country I am not only peaceful and loyal, moral and constitutional, but most strictly conservative. So that I set attorney-generals at defiance. Besides, this attorney-general is in nowise like Monahan. He is no night-bird, but a tall and handsome soldier, bearded up to the eyes, who has fought in Mexico under General Shields, and has a bullet in his right leg—gentle souvenir of Cerro Gordo. Most of the men here, however, are mere money-making machines, and of society there is very little. The ladies very seldom come out except to church. There is a gloomy clerical incubus weighing them down, and they are benighted Protestants of one sect or other—Presbyterians being most numerous, then Baptists, Methodists, and Episcopalians. Of benighted Catholics there are hardly any, only a few Irish railway labourers. Within the last year they have got a chapel, and their priest is a Belgian. In and around the town are a good many Germans. But perhaps the most agreeable ingredient of the population consists of some Swiss families from the Canton of Vaud. Some of these people are highly accomplished, and preserve their own customs in a great measure. But I think a copy or two of a Knoxville newspaper, which I will send herewith, may give you some further notion of the place, though, I fear, not a high idea of its literary and intellectual condition.

The attorney-general referred to in the above was the Mr. McAdoo, from whom I have already quoted, a gentleman whose friendship he valued highly. On the 10th of August next following we find him back again at Tucaleechee, and writing to his sister Mary about a visit he had just made to Montvale Springs, where he stayed a fortnight, and drank copiously of the waters. There was something about the society of the South which made it much more congenial to him than that of the North. He alludes to this more than once in his letters. The following is taken from the letter to his sister Mary above referred to :—

I met there many very agreeable southern families, mostly Georgians, very different from any experiences I have had of northern Americans. They were all very polite to me, but you know I am endeared to them by my border-ruffian principles. Montvale is an immense house, standing on the very root of the Chilhowee, and surrounded, of course, by noble woods. There were in the house two hundred and fifty persons, besides a great number in detached cottages. There was a brass band, and dancing every evening. Such gorgeous dressing I have never seen in America or anywhere else. Everybody was pleased, and seemed disposed to make the time pass jovially. Nevertheless, I can't say that I had much pleasure. Next summer, if I can afford it, I will bring all my flock there for two or three weeks. We have had the hottest and driest summer in Tennessee that anybody remembers, and there is almost a total failure in the Indian corn crop, but wheat and oats (if it be any comfort to you) have been abundant and fine. On the whole I will not have lost much by my farming, though I have not amassed a fortune. In fact, one evening's *average* lecturing is a more profitable harvest to me than all the cereal grains and live stock I can raise in a year. That field, therefore, I intend to cultivate, at least for this coming winter, and am to commence my tour the first week in October, beginning with Nashville. When I may reach New York I know not yet, nor what I am going to vociferate about.

The move from Tucaleechee to Knoxville did not take place until the end of September, 1856. The farm was sold for something more than was given for it. The moving itself was a somewhat formidable business :—

Our three horses carried myself and the two boys, while a comfortable arrangement was made in one of the covered waggons for the female part of the family ; while a little herd of cattle was brought on after. If we had been starting "across the plains" to California, we could not have looked more like an emigrant caravan than we did. The weather was delightful, and the woods were flaming with purple, crimson, and gold. I believe the party, on the whole, enjoyed these two days very much ; chiefly, perhaps, because they felt themselves to be escaping from the delightful vale of Tucaleechee. Yet, as I took my last look backward at what had been our home for a year and a half, I knew that I should never again call my own so lovely a spot of earth.

So ended John Mitchel's last attempt at farming. From this time forward, whatever his private opinion may have been, he was content to accept and act upon the judgment of his family and friends—that nature had not intended him for a farmer.

CHAPTER III.

KNOXVILLE—THE "SOUTHERN CITIZEN."

1856–1858.

THE new house at Knoxville was a commodious and comfortable one—a very decided improvement upon the Tucaleechee abode. The first thing that Mr. and Mrs. Mitchel did, as soon as the last painter was cleared out, was to summon some thirty of their friends—mostly young people—and have a good time. "For," said Mitchel, "until something of this kind has been done, a new house is unwholesome to sleep in."

For the first year after they went to live at Knoxville, Mitchel had no regular occupation. He had a long spell of lecturing during the winter of 1856–57, and he visited quite a number of leading cities in both North and South. But during the greater part of the year he was more or less at leisure. He, of course, regarded this as a state of transition which could not last long. He formed many plans for the future, and, as was usual with him when he had leisure, he wrote often and at length to his relatives and friends. In letters written to his sisters and to friends in Ireland, I find detailed accounts of the lecturing tour just referred to. He travelled first to Nashville—the capital of the state of Tennessee—and thence by steamer on the Ohio and Mississippi to St. Louis. This mode of travelling by river steamboat he much enjoyed ; and indeed, as done in the

United States, it is probably the most enjoyable mode of locomotion yet invented. He describes with some minuteness in his letters the scenery of the Cumberland, the Ohio, and the Mississippi. Speaking of St. Louis and of the impression it made upon him, he says :—

The city is very fine. One pleasing feature in these large American cities is the wonderful mixture of races and languages. Here is (besides the old French colony who founded it, and whose representatives now are very wealthy) a matter of twenty-five thousand Irish and forty thousand Germans. The latter belong almost entirely to the last German immigration, that is, since '48, and these fellows are generally socialists and the reddest of republicans—a great scandal to America, and not without reason. For there is here no necessity for these red theories. . . . They bring one blessing, however, with them—music. The best bands in every city, and in some cities and towns (as in Knoxville) the only band is German. Thus they harmonize the republic. They are greatly devoted to amusement on proper occasions, that is, on Sunday evenings. . . . I dwell so much on St. Louis because the truth is I was very much tempted to go and settle there instead of in New York. It would have many advantages for me over New York, yet I suppose the latter is to be our home.

From St. Louis he went to Chicago ; thence to Detroit, and thence to Cleveland. This last place he describes as "the most beautiful city perhaps in America, seated on the high bank of Lake Erie, with upwards of fifty thousand people, and a great trade on the lakes." At each of these cities he lectured. I cannot find in his journal or letters any statement as to whether or not he was satisfied with the success of his lectures. But I rather infer from some things he says that the lectures were at least fairly successful, and that they realized a considerable sum. In the north-western cities, he was much struck by the energy of the inhabitants. On this subject he observes :—

The wealth, the energy, the intense vitality plainly visible in all these places are very impressive to a stranger. The rapid advance in architectural taste is also remarkable, and I make no doubt that within ten years this continent will have more elegant cities than all Europe.

From Cleveland he went to Buffalo, and thence to New York. At New York, as on the previous tour, he stayed at his mother's house. His mother had differed from him on several matters since he came to America; but they were as much attached to one another as ever. On this occasion he stayed at or near New York some three weeks, during which time he delivered one lecture. His time was spent mainly in the society of his mother and sisters.

He had abused and fled from New York; and yet, after all, he had at bottom a certain liking for the place. In a letter written to Miss Thompson in the month of May, 1857, he refers to his visit to New York in the previous winter :—

At New York I always feel at home. . . . It is a vast cosmopolitan place, in which all kindreds and tongues and nations employ and amuse themselves under the first-rate constitution we have got here ; and this circumstance adds to its attraction. . . . When you hear in Europe of New York society, you associate the idea of it with the vulgar pretentions of new-made wealth; and no doubt there is much of this ; but be assured that city contains all kinds of society, and all sorts of circles except only that sleek abomination, the courtly official circle. In short, I maintain that there is nothing in city life that a man ought to desire which may not be found on Manhattan island, and all heightened and sweetened by the atmosphere of liberty.

On leaving New York, he went on to Washington, where he had also engaged himself to lecture. This Washington lecture was an emphatic success, and for once he alludes to his success in his correspondence. Writing to his sister Henrietta, under date February 17, 1857, he tells of this lecture. The opening sentences in the following extract refer to an incident that had occurred during his recent sojourn at New York :—

I am very glad that accident brought me for once into a regular New England family, even for a few days. People are so liable to become violent partisans and sectionalists in these times. However, if your friends in those parts were a little while in some good southern house, they would fall in love with the South too. Tell them so; and tell them, further, that I remember with gratitude the quiet hospitalities of Cape Ann.

Now, I am to give you some account of myself. After leaving New York, I had a series of misfortunes. At Washington I was laid up with a violent sore throat, but luckily it was in the house of Dr. Antisell, who, seeing it was absolutely necessary I should lecture on a certain night, took care, by burning the inside of my throat with caustic, to keep open an orifice large enough to let the lecture come out. It did come out accordingly, and before a very fine audience—half of it composed of senators and congress people with their families. It was bad, however, that I should be sick and half choked on an occasion when I wanted to make the best impression in the world. Was at a little party in the house of Mr. Toombs, of Georgia. Met there some very prominent senators of *our* side, viz. Howell Cobb, Alex. Stephens, Judge Douglas, and others—all very polite to me, by reason of my constitutional principles. General Cass called on me, etc. . . . Well, I need not tell you how kindly Dr. Antisell tended me, and his wife too. The doctor worked about all the arrangements for my lecture like a little lion. It was a very unusual occupation for him, and one that usually falls to one of the more enthusiastic patriots. But he gave himself no rest till it was over; though, of course, now and then he grinned, sneered, and snapped— demonstrations which I took constant care to elicit and provoke. Then I accused him of a want of sympathy, charged him with neglecting to cultivate the finer sensibilities of the heart, and reminded him of all those amenities which lend a charm to life and do honour to our common nature. If you had only seen his vindictive sneers then, and the diabolical curl of his moustache ! . . . Nothing decided yet about my future movements. When it

is decided, I will write. You may think it is full time that I should
know when and how I am next to begin the world—a wicked and
ungrateful world, which I am always *beginning*, and see no immediate prospect of getting to the end of. Like the camp-meeting
psalmists, I cry out—

> " Oh, heaven, sweet heaven, I long for thee—
> And when will I get *thar?* "

After leaving Washington, he visited several of the
cities of the South. As a rule, the attendance at his lectures
was not as good in the southern as in the northern cities.
In a letter written to his mother on February 17, 1857, I
find the following :—

I found Savannah and Charleston both very agreeable places,
but the people have generally too good sense to go to lectures.
So I bid that business adieu, yet not till after I have lectured
three weeks hence at Macon, in Georgia—about four hundred
miles off—and also at Atlanta. The people in those places wished
me to stay on my way home, but I was impatient and sulky, so I
pressed on, but promised to come back there in three weeks.
Nothing further about my future whereabouts. I will probably
defer my decision till I have sold my place, and then take our
places in the train leading to some quarter of the compass.

So ended his lecturing tour for that season. In after
years he lectured occasionally, sometimes delivering as
many as three or four lectures successively at different
places ; but, so far as I can gather, he from this time
forward gave up all notion, if he ever had any such, of
pursuing lecturing as an occupation or looking to it for the
means of subsistence.

The reader will gather from the foregoing extracts
from correspondence that, during the winter of 1856–57,
Mitchel's thoughts were much occupied with the important
question—What was he to turn to next ? A few more
extracts taken from various letters written during this
transition period, will serve to give the reader a better idea

of what subjects were then occupying Mitchel's thoughts, and how he spent his time.

On May 3, 1857, he writes from Knoxville to Miss Thompson :—

I think of resuming the practice of my profession of the law, and I have advertised my new house at Knoxville for sale. Jenny is nearly tired of wandering, and I think would be well content to stay here, as we really have a very pretty place, and the climate is lovely, if we were but independent enough to live where we choose. However, I must work, and I, too, am tired of wandering, and greatly desire a permanent occupation. It is twelve years since I threw away my profession, and now I suppose I had better take it up again. It will not hinder me from journalizing after I shall be a citizen, if I choose.

And again, in another part of the same letter, which by the way, is an exceptionally long one for Mitchel :—

Your first letter gives me an entertaining account of the state of the religious world at Kingstown, the chaotic condition of which seems to have somewhat unsettled your own convictions. Suffer me to press, in this transition state of your mind, the claims of my own church. I profess myself an unworthy member of the pagan persuasion, and am even becoming rather bigoted. There is no sect of Christians whom I might not be tempted to persecute, if I were in power, for their cup of balderdash is nearly full : except, however, for the present, the Catholic Church. I wish you could see some benighted people in *Nox*-ville, and could hear some of the pastors that guide them—destined both to fall into the ditch. It is strange to find myself writing such atrocious impiety to you, and to change that subject, I will tell you about my last tour.

Then follows a detailed account of his lecturing tour during the previous winter. He seems, as a rule, to have written longer letters to this Irish lady than to any one else. In a letter to his sister Henrietta, I find the following description of a visit to Chattanooga in the spring of 1857 :—

I had a pleasant excursion lately to Chattanooga, attending a "convention" on the top of a high mountain which overhangs the Tennessee river. There is a fine hotel on the summit, and here I met the bishops of the southern states (Protestant bishops), to organize a great southern university. We intend to be not only independent of your Harvards and Yales, but to offer to northern youths the sort of education that will do them good, amend their morals, enlighten their intellect, and purify their heart. I went merely as a spectator, along with some other Knoxville people, and found a very large and elegant company assembled in the hotel, where I spent three days. Since then I sent Meagher (for publication in his *News*) two long letters touching universities, the south, slavery, British villainy, and things in general. The first of them ought to appear this week, if, indeed, Meagher do not take fright at some of the sentiments, and shrink from making his paper even the medium of promulgating them. You may think how horrible they are ; yet they will probably amuse you.

One of Mitchel's friends—John Dillon—after a residence of some eight years in New York, had recently returned to Ireland. To him Mitchel writes from Knoxville, on May 30, 1857 :—

I often try to realize, as we Americans say, the mingled sensations of troubled emotions (see Wolf Tone, *passim*) with which you, having got clear out of the whole chaos of Irish patriotism, and standing safe on the other side, look over the scenes of the last ten years. Not, I suppose, that you do so very often—as seldom as you can, perhaps ; yet very few of all the crew can look back with so little self-reproach as you. My judgment is that you were right all through those ten years, and that you are right now. *Cela étant*, you may enjoy private life, and busy yourself with professional toils, and send public duty to the devil ; perhaps even, may come to wear ermine and horsehair—yet no, the line must be drawn somewhere. . . . Do you wish to hear anything about me and my little family? Well, then, we are still living a mile from Knoxville, where I now write this note, in a quite pretty new house which I have built. It has cost me nearly $3000, and is as good as I could build near New York for $5000.

I have not been able, however, to get it sold this spring, partly because it was unfinished, and partly because money has been scarce, owing to the breaking of some banks. So I have finished it, or nearly, and we are occupying the back building, which I finished last year. It will be a very pleasant place to spend the summer; but I can do little or nothing here except teach the children their lessons. House once sold, then to New York; at least, that is my present intention, and get admitted to practise law there, in which, you know, I will soon make a fortune. I will put James into the office of some lawyer (some other lawyer, less profound, perhaps, but whose business will be larger) for a year or two. I have had not a bad proposal here—partnership with a gentleman who was lately Attorney-General of the State; a highly respectable man, with whom I have been very intimate since I came to Knoxville, but I declined, Knoxville not suiting me. He has since become one of the circuit judges. I have no right to speak very ill of this Knoxville, yet no bribe would induce me to live in it a day longer than I must.

To his mother he writes on the 20th of June: —

I am getting on with the plastering of my house as fast as I can hurry the rascals of plasterers. There has been an immense deal of religious excitement here this spring; in short, a "revival." All the churches (except the Episcopal) open every day, and in some of them, especially the Methodist, horrible noises. We go every Sunday to the Presbyterian church, where I have a pew. No news here. All are well. Lessons going on with rather more activity than usual; and occasionally we go out to ride, for I have still two horses on my hands.

In the spring months of 1857 his mind seems to have inclined most to the plan of going to live in some one of the large cities, and resuming the practice of the law. But this plan was never carried out. It was probably as well he never tried it, for I think he would most certainly have given it up again before long. John Mitchel was not intended by nature for an attorney, and the wonder is that, even in early life, he remained at the profession as long as he did. In behalf of any cause which he thoroughly believed in, he could write as few other men of his day could write. But he needed to be in earnest before he could bring into action the power of his intellect. To sham earnestness in behalf of a cause about which he cared little or nothing was what he had neither the faculty nor the will to do.

I have already alluded to the friendship which came to exist between John Mitchel and Mr. Swan. Swan lived close to where Mitchel had built his new house, and the two friends were much together during the spring and summer of 1857. They talked over the questions which were fast dividing the United States into two hostile sections. They agreed in their views upon these questions, more especially in their thoroughgoing advocacy of slavery and dislike of abolition. It was obvious that abolition was making rapid progress in the North ; and as Mitchel came to see more clearly the danger to what he called "the good and wholesome institutions of the South," his interest in the coming struggle became all the keener. To both Mitchel and Swan it appeared that the southern people were somewhat too indolent and too good-natured in their way of meeting the abolition movement ; that they were not sufficiently awake to the reality of the danger which threatened their whole social system. Finally, in the late summer or early fall of 1857, Swan suggested to Mitchel that they should together start a weekly paper to champion the views which they held in common upon the leading public questions affecting the South. Mitchel, with his usual promptitude, decided at once to close with his friend's offer. The writing for the paper was to be done mainly by Mitchel ; the business part by Swan. Thus, instead of returning to his first profession of the law, John Mitchel ultimately decided to return to his second profession of journalism. Journalism was not, in my opinion, the profession he was best qualified to shine at; but, then, it certainly suited him much better than the law; and the conduct of a journal in behalf of a cause in which Mitchel earnestly believed, afforded frequent opportunities for the display of his singular gift of writing.

The first number of the *Southern Citizen* (so the new paper was named) appeared in the month of October, 1857. The paper contained an address to the public, stating its objects and the views it proposed to defend. Instead of reprinting this address here, I prefer to give Mitchel's account of his aims in starting the *Southern Citizen*, as given in his journal. He there speaks of his proposed paper as—

An organ of the extreme southern sentiment, which is to address itself to the task, *first*, of rousing the somewhat indolent and too good-natured southerners to their danger; *second*, of discussing in all points of view the whole matter of negro slavery, both in Africa and here, so as to make hesitating and frightened people better satisfied with the institutions which their fathers handed down to them; and *third* (as means to both these ends) to advocate earnestly the re-opening of the African slave trade in the interest both of blacks and whites.

And again, in giving an account of the starting of the paper, he says :—

We commenced our *Southern Citizen*—Swan and myself—with much spirit, and produced a very handsome weekly newspaper, as to its outside. For the inside, State rights; the value and virtue of slavery, both for negroes and white men; the importance of procuring more and more negroes direct from Africa, and elevating those poor devils to the comparatively high position of plantation hands; the necessity of resisting, by any and by all means, the pernicious doctrine of "squatter sovereignty," and all other open or insidious methods of preventing our southern institutions from extending themselves into the territories of the United States

(which belong as much to the South as to the North) ; decrying and
defying the unconstitutional law making importation of negroes
" piracy " and " felony " ; exhorting and encouraging the southern
people, by means of " commercial conventions " and otherwise, to
take measures for the promotion and vindication of their own
industrial system, as the best, wholesomest, and most conservative
in the world ;—these were our topics and our texts.   But all this
while I was thinking of Ireland, and contending for the South as
the Ireland of this continent.

For nearly two years—that is, from the fall of 1857 to
the late summer of 1859—Mitchel continued to conduct
the *Southern Citizen.*   For something more than half that
time the paper was published at Knoxville ; for the rest
of its existence, it was published at Washington.   From
occasional statements in Mitchel's correspondence, I infer
that the paper was not a decided success in a pecuniary
point of view.   Yet it had a fairly good circulation, and
the writing in the paper, more especially after its removal
to Washington, excited much attention both in the South
and in the North.

So far as regards the political tone and work of the
paper—that is sufficiently indicated in the two extracts
from the *Journal* given above.   John Mitchel, as was usual
with him, threw his whole strength into the cause which he
advocated, and wrote in aid of that cause with much of his
old force and fire.   Upon this head, I may further mention
that the best statement that Mitchel has left us of his
views upon the institutions, the politics, and the social
system of the South, and of the causes which led to the
Civil War, is to be found in two series of letters written by
him to his friend John Martin and published in the *Southern
Citizen*—the first series being called " A Tour through
the South-West," and the second, " Letters on President-
making."

But, besides politics, there was another feature about the *Southern Citizen* which calls for further notice. The prospectus of the paper said :—

Literary articles and reviews will form a main feature of the *Southern Citizen*. Intellectual grandeur, wherever it appears in the world, shall meet prompt and zealous recognition. We do not need to shut out light or stifle inquiry ; but, in this department as well as in politics, we shall take leave to examine and judge from our own point of view ; not importing our opinions from England, still less, at second-hand from New England.

The promise here given was strictly fulfilled. Relatively to the size of the paper and to the period of its publication, there is more literary work in the *Southern Citizen* than in any other paper that Mitchel conducted. And the quality is no less conspicuous than the quantity. Some of the best literary work that John Mitchel has done is known only to the readers of this paper. In a judiciously compiled selection from Mitchel's miscellaneous writings, quite a number of papers from the *Southern Citizen* would find a place.

I cannot find space here for any criticism of Mitchel's literary work in the *Southern Citizen ;* but I may mention that the reviews of books to be found in the paper are very numerous and include the following :—

" Livingstone's Travels," reviewed January 14, 1858.
" Africa and the Africans," reviewed January 21, 1858.
" Bacon's Essays " (Whately), reviewed April 22, 1858.
" Poetry for the Million," reviewed May 13, 1858.
Buckle's " History of Civilization," reviewed October 23, 1858.
" Tennyson and Bulwer," reviewed October 30, 1858.
" Wild Sports of the West," reviewed January 1, 1859.
" Transactions of the Ossianic Society," reviewed April 9, 1859.
" Dufferin's Yacht Voyage (Letters from High Latitudes)," June 11, 1859.

John Mitchel's faculty of reviewing books was quite exceptional. Indeed, I do not know of any writer of the English language, during the last generation, whose powers as a reviewer and critic I would call equal to Mitchel's. There were one or two French writers who, in this department, were probably his superiors.

As Mitchel had to do nearly all the writing for the paper, he felt little inclination to use his pen in correspondence during his periods of leisure. Whilst he conducted a journal, he was always in the habit of sending copies of the same to his relations and friends; intending, as he was at pains to explain to some of them, that this proceeding should be accepted in full discharge of all epistolary obligations. He did, however, find time, every now and then, to write a letter even during his periods of journalism. Among his letters of this period, I find one written some six weeks after the starting of the *Southern Citizen.* It is a letter to his dear and valued friend, Father John Kenyon, and it is decidedly the most remarkable letter in all the correspondence of John Mitchel that has come under my notice. Certain portions of it throw much light upon that phase in Mitchel's life which many of his admirers find it hardest to understand—his connection with the South and with slavery. I give this remarkable letter at length, as I find it. It appears, from the opening sentence, that Mitchel had sent Father Kenyon a copy of the prospectus of the *Southern Citizen :—*

MY DEAR FATHER KENYON,

So you don't understand my prospectus or my letters to J. Martin, save on " one theory," and that the wrong theory. You and I, then, are not only in different degrees of longitude, but are out of one another's latitude. Do we look at the world now, not only from different points of view (that we probably always did), but from such remote points, and through such variously contorted *media*, that we can't even perceive it is the same world we are looking at? Have our two paths been diverging —or has one of us been sitting still while the other has gone forward, or back, or round? And which has been sitting, which expatiating? I admit that in the case of a man (è grege *me*) who has never been but once absorbed and engrossed and possessed by a great cause, whose whole life and energy and passion converged themselves once to one focus, and were then dissipated into the general atmosphere, who dashed himself one good time against the hard world, and was smashed to smithereens—in the case of such a fellow as this, I admit that the probability is *he* may be the stationary and sitting-still individual. His life, or the fragment of it, then and there crystallizes, and he never grows older, but is truly dead and a ghost. There, now, is an admission for you.

Nevertheless, here I am, or the fragment of me, dwelling in the heart of the United States, likely to be a citizen of the same, surrounded by a world of people, all alive and lifelike, dealing and talking with them every day—for they do not know that I am a ghost, and even if they did, would not be at all afraid—and I cannot but take an interest (of a certain spectral sort) in them and their fortunes. Not only that, but I must work also at something, in a somnambulistic manner, while above ground. And I seem to myself to be actuated by the very same sort of motives, and to be moved by the same impulses, passions, and affections, as ever. I do still (I think) abhor injustice and oppression, and hold the same notions of right and wrong. Now, in looking back, and trying to analyze my own feelings, or principles, or whatever it was that made me act and write as I did in Ireland, I have found that there was perhaps less of love in it than of hate—less of filial affection to my country than of scornful impatience at the thought that I had the misfortune, I and my children, to be born in a country which suffered itself to be oppressed and humiliated by another; less devotion to truth and justice than raging wrath against cant and insolence. And hatred being the thing I chiefly cherished and cultivated, the thing which I specially hated was the *British system*—everywhere, at home and abroad, as it works in England itself, in India, on the continent of Europe, and in Ireland. Living in Ireland, and wishing to feel proud, no t ashamed of Ireland, it was there, first and most, that I had to fight with that great enemy. For it is a great, or at least a big and strong thing, the British system. It has money in its purse, and a code of opinion received to a really wonderful extent by all mankind, that is, by the richest, that is, by the strongest, part of mankind. It is so big that it keeps many things in their place by attraction, and many other things, me, for example, by repulsion. I also depend upon it and revolve round it, not like a satellite, but at least like an aërolite, wishing always that I could strike it between wind and water, and shiver its timbers.

As for Ireland, and her destiny, all that now depends absolutely upon the destinies of the British empire. So far as I can judge now by all the *indicia* I am aware of, Ireland is not even likely to be one of the powers or agencies that will destroy the enemy ; rather she will help and is helping to save him. The stillness and deadness of Ireland are wonderful to me. I don't believe that I can pretend to understand the phenomenon—but there it is. Whatever is now moving action and articulation in Ireland (for I count nothing on the *Dundalk Democrat*, or a few seditious placards), seems to me not only British, but more British than the British themselves. On that subject I have not patience to dilate.

Well, all my behaviour from November, '45, down to this November, '57, seems to myself to be consistent, to be of one piece. I have not only contended with the enemy of mankind constantly, but on the same argument, varying it only with varying circumstances, " cœlum non animam mutans." In Ireland I sought to rouse up national pride to such a point that we could "dismember the empire," which would have ruined the whole affair, and sent the enemy (that is, the British system) a naked beggar on the world. Ireland, just then, was suffering the worst by that system ; would have gained the most by its overthrow. I was Irish, and intensely Irish, so my business then was clear and plain. But now I meet that evil power here also ; he is everywhere, and nowhere more active and mischievous than in these United States. I perceive in the institutions, and of late in the tendencies, proclivities, aspirations (these are vile, vague words) of the southern states, a special hostility to the British system ; not hostility arising from the accident of England being active in suppressing, and loud in denouncing slavery, but hostility founded on essential differences in the two types of human society. You seem to imagine that my plans look to an arraying of the United States, or at least the southern states (after disruption) against England. Yes; but not in the way you mean. England would rather quarrel with the North than with the South, and so long as she is able to order cotton and pay for it, the South will never quarrel with her. But the South is trying one form of civilization, and with signal success; England has tried another (I should say *the* other), and is going shortly to ruin. I want to promote the success of the one and the ruin of the other. Consider this one point alone—the danger, weakness, and unsoundness of England arise in great measure from her vast manufactures. She keeps two millions of people clothing the world, and so has become a nation of hucksters. Let her be furnished just these few years to come with more and cheaper cotton—crammed, surfeited, choked with cotton, and she will soon lose entirely what is even now so much impaired, the military spirit, without which a nation cannot live. Besides, if there were no grudge to be satisfied against the enemy at all, for the mere well-being of these southern states, and of the Africans who now are or hereafter may be slaves therein, I should zealously maintain the cause of slavery, and try to make the people here proud and fond of it as a national institution, and advocate its extension by re-opening the trade in negroes. You say, in this letter of yours, "Actively to promote the system for its own sake would be something monstrous." *Why?* I cannot so much as conceive any reason for this judgment. Actively I promote it, for its own sake, and shall promote it. It is good in itself, good in its relations with other countries, good every way. And I do much want to know what was in your mind when you wrote? I bethink me that I do not perfectly know the position held just now by the Catholic Church with respect to the *enslavement* of men. Whatever that may be, however, it has no application to negro slaves bought on the coast of Africa. To enslave *them* is impossible, or to set them free either; they are born and bred slaves.

About a month later, there is another long letter, this time to Miss Thompson. She, also, had evidently remonstrated with him about his writings on the slavery question.

He says that he feels her remonstrance all the more because he knows her to be sincere.   He then proceeds :—

To be sincere, that is, to deal honestly with one's self and with all the world, seems to me the greatest of all qualities.   And for my part—save that I know myself to be exaggerative both in expression and in sentiment—I am conscious of endeavouring to preserve or attain that virtue.   When I admit myself to be exaggerative, I mean that whatever I take in hand, whatever cause I favour, comes to occupy, for the time being, too much of my field of vision.   It possesses me too much.   But still, I mean what I say and all I say. . . .

Now for "southern institutions."   You know I have declared my intention of becoming an American citizen—an act which involves certain obligations.   If I move tongue or pen at all on public affairs (and the vocation of an editor seems my fate ; I have tried farming three times in my life, and it would not do), I am bound to maintain what I think good and just; rebuke what I think bad and stupid.   Moreover, I have selected, and that with deliberation, the southern states to live in.   Nothing but necessity could drive me north.   And I have even engaged myself in a local newspaper speculation, not quite to my taste, to prevent the necessity of going north.   The South and the North are two nations, and cannot, as I believe, go on long together. Every year widens the breach, and reveals the incompatibility of the two sections.   I prefer the South in every sense.   I do really believe its state of society to be more sound, more just, than that of the North ; and whatever measures the South calls for and truly needs to secure and establish itself, I advocate.   Mind, I deny that any nation can ever *need* to do that which is unjust, any more than an individual can.   Well, then, I consider negro slavery the best state of existence for the negro, and the best for his master ; and if negro slavery in itself be good, then the taking of negroes out of their brutal slavery in Africa and promoting them to a humane and reasonable slavery here is also good.   But I need not repeat what you will find in the various numbers of the *Southern Citizen*, which, I believe, is regularly sent to you. All that I want to impress upon you is that I honestly mean all that I say.   You must not deny me this credit.   And it is no use crying, "What have you to do with it?" I have to do with all the interests and exigencies—more especially with the great leading interest and exigency—of the community wherein I undertake to conduct a weekly newspaper, and where I have declared my intention to become a citizen. I will not deny, however, that in my mode of prosecuting my object, that same exaggerative temperament may make itself visible—a thing to be guarded against. And, further, I do not deny that the natural pleasure I have and always have had in hunting down and tearing to pieces all sorts of solemn cant—a kind of sportsmanlike instinct that was born in me—may give me the appearance of too great eagerness in this existing pursuit.

In these letters we find suggested, rather than explained, the main ground upon which Mitchel's pro-slavery view rested. Neither of the letters is intended to be a full statement of the case for slavery. They are intended to furnish food for reflection; to suggest the lines of thought by which certain conclusions may be reached.

The reader will notice that in both letters the point mainly dwelt on is that the general system of society, as it existed in the South on a basis of slavery, was better for all classes than the social system which existed in the "free-soil" and commercial North, or in England.

The slavery question may conveniently be considered under two heads. Firstly, there is the question, Can slavery be justified, viewing the matter from the standpoint of the slave, and assuming that the negro has rights as well as the white man? And next, there is the wider question of the effect of the institution of slavery upon the general system of society. Is a social system, where the relation of master and servant rests upon a basis of slavery, better or worse for all classes and colours than a system where the same relation rests upon freedom and free competition as modified and controlled by the existence of property in capital and in land?

As regards the first question, Mitchel's answer was ready
and· simple.   The formula of the abolitionists—that property in human flesh was always and under all circumstances an abomination—was to John Mitchel simply
balderdash.   He hated cant, and this formula, as propounded
by the abolitionists, seemed to him to have a decided
flavour of cant about it.   The real question with him, so far
as the negro was concerned, was a question of happiness
and usefulness.   Was it, or was it not, the fact that the
average negro was both a happier and a more useful
member of society as a slave than as a free man ?   Mitchel
had no hesitation in affirming that this was the fact ; and,
that being so, he made very little of formulas about property in human flesh.   In after years, during the Civil War,
when it was proposed by some of the Confederate leaders
to arm the slaves, and to hold out freedom to them *as a
reward*, Mitchel wrote upon this proposal in a way which
showed very clearly what his view was and how consistently
that view was held :—

The general further urged that the Government should hold
out *emancipation* as a reward.   Now, if freedom be a *reward* for
negroes—that is, if freedom be a good thing for negroes—why,
then it is, and always was, a grievous wrong and crime to hold
them in slavery at all.   If it be true that the state of slavery keeps
these people depressed below the condition to which they could
develop their nature, their intelligence, and their capacity for
enjoyment, and what we call "progress," then every hour of their
bondage for generations is a black stain upon the white race.

Mitchel had lived in the southern states.   He had seen
black slaves at work, and had observed their relations with
their masters.   He had also been in countries and in cities
where he had seen white slaves at work, and had noted
how *they* felt towards *their* masters.   His observation had
led him to conclude that, with the black slave, happiness

and affection for his master were the rule ; the opposites
of these the exception. If, and in so far as it was true,
that brutalities of the kind described in "Uncle Tom's
Cabin" were practised, the remedy was by legislation to
prevent and punish ill-usage, not by abolishing the whole
system.

In order to see the matter more clearly, let us take two
cases, and put them side by side. Firstly, take the case
of a slave girl in Virginia or Alabama, working for a fairly
kind master ; and secondly, we will take the very common
case of a seamstress in Boston or New York, working for
wages which are hardly sufficient to supply her with the
necessaries of existence. What, Mitchel might ask, is the
essential difference between these two cases? You answer,
The white girl is free, and the black girl a slave. Fine
words these, but what do you mean by them? Each one
of the two girls is equally forced by circumstances, over
which she has no control, to work all day long ; each one
gets in return, food, clothes, and shelter. The advantage,
if any, in these respects, will be on the side of the black
girl. Her master has a direct interest not to overwork
her, and to give her enough of wholesome food. The
interest of the white girl's master is to get the maximum
of work at the minimum of wages. If she die in the process, he is at no loss, and can supply her place without
expense. So far as concerns happiness, and all that makes
life worth living, does it really matter to these two girls
that in the one case the coercive force rests upon a bargain
and sale, in the other case, upon the action of free competition and monopoly of capital? If the black girl be
joyous and healthy, and the white girl miserable and sickly,
must we still conclude that the white girl is really the better
off of the two simply because she is not liable to be bought
and sold? Lastly, if the action of free competition and

private property combined be to reduce even white men and women to a state which is in reality a degrading slavery, is it likely that an inferior and weaker race will prove able to hold their own under a like system ; can we say with confidence that it will prove for them a condition better than that in which, as experience proves, they can be at once useful and happy ?

If it were said that, even granting the negro to be more happy and more useful as a slave, still the white man has no right to make a slave of him against his will, Mitchel would answer, What do you mean by right ?   If you see a black man—or a white man, for that matter—going to blow his own brains out, have you a right to stop him ?   Yet, is not his life his own as much as his liberty, and has he not, on your principle, a right to do as he pleases with it ?   The most fanatical abolitionist must admit, at some point, the right of the wise man to judge for the foolish man, and to make his judgment valid ; or rather, as Carlyle would put it, the right of the foolish man to be guided by the wise man, and made to do what is good for him.   The widest extension of the principle of *laissez faire* cannot entirely get rid of that other principle.   It is, as usual, a question of drawing the line.   Mitchel would draw the line so as to affirm the right of the white man to force the negro to be useful and happy, although, if left to his free-will, he might prefer to be idle and miserable.

There remains the wider question—the general merits of the social system which prevailed in the South as contrasted with that which prevailed in the North.   As already noted, it is this aspect of the question that is mainly dwelt on in the two letters quoted above.   I do not know whether John Mitchel had, at this time, read the speeches and writings of John C. Calhoun.   There is certainly a very striking similarity between Calhoun's and Mitchel's ways of handling the social aspect of the question. Like the great son of South Carolina, Mitchel made no compromise with abolition. He did not defend slavery as a necessary evil ; on the contrary, he held, with Calhoun, that it was "a good, a positive good."

The social aspect of the slavery question is a wide subject—much too wide to be fully discussed here. Yet, in the position taken up by Calhoun and by Mitchel upon this question, the following leading points may be noticed :—

1. The relation of master and servant has existed in every social system that we know of, and, so far as we can see, must always continue to exist.

2. There are three leading sentiments or motives in our human nature upon which this great relation ought mainly to rest. These are (1) Duty, including in that term the conception of Justice in so far as applicable to the relation in question ; (2) Affection ; and (3)—so far as may be consistent with the other two—Self-interest.

3. There have been times in the history of the world when the relation of master and servant was ruled in a quite perceptible degree by motives arising from Duty and Affection.

4. The tendency of our modern system is to entirely eliminate all motives of Duty, Justice, or Affection from the relation of master and servant, and to cause that relation to rest exclusively upon self-interest, and that too of the most sordid kind. When I speak of our modern system, I mean, of course, the system which bases the relation of master and servant upon "free competition" under existing circumstances as to property in land and capital; the system which takes one of the most purely selfish and most sordid instincts of our nature and sets this up as *the* principle upon which social arrangements are and ought to be based ; the system which puts before both master and

servant as the sole end of their endeavour to get the greatest amount of wealth at the least cost of labour or inconvenience ; the system, in fine, which makes "cash payment the sole *nexus* between man and man."

Of this " free competition " principle and its workings, Mitchel wrote in the *United Irishman,* years before he had any idea that he would ever be concerned to defend slavery in the southern states.   He described it as—

> The detestable system of " free trade " and " fair competition," which is described by Louis Blanc as "that specious system of leaving unrestricted all pecuniary dealings between man and man, which leaves the poor man at the mercy of the rich, and *promises to cupidity that waits its time* an easy victory over *hunger that cannot wait ;* " the system that seeks to make Mammon, and not God or Justice, rule this world—in one word, the English, or Famine system, must be abolished utterly—in farms and work-shops, in town and country, abolished utterly ; and to do this were worth three Revolutions, or three times three.

In countries such as England and America, where the commercial or " free competition " system reigns with greatest power, if the relations of employer and employed be still in any degree ruled by justice, duty, or affection, that is in spite of the system and because it has not yet entirely prevailed.   In so far as it does prevail, the tendency always is to this type—a relation in which the master's sole object is to get as much work from, and to give as small a return to his servant as possible ; the servants to do as little work and to get as much wages as may be ; the feeling between master and servant being such as, with such objects on either side, might be looked for.

5. Mitchel, having seen the working of slavery, was of opinion that in the slave-holding South the relation of master and servant was upon a much more satisfactory

footing than in the free and commercial North. If the relation did not entirely conform to ideas of justice or duty, it was at least, in a very large degree, based upon mutual affection.

If it be said that the comparison here made is between slave service and free service as it is and not as it ought to be, my answer (sufficient for my present purpose) is that John Mitchel had no faith in social Utopias of any kind. In reply to the reproach that he "did not believe in the future of humanity," he once wrote to a friend—"I *do* believe in the future of humanity. I believe that its future will be very much like its past; that is, pretty mean." For him, the practical issue in the South was between a social system based upon the institution of slavery, and a social system in which the relation of master and servant would be regulated by free competition as in the North. He took his stand in favour of that system which seemed to him the better of the two; and, as was his habit, he took it decisively.

Slavery is now, so far as the Union is concerned, an institution of the past; an institution which no one expects and few would desire to see revived. Arguments and discussions which had a practical value twenty-five years ago have no practical value now. Yet the deeper social questions which lay at the root of the slavery problem, and which mainly influenced the judgment of men of insight, are to-day as urgent for solution as they were when the slavery dispute was at its height. These deeper social questions are not to be answered without long and anxious thought. Not unassisted thought, however, for in making the inquiries I speak of, we now have available the most effective kind of aid—the aid of a great teacher. At the time that Mitchel's views on the slavery question were exciting the wrath of northern abolitionists, a series of essays on the principles of political economy were appearing in an English magazine which puzzled most readers, delighted a few, and, by the orthodox teachers of the science, were received with a perfect storm of anger and derision. These papers—afterwards collected and published in book form— are very decidedly the best work done on the subject of political economy by any Englishman during the present century. And, indeed, if there be any of my readers who desire to enter into (if not to agree with) Mitchel's view on the slavery question, the best advice that I can give to such is,—read Mr. Ruskin's " Unto This Last." *

During the winter of 1857–58, Mitchel continued to reside at Knoxville. His time was mainly taken up with the work of the *Southern Citizen,* yet he found time to visit some southern cities and to deliver a few lectures. At the beginning of the year 1858, he received an invitation to lecture at New Orleans and one or two other cities. Of this invitation, and of his reasons for accepting, he writes to his sister Henrietta on January 9, 1858 :—

I am very busy now, for on Monday the 11th I set out on a southern lecturing tour—a loathsome business which I thought I had renounced for ever ; but I want money, and can only think of preying on the public. So, I am going to try a new field, where I have never been before. I never saw New Orleans or Mobile, and, what is more to the purpose, New Orleans and Mobile never saw me ; so that I shall have " houses " not so much to hear what I have to say as to hear how I say it, and to have a look at me. They would come just as well if I advertised that on a certain evening I would appear upon a platform and stand upon my head there. This is a humiliating reflection to an illustrious patriot, but it can't be helped.

* In this discussion of Mitchel's position on the slavery question, I have not considered it any part of my duty to state or even to imply my own view on the subject. However, the possibility of being misunderstood may justify me in saying here that, since I have had any opinion on the subject, I have been against slavery, though hardly, I think, on the same grounds as most abolitionists.

The *Southern Citizen*, I think, is establishing itself pretty well, considering the nature of the *times*, for you may possibly have heard, or may have met the statement in the course of your reading, that there is a monetary pressure and a financial crisis. I work pretty hard, harder than ever I did for the *United Irishman*, and now I have to write some literary articles in advance, to be used while I am absent, and at the same time to prepare lectures, so that I am seldom in bed this last week before three o'clock in the morning.

On this occasion he lectured at Memphis, New Orleans, and Mobile, starting from Knoxville about the middle of January. He left Tennessee "all rigid in frost," and in Louisiana he found the weather mild and balmy He was much struck with New Orleans. The French part of the city pleased him especially. To one accustomed to the monotonous uniformity of the newer American cities, the variety presented by New Orleans cannot fail to be pleasing. Passing from the American to the French side of Canal Street, one feels as if suddenly transported into some old city of Southern France or Italy. And what made this visit still more enjoyable to Mitchel was the fact that he had several friends in New Orleans whom he was really glad to see. Foremost amongst those was Richard Dalton Williams. Of him he says, "Met R. D. Williams, who has a wife. The poor fellow is not rich—such chaps never are—and is teaching a Catholic school. Spent an evening with him, for the first time since our parting in Ireland, and alas! for the last." Of friends visited in New Orleans he further notes : "Visited at the house of my friend the good Bishop Polk, whom I had met in Tennessee ; a good southerner, slave-trader, and 'pirate.' This worthy bishop has since fallen at the head of his troops, fighting for his country. God rest him!" From New Orleans he passed on to Mobile, which he describes in his correspondence as "one of the gayest and most luxurious cities he had ever seen." As regards the subjects of his lectures and his success in persuading his audience, he observes in his "Journal" :—

Both here and at New Orleans, my lecture was on India and the events of the past summer. I tried to expound to my audience the odious and predatory policy of England in the East ; but although I was listened to with applause, it was but too evident that this cotton-growing, cotton-selling community could not be brought to feel any serious indignation against so good a customer as England ; for the heart of the cotton-bale beats responsive to the throb of the Manchester mill.

By " the events of the past summer " he here means the Indian Mutiny. From Mobile he travelled by river steamboat to Montgomery, the capital of the State of Alabama, thence by rail into and through Georgia, and so home to Knoxville.

Early in 1858, I find a letter to Miss Thompson containing some interesting passages. She had evidently been expostulating with him for giving up Ireland, and devoting his efforts to aid the cause of the southern states. To this he answers :—

Now you expostulate with me on having given up Ireland. Which of us has given up the other ? What indication do I ever receive from Ireland (save from yourself and one other) that does not show me how absolutely and how scornfully Ireland has condemned herself and repented in sackcloth and ashes for having ever listened to the wild counsels of such as I ? Yet I do not believe that Ireland, in her secret heart, hates those counsels ; and do not you believe that I, in my secret heart, have forsworn all care for the land where I was born, and for a cause in which I suffered much, though I did but little ? An exile in my circumstances is a branch cut from its tree ; it is dead, and has but an affectation of life. Neither are you to think that I have any tie, or am likely to have any here, which could prevent me from throwing myself into that cause again, if it were again showing life ? But I do not

II.

feel impelled to keep harping on a string to which everybody is deaf.

It would seem from another letter to the same lady that the "one other" here referred to was John Edward Pigot. It must not, however, be inferred from this that Miss Thompson and Mr. Pigot were the only persons in Ireland who corresponded with him. Besides his own relations, he had frequent letters from John Martin and Father Kenyon, and occasional letters from other friends.

From the time he returned from his lecturing tour in February, 1858, until late in the fall of the same year, Mitchel continued to work steadily at the *Southern Citizen*. It was during this time that a series of letters appeared in the paper giving a history of the "Young Ireland" movement, and of the events of 1848 in Ireland. The letters were addressed to the Hon. Alexander Stephens, of Georgia. They were subsequently—in 1860—collected and republished in book form under the title of "The Last Conquest of Ireland (Perhaps)." This book is, next to the "Jail Journal," the most widely read of Mitchel's works. Of the subject of the book, he says in his preface :—

There has not been, to my knowledge, any other attempt to give a connected narrative of the decline and fall of "repeal;" of the English famine-policy and its complete success ; of the steady progress of demoralization and denationalization, which have brought Ireland into her present abject state. These letters may fill up that *desideratum*—at least provisionally—till the task shall be better accomplished by somebody else.

The twenty-second letter contained an account of the attempted rising in the summer of 1848. Mr. O'Brien, the principal actor in that transaction, took exception to Mitchel's account of it. He addressed to Mitchel a letter from Cahirmoyle, dated October 4, 1858. The letter was friendly, and indeed complimentary, in tone. He acquitted

Mitchel of all intention to mislead, but stated generally that he did not admit the accuracy of the narrative. Mitchel published the letter in the *Southern Citizen* and answered it. In this answer he says that his account of the attempted insurrection had given rise to considerable controversy ; that he had resolved to ignore all this controversy, and to be corrected by no one except Mr. O'Brien himself. Of Mr. O'Brien's letter he says :—

It does not state wherein we were misinformed ; but whenever it shall please Mr. O'Brien to give an account of his own movements and motives at that period, the writer of the letters to Mr. Stephens undertakes to adopt that account, to alter his narrative by it, and to uphold it as absolute truth against all the world.

During the year 1858, the *Southern Citizen* continued to do fairly well, but it became more and more evident to both Swan and Mitchel that at Knoxville they were decidedly outside of the main current of events. If the paper was to exercise a perceptible influence upon the general public opinion of the southern states, it would need to be published in some place more central than Knoxville. Accordingly, in the fall of 1858, Swan and Mitchel agreed, after consultation, to remove the paper to Washington.

Once more, then, John Mitchel had to change the place of his habitation. It seemed fated that he was never to have a permanent home. The house in Knoxville, which he and his family had begun to regard as a home, was put up for sale. All necessary preparations were made, and it was arranged that they should move to Washington at the beginning of the month of December. Very shortly before the move was made, and while they were in all the agonies of moving, Mitchel had a visit from a man who afterwards became known to fame :—

About two weeks before our migration a gentleman appeared

at our door who announced himself as James Stephens. I had never seen him before, and knew him only as having turned out with Smith O'Brien in 1848 with his pike in good repair. Glad to see an Irishman of such antecedents at Knoxville ; and for two days he remained with us, telling me romantic tales of his armed, sworn, organized forces in Ireland. All he wanted was that I should publicly call on my fellow-countrymen in America for money, and more money, and no end of money to be remitted to him for revolutionary purposes.

Mitchel declined to join in any public appeal for money. But he gave Stephens what money he could spare—some fifty dollars—and a letter of recommendation to certain gentlemen in New York who had the control of funds intended for revolutionary purposes.

Early in December, 1858, the move to Washington was made. There was now a railway running into Knoxville, and Mitchel and his family were able to travel all the way by rail from Knoxville to Washington.

They left several valued friends behind them when they quitted Knoxville. I have already mentioned Mr. Swan. There was another whose friendship was hardly less valued by Mitchel. This was M. Esperendieu, a Swiss clergyman from the Canton de Vaud. He had been banished from his country during the troubles of 1848, and had come with some members of his flock to live in East Tennessee. He had a farm some four miles from where Mitchel lived at Knoxville. The Irishman and the Swiss had certain opinions and tastes in common ; and in particular, they were exceptions to most of their neighbours in having, both of them, a wide acquaintance with literature, ancient and modern. They became and remained fast friends.

Mr. McAdoo and Colonel John H. Crozier were also of the number.

To the passage already quoted from Mr. McAdoo's reminiscences, I may add the following. After some description of Mitchel's life at Tucaleechee Cove, the writer proceeds :—

· "My office, and my home, was on Main Street, in a quiet and comfortable building, wherein I lived and kept my library. On Mr. Mitchel's frequent visits to Knoxville, he would often come to my office ; and there he would, in answer to my inquiries, pour forth such a flood of information touching the thousand and one topics of conversation that came up between us as surely marked him as being a very extraordinary man. I was then a subscriber to the London *Times* newspaper, and to *Blackwood's Magazine*, and the 'four reviews'—the *Edinburgh*, the London *Quarterly*, the *Westminster*, and another. These he would read by the hour.

"Once he was reading in one of these a review of some work that had then just appeared on the origin and signification of English *surnames*. In one of the extracts 'Mitchel' was derived from the Saxon adjective 'Muchan.' Mr. Mitchel's anti-Saxonism at once rushed to arms ; he claimed for his name a Celtic origin (though I do not remember the derivation he gave), and was thoroughly out of humour with the writer of the book.

"It was in the time of his residence in Tucaleechee Cove that I had a ride on horseback with Mr. Mitchel from Maryville, seat of justice in Blount County, to Knoxville, my home. The Circuit Court in Maryville had just adjourned ; the judge and the other lawyers residing in Knoxville. I was detained an hour or two by some official business with the clerk of the court. To my delight, I found that Mr. Mitchel was in the village, on his way from his mountain home to Knoxville. He consented to wait an hour for me. We set forth in the afternoon to make the journey, fifteen miles, over a rough country road. He was mounted on his favourite grey mare, a spirited and

brisk traveller ; I on a powerful animal, such a one being
necessary to carry me well over the very rough mountain
roads found in some parts of my circuit of seven counties,
extending across Tennessee from North Carolina to
Kentucky. We trotted along merrily, Mr. Mitchel being
in his best conversational mood. At length the sky, which
had become overcast, startled us with a few drops of rain.
The day was not cold, and neither of us had any overcoat,
umbrella, or other protection against the invasive damp-
ness. We trotted along more briskly as the shower grew
harder, and settled itself into a whole afternoon's work.
We were then some twelve miles from Knoxville. As our
spirits, however gay, were not so philosophic as to resist
some dampening effect as we felt the water trickling down
our persons underneath our clothing, we fell, after a while,
into a silence—a silence relieved only by the monotonous
sound of the rain through the forest leaves, and the sounds
of our horses' hoofs splashing along the muddy roads. Our
silence was at length broken by Mitchel, who, as we rode
along, recited in the finest manner possible, James Clarence
Mangan's translation of the German poet, Emanuel
Geibler's ballad of ' Charlemagne and the Bridge of Moon-
beams.' Pausing a moment, and before I ventured to
criticise the first performance, he commenced again, and
recited ' The Battle of the Lake Regillus,' from Macaulay's
' Lays of Ancient Rome.' Line by line the magnificent
stream of the story rolled on under Mr. Mitchel's wonderful
utterance, until the heart felt all the exultation of victory
and all the solemn sense of parting from friends, as he
recited the quatrain in regard to the departure of the twin
brothers, Castor and Pollux—

> ' And straight again they mounted,
>   And rode to Vesta's door ;
> Then, like a blast, away they passed,
>   And no man saw them more.'

" I had read Macaulay's ' Lay,' but I had no conception of its power until I heard that recitation, always memorable to me, from the lips of my friend, John Mitchel. I had not heard or read the ballad of ' Charlemagne.' Mr. Mitchel informed me respecting its authorship and its translation, stating that the translation was made by Mr. Mangan, an Irish friend of his. I ordered the work, and in due course of time obtained from Dublin the copy of Mangan's ' Translations from Various German Poets,' which now lies before me. While we discussed questions growing out of these delightful recitations, we reached Knoxville, cheerful, notwithstanding the gloom and disagreeableness of the day. Mr. Mitchel's genius had triumphed over these ! "

Colonel Crozier, the other friend named above, often gave Swan and Mitchel valuable aid in the editorial work of the *Southern Citizen.*

Those I have named were the principal ones—by no means all—of the friends whom John Mitchel left behind when he moved from Knoxville to Washington.

CHAPTER IV.

WASHINGTON—PARIS.

1858—1862.

AT Washington, John Mitchel and his family lived in the old house on Capitol Hill which had once been inhabited by Henry Clay. They were quite close to the Capitol. The city was spread out beneath them, and in the distance they could see the Potomac and the dark woodlands of Virginia.

The entire period of Mitchel's first residence at Washington did not exceed nine months. During that period most of his time was occupied with the work of the *Southern Citizen.* Yet he found time to see a good deal of society, and he seems to have enjoyed the society at Washington more than at any other American city he had yet lived in. His most intimate friend in Washington was Dr. Antisell, who, as the reader will remember, is mentioned in a letter of Mitchel's quoted above. Of this friend, he writes years afterwards :—

Dr. Antisell is a genuine man of science, if he *does* read Darwin ; and, what is better, has been always a warm and sincere friend of ours since we arrived upon this continent ; sometimes, as we thought, too sincere, for he has not scrupled to say disagreeable things—most sardonic, cynical, misanthropic remarks indeed, which, however, in the long run, make his friends like him the better. More genial misanthrope, in his own house—more jovial cynic was never known.

Next to Dr. Antisell he mentions General Shields as an intimate and valued friend. Of General Shields it is not necessary to say much to American or Irish-American readers. Mitchel has a good deal to say about him in the "Journal"; but I prefer to give here a description taken from a private letter. Writing to Miss Thompson under date April 24, 1859, Mitchel says :—

I told you I would expound General Shields to you. I have known him for five years, but never so intimately as during this last session of Congress, and find him a very remarkable person. But I bethink myself that I have given some account of him in the last *Citizen*, to which I may add that his relations—two brothers, with their families—live in Altmore, a mountain district of Tyrone, between Dungannon and Omagh, that he himself came to this country a little boy "without a cent," that he is a man of great and deep enthusiasm, as well as great accomplishment, and would at this moment most gladly devote the remainder of his life (otherwise useless to him) in revolutionizing Ireland, if we had but a chance. He was the most brilliant and dashing of the leaders in the Mexican war, although, in American accounts of that affair, his name is as far as possible suppressed ; but he commanded the brigade which contained some of the finest regiments, and after the war, one of the finest pageants was his visit to Charleston, where his progress through the streets was embarrassed by bouquets, and the state of South Carolina presented him with a superb jewelled sword. He had led the Palmetto regiment, in which that state takes great pride, and received a desperate wound through the lungs while charging at their head. During this winter and spring the general has been very much with us, but has now set off for his home in Minnesota. He appears very much interested and attracted by Mr. O'Brien.

These, then, were their two principal friends. As to the rest of their Washington society and their enjoyment of it, I take the following from the "Journal" :—

Meagher came often from New York. John Savage was a resident here some time before me, and his gaiety and jollity often enlivened the little society. He was then engaged in writing upon a Washington newspaper, what sort of politics I forget, if I ever knew. He was very festive, frank, and funny in those days; had not yet been caught right into the very head-centre of a Fenian spider-web. Several families of our American neighbours on Capitol Hill have called on us, and we have found their company highly agreeable. We know many of the southern senators and representatives and their wives, from far away by the banks of cotton-bearing rivers or shores of the Mexican Sea; no northern members of either House at all—at least, at first—except Mr. Cox, from Ohio, whose wife then resided at Washington.

He says here that they knew no northern members of either house—at least, at first. The qualification is inserted in view of the fact that Mitchel afterwards came to be on friendly terms with several of the leading northerners— more especially with Mr. Seward.

The passage descriptive of General Shields, above quoted, ends with a reference to Mr. O'Brien. We have already seen that some few years previous to this year 1859, O'Brien and his comrades were released from their banishment in Van Diemen's Land, and allowed to return home. In the spring of 1859, O'Brien paid a visit to the United States. He arrived at New York towards the end of February, 1859. Congress was then still in session at Washington, but was to adjourn in four or five days. Mitchel at once wrote to O'Brien exhorting him to come on to Washington at once, as he might not soon again have as good an opportunity of meeting the leading men on either side. O'Brien came, and Mitchel was at the train to meet him.

John Mitchel and William Smith O'Brien had not met since Mitchel's escape from Van Diemen's Land. The meeting was extremely cordial on both sides. Mitchel brought O'Brien to spend the evening at his house. It was a pleasant evening for O'Brien; and as for Mitchel, I have no doubt that he was happier that evening than he had been for years. What pleased him most was to observe how the distinguished Americans who crowded in to see O'Brien, at once and instinctively appreciated the innate nobility of his nature, and treated him accordingly. Here is his account of the evening in the " Journal " :—

His coming was soon noised abroad; I had myself informed many friends that I expected him ; and so, after tea, distinguished statesmen began to pour in by twos and threes. The House and Senate were both in evening session ; and our house being within two minutes' walk, members took occasion to step over and greet the noble exile. General Shields was there, of course, and his brown face was lighted up with pride ; Seward, with his thin jaw and bird-like beak, spoke to O'Brien with extreme courtesy and cordiality. Old Mr. Crittenden, of Kentucky, was there ; and my little squatter-sovereignty friend, Mr. Douglas ; and Clay, of Alabama, looking more like a student than a senator ; and Alexander H. Stephens presented his small keen face, much like that of Curran ; and his brawny colleague, Robert Toombs, of Georgia. Carolinians and Mississippians ; people from Louisiana and Massachusetts, from Virginia and Illinois, were there ; and all testified most cordial respect and felicitation, which could not fail to be gratifying to our friend. " It is truly pleasing," he said to me afterwards, "to see all those gentlemen, of widely different politics, representing opposite poles of your American life, and on the eve, perhaps, of a contest more bitter and violent than ever before—yet meeting together with so much good-humour and exchanging courtesies."

During O'Brien's stay at Washington there was a dinner-party at Mr. A. H. Stephens's, and another at Mr. Seward's, at both of which Mitchel was also a guest. Then there was a visit to the President, and a very friendly reception by him. Mr. Seward, no doubt, really liked O'Brien, but he was probably also anxious to do a stroke of business. He foresaw the possibility of a struggle between the North and South, and he desired to secure that Mr. O'Brien's influence with the Irish population should be exercised in favour of the North. At the dinner-party at his own house, Mr. Seward devoted all his attention to O'Brien, and put forth all his powers of conversation in discussing the political issues of the day. He turned good-humouredly to Mitchel, and boasted that he, Mr. Seward, had more influence with the Irish than John Mitchel had. His eloquence, however, was somewhat superfluous, since O'Brien was already a pronounced abolitionist.

When O'Brien left Washington, Mitchel accompanied him as far as Richmond, where O'Brien was again most cordially received by the governor and other leading citizens. There is a great deal in Mitchel's "Journal" about this visit. It was a subject upon which he loved to linger, for there were few living men whom he respected more than O'Brien. I can only find further space here for an extract from one of his letters, written shortly after O'Brien's departure. It is a letter to Miss Thompson :—

I knew you would be glad to see how cordially Mr. O'Brien was welcomed here by Irish and Americans, and men of all parties. But you seem not only pleased, but also a little surprised that he and I should have met on terms so perfectly friendly. Dear lady, we were never anything else but friendly personally since we first met ; and widely as we differ, and heartily as we censure one another, we can never be other than friends. In Van Diemen's Land, where we had no occasion to trouble ourselves with Irish politics (the onus being off our shoulders for a time) we had much and unclouded social intercourse, and came to know one another so thoroughly that there is no danger of our ever misunderstanding one another any more. Indeed, if I and my faction ever attempt anything in Ireland, he would be amongst the most strenuous of our opponents, and says he would feel it his duty to hang us. I, on the other hand, let him know that he might be spared (supposing us uppermost) by swearing allegiance to the Irish Republic and signing a proclamation for instant abolition of landlordism. Of course, he would not do it, and we should be forced reluctantly to hang him.

I think he was very much pleased with his visit to Washington and Richmond; the only two places where I went with him. . . . It gives me pleasure also to find that the southern planters and members of Congress who have been most attentive to him, are all very special friends of mine ; and one of his pleasantest visits in the South was to Colonel Maunsell White, a princely old Tipperary planter in Louisiana, who has written to me since O'Brien's visit a long account of it, from which it is evident that both host and guest were well pleased. On the whole, his visit will do service to his countrymen on this continent, and will enable him to set right several misapprehensions in Ireland when he goes home.

O'Brien's tour in the United States and Canada lasted some three months. On the 28th of May he sailed from New York by the *Vigo*. It was a gala day with the Irish of New York, and Mitchel, with his friend Dr. Antisell, came from Washington to be present at the leave-takings. There were receptions, parades, addresses, and so forth. After the farewells were over, and the vessel had sailed, an amusing incident occurred :—

As Meagher and I walked up Whitehall Street together, in company with a young American of our acquaintance, the latter said to us in a good-humoured kind of way, yet not without a *soupçon* of earnest mingling with his jest, " Your friend has had a very imposing and flattering farewell; but if you Irish would *all* take your departure for your own country, we would give you such a parting procession down Broadway as this continent has never seen." At which we all laughed ; and Meagher said, " We should have to bring *you* all with us, then ; for you have never been able to take care of yourselves without us."

Having thus seen the last of O'Brien, Mitchel returned to Washington and to work on the *Southern Citizen*.

Under date April 10, 1859, there is a letter to his sister, Mrs. Dickson, from which I take the following :—

. . . We have little to tell here in the way of news. John is going out with General H—— to begin a settlement in Arizona, a territory lying immediately north of Mexico.   James keeps the books, and does the business of the *Southern Citizen*.   Henrietta is taller than her mother, and plays pretty well.   As for me, I am " saving the South " with all my might—indeed, so violently, that a great part of the South (besides the whole North) thinks me mad. We had a highly agreeable visit from Mr. Smith O'Brien. . . . While Congress was in session, and the town was crowded with the families of congress men, we saw a little of the excessively fast Washington life.   But, independent of the congressional people, there is a large permanent population in the city, and they seem to me very good sort of people.   I have not seen my mother or any of them for eighteen months, nor Mary Jane since her visit to Ireland.   She seems to have enjoyed the Irish trip very much. It is a pleasure in which I cannot indulge myself; but I find there are still representations and intercessions made, with a view of having the ban upon us removed.

On the 20th of June, he writes again to a friend in a strain which shows that his thoughts were still running much upon O'Brien and his visit :—

You lecture me on the duty of Irishmen " sinking differences," and working together for a common national purpose, and you say you won't believe but that I could work zealously with Mr. O'Brien.   Yes, zealously and proudly with him or under him, so far as the difference between him and me.   I am no republican doctrinaire, and would accept an Irish monarchy or Irish anything; but our difference, as before, is not as to theories of government, but as to possibilities of action ; not as to the political ideal we should fight for, but by what appeals to men's present passions and interests we could get them to fight at all.   I am convinced, and have long been, that the mass of the Irish people cannot be roused in any quarrel less than social revolution, destruction of landlordism, and denial of all tenure and title derived from English sovereigns.   This kind of social revolution he would resist with all his force, and patriotic citizens could do nothing less than hang him, though with much reluctance.   I know you will be shocked when you come to this point in my letter, for I know how deeply you respect the name of O'Brien ; but, believe me, that I venerate it not less.   His tour through the United States was almost as great a pleasure to his countrymen here as to himself. I think, on the whole, he was pleased; but we were all proud as well as pleased.

The beliefs expressed in the foregoing letter as to the true method of working in Irish politics, and the only way of rousing the people, are interesting in view of recent events in that country.

It was during the time of his residence at Washington, in 1859, that there was published in New York his selections from Mangan's poems. The book is well known to Irish readers. Prefixed to it is an introduction—partly bio-graphical, partly critical—written by Mitchel himself.. I have always regarded this introduction as being, of its kind, the most perfect thing Mitchel has written. If there be any one amongst the readers of this book who desires to obtain, in the quickest and easiest way, an adequate idea of John Mitchel's power over the English language, I would say to him, read the introduction to Mangan's poems.

During the spring and summer of 1859, the *Southern Citizen* continued to discuss the questions of squatter sovereignty, free soil, and so forth, with its wonted vigour, and Mitchel was glad to perceive that the leading southern statesmen, as the time of the presidential election approached, were fast coming round to the extreme views which he advocated. But all the time the current of Mitchel's thoughts was setting in another direction. After all, as he said in his letter to Father Kenyon, the interest which he took in American politics was but a spectral interest, a mere shadow of the interest which he had taken in Irish politics. And from time to time, as affairs in Europe would take a turn that seemed to promise some hope for Ireland, the old interest would revive with the old force, and the effort to keep his mind busied with other matters would become irksome. The summer of 1859 was an exciting time in Europe. The French emperor had declared war against Austria on behalf of Italy. In the months of June and August, the European news was all of great battles and French victories. But it was not the prospect of a " free Italy " that interested Mitchel so much as the prospect of a breach between France and England. Shortly before the outbreak of the war in Italy, certain events had occurred which threatened to break up the *entente cordiale*, and lead to a Franco-English war. The tone of the press in either country had become bitterly hostile. The volunteer movement had been started in England to provide for the defence of the country against the French. And now, after all his brilliant victories in Italy, the French emperor seemed nervously anxious to patch up a peace with Austria as soon as possible, and to get back to Paris. People said that he must be looking forward to the immediate outbreak of another war, and whom could he intend to fight next, if not England? Mitchel became excited and uneasy, and longed to be on the other side of the Atlantic. Towards the end of July he had a consultation with Mr. Swan, his partner in the *Southern Citizen*, and, with Mr. Swan's assent, he determined to discontinue the paper. Arrangements were made to have the subscribers supplied with another weekly paper of similar politics, until their subscriptions expired. Of this contemplated change, he writes to his mother under date July 30, 1859 :—

I have delayed writing to you for some days, in order that I might have something definite to tell. I have something definite now. We have arranged with the *New York Day Book*, a strong southern paper, to supply our subscribers with the *Weekly Day Book* in lieu of the *Southern Citizen* for the unexpired time of their subscriptions. This we have accomplished at some sacrifice ; but it enables me to wind up the concern, without laying myself liable to any reproach. Next week's number of the *Southern Citizen*, then, will be the last number ; and then farewell to the Dred Scot decision and squatter sovereignty. The poor injured South will have to do without me and take care of itself.

I am going to Europe—which will be generally accepted as a sufficient reason for discontinuing the paper ; otherwise it would be set down merely as a broken and bankrupt concern. How long I may stay must depend on circumstances ; but as to this I will explain to you more fully, as I shall see you before leaving. Of course I am not going to Ireland. Mr. Swan is acting very well in all this business, though he is a heavy loser by our news-paper undertaking. He wishes me to go, and leaves the entire winding-up of the affair to me. I am now taking measures for turning into money all the materials and machinery. After paying all that is due, I hope to settle matters so that the family shall have the means of living quietly for a year or so. In the mean time, all the boys must instantly get into a way of earning their livelihood. . . . Of course some northern newspapers will abuse me ; but I don't mind that. If I satisfy my own subscribers, that is all that is necessary, and any remarks or speculations will be only impertinent.

The *Southern Citizen* accordingly ceased to exist, after a career of something less than two years ; and early in the month of August, 1859, John Mitchel sailed from New York in the sailing ship *St. Nicholas*, bound for Havre.

After a sea voyage of three weeks, and a railroad journey of a few hours, John Mitchel arrived in Paris about the end of August, 1859. He had never been in Paris, or indeed in France before. Under ordinary circumstances, to a mind so familiar as his with the historic associations of the place, the first sight of Paris would have been very interesting. But when Mitchel first saw Paris, and for some little time afterwards, his thoughts were so engrossed with political matters that he found it difficult to take a keen interest in anything else. Accordingly, we learn from his "Journal" that on the morning after his arrival, the first thing he did, after breakfast, was eagerly to consult the newspapers. Things still looked hopeful enough from Mitchel's point of view. The peace of Villafranca had been concluded a month before. The hands of France were free, and, judging by the press, the bitterness of the French against the English was more intense than ever. "There is an Anglo-French war in the air," says Mitchel. "When will it come down in bodily form to the earth?"

It was not destined to "come down in bodily form to the earth" for that time, nor, indeed, during Mitchel's life. A couple of months' residence in Paris sufficed to satisfy Mitchel that, however fiercely they might talk, neither party really meant or wished for war. And so soon as he was satisfied of this, he desired to be back again in Washington with his family. As he puts it himself, he began to feel that he might as well have stayed at home. All was too quiet; and he read his newspapers every morning dismally.

In the month of October he had two very welcome visitors—his brother William and John Martin. He had not seen John Martin since they parted at Nant Cottage, Van Diemen's Land. They had, therefore, much to talk about. Mitchel was now staying at a small hotel in the Faubourg St. Honoré; and John Martin, during his visit, stayed at the same place. There they spent long evenings together, talking and smoking as of old. In the daytime, too, they found plenty of occupation. Martin had been in Paris frequently before, and knew the city well. Under his guidance the other two saw a fair share of the principal sights.

After the departure of John Martin and William Mitchel, which took place about the beginning of November, John Mitchel's life in Paris was gloomy enough. On the 2nd of December, he writes to his sister Mary :—

I am living like any hermit ever since William and John Martin left Paris ; seldom see anybody, and the weather is so excessively bad and dreary that there is small temptation to go out. I have been two or three times at Versailles to see Mrs. Kelly and her family, who are highly agreeable people, and occasionally I sit an hour in Colonel Byrne's. To Mr. Leonard's I go but seldom, and have not even cared to improve the only French acquaintance I have made, that of M. Marie Martin, one of the writers in the *Constitutionnel.* In short, I am not in brilliant spirits, and have small reason to be, either on public or private account. I can see very clearly that I will shortly be wanted at home, and cannot perceive that I am much wanted here. So that, unless something quite unexpected befalls within the next two weeks, I shall certainly recross the Atlantic at once.

The Colonel Byrne referred to in this letter was Miles Byrne, *Chef d'e Bataillon* in the French army. He was an Irishman by birth, and had [fought with Father John Murphy in the rebellion of 1798. When that was over, he had left Ireland, and entered the French service in the Irish legion. He had served under Napoleon in most of his campaigns, and had won his rank and cross of the Legion of Honour by hard fighting. He was now a noble-looking old man, eighty years of age, but still erect in body and in mind. The old colonel and Mitchel became warm friends ; and both in his " Journal " and in his private correspondence, Mitchel always speaks of Colonel Byrne in terms of affection and respect.

The French acquaintance whom he speaks of in the above letter, M. Marie Martin, was an able writer on the staff of the *Constitutionnel.* While Mitchel was in Paris, M. Martin, at his suggestion, wrote some articles on the subject of "Liberty of the Press as it exists in Ireland." The liberal journals of Paris were taunting the emperor with being afraid to allow in France such liberty to the press as was allowed by the English Government. John

Mitchel gave M. Martin some account of his experiences of the kind of liberty that was allowed to the press in Ireland ; and M. Martin embodied Mitchel's narrative in a series of articles. Emile de Girardin replied in the *Presse* that Ireland was a conquered country and was treated as such ; he had been speaking of the press in England. Of which declaration Mitchel observes that this was just the effect he desired to produce. He wished all men to know and to acknowledge that Ireland was governed without law and as a conquered country.

On the 15th of December, he writes to a friend in Ireland from the Rue Lacépède, where he was then staying :—

As to Irish movements, I cannot say that I am much exhilarated, though my friend, Mr. Pigot, is sanguine. It is rather unlucky, this agitation about the Pope, though, in fact, any kind of opposition to English policy upon any question is in my eyes so far good. And, moreover, I deny that there is the slightest inconsequence in the Irish people demanding a restoration of their own nationality, and at the same time refusing to sympathize with Italian insurgents against an Italian sovereign. For my own part, I should heartily sympathize—if sympathy were of any use—with the people of the Romagna in all this affair, if it were any business of mine; but I feel discharged from attending to it. With respect to English liberality in Italy or anywhere else, nobody knows better than you that it is an imposture. Well, then, the amnesty movement in Ireland pleases me still less. It is with difficulty I restrain myself from speaking out what I have to say on that point. And, indeed, I have not restrained myself altogether. I perceive the Irish Tory newspapers are exciting themselves a good deal against me. My near neighbourhood seems to affect those people much as a red flag affects bulls or turkey-cocks.

On the 22nd of December he writes to Mrs. John Dillon, who was then living at Dublin :—

Shortly I go over to what I suppose you would call the wrong side of that sheet of water. And the truth is I do feel somewhat more affinity for this old hemisphere. Yet the contemptuous tone in which most of my acquaintances in Dublin—even you— speak of the United States, excites my rage. The Irish despising the Americans! You know this is too strong. . . .

Did you ever see the tall gloomy old convent, now *pension bourgeoise*, which I now inhabit, in one of the vilest streets in Paris? Half of the inmates are very aged women, and one of them died in the house this week. Indeed, when I go into the dining-room, and see these poor old bodies ranged at table, each with her napkin fixed under her chin, it makes me shiver with a sudden thought of the *morgue* and the cemeteries. Do you know that the only formal written invitation I have received since I came to Paris was an invitation to the old lady's funeral, and that in the grimmest, gloomiest weather. Is it not ghastly? If I were a woman, I would sit down and take a good cry. . . .

He then proceeds to acknowledge a book which Mrs. Dillon had sent for his sister Mary. It was a work by some well-known Catholic author in defence of the Catholic belief. Mrs. Dillon was herself a devout Catholic. Alluding to a recommendation that he should first look into the book himself and judge of its fitness for his sister's reading, Mitchel says :—

Ah, lady! I know the wickedness that is in your thoughts. You wish to save Mary's soul, and have no objection to give— *chemin faisant*—a lift to mine also. You want to undermine our great right of private stupor through the seductive philosophy of this Catholic author. The truth is that there is a kind of hankering in all our family after the "errors of Romanism." Well, perhaps I may read the book on my voyage, and mark the objectionable passages for Mary's avoidance. . . .

Don't be angry, if I say that I think our people are making fools of themselves with their MacMahon swords, and papal agitations, and amnesty movements. Marshal MacMahon will never see the sword, the Pope will never get back the Romagna, and there never will be any amnesty. Indeed, as to the aforesaid sword, that foolish idea—so foolishly puffed by silly letters—has done serious harm to the man it was intended to honour. The bad taste of singling out one of the emperor's generals, and making a demigod of him, is fully appreciated here. . . .

On this matter of the sword he must have changed his view, since he was afterwards himself a member of the deputation which presented the sword to the marshal.

On January 8, 1860, he writes to John Dillon, the husband of his last-named correspondent :—

> The *entente cordiale*, though it is false and treacherous on both sides, is for the present in full credit. It will burst up one of these days, to be sure ; but I can't afford to wait for that. Lurking in Paris, waiting for wars, and looking out for squalls, won't do for a long time, and I am wanted at home. . . . I don't like the *Irishman*, except those things in it which are written by " Gall." He always writes with good sense and good feeling ; yet his manner of writing is not well adapted for journalism. . . . You tell me I have made many bitter enemies. What is this for ? However, they, the enemies, may all go to blazes, provided I keep the few friends.

The person here referred to as " Gall " was John E. Pigot, who has been already mentioned as one of Mitchel's most valued friends. The reason of the reference to the *Irishman* is that Mitchel was, during his stay in Paris, an occasional correspondent of that journal.

Ten days after this letter was written, Mitchel sailed from Havre by the ship *Mercury*. He was the only cabin passenger, but there were some two hundred and fifty emigrants, mostly Germans. They had bad weather and a long voyage. It was about the middle of February when the *Mercury* arrived at New York. Immediately on landing, Mitchel hurried over to Carlton Avenue, Brooklyn, to see his mother, brother, and sisters, as well as his two youngest daughters, who had been staying with his mother all the time he was away. I believe that this was the last

time that John Mitchel ever saw his mother. She shortly
afterwards left America. After a brief stay at his mother's
house, he went on with his daughters to Washington.

This time, Mitchel only remained some five months in
America. During that time several public events of
importance took place. Abraham Lincoln was nominated .
at Chicago as the candidate of the abolitionist or republican
party for the presidency. Mitchel admits that he was sorry
they did not nominate Seward. He speaks of Seward as
being " by far the ablest of the radical or abolitionist statesmen," and as " the man who built up the party, and by his
talents and energy made it the powerful (and noxious)
thing which it unhappily is." The Democratic Conventions met shortly afterwards, and two candidates were
nominated, one Stephen A. Douglas by the northern
democrats ; the other Breckinridge, of Kentucky, by the
southerners. This division insured the election of Lincoln.

All these events Mitchel watched with interest. The
southerners, in rejecting the candidate of compromise, and
starting one of their own, were following the course which
he had always urged in the *Southern Citizen*. All the
indications were in favour of civil war.

In June, 1860, Mitchel had a short lecturing tour. He
first visited Richmond and lectured there. Thence he
went to St. Louis, and thence to Chicago, Milwaukee, and
Cincinnati ; and at each of these places he delivered
lectures.

On Mitchel's return from Paris, he had found his family
still in the same house on Capitol Hill, and all well. They
continued to reside at Washington until after Mitchel's
return from the lecturing tour above referred to. It was
then decided that they should remove their place of abode
to New York. The family now consisted, besides Mr. and
Mrs. Mitchel, of the three girls and the youngest boy,

Willie. John, the eldest son, was now engaged as an engineer in Alabama; and James, the second son, was in Richmond, where he had obtained employment from an insurance company. Before looking for a house in New York, it was resolved that the family should have a few weeks at the sea during the heat of the summer. They first went to New Rochelle, one of the regular summer resorts for New Yorkers. Not liking this place very much, they soon removed to David's Island, an island of some one hundred acres in extent, situate in Long Island Sound, eighteen miles from New York, and one mile from New Rochelle. There was good sea bathing to be had at David's Island, and the place was more quiet and retired than New Rochelle. So they determined to enjoy a few weeks in this retreat, pending the determination of the great question—where next?

From David's Island, Mitchel writes to his brother William on July 6, 1860 :—

The island has a most beautiful grove, very fine fields, plenty of springs, and as fine a shore for bathing as ever I saw—smooth sandy beach at one side for women and children; at the other steep rocks and deep water, where Willy and I can plunge. It is within twenty minutes row of the shore at New Rochelle, which accordingly is the proper post-office to address. The proprietor has a fleet of boats, and they are to be at our disposal. Jenny and the children are all perfectly delighted with it, and, in short, I do not see what it wants as a perfect summer sojourn. I had quite a capital trip to the north-west lately, and amongst other places visited Milwaukee, which I found a handsome, large, well-built town. To show you in part what they have been doing there since your sojourn, I send you a faithful picture of the hotel, which I clipped off one of the dinner bills-of-fare. I was also in St. Louis, and Chicago, and Cincinnati, and became the fortunate discoverer of a town called Lafayette (Indiana), of which I had never heard before, nor, I suppose, anybody else; but where I vociferated before a large and fashionable audience.   Everywhere I found large promise of bountiful crops, especially throughout Indiana, where it is very evident to me that the citizens will not starve.

But, pleasant as was David's Island, they could not stay there for ever.   Something had to be determined upon. Mitchel had still some thoughts of returning to law-practice ; but all the time he knew well enough that nature had never made him for a lawyer.   The only alternative in America seemed to be another newspaper venture, and for the present, at all events, he was quite decided not to try that.   At times he thought of returning to Paris and bringing his family with him.   He had reason to believe that, if living in Paris, he could get employed as corre-spondent of certain American and Irish papers, and thus earn enough to support his family.   Still, he had by no means decided on this course, and was in fact engaged in studying law, when an incident occurred which brought him to a decision in a manner very characteristic.

One day, about the middle of July, Mitchel was in New York.   As chance would have it, he met upon the street his friend Captain French, of the *Mercury*.   The captain asked Mitchel to go with him on board his ship.   She was at the wharf, sitting the water like a sea-gull, all trim and taut.   In about eight days she was to sail for Havre. Mitchel at once made up his mind.   He would cross the Atlantic again in the *Mercury*, and take his family with him.   He went back to David's Island that evening, and announced his decision.   Mrs. Mitchel was rather glad to hear that Paris was to be their destination.   She would have to leave her two eldest sons behind in the United States, but, on the other hand, she hoped that in Paris she would have better facilities for educating her daughters. They had to set to work at once to make their preparations.

The second son James came from Richmond to spend a few days with them before they left. On the day appointed for the sailing of the *Mercury*, they were all ready. It was about the end of July, 1860, when they bade farewell to David's Island. They passed over to New York, got on board the *Mercury*, and started on their voyage for Havre.

The voyage was uneventful. They arrived at Havre about the end of August. The scenes and customs of the old world were in many respects strange to the young people of the family :—

The aspect of a French seaport, with its tall, narrow houses of six or seven storeys on the quay, was new to our young people, who were immensely impressed by the majesty of two or three *gens-d'armes* who came on board our ship, with their tremendous cocked hats and broad yellow sashes, and profusion of lace, swords, epaulettes, and so forth. My youngest little daughter, who saw these personages stepping on board, ran into the cabin to announce that the emperor was come to meet us.

They passed on to Paris. For a few days, they stopped at a hotel, until they could find suitable apartments. During these days Mitchel took great enjoyment in "witnessing the eager curiosity and wondering delight which always intoxicate young people at first sight of this astonishing city." After a short search, they found rooms to suit them in the Rue de l'Est. Their windows looked out on the gardens of the Luxembourg ; and in these rooms they resolved to spend the winter.

This second residence of Mitchel's in Paris lasted just two years, from the beginning of September, 1860, to the beginning of September, 1862. He did not continue during all this time to live at the Rue de l'Est, but he resided either in the city or in the suburbs of Paris.

Mitchel's regular occupation during these two years— so far as he had a regular occupation—was that of a newspaper correspondent.   He wrote a letter every week to the *Charleston Standard* until the outbreak of the war and the blockade of the southern ports ; and I believe he also corresponded during most of this time with the *Irish-American* and the Dublin *Irishman.*   This was the work he relied on for the means of livelihood ; but it did not occupy his time so entirely as the work of conducting a journal.

During the winter of 1860–61, their life in the Rue de l'Est was monotonous.   The novelty of Paris and of sight-seeing soon wore off, and they settled down to the ordinary cares of housekeeping in these new quarters.   It was arranged that the youngest boy, Willie, should attend a day school, and a governess was to come three times a week to the girls.

During this period, Mitchel was fairly industrious as a correspondent, and his letters, as usual, give a good picture of the sort of life he led and the subjects which occupied his thoughts.   On October 4, 1860, he writes to his sister Mary from the Rue de l'Est.   I should mention that his mother and her family had left America in the spring of 1860.   They were now living in London :—

We have a quite good-enough lodging here (for Paris), with a most beautiful outlook over the splendid garden, or rather park, of the Luxembourg.   We have little enough room, and Billy particularly is obliged to *niche* himself in a precarious fashion ; but, on the whole, it will do.   The rent is one thousand francs a year, that is, two hundred dollars ; for which sum, you know, we could not get a decent house in New York.   It is astonishing to see the nooks that people will live in at Paris, and consider themselves well off too.   Is there any chance of our seeing any of you over here, were it but for two or three days ?   Our girls, in such a case, would be able to so dispose themselves in their room as to give one of you a bed in their place.   We have but two good bedrooms besides the servants' bedroom ; but, with goodwill, there is wonderful accommodation to be got by stretching.

I am hardly yet set to my work regularly. Indeed, it is only the last three days that I could so much as put down a desk anywhere to write. The weather has been gloomy and chill—is bright now, but cool—and our Luxembourg trees, which have been till now rich and green, begin to grow brownish—not crimson and gold, like the woods of that capital old America, which I always like best when I am not there. As to my ever being a lawyer in America, I have put that finally out of my head. I knew all the time that I must come over here, and it might as well be done at once. What hurried me at the last, if you must know, was that I found my particular ship, the *Mercury*, was in port, and to sail for Havre on a certain day. They brought over all our packages, just as they had been made up at Washington, piano and all, in their packing-cases, as they were, without charging freight, they all came as our personal baggage. The piano is not a bit the worse. I am going to send Billy to school for the winter, at least, and also get a person to come three times a week to give lessons to the girls.

On the 24th of the same month, there is a letter addressed to Mr. and Mrs. John Dillon :—

My dear John Dillon and Mrs. Dillon,

    One can hardly hope to be pardoned who receives a letter dated 9th of September, and only sits down to acknowledge it on the 24th of October, especially a very good, gracious, and double letter from two of his best friends. Especially his chance of forgiveness must be small when he has no excuse to offer, except a vile, procrastinating, lazy habit. I hate a desk, I loathe a pen, and anathematize an ink-bottle. It seems like an effort to drag my heart out, if I draw over to me those hated utensils, even to write what people pay me for by the line. Then I wish that I were working with any other sort of tool—a spade, an axe, a shoe-brush, a sword, a currycomb, trowel, or harpoon. Yet I can't do anything except with a pen, and it's the old story, as stated in Horace's rattling line—

    "Optat ephippia bos piger, optat arare caballus."

John O'Hagan was here and Father Kenyon. They both welcomed us very hospitably to their hemisphere. J. O'Hagan is very little changed indeed ; Father Kenyon not at all. . . . I note what you tell me about the state of political feeling in Ireland. It accords pretty well with what I have gathered from other sources. If the case were even worse, if the people—upper, middle, and lower—were even in a more hopeless state, it would not alter *my* conduct in any respect. What I know is that I will not stay patiently exiled and banned from my own country by the British, and shall steadily work and labour to set that matter right by any means that may occur to me, provided I deem those means just. And the best thing I can think of now is to help and stimulate the quarrel between France and England, with a view to having the chance of joining, before I die, in an invasion of Ireland, and so endeavouring to set you all free whether you like it or not. It is useless telling me all this will never come to anything—I think that quite probable—but it does not affect me in the least.

There now, you have the whole of my theory and principle. It may be resumed in this formula.

I (John Mitchel) have an absolute right to live in Ireland, which is my own country.

If there be no other way of asserting that right but destroying the British Government, then I have a right to do that too—by means of the French or any other allies.

If there be any persons in Ireland who maintain that I have *not* the right to live in that country, and who will set themselves to oppose it, why I have a right to cut (or procure to be cut) all those persons' throats.

So look out. I like this formula so well, that I will try to elaborate it a little, and make it more categorical, and stick it somehow into the *Irishman.*

Paris is a hateful place. So is every place, when you are once in it. Sometimes I wish I were back in the "land of the free and the home," etc. ; but then I should immediately wish myself back here again. After all, you know, Dublin is my real place of abode. All the world can't alter that.

The visit from Father Kenyon here referred to was a source of keen pleasure to Mitchel. Next to John Martin, John Kenyon was his dearest friend.

During the autumn they also had a visit from Mr. John Martin. He stopped at the Rue Lacépède during his stay in Paris, but spent most of his evenings with the Mitchels. The children had not seen him since they left Van Diemen's Land, and they were delighted to see him again. John Martin was always a great favourite with children. He took them out for walks, and showed them what there was to see.

In November, Mitchel writes to his mother from the Rue de l'Est :—

We are comparatively comfortable here on our little flat ; but we have had two servants both bad, yet not to be compared for badness to the Washington young ladies. Jenny's heart is broken because she cannot as yet scold them in French, and she is studying a vocabulary and learning verbs for that express purpose. Henrietta and Minnie are attending school, which school happens to be in our very house; but it was recommended to us well. Billy also goes to another school, and I think they all get on pretty well.

We hear from James occasionally—more seldom from John, who was about, at the date of his last letter, to change the railway he was on for another.

And on the 22nd of December, to the same correspondent :—

I am slow and remiss in my correspondence, but at the approach of Christmas I must make up my defaults. You are, I hear, very brisk, and must be seeing sights all the day and every day, just like Father Kenyon when he was here in Paris. I am happy to hear you are so active, and have still the spirit to go and see sights. I suppose you are familiar with the Tower, St. Paul's, and Guildhall, and it is a pity the Parliament is not in session that you might see the august legislators of England, and even of Ireland.

Under date of the 28th of December, he writes to his sister Matilda (Mrs. Dickson) :—

As for us, here in Paris, there is little news to tell you. We are living in a flat (*un étage*) not much bigger than one room of Tullycairne. We have some good acquaintances, especially the Byrnes and Mrs. Power, and the Kellys of Versailles (if you know who they are), and one or two others. Hardly any French, and those of the masculine sort. In fact, we live very quiet and obscure, hiding our light under a bushel. Henrietta has been for two years a devout Catholic. She has become extremely intimate with the ladies of the Sacré Cœur—a splendid convent here—and I believe she is to make abjuration of something one of these days, with the accompaniment of a religious service—to all which I offer not the least opposition.

The young lady referred to in this letter as Henrietta, was Mitchel's eldest daughter. While the family were living in Washington, she had become intimate with two young girls, who were about her own age, and who were devout Catholics. After this intimacy had lasted some little while, Henrietta told her parents that she wished to become a Catholic. John Mitchel thought she was then too young to make up her mind on so important a question. He told her he could not allow her to make any formal change of religion for the present ; but that if, after a few years, she still desired to become a Catholic, he would offer no opposition. Towards the close of 1860, Henrietta became intimate with the ladies of the Sacré Cœur Convent in Paris. She again spoke to her father expressing an earnest wish to enter the Catholic Church at once. This time he offered no opposition, and the day was fixed for Henrietta's reception into the Church.

When this fact came to be generally known, some of John Mitchel's relations and friends in the North of Ireland remonstrated very earnestly with him. The persons who so remonstrated were entirely free from that anti-Catholic bigotry which is so common amongst the Protestants of the North of Ireland. But they had an objection—by no means unnatural—to the idea of a young girl taking upon herself publicly to renounce the religion of her forefathers. Still, I think it is impossible to read Mitchel's letters upon the subject without feeling that he was entirely in the right. Early in the year 1861, he writes to his mother, in answer probably to some remonstrance of hers :—

As to Henrietta's religious proceedings, you are aware that it is no new thing. The matter is put off for the present; but if, hereafter, she should be bent upon it, I don't know with what conscience I can interpose parental authority to prevent it. I have never taught my children any religion, nor even spoken to them on the subject. If I had any system of my own to inculcate, I might endeavour to hold them to it; but would really feel that I could not be justified in merely prohibiting their profession of any particular faith which they may be inclined to without direct- ing them to any better or any other. As to my own position, on that matter you need have no apprehension. There is not the least chance of my being a Catholic, and so much the worse. But it is not very kind of you to intimate that respect for my father's memory is anyway concerned in the matter. He vindicated the right of private judgment above all things. If one's private judgment leads him into the Catholic Church, it is private judgment still.

The superioress of the convent of the Sacré Cœur (referred to in the letter to Mrs. Dickson) was one Madame Davidoff. She was a very clever and very energetic lady. Having succeeded so well with Henrietta, she thought she would try what she could do with Henrietta's father. She made energetic attempts to convert John Mitchel; and arranged for an interview between him and a learned divine. But nothing came of it.

I may finish here the brief story of Henrietta Mitchel's life. With the sanction of her parents, she carried out her intention and entered the Catholic Church. She then went to school to the convent of the Sacré Cœur, and there

she remained until her death, which occurred in the early
summer of 1863. From the time of her conversion she
was noted for extreme piety, and she endeared herself
much to the ladies at the Sacré Cœur. After her death,
a short account of her life was written by a Mademoiselle
Bramêt, at the request of the ladies of the convent. From
this memoir I would infer that by many of the inmates of
the Sacré Cœur Convent, Henrietta Mitchel was regarded
as a saint.

In a letter of Mitchel's to his sister Henrietta in the
month of January, 1861, I find the following account of his
occupations :—

I have a great deal of writing to do. In fact, write more
" original " matter every week than ever I did while I conducted
the *Citizen* or *Southern* ditto. You see in the *Irishman* (if you
get it) only one-third of my performances ; and I am at the same
time giving capital matter to the *Charleston Standard* and *Irish-
American.* Of course, I have a good deal of reading to do. In
fact, I suppose I write a good deal of trash ; and John Martin is
savage with me for my intolerant and reckless habit of denouncing
everybody who does not agree with myself. I cannot help it.
Whoever does not agree with me is an idiot, you know. Very
likely John Martin will have passed through London on his way
hither by the time this reaches you. He said he would call and
see you. I hope you have softened him a little towards me ; for,
if not, I expect much bad usage from him when he comes. I
hope you admired my French in the *Ami de la Religion?* Well,
having duly admired it, I may tell you that it was not my French
at all ; but that it was put into presentable shape for me by
M. Marie Martin.

On Easter Sunday, 1861, he writes to his mother :—

The weather begins here to be a little like spring, and the trees
in the parks are growing green. We had some thought of moving
from our present lodgings about the middle of April, but have
changed our minds, and are to remain here another three months,
that is, till the 15th of July. Then I will try to get a little place

outside of Paris, where rents are not so high. We had a letter yesterday from James. He seems to get on very well, and gives a flourishing account of the prosperity of the insurance company. He says that everybody in Virginia is soldiering in one form or another, and that he himself is now in the Montgomery Guard, a very fine company of the first regiment of Virginia volunteers; but I suppose in the rank of a full private. A few days ago also we heard from John. It seems they keep him pretty busy. The only serious work now in South Carolina appears to be preparation for defence; and although the Federal Government was to abandon Fort Sumter, yet matters are very far from being settled. We have letters, too, from Henty and Minnie, who seem to be spending a pleasant though quiet time. They sent us a very kind letter which they had received from Mrs. Dillon, asking Margaret to bring them to Dublin to spend a few days with her; but I don't think that is likely to take place. John Martin had called on his way back from Dublin, and seemed in bad humour about public affairs.

We were present last Monday, in the midst of a tremendous crush, to hear the Bishop of Orleans preach his charity sermon for the Irish poor. We are all well here, except myself, who have had a succession of bad colds for three or four months—nothing more than colds, however; but that is sufficiently troublesome. Mr. Leonard has gone over to Ireland, bearing the proceeds of the charity sermon, about £600, which is considered a fine collection.

This, I think, is all my bundle of news.

The events in America during the spring and early summer of 1861 interested Mitchel extremely. It is not necessary to repeat here the narrative of those events. Every one knows that it was in the spring of 1861 that the great civil war broke out; and, in America, at all events, most people are familiar with the events which led up to that result. Mitchel's two eldest sons were both in the Confederate army from the very outbreak of the war. John, the eldest, held a commission in the First South Carolina Artillery; James, the second son, served first as

a private, and afterwards as an officer in the First Virginia
Infantry. This fact, in itself, made the outbreak of the
war a matter of terrible interest to the Mitchels; but it is
certain that even if Mitchel had had no personal stake
whatever in the struggle, he would have looked on with
the keenest interest. His "Journal" at this time is full of
reflections and comments upon the course of events in
America.

Early in the month of May, 1861, they left the Rue de
l'Est, and went to live at Choisy-le-roi, a suburb of Paris,
situate on the banks of the Seine above the city. In a
letter written to Miss Thompson, shortly after the removal,
he describes the new abode :—

Last Tuesday we removed from that dungeon-dark abode of
Rue de l'Est, and have got here a cottage all to ourselves, with a
little garden. The rooms are better, and more of them than we
had before, and at least we have good daylight and fresh air,
which, you remember, were commodities not to be had at Rue de
l'Est, except in the front rooms. We are fifteen minutes from
Paris on the line of the Orleans railway, and we are in the middle
of a pretty enough country, and on the banks of the Seine, which,
above Paris, is a clear and natural sort of river. Now, you have
an inventory, and what the *proprietaires* call *état de lieux* of our
new premises, which, on the whole, I think will be very agreeable,
at least, during the summer, however we may find it in the winter.
Choisy is a neat little town, with good shops, and all sorts of
resources for living, except the opera and the boulevard *cafés*, of
which sort of institutions, you know, we did not much avail ourselves, at any rate. Our *déménagement* was all effected in half a
day, the *déménageurs* of Paris being perfect magicians; but Jenny
has been ever since settling herself in her new place, and this
Sunday we begin to feel at home.

The life at Choisy is also described in the "Journal" :—

We are here but a quarter of an hour from Paris; in little
more than half an hour we can go to the Palais Royal. From
the high ground over this little town we can see the towers of

Notre Dame and the dome of the Pantheon; yet the country around is perfectly rural and tranquil, with vast wheat-fields on the plain, and vineyards clothing the sides of the gentle hills which bound the Seine valley on either side. I have several times started hares, almost under my feet, in the fields. Hares are fearless and familiar in this country, knowing that there is a law against keeping greyhounds. We have explored both banks of the river, upward and downward, and Willy collects beetles. He also attends lectures by professors of natural history at the museum of the Garden of Plants.

I go into the city three or four times a week, to see all the papers—American, English, and French—at Galignani's; and follow with eagerness the progress of events in the United States.

In the month of July, they had a visit from Mr. W. S. O'Brien. He was on his way to visit the camp at Chalons, on the express invitation of Marshal MacMahon. He came out one morning from Paris to Choisy to spend the day with the Mitchels. It was the last time that John Mitchel and William Smith O'Brien ever met. They talked much of American and much of Irish affairs. There were few matters about which they could entirely agree. Mitchel lingers over this day in the " Journal " as though the memory of it were dear to him; and indeed he always writes with a certain affection and pride about everything connected with O'Brien. I can only extract the concluding passage :—

The delicious summer evening passed quickly, as he and Leonard and myself sat smoking in our cottage garden. My wife summoned us to tea. Then for an hour O'Brien was his old self, his darkened brow cleared, the high courtesy of the man—and, I think, somewhat of real regard for us all—made him desirous to make this last hour pass gently and kindly. All my little household idolized him; and although we could never agree upon any single question (save *one*), I felt that he had a kind of presentiment, as I had, that we should never meet again. So our parting was affectionate, though silent. Willy and myself went with our two friends to the railroad station, and the last words of O'Brien to me were : " As for your Southern Confederacy, you will hear of the collapse of *that* in a few days." The train thunders into the station, and with a benediction we part. Farewell, then, royal heart !—the best and noblest Irishman of our generation, and for this reason, and for this reason alone, sentenced to be hanged, drawn, and quartered !

During the summer of 1861, Mitchel's interest was divided between the news from America, and certain plans suggested by leading men in Ireland for the purpose of reviving the national spirit there.   Mr. George Henry Moore had certain projects of organization which were communicated to and discussed with The O'Donoghue and others. Mitchel's advice was asked, and I believe that The O'Donoghue came over to Paris to talk over the matter with Mitchel. Mitchel's views upon the project were mainly expressed in letters written to his friend John B. Dillon. He criticised adversely Moore's plans, and suggested himself, amongst other things, an address to the French people, which he drafted. This address seems to have called forth from some quarter the charge that the one thing essential in Mitchel's idea of policy was to be illegal. Against this charge he defends himself with warmth in his letters to Dillon. Speaking of his draft address to the French people, he says :—

It was a plain statement of facts as to the actual condition of the country. . . . And there is no law yet against divulging the results of the Irish census to foreigners, or the provisions of statutes in force in Ireland, or the public proceedings of courts of justice. Somehow or other, many of my friends have got it into their heads that my sole policy is to be illegal. But I have now got very strong reasons for not advising people in Ireland to do what is illegal (before the country is ripe for it), seeing that I am myself out of the enemy's reach.

And again, a few days later, to the same correspondent :—

I see you have been heretofore under the impression that all I thought of was instant and constant collision with law at all points. And now, when I cite an Act of Parliament as a reason for a thing not being done, you say that, in my "present mood," I agree with you. My present mood is just the mood I always was in, and I despair of agreeing with you until the moment of —— arrives, when I know we shall be in admirable accord.

There are several more letters on this subject. I cannot give them all, but I select the following passage as giving an idea of the nature of Mitchel's objections to Moore's scheme. I gather from Mitchel's letters that Moore must have been endeavouring to get permission for Ireland to raise a force similar to the volunteer force then being created in England, and ostensibly with the same object—to resist apprehended invasion :—

Neither do I at all stand upon "phraseology;" but in substance his draft address contained the representation—that Ireland, being a part of the British empire, is threatened by the same enemies; that, being the outworks of the empire, of which England is the citadel, Ireland is likely to be in greatest danger (from the French, of course); and that Irishmen should testify their wish and readiness to be armed, in order to resist (the French, of course). All these things do not amount to "reserve;" they amount, in my mind, to a servile proclamation of attachment to the empire, and a declaration that the "empire's" cause is our cause. I confined myself to cutting out phrases in this sense. . . . It is one thing not to avow the real intention, and another thing to suggest that which is *not* the intention. . . .

The address to the French is also perfectly legal, and is not only the natural sequel to the national petition movement, but is the thing that is required to give a *meaning* to the projected organization, which would otherwise have none. Indeed, most people would laugh, and very excusably, at the enrolment of men forming an army *in all but the arms*. . . . Perhaps when he (Moore) and you see the inoffensive document I have given to

O.D., you will both accept them. At all events, they are the best I can think of. The *phraseology* is nothing. Take them both, and alter every phrase, if you like, but leave the idea.

So far as I am aware, nothing came of these proposed addresses and organizations. But the reader will be able to see from these letters that even when events in America were most exciting, Mitchel did not lose his interest in Irish politics.

Describing his life at Choisy in the summer of 1861, he writes to his sister Matilda :—

The country about you must be most beautiful in this glorious weather. Here also we have a lovely, rich country all round us, and the Seine, which flows past here, is perfectly limpid and beautiful, Paris being lower down. There are hardly any fences, the roads are very firm, and shaded by double rows of trees on each side. On the whole, it would be splendid for riding, if one only had horses, but horses are too expensive to keep here, for my finances. In Van Diemen's Land, or Tennessee, the keep of horses was little or nothing. We are within fifteen minutes of Paris by the Orleans Railway, and I often go in. Our little bit of garden is blooming, and we shall have plenty of grapes, if the *oïdium* don't come on them ; this consideration is very important to France in general, though not extremely momentous in a garden forty feet by thirty.

We have no late news from the two boys, and I suppose shall have none soon, for I think the mails are stopped between South and North. All the news that comes here of the course of events will be northern news, so you may prepare to swallow more and bigger lies than you ever heard before ; the truth will be told after we are all dead. In the mean time, I know so much of the matter as to be exceedingly well content that my boys are on the southern side. When I go to America again—if ever—it will be to Charleston, Mobile, or New Orleans. At present we are anxiously looking out for some intelligence of James. He is on more dangerous ground than John for the present, as I am quite certain his regiment is out on service, and the first serious fighting will be on the Potomac.

On August 14, 1861, he writes to his sister Mary :—

You ask, as it is very natural you should, whether I have any plans for the future. Not I, no more than Mr. Lincoln has. You hear that I intend to go back to the Confederate States. Not I. I never said so; neither do I intend to go, nor intend to stay. All that depends on what may take place in Ireland and in France and Amerca. In the mean time we vegetate here. I still correspond with both the *Irish-American* and the *Charleston Mercury*. My communications with the latter were interrupted for a time, but are resumed through a channel unknown to Mr. Lincoln. I receive a little money from those offices, but am finely cheated by the *Irishman*. . . .

I know the comment you are likely to make on all this— " They are a vile set, those Irish, particularly those rebel Irish." Indeed, you tell me plainly, " Irish people are despised all over the world, at least, Irish rebels, and no wonder." This is a very complete mistake of yours. It is for *not* being rebels the Irish are despised, and no wonder. Those who are most despised are those who pretend to be loyal subjects.

The paragraphs about John at Bull Run are all a mistake. So far as I have any reason to know, he was not in Virginia at all. James must have been there, indeed, but as yet we know nothing of their fortune. Every day we await, with what anxiety you may guess, to learn how it has fared with them. . . .

We can scarcely be said to know any one here, though, as our garden communicates with two or three other gardens, we some- times sit of an evening with the people of one or other, or else they with us—people of whom we know nothing except their names, and that they are polite and well-bred. We go seldom to Paris. All our acquaintances in Paris are off for the summer. The Leonards at Courcelles, on the coast of Normandy ; the Conollys at Venice ; the Pallachés are gone from Versailles alto- gether. I think they are in England. Only the Byrnes are still in Paris.

The brief catalogue of friends and acquaintances given at end of the above extract may be supplemented by the following account of some of their neighbours, taken from a letter (also to Mitchel's sister) written in the spring of 1862. In this letter he mentions that his eldest daughter, Henrietta, was at school at the convent of the Sacré Cœur. He then proceeds :—

The others say lessons in a desultory sort of way here at home; some to me, some to M. Bayer, our worthy old neighbour, who makes it his pleasure and delight to lecture on the French language, and we indulge him. He loves company, too, being a Parisian, and he is now living in exile. For every Parisian conceives himself to be in exile and in the wilds when he is once outside the barriers. He wants occupation and somebody with whom to *causer* and *jaser*. He is also perfectly well-bred, and a wonderful legitimist, having a very slender opinion of *celui-ci*— " this man "—and he wears the white lily in his genteel heart of hearts. He has had in his day relations of some sort with the Polignac family, and keeps hanging in his *salon* a portrait of that Prince Polignac who was sent to Ham, having been prime minister of Charles X., and, of course, clapped in gaol after the three glorious days. Now, Minnie has the good luck, it appears, to resemble a princess Polignac, and therefore the old gentleman takes especial pleasure in correcting her exercises.

And lastly, regarding the friends they had, and the sort of life they led at Choisy, take the following from the " Journal " :—

The summer creeps along slowly. We have some few acquaintances, both at Choisy and at Paris; the good family of Rue de Montaigne, old Colonel Byrne and his devoted Scottish wife; also the agreeable family of Mr. Leonard. Within four miles of our Choisy cottage is the village of La Rue, in which dwells Mr. Bréant, a Frenchman, married to an American wife. They are vehement southerners; but the lady's mother and sister, who live in the same house, are as violent Yankees; so the very subject which most deeply interests them all is tabooed; nobody mentions the American war; and each faction reads its morning newspapers in silence. Madame Bréant, however, is well pleased to meet with southerners as decided as herself; and in us she reposes her confidences. In Choisy itself we know three French families, and have a good deal of social intercourse with them; they all keep pet cats, and all love a quiet game of *wisk*. I keep myself tolerably busy writing my " correspondence."

So passed the summer and fall of 1861. Mitchel himself continued to go to Paris regularly two or three times a week ; the rest of the family very seldom.

Early in March, 1862, John Mitchel went down to Dieppe to meet his brother William, by appointment. William was to come from Ireland, and they were to meet at Dieppe and go for a walking tour through Normandy. The walk lasted some three weeks, and both of the brothers enjoyed it keenly. Four consecutive numbers of the " Journal Continuation " are devoted to giving a quite minute account of this walking trip ; and very interesting numbers they are. They visited quite a number of the old Norman towns, saw and admired their grand old cathedrals, and talked over their historic associations. But for the details of this tour, I must refer the reader to the " Journal." To give an account of it here would only be to rehash and to spoil a narrative which John Mitchel evidently lingers over with loving remembrance, and parts of which are written in his happiest vein.

While I am on the subject of walking tours, I may mention that in the following summer (1862), John Mitchel had another walk in France, but this time in the south. He had again his brother for a companion, and also John Martin. Of this tour also, John Mitchel published an account entitled an " Exile in France," also very well done, but too long to be reproduced here The following brief sketch is taken from a letter written from Richmond to M. Esperendieu (the Knoxville friend mentioned in Chapter X.) in the spring of 1863 :—

Yes, I was in Lausanne last July, at the most beautiful season of the year, after perambulating all Dauphiné and Savoy, and bathing in the lakes of Annécy and Bourget. On coming one evening to Lausanne in a steamboat from Geneva, you may be very sure I thought of you. . . . It is a most beautiful place indeed ; and the picture of the old town, with its grand church tower looking down upon the blue lake and faced by such a grand rampart of mountains crested with snow, will remain always photographed in my memory.

Late in the evening, we proceeded by railway to Yverdon, passed the night there, and next morning, on foot, breasted the Jura, found the little town of St. Croix almost on the summit and immediately under the peaks called Chasserets, and from thence walked on across the frontier, down into the valley of Joux, and so to Pontarlier, coming back to Paris by way of Dijon. It was a most delightful tour altogether. Nothing impressed us more than the splendour and wealth of the city of Lyons, which has become almost the rival of Paris. Geneva also must be greatly changed since your time, as there are many streets and places quite new and very elegant. Travelling generally on foot, and stopping at villages, we saw a great deal of the country people, and liked the French extremely. We saw less of the Swiss, and, candidly, liked them less than the French. At Lausanne, however, we got some very good wine at dinner.

All through the spring and summer of 1862, there was constant anxiety in the cottage at Choisy about the two boys who were fighting far away in the Confederate army. Mitchel's "Journal" at this time consists largely of summaries of and reflections on the news from America. McClellan's great campaign against Richmond was in progress. James Mitchel was in Lee's army, in the thick of the fighting. John was at Charleston, doing garrison duty in some of the forts there. Mitchel's letters contain constant references to American affairs, and to the prospects of his sons. Late in the spring of 1862, he writes to his brother William :—

Looking over your letter again, I see you are furious with the southerners for not "waiving their damned policy of conciliating public opinion in foreign countries for a moment," and making some acknowledgment for my services to their cause. That's too romantic; nobody is so "high-toned" as that. No doubt I did service in blowing up Douglas, but southerners at the time regarded me as a species of bore, and if they owed me anything they are of opinion that it is more than repaid by giving Jack a commission in an army of such whole-souled cavaliers. He is the only commissioned officer of foreign birth in the regular army of South Carolina, and it was regularly announced to me that the distinction was conferred on my account. Well, he wished such a position, and has got it, and the exertions of my friends in South Carolina to procure it for him must be set down to their credit in the account between us. It would be highly impolitic in them to make my name prominent, because there is no name so hateful (I flatter myself) in England. And they are right. It is not a damned policy to conciliate both England and France. I do not believe Russell, however, who says he found so many Carolinians sighing for a monarchy and longing for a British prince.

As the autumn of 1862 wore on, Mitchel became more and more anxious to join his sons in the Confederate States. Besides his anxiety about his sons, and his eagerness to take some part in the great struggle, there was another motive which helped to determine his decision. In the summer of 1862, he had ceased writing letters to the Dublin *Irishman*. During the greater part of this sojourn in France, Mitchel's correspondence with the *Charleston Mercury* was his main source of income. But as the blockade of the Confederacy, by sea and by land, became closer, correspondence with the *Charleston Mercury* became no longer possible. As Mitchel put it himself, he had no wish to make lively remarks for the benefit of the United States dead-letter office ; so that the only means he had of supporting his family while living in Paris had now failed him. It was necessary to do something, and the something which Mitchel himself most inclined to was to attempt the difficult and dangerous task of getting into the Confederate States. But what to do with his family ? He was ready enough himself to incur the risk of passing the Federal lines; but to take his wife and family with him on such an expedition was hardly to be thought of.

Towards the end of August, 1862, the Mitchels had a visit from Father John Kenyon. Father Kenyon was always a very welcome visitor at their house. On this occasion he was able to help Mitchel out of his difficulty. It was arranged that Mrs. Mitchel and one of her daughters should go to Ireland under the escort of Father Kenyon, and that the two other daughters should remain in Paris at school at the Sacré Cœur. As to the youngest son, Willy, it was at first intended that he should go to Ireland with his mother; but to this proposal the boy made a most determined opposition. He was now eighteen years of age, and he very resolutely told his father that he must go and join his brothers in the southern army. John Mitchel consented to let the boy have his way. He afterwards bitterly regretted that he had not insisted on Willy going with his mother and sister.

Once more, then, John Mitchel was a wanderer. This time, too, the family was divided up as it never had been before. Of this separation, Mitchel says in the "Journal":—

So there is another break-up of our household. When shall we be at rest ? Two trembling and saying their prayers in Ireland; two passing anxious hours in the Paris convent; two in camp and garrison beyond the Atlantic; and two making ready to penetrate the Yankee blockade in disguise, and by way of New York.

Early in September, 1862, John Mitchel and his son Willy left Paris for Havre, intending to embark at that port for New York. It appears that they were at Havre on the 7th of September, for I find a letter from Havre of that date addressed to Mitchel's sister Henrietta:—

Here we are, Billy and I, for the last three days. We are

going to sail somewhere to-morrow if possible. It is a hazardous experiment I am making, and I am leaving my poor folks in a painful situation enough, but anything must be better than as we were, or at least must soon have been, if I had lingered at Choisy. I saw the poor little girls every day before leaving Paris. They are well fixed, and seem well and contented. Madame Bréant and a few other ladies are to have leave to visit them, and even to bring them out when there is *congé*. They have their piano at the convent for practising, and the superioress asked that I should be presented to her, in order that she might beg of me to be perfectly easy in my mind about them, even in the worst case that could happen, and I try to be so. As for my own movements, I can tell you nothing, except that I am here, and hope to be no longer here to-morrow night. I send you all the remaining copies of the little photograph that I have, perhaps somebody may be glad to have them hereafter. I was much obliged to William for coming over to see me before I started ; and he will tell you what arrangements I have made for sending my news from the other side, supposing we get there.

On inquiry at Havre, Mitchel ascertained that the *Borussia*, one of the Hamburg line of steamers for New York, was to touch at Southampton. French passengers were brought over in a small steamer from Havre, and put on board in the harbour of Southampton without the necessity of landing. This suited Mitchel very well. He did not much relish the idea of being put ashore on English soil. Not that there was much danger of his being molested. It was very unlikely that any one would know him, for he was travelling under an assumed name, and was somewhat disguised. And even if the English authorities did know who he was and where he was going, it is not very likely that they would have cared to stop him. Still, he was glad to avoid giving them the opportunity. As matters turned out, however, he did not avoid it. When the little French steamer arrived in Southampton Water on the morning of the 9th of September, the

Borussia had not yet arrived. The passengers from France were put on shore at Southampton to await the arrival of the Hamburg liner. Thus, for the second time, and for the last time in his life, John Mitchel found himself in England. The reader will recollect that the former occasion was when he went over to present an address to Smith O'Brien in the cellar of the House of Commons.

They learned that the *Borussia* was not to arrive till the next day, the 10th of September. Mitchel and his son took up their abode in a neat hotel near the quay. The landlord is described as a "fat and jolly man, disposed to be quite talkative." He treated his guests remarkably well. When he heard that Mitchel was going to New York next day by the *Borussia*, he at once concluded, from these somewhat insufficient premises, that his guest must be a southern Confederate. Next morning, Mitchel sauntered out to see the town. At a newspaper office, he saw a large placard announcing that "the second battle of Manassas" had just been fought, and that the rebels had been totally defeated. This was, of course, a northern despatch, and it would seem that by this time people in England had learned to take northern despatches *cum grano*. Mitchel heard various incredulous comments from the crowd in front of the placard. And when he returned to the hotel, the fat and jolly landlord at once proceeded to interpret the despatch for him. Here is the account in the " Journal " :—

Returning to the hotel, I was met by my landlord, who was rubbing his hands, and his cheeks were inflamed with the energy of his smiling. " Bravo, sir," he cried, " you have heard the good news ? " " No, landlord—what news ? " " Lord bless you— glorious victory; the enemy thrashed to death." " But on which side is the victory ? " " Why, on *yours*, of course. Old Lee has punished the Yankees; given them their gruel, sir; routed their whole army before him; and he's now driving them all through the upper end of the State of New York!" It would seem that the lying style of news cannot answer; for people soon come to interpret it, like dreams, by contraries. Here was the reading which the worthy landlord put upon the New York despatch; whereby I found that it must also be the common reading accepted by the general public who used his house. I was pleased, at any rate, that the old fellow set me down as a southerner.

By two o'clock in the afternoon of the 10th of September they were on board the *Borussia.* Nothing special occurred on the voyage. On September 23, 1862, John Mitchel with his son Willy, once more landed at New York.

CHAPTER V.

IN THE CONFEDERATE STATES.

1862—1865.

FOR the period of John Mitchel's life which we are now entering upon the biographical material is somewhat scanty. The best material for writing his life I always find to be his own letters. Even that portion of Mitchel's correspondence which is not reproduced here (by much the greater part of it) has been of the greatest use in furnishing facts and suggestions for this biography. Now, during his residence in the Confederate States, his letters to friends and relations were necessarily few. None of his customary correspondents resided in the Confederate States, and the blockade was so close that it was only now and then an opportunity occurred of getting a letter out. With a very few exceptions, the only letters of John Mitchel, written between the date of his arrival in America and the close of the Civil War, that have come to my hands, are letters to his sons, then in the Confederate army. These letters are interesting, but they do not furnish much material for biography. They are mainly taken up with discussions of the military situation.

No sooner did Mitchel arrive at his hotel in New York than he became aware that there was some important war news. "Many absurd-looking officers, with plumes in their hats, were strutting around in the reading-room and office, expounding to civilians some startling newspaper army reports." It proved to be the news of the great battle of Antietam. General Lee had advanced into Maryland after Pope's defeat. McClellan had met him at Antietam, and if he had not gained a decisive victory, he had, at least, stopped Lee's advance and forced him to retire.

Life in the United States had changed much during Mitchel's absence. He was at once struck by the change, and he thus comments on it in the " Journal " :—

Am I in Austria? or in Ireland? It would not have surprised me if some of these fellows had stopped me and invited me to go before some provost-marshal and give an account of myself; but, in fact, we passed on quite uninterrupted and took our places. Many officers and soldiers were in the cars ; and at every station there was an unwholesome air of military *surveillance.* All night we travelled through the well-known and, to me, rather ugly country; and I have seldom made a more disagreeable journey. The military creatures—all of them, as it happened, most vulgar persons—talked loud slang and told anecdotes of camp and field, not always savoury. It is a changed America ! These shoulder-strapped beings are of the sort that would have travelled in modest silence or quiet talk with an acquaintance three or four years ago, but now talk loudly to one another at the distance of all this long car, and attract attention by their questionable semi-military jokes.

The night journey here referred to was from New York by rail to Baltimore. At Baltimore, Mitchel had been told, there was a kind of committee of southern gentlemen who facilitated in various ways the process of crossing the lines, here the river Potomac. To some of these gentlemen Mitchel had introductions. He saw these, and by them was introduced to others. They all consulted together, and various plans were discussed for getting Mitchel through the lines. It was finally decided that he should go on to Washington, where some other persons of Confederate sympathies would find means to convey him through the lower parts of Maryland and across the broad estuary of the Potomac near the sea. To go to Washington was somewhat risky, as Mitchel had lived there a considerable time, and was pretty generally known. It is true Mr. Seward was an old friend of his; but just then John Mitchel was not at all disposed to renew the acquaintance. He ran the risk, however, and went to Washington. The first experiences there were not encouraging. Mitchel went to an obscure hotel, and sent a message to a friend of his—a young lawyer, whom he knew to have Confederate sympathies. The result is thus told in the " Journal":—

My friend did not come very soon; and when he did it was with a face as pale as death. "What is all this?" he said almost in a whisper. "Why are you here? You will be seized and imprisoned. This place is peopled with spies; they are in every man's house; they dog every man's steps. I could not come here at once after receiving your note; but went round to various other places; came to this hotel from a direction contrary to that of my office; and even *so* I fear I am traced, and you are lost." And this is the free and easy Washington of old days! Not Washington, but Warsaw! Willy went out to walk through the streets, never dreaming that *he* would be recognized after two years and more of growth. He was hailed by his name all across Seventh Street, by a gentleman who inquired very kindly all about the family in Paris. So he came back, and gave me his decided opinion that Washington was an untenable position. My friend the young lawyer was clearly of the same mind; advised me to return to Baltimore for the present, and assured me he would make such an arrangement in a few days as would be almost certainly successful in getting us through the lines.

Mitchel and his son returned that same evening to Baltimore. There they stayed at the house of an old friend, a Limerick man, who welcomed them very cordially, and did all he could to forward their plans.

At this time the greater part of the population of Baltimore sympathized with the Confederates. The city was, therefore, kept under very strict *surveillance*—in fact, the people of Baltimore were watched nearly as closely as the people of Washington. Recently, when General Lee was in Maryland, the Baltimoreans were much excited. The greater number were preparing to welcome the Confederates ; while the minority, who were for the Union, were getting ready to leave the city.

John Mitchel remained in Baltimore about a week. During this time his friends at Baltimore and at Washington did not succeed in making any arrangement to get him through the lines. Mitchel became impatient. He determined to go on again to Washington, and thence to the lower part of Maryland. He would make the attempt by himself, relying on the friendly offices of the planters of southern Maryland, who were all strong Confederates at heart. The story of this all but desperate attempt is very fully told in the " Journal."

Mitchel, with his son and two others, succeeded in getting out of Washington without attracting observation, and spent some days in southern Maryland, watching for an opportunity to cross the Potomac. During these days they stayed at the houses of various planters—all in sympathy with the Confederates, and all very well aware of the object which their visitors had in view. There were a good many others in southern Maryland who had the same object as Mitchel ; and the party increased from day to day until it numbered eleven, including two Confederate officers who had crossed over to Maryland on some secret mission. The river was closely guarded by Union gunboats, and it was no easy matter to get over to the Virginia side. At last they heard of a chance to cross. An old man, who had a house on the northern bank of the Potomac, was said to have a boat and to be open to argument. To the house of this old man the entire party made their way. At first he would have nothing to say to them. But, after arguments of a most persuasive kind had been used, the old gentleman agreed to take them in. He was to give them supper and bed, and, shortly after midnight, he promised that his boat would be ready. In the house, which had six rooms, there were two Jews and another man dressed in blue Yankee cloth. These also were waiting to cross the river. The Jews had bales of goods which they hoped to sell at a profit in the Confederacy, and the individual in blue was said to be a trader also who supplied the Confederate sutlers with cloth and boots on the one side, and the Federal sutlers with tobacco on the other. In the course of the evening the man in blue several times looked at Mitchel somewhat more curiously than was pleasant. At length he came up to where Mitchel was standing apart from the others, and the following conversation took place :—

" I know you, sir," said he, in an Irish accent. "You know me? Who, then, do you say I am?" "No matter, sir, I have seen you in Dublin ; and very glad I am to see you now." With that he gave me an account of himself; told me he knew more about the crossing of that river than anybody else, as he was still coming and going; being neither Yankee nor Confederate, trading with both and caring for neither. He further assured me that old Mr. ―― would put us safely over, etc.

Shortly after midnight, they all went down to the river-side, expecting to find the boat. There was a boat there, but not exactly the sort of boat they wanted. Even if in good repair, it was much too light to carry the entire party ; and it was far from being in good repair. There was a large hole in the bottom of it, and it was obvious enough to Mitchel and his companions that if they put off in that boat they would certainly sink within twenty yards of the shore.

They returned to the house and abused the old man.

He assured them he had another boat hidden away some-where, which he would certainly have ready for the following night. There was nothing for it but to wait. During the following day, however, they noticed a very suspicious activity on the part of the gunboats and their launches—examining the shore with glasses, and so forth :—

Meanwhile our appointment with our old host stood for eight o'clock in the evening ; and after dusk his second boat was really brought out of its hiding-place and hauled upon the beach below the house. Now it was that some of our party held a council of war ; we had separately observed the same ugly phenomena amongst the gunboats and their boats' crews ; and had no doubt that we were to be betrayed and delivered up. The two Hebrew gentlemen at once shipped their goods on board the boat, and seemed to have no misgivings ; but we Confederates prudently retired into the wood, about a quarter of a mile off. We were not, of course, at hand when the hour of starting came ; the Jews were impatient, and they and two rowers had just put off, when a large man-of-war's boat, with over twenty armed men in it, swept round noiselessly and swiftly ; two men jumped on board the little boat, drove it ashore, rolled out the Israelites' goods, stove the boat with an axe ; then all the party leaped ashore, and—I regret to say—my friend who knew me in Dublin, who was sitting in the stern-sheets of the man-of-war's boat, came ashore with the rest, and led the party up to the house, which they instantly surrounded ; ten men in the garden, and ten in the front demanded that the door be opened ; enforced the demand with a volley ; burst in, and in three minutes searched the little place thoroughly. The old man, on the first alarm, had taken to his bed, where his wife said he lay at the point of death. His rude visitors smashed all presses, trunks, and cupboards, still demand-ing *the other eleven*—meaning *us*.

We did not know all these details until the next morning ; but where we were in the wood we could hear the firing about the house and some loud words of command.

They had to spend the night in the wood. It rained all night, and they could not even light a fire. One of the party—a young Confederate officer—was missing, and they feared he might have been taken prisoner. He turned up, however, in the morning. He had been concealed in the garden during the storming of the house, and on several occasions had very narrowly escaped being taken. He told his companions that, after the house had been searched, the leader of the Yankee party had loudly demanded of the two Jewish pedlars, "Where were the other eleven?" from which Mitchel inferred that his Dublin friend must have given an exact account of them to the enemy. The young officer further told them that the commander of the search-party had given orders to have an additional force brought ashore in order to picket the woods all round in a wide semicircle, so that any persons concealed in the wood might be enclosed between the guard and the river. This was not very pleasant news. The party in the wood had no food to eat, and no means of crossing the river. It seemed almost certain that they would all sleep in more confined, if not more comfortable, quarters before very long.

During the forenoon, two of the party went cautiously down to a place upon the river bank where there was a small hut owned by a fisherman. They succeeded in getting some provisions, and then asked cautiously about a boat. The man had in an outhouse a small, flat-bottomed skiff, wanting a plank at the bottom. But he was willing to mend the boat and to let them have it, provided he received a sufficient consideration. They agreed to his terms, and he promised to have the boat ready by nightfall. The two ambassadors then returned to their companions.

When night came they went down again to the river-side. The man was there with the little boat. It was much too small for the party, and they never could have crossed in it if the water had been rough. But, fortunately, the night was calm and the river perfectly smooth. Far out upon the river they could see the lights of two gun-boats keeping watch. But neither was directly in their course, and the night was dark :—

Quietly and as silently as possible we pulled out into the river; the chief danger being the noise made by the oars, which with all their noise gave us very little way. When about two-thirds of the way across, we suddenly found ourselves just under the bows of a small vessel, which we could not see in the darkness until she was almost upon us. She was making no way, however, in the dead calm, otherwise she must have run us down. Our friend, the fisherman, informed us that this was a revenue cutter. Notwithstanding the rattle of our bad oars, no notice was taken of us until after we had run across her bows and were two or three boats' lengths off. Then came the hail, "Boat ahoy!" We made no answer, but pulled hard; and now we expected a visit from a few musket bullets, but instead of this the cutter only ran up a light at her stern as a signal to the steam vessel two miles down the river, and we could see the light of the gunboat move almost instantly as she ran down at once to communicate with the revenue cutter. When this had all been done, we were some distance off, but still a good half-mile from the Virginia shore; and if a six-oared man-of-war's boat had at once been sent after us, she must have picked us up. I suppose the pitchy darkness favoured us more than anything else; at any rate, we made the rest of our toilsome way undisturbed, and leaped upon the gravelly beach at the foot of Mathias Point. At last we were on Confederate ground, and shook hands with one another all round.

About a mile from the shore was a farmhouse, to which the party made their way, arriving about nine o'clock. Their supper was a somewhat meagre one, and Mitchel could not but smile as he thought how they had all been so eager to get into that blockaded Confederacy whilst, at the very same time, so many others were equally anxious to get out of it.

Leaving the Virginia shore of the Potomac, John Mitchel and his son travelled in a spring waggon until they struck the Richmond and Fredericksburg railroad at Milford ; thence by rail to Richmond. At Richmond they stayed first at the house of a Mr. John Dooley, an old friend, whom Mitchel describes as " one of the best Irishmen he had ever met on that continent; greatly respected in Richmond as a citizen, and in the army as a gallant officer." Mr. Dooley had been a major in the First Virginia Regiment, but had been obliged to resign by reason of ill-health. He had two sons in the same regiment ; in which also James Mitchel was serving. James had been a private, but was now a captain. Willy Mitchel, the youngest son, who had just come with his father from France, was determined to serve in the same regiment with his brother James. And very shortly after his arrival at Richmond, Willy proceeded to carry out this intention. He enlisted in the First Virginia as a private. All three of John Mitchel's sons were now serving in the Confederate army. John was a captain of artillery, and was stationed at Fort Sumter ; James, also a captain, was in Lee's army on the Potomac ; and Willy was a private in the same army. As for John Mitchel himself, I believe he at first intended to enter the army also ; but he soon found that he was disqualified by reason of his nearsightedness. Afterwards, as we shall see, he served often in the field on the ambulance corps.

Shortly after his arrival at Richmond, Mitchel called on President Davis, whom he had formerly known in Washington. Mr. Davis received him very cordially. Mitchel at this time was a great admirer of the president. Afterwards, he came to modify his opinion considerably, and many of Mr. Davis's acts he severely censured. But, notwithstanding strong difference of views on points of policy, they remained on friendly terms during the whole period of Mitchel's residence at Richmond.

Finding that he was not qualified for actual service in

the field, Mitchel once more turned his thoughts towards journalism. His powers as a writer were well known to many leading men on the southern side, and he at once had offers of employment. There were then in Richmond two principal daily papers—the *Enquirer*, which supported the government and, as a rule, sustained the measures of President Davis; and the *Examiner*, which, upon the whole, was hostile to Davis and often fiercely attacked the administration. The owner and editor of the latter paper —John M. Daniel—was a very remarkable man. Of him Mitchel gives the following sketch in the " Journal " :—

Of this John M. Daniel I shall have more to say probably, hereafter, as although in some sense rival journalists, circumstances have produced a very friendly intimacy between us ; and I find him decidedly the most singular and original—I may add most accomplished—American whom I have ever yet known. He was minister at Turin for eight years before the war broke out. On that event he at once came home to Virginia, and threw himself most heartily into the conflict. When I arrived from France, I found him confined to his bed with a broken arm, a wound received while he served with Floyd. Daniel is a man of middle height; straight, slender, very swarthy, with keen eyes and a somewhat ferocious mouth, which is partially hidden by a black moustache. It has been to his urgency that the present military system of conscription was mainly due; and if he quarrels sometimes with the conduct of the president, it is chiefly on account of a certain slackness and timidity in enforcing upon the enemy due respect for the laws of war, by an unrelenting course of retaliation.

Later on in the war, Mitchel came to hold much the same views upon questions of war-policy as Daniel ; but his opinions had not yet reached that stage of development. He was asked by the owner of the *Enquirer* to take charge of that paper as editor, and he accepted the offer.

Not long after Mitchel's arrival in the Confederacy, General McClellan was superseded, and General Burnside was appointed to the command of the Federal army of the Potomac. The Confederate officers were strongly of opinion that McClellan was the ablest commander the northerns had. Naturally, therefore, they rejoiced when they learned the reward which the general had received for saving the North at Antietam. It was generally understood in the Confederacy that Burnside had been appointed for the express purpose of fighting Lee and putting an end to the business ; and accordingly he did fight Lee at Fredericksburg, but not exactly with the desired results.

A few days before the battle of Fredericksburg, Mitchel and his friend Mr. Dooley—each having two sons in Lee's army—went down from Richmond to visit the camp and see their sons. It was dark when they arrived at the first group of tents. They walked through the camp by the light of the camp-fires, inquiring as they passed along for the quarters of the First Virginia. Mitchel found his son Willy sitting by one of the fires with some comrades. He sat with them for an hour or two, and then went, by invitation, to spend the night in the tent of the commissary of the regiment.

The following two days were spent by the Federals in bombarding Fredericksburg. On the third day after Mitchel's arrival in camp, Burnside crossed the Rappahannock and drew up his army in front of the Confederate position. Mitchel and Dooley were in about the centre of the position and had a good view :—

We sat awhile with our friends of the Richmond Howitzers, viewing the gathering hosts of the Yankees filling up the plain, and admiring their order and celerity, when, about one o'clock, I think, an aide-de-camp rode up to Ned McCarthy, and conveyed to him some order. He bowed, and turned to his men, when every artilleryman was at his gun in a moment. " We are to open the ball," he said. " You had better retire to that other knoll alongside of us." A splendid battalion of Yankee artillery was right opposite upon the plain; and had just got their guns in position, when two guns of the Howitzers were pointed at the spot, and sent the Yankees a first message. It was at once answered by a very rapid discharge of shell. The artillery duel proceeded for some time, but without any marked effect that I could see, either on the one side or on the other. Soon we found that the knoll on which Major Dooley and I were standing seemed to become a special object of the enemy's shot; they evidently took us for two officers of distinction. The horrible screaming missiles came very close to us, and tore up the earth near to where we stood. Dooley and I descended a few paces on the safe side of the hill, and lay down, showing only the tops of our heads. The shells came thick and fast, sometimes throwing some of the earth over us. All this while McCarthy was hammering away from our side; and soon both parties slackened their fire, and the duel was over for the time. "Ned," I said, "their practice is a little better than ours—is it not?" "They have better powder, confound them!" was the answer.

Nothing further of importance occurred for that evening. The next morning all was quiet, and the Confederate officers began to think that perhaps Burnside was not going to fight, after all. Mitchel and Dooley left the camp early in the morning on their return to Richmond. They had six or seven miles to walk through the woods before they struck the railway. As they were nearing the railway station, the roar of artillery suddenly burst on their ears: the great battle of Fredericksburg had commenced. Shortly after Mitchel and his companion reached Richmond, the news came of the Confederate victory. This was about the middle of December, 1862. Willy Mitchel was in the thick of the fight, but was, fortunately, not hurt.

Through the winter of 1862–63, Mitchel was for the most of the time in Richmond attending to his duties as editor of the *Enquirer*. In the spring, he joined the Ambulance Committee, which imposed additional duties upon him. I give his own account of the work of this committee :—

I have joined a committee of Richmond gentlemen, who have associated together for relief and transportation to hospital of the wounded, whether of our own army of Northern Virginia or of the Northern Army of the Potomac. It is called the Ambulance Committee; and besides its civil functions, is armed as a company connected with the city guard, and under the command of Major Dooley. In this latter capacity we have been several times called out to take share of guard duty in the trenches around the city; but the real service of the company is done immediately after some battle or skirmish, when multitudes of wounded men are carried to the rear, destined for different hospitals. These poor fellows are placed in our care; and, when necessary, some men are detailed to help us. We are provided with supplies of various kinds, partly by the Commissary Department, partly at the cost of the committee; and transportation is also placed at our disposal to carry our patients to various hospitals. Pitiable and horrible cases of ghastly wounds are so frequent on these occasions that one might grow callous to the sight of human agony. Surgeons are assigned to duty with us to perform operations; and sometimes around our quarters are seen severed fragments of limbs.

Among the few letters to persons outside of the Confederacy, I find one to Mitchel's brother, written during the month of March, 1863 :—

I address this to you, as I know not where Jenny may be when it reaches Europe. It is but a chance if it ever reach, so I just give much the same intelligence which I have tried to send, through several channels, several times before. All are well— John still at Fort Sumter, where they constantly await attack; James with the army at Fredericksburg with rank of captain of cavalry. Billy is in North Carolina, and is a private as yet in the First Virginia Regiment. He has had hard duty this winter, and some terrible weather; and he was in the battle of Fredericksburg. He stands the campaigning very well, and is more robust than ever he was. Lately, indeed, he spent a day or two in Richmond, where (as is usually found to be the case) the exposure to a warm house and a dry bed at once gave him a severe cold. Since then he has returned to bivouacking in the snow, and is as well as ever. For me, I am doing the principal writing of the Richmond *Enquirer*, which is *supposed* to be in the confidence of the government, and I am able to divide a little with Bill, so as to procure him some little comforts, especially coffee, which is the greatest luxury. It cost $4½ per lb. The prices here have become monstrous, and scarcity is threatened of everything but the very necessaries of life. Board from $75 to $100 per month, etc. Things are by no means ripe for Jenny to come over ; nor do I believe she would be allowed to pass the lines if she came by way of New York. I am anxious to hear how all are.

In the spring of 1863, Burnside was superseded by Hooker in the command of the northern army of the Potomac. Hooker, like Burnside, was appointed to fight, and, like Burnside, he did fight. On the 2nd, 3rd, and 4th of May, 1863, the battle of Chancellorsville was fought, and again the Federals suffered a crushing defeat. But this time there was a compensating circumstance. Stonewall Jackson, the famous Confederate general, was killed by a chance shot from his own men. In this battle Mitchel's son Willy was not engaged, being, as we have seen, with Longstreet in North Carolina. James, however, took part in the battle as chief-of-staff to General Gordon, of a famous Georgia brigade. This brigade participated in the storming and retaking of Marye's Height, which had been occupied early in the day by the Federals. In the charge up the hill, James Mitchel was struck in the breast by a fragment of shell, and received an ugly wound. He had to be sent to Richmond as soon as he was able to bear the journey ; and it was several weeks before he was fit to return to duty.

From the eldest son, John, letters came every now and then. He was captain in the South Carolina Regular Artillery, and was all this time on duty in the harbour

defences of Charleston.   In the spring of 1863 he got a few
days' leave of absence and came to see his father at Richmond.   He gave a glowing account of his regiment, and
was able to tell his father some of his experiences at the
great bombardment of Fort Sumter, which had taken place
shortly before this visit to Richmond.   John's regiment had
been in the fort, and had taken an active part in the
defence.

Of another one of his children Mitchel, about this time,
heard a different and a sadder account.   I have already
spoken of Henrietta Mitchel's conversion to Catholicity
and of her early death.   Here is Mitchel's account of how
the news of his daughter's death was conveyed to him :—

One day I sat in my room in the *Enquirer* office, when an
officer came in who was unknown to me.   He introduced himself,
would not sit down, and showed a nervousness of manner.   At
last he rose, placed in my hand a newspaper closely folded up,
shook hands with me, and went quickly out without another word.
I found it to be a Dublin *Freeman's Journal ;* and I soon found
the paragraph which had induced my visitor to give me the paper,
but which he would not stay to see me read.   It was to announce
the death of my daughter Henrietta at her convent school in Paris.

It is the first break in our family of six children ; and there
are three more " on the rough edge of battle."

In the midsummer of 1863, General Lee once more,
and for the last time, crossed the Potomac.   He seems to
have supposed that the two great defeats which he had,
during the previous winter and spring, inflicted on the
Union army, would dispose the Northerns to come to
terms, and that the war might be brought to a close by a
rapid advance on his part into Maryland and Pennsylvania.
While this decisive movement of Lee's was in progress,
John Mitchel was with the Ambulance Committee on the
banks of the Chickahominy.   From time to time the news
reached them.   Lee was in Maryland ; Lee was in Penn-

sylvania ; he would soon be threatening Philadelphia. Then came rumours of a great battle that was raging near a town in Pennsylvania called Gettysburg. For a few days the accounts were varying—sometimes announcing victory, sometimes defeat. At last the whole truth came out. The Federal army under Meade had taken position at Gettysburg to stop Lee's advance. Lee had made a most desperate and determined effort to dislodge the Federals, but had failed to do so. His army had not been by any means put to rout ; but he had received a decisive check, and was obliged to relinquish all idea of ending the war by an invasion of the North. This was bad enough for all Confederate sympathizers ; but for Mitchel individually there was worse news still. I tell it in his own words :—

My two sons have been in the battle, and one dismal piece of news comes in—Pickett's division of Virginians, including the First Regiment, has been almost annihilated in the attempt to gain the Cemetery Heights. But nobody can yet tell who have been spared and who slain. James, with Gordon's brigade, was in that division of our army which drove the enemy through and out of the town of Gettysburg ; and he has not been wounded this time ; but he knows nothing of the fate of his brother. After a while, however, the truth came to us ; our poor Willy, in that terrible slaughter of Pickett's division, was shot through the body and at once killed. Those who were in that advance lay where they fell ; his remains were never identified ; and for a few days there was even some hope that he might have escaped or have been taken prisoner. But no, he died there ; and he could not have fallen in nobler company, nor, as I think, in a better cause.

So I have this dreary news to send to Ireland, if I can get a letter smuggled through the lines.

For some time after the battle of Gettysburg, John Mitchel remained in a state of uncertainty as to the fate of his son. That he was still uncertain at the end of July appears from the following letter written, on the 29th, to his son John :—

I have been delaying to write to you in the hope that I might have some news of poor little Willy. Not one word, more than we heard at first, namely, that he was wounded and left on the field. Some of his regiment, who are down here, say even that they saw him fall, but nobody can tell anything of the nature or extent of the wound. I begin to be very anxious about him, for it is now near four weeks since the battle, and if he and J. Dooley were in any hospital or place of confinement at the North, one would suppose that one or other of them would have found means to get a note slipped through the lines to let us know they are alive. At this moment there is not the smallest ground even for a guess, whether the poor fellows are alive or dead. Billy had just overtaken his regiment at Chambersburg a few days before the battle ; for he had been here sick a little while, and when he heard the regiment was off to Pennsylvania, he hurried away, to walk from Staunton to Chambersburg, which he had done in six days—one hundred and thirty miles.

A few weeks later he writes again to John. He says he has still some hope that Willy may turn up, and then proceeds :—

I see you are kept busy about Charleston. Colonel Moore and I had projected a trip to Charleston lately, but Mrs. Moore would not hear of it, and he had to give it up. He is down here for a month on leave. We thought it might be difficult for us, even if we had gone, to get into the city, on account of the strict orders ; and, in fact, we would only have been in the way. I am very specially interested about Charleston, and want it to show a splendid example. The Confederacy wants an example of heroism now to stimulate it, and no place has so good a right to give the example as Charleston. You ought to be very well pleased at being one of the defenders. I don't believe the place is going to fall, and if not it will be a splendid triumph to beat off such an attack. It will force all parties to do justice to Beauregard. As to yourself and your service, never mind the newspapers. All will be right if some stray bit of shell do not hurt you. James was down here for six days on furlough. He is gone up again, and is perfectly well. I have written to your mother since your letter came. I enclosed some of the newspaper descriptions of the fighting on Morris Island, that she may see you are not asleep.

The reference in this letter to the possibility of John being hurt by a " bit of shell " is curious, in view of his ultimate fate. A few days after this last letter was written, the uncertainty as to Willy's fate came to an end. On the 30th of August, Mitchel again writes to John :—

MY DEAR JOHN,
I know poor Willy's fate at last. He was killed on the field at Gettysburg. It was only to-day I learned it, by a letter from a gentleman in Philadelphia, to whom Mr. Dooley had written to make inquiries about his own son Jack, about Willy, and about Halliman, a captain in the same regiment. Captain Halliman was also killed. So poor Bill finished his first and last campaign.

During this summer of 1863 there was hard fighting around Charleston, which city the Federals made a most determined effort to capture. In one action, Captain John Mitchel and some other officers of the South Carolina artillery particularly distinguished themselves. Indeed, so conspicuous was their gallantry, and so important was the service they rendered, that the legislature of South Carolina deemed it right to award them a special resolution of thanks. Captain John Mitchel's name appeared upon the list of those to whom the thanks of the legislature were voted. He was naturally proud of the distinction, and he sent a copy of the vote to his father. Mitchel was much gratified. He immediately answered his son's letter :—

I received yours with enclosure of the South Carolina legislature's resolution of thanks. I was very glad to see it, and must say that I think you deserve it. You have had great luck in escaping so far, while so many fine fellows of your regiment have fallen either in battle or by sickness ; great luck every way except in the way of promotion, which, however, must surely come to you soon.   I am sending the resolutions to your mother.

No, James has not got his majority.   He is off now, with Ewell's corps, getting round Meade's left flank, and it is believed that General Lee meditates active movements.   Everybody speaks highly of James, and, like you, he gets every luck except promotion. I trust you and he may both be spared through this horrible business.   Poor Willy's death will be a shocking blow to your mother and sisters, and I feel it very much too, because I might have insisted upon his remaining behind in Europe ; but nothing would serve him except coming and taking his chances with his brothers.

I had a letter lately from Ireland, dated late in August.   Your mother had gone over to Paris, along with John Martin, and had brought away my dear little Isabelle from the convent.   She is now with them at Omeath, or was when the letter was dated. The little thing is very well, and delighted to be at home, though she was very happy also with the good ladies.   She speaks French now better than English.   Your mother and Minnie were well, and very impatient to be brought out here.

When John Mitchel left Paris for America in the fall of 1862, Mrs. Mitchel, with her daughter Minnie, had gone to Ireland in charge of Father Kenyon.   The eldest daughter, Henrietta, remained at the Sacré Cœur Convent to prosecute her studies, and the youngest, Isabel, was also left at the convent with her sister.   Mrs. Mitchel and Minnie remained at Father Kenyon's house at Templederry, until a few weeks before the Christmas of 1862 ; then they went to Dublin to spend the Christmas with a sister of Mr. John Martin.   Father Kenyon was much grieved at parting with them.   He seemed to have a presentiment that he would never see them again ; and he never did.   At Dublin, Mrs. Mitchel had visits from several old friends of the '48 time, amongst whom were Mr. O'Brien, Mr. John E. Pigot, and Mr. Dillon.   She would have enjoyed all this much, were it not that she was at the time in a state of the utmost anxiety owing to a report which had reached Ireland to the effect that her son James had been killed in the second battle of Bull Run. The report proved to be false, but James had in fact been very severely wounded in that battle.

After Christmas, Mrs. Mitchel went to Newry to visit her husband's sister, Mrs. Irvine, at Dromalane ; and from this time until she left for America, she and her daughter lived either with her husband's relatives or with his oldest and dearest friend, Mr. Martin. In the spring of 1863 came the news of Henrietta's death in the convent at Paris. Mrs. Mitchel was very ill when the news first reached, and it was not communicated to her for some time afterwards. The summer of 1863 was spent with Mr. Mitchel's sister, Mrs. Dickson, at Tullycairne, near Belfast. It was during this time that the youngest boy, Willy, was killed at Gettysburg, though his mother did not hear the news for some months afterwards. From Tullycairne she went to Paris to see the grave of her eldest daughter, and to bring home the youngest, Isabel. From Paris she returned to the old home at Dromalane, stopping a few days on the way to visit her husband's old and valued friend, Miss Mary Thompson at Ravensdale, near Dundalk. All through this terrible time, Mrs. Mitchel was in a state of constant suspense ; and, indeed, her trials and anxieties were such that she must certainly have broken down had it not been for the constant sympathy and unwearying kindness of her husband's relations and friends.

John Mitchel's letters to his wife during this period were among the papers lost when Mrs. Mitchel ran the blockade. A few letters to his daughters have been preserved, owing to their not having reached Ireland until after Mrs. Mitchel and her daughters had sailed. The following letter to his second daughter, Minnie, is dated October 22, 1863 :—

I hear you are most impatient to be over here with us. I do not wonder at it. Your present position is not what I wish, no matter how kind our friends may be to you all—and I am very grateful to them. Your mother and you, and my darling Isabelle, ought to be in a house of your own, and under the protection of your own people. When this winter is over, even if the war should be still going on, I intend to make an effort to bring you all over. James wishes to get a furlough to go for you, and it is possible that he may get it. Another Irish officer, a Captain Atkins, of the county Cork, got lately a four months' furlough to go home, and I wrote by him to your mother. The worst of it is James would have to go, and you would have to come, by way of Wilmington, in a blockade-running steamer, which is dreadfully expensive. But some happy change may take place before spring. This is by no means a comfortable or desirable place for a family ; but we must live as best we can, and as many respectable people are doing near Richmond. In the mean time, keep up your poor hearts as best you can.

And, again, about a fortnight later, to the same daughter :—

After my letter of the 22nd of October was written, the gentleman who was to bring it across the lines went off without it. I have found another now ; so I hope this will have the luck to reach you. Since I wrote that, there is no great news. I went up a few days ago to the army, and spent a couple of days with James at the head-quarters of General Gordon. James is very well. I arrived at the camp at night, and found my way to the camp-fires of Gordon's brigade. A private soldier, an Irishman, volunteered to guide me to the general's quarters. Then I found in front of a tent, before a large fire of logs, James and another officer. James was in high cavalry boots and spurs ; the horses at pasture in a large field, and two or three negro servants cooking supper. Next day I rode with him to the quarters of General Ewell, Jackson's successor, and we dined with him. He has a wooden leg, but rides admirably. We also called on General Early, the commander of James's division, and had a good time generally.

Yesterday, it appears, there was a sudden advance of a part of

Meade's army; and two of our brigades were overpowered and captured. It seems likely that there will be another great battle in that neighbourhood. God grant that our good James may pass through it in safety.

I will write again immediately, by several ways, after I know the result of the fight.

The course of events in the summer and fall of 1863 was not favourable to the Confederacy. Not long after the battle of Gettysburg came the fall of Vicksburg, the most damaging blow the Confederacy had yet received. General Grant, who had conquered at Vicksburg, was then appointed to the command of the army opposed to Bragg in Tennessee. On the 24th of November was fought the great battle of Chattanooga, in which Grant gained the most brilliant victory yet achieved by any northern general, and drove Bragg with great loss from a position by many regarded as impregnable. These disasters were very discouraging to the Confederates; and many leading men expressed strong dissatisfaction with the acts of President Davis. Pemberton, who surrendered Vicksburg to Grant, was one of Davis's favourites; and men said of Mr. Davis that he was most obstinate in pushing on his favourites, whatever opinion as to their capacity might be entertained by more competent judges. It was also said of Mr. Davis that he had upon several occasions declined to retaliate for outrages committed by the Federals. About this also there was much dissatisfaction.·

Up to this time—the fall of 1863—John Mitchel had continued to edit, and to do the principal writing for the Richmond *Enquirer*. This paper, as we have seen, was friendly to Davis and his government—indeed, it was regarded as a sort of semi-official organ. But during all the time that he wrote for the *Enquirer*, Mitchel had continued to be on friendly terms with Daniel, the owner of the *Examiner*. And during the summer and fall of 1863, Mitchel's views regarding the policy of President Davis underwent considerable modification. He began to feel that he was now more in accord with the *Examiner* than with the *Enquirer;* and he therefore had thoughts of transferring his services from the latter paper to the former. Daniel, he had reason to believe, would welcome his assistance on the *Examiner*.

Meantime, in Ireland, as the autumn of 1863 wore on, Mrs. Mitchel became more and more impatient. She had heard of the death of her youngest son; she knew that her other two sons were in the thick of the fighting, and that any day might bring her the news of their deaths also. At last the suspense became intolerable. Mrs. Mitchel determined that she would, at least, see her sons again before they were killed. She hoped also that she might be able to help them by bringing over a store of clothes and of certain articles of provisions. Exaggerated accounts had reached them in Ireland of the suffering and privations of the people in the blockaded states. The scarcity and high prices of tea and coffee had been specially dwelt on. Of these luxuries Mrs. Mitchel laid in quite a large store, and she also provided herself with materials for clothing, boots, shoes, etc. She caused her stores to be packed in cases and shipped at Falmouth by a blockade-runner called the *Vesta*. Taking her two girls with her, Mrs. Mitchel herself embarked in the *Vesta*, and started on her perilous journey. This was about the end of the year 1863. Of this proceeding John Mitchel knew nothing whatever.

The voyage was pleasant enough as far as Bermuda. There they stayed a few days, and then started on the dangerous part of the journey. I copy John Mitchel's own account of what followed :—

Coming near the coast of North Carolina, the little *Vesta* very soon found herself chased by some eight or ten Federal ships of war. For several hours she was under fire, and shot and shell tore through her rigging; but the *Vesta* was very fleet, was gaining ground on her pursuers, and having good prospect now of running into Cape Fear River, when it was found that the fuel was exhausted. A large part of the cargo consisted of bacon, shipped for the Confederate Commissary Department. This bacon was, without scruple, used as fuel, and was thrown into the fire. Steam was kept up, and the little *Vesta* actually ran past and through her pursuers; and when night fell was out of their reach, and on the direct course for Cape Fear River.

So far so good. But, unfortunately, at this very critical stage of the proceedings, the captain and the first mate took it into their heads to get drunk. Whether this was in the exuberance of victory or because they meditated treachery, does not very clearly appear. But be this as it may, they got drunk; and, being drunk, they deemed it necessary to run the vessel ashore. And having run the ship ashore, and landed the passengers with nothing but their clothes, they further deemed it necessary to set fire to the ship. If they had been hotly pursued at the time, one might understand the proceeding. But they being at the time clear of all pursuit, it is hard to explain the burning of the ship, unless we regard it as the reckless act of drunken men. All the stores which Mrs. Mitchel had purchased for her family were burnt up with the ship. And, what was worse than all, the box in which Mrs. Mitchel had packed her husband's private papers and correspondence, was also destroyed. On a bare sandy beach, and on a cold winter's night, Mrs. Mitchel sat with her two little girls and watched the destruction of all her property. On that beach they had to spend the night, without shelter and without fire. When morning dawned, they found that they were not even on the shore of North

Carolina, but on a sort of sandy island divided from the mainland by shallow water.   During the day they found means to cross to the mainland ; but even then they were some forty miles from Smithfield, the nearest town, and forty miles of pine swamp.   They succeeded in getting shelter in a sort of hut, and then some gentlemen, who had travelled on the *Vesta*, and had been very kind to Mrs. Mitchel, went to look for a waggon.   They succeeded, with some difficulty, in getting one, and the party started on their dismal journey through the swamps to Smithfield. When they arrived there, Mrs. Mitchel and the two girls were nearly half dead from hardship and fatigue ; but they were now all but arrived at the end of their long and perilous journey.   From Smithfield they travelled by steamer to Wilmington, and Mrs. Mitchel's first act on reaching there was to telegraph to her husband announcing her arrival.   This telegram was the first notification John Mitchel had of the journey his wife and daughters had made.   Up to this he supposed that they were all quietly living in Ireland.   From Wilmington, Mrs. Mitchel travelled by rail to Richmond, where she found her husband expecting her.   Her two surviving sons she did not see for some time afterwards.

Mitchel gives the following account of the condition of his wife and daughters on their arrival :—

No more destitute refugees ever came to Richmond, even in these days of *refugeeing*, than my wife and two little girls, after the burning of all the cargo of that ill-omened ship the *Vesta*.   After having hoped to supply the Confederacy (their own share of the Confederacy) for three or four years, they were cast upon its shore, and on the most desolate shore in the world, at midnight, and saw the vessel which contained their stores, and even their trunks of clothing, burnt to the water's edge.   Three gentlemen on board, two of them being Confederate officers and one an Englishman, were very kind and attentive to the unprotected ones, and stayed by them until at last, through much discomfort and by a swamp road, they brought them safe into Wilmington, from whence the telegraph brought me the first news of their arrival on this side of the Atlantic. They came on by railroad, and were hospitably received at first in a friend's house, until I should be able to make more permanent arrangements.

Before the arrival of his family, Mitchel had resigned his position as editor of the *Enquirer*, finding himself no longer able to give an unqualified support to the measures of President Davis. Mr. Daniel was very glad to secure Mitchel's services on the *Examiner*, and it was arranged between them that Mitchel should write the leading articles for that paper. He was gradually coming to think very much as Mr. Daniel thought regarding the policy of the administration.

During the spring months of 1864, things were quiet at the seat of war. The Confederates were standing strictly on the defensive, and the Federals were making their preparations for a grand attack. Grant was appointed commander-in-chief of the Union armies. At Richmond there was every show of confidence in the result ; and no doubt there was a good deal of real confidence. But people could not conceal from themselves the fact that their position had certainly not improved during the past year. The resources of the North were practically inexhaustible ; while to the resources of the South there was a limit, and the limit was already within measurable distance. The Confederates had hoped that their repeated victories would have the effect of tiring out the North. But of this there did not seem to be any sign. Moreover, with all his admiration for the social system of the South, Mitchel was perfectly well aware that it had one serious drawback which was sure to manifest itself in a dangerous way the moment there was any sign of a turn in the tide of fortune. On this subject Mitchel writes :—

I am quite sensible that there is one vice in this Confederacy ; one weak spot in its harness ; one taint in its heart—namely, that the poorer people—the mean whites—have not the same interest in the contest which wealthy planters have.   They cannot, indeed, bear the thought of being, what they call, whipped ; and have fought well these three years, still hoping that the northerns will tire of their many defeats and humiliations, and will turn upon the dominant faction which has plunged their country into war.   But now they begin to see that the North is growing stronger every day, while they are growing weaker.

*   *   *   *   *   *   *

But, as I said, the greatest weakness of our cause lies in that one consideration—that the great mass of the people do not find themselves so deeply interested in the success of the Confederacy as to make them endure for an indefinitely longer time, perhaps years to come, the hardship and the hunger, and the marching in bad shoes, or no shoes, and the picket-guard on frosty nights. They say to one another, indeed, that they must not be beaten, that it will never do to give the thing up ; but they do not always mean it now when they say it.

After the arrival of his family, Mitchel moved into a house on Fifth Street, at the corner of Carey Street ; a large old house which had belonged to a leading Virginia family. Both John and James contrived to get short furloughs, and came to see their mother and sisters.   It was of course a time of cruel anxiety to Mrs. Mitchel, however proud she might feel of the distinctions won by her sons.   She and her daughters did their part with the other ladies of Richmond in caring for the wounded.

There was a good deal of social gaiety in Richmond during these years.   Indeed, as often happens in war times, people seemed to think it incumbent on them to keep up an appearance of gaiety and lightness of heart.   Mrs. Davis entertained frequently, and Mr. and Mrs. Mitchel were often at her house.   There was another lady in Richmond whose house was frequented by the best society almost as much as Mrs. Davis's, and who was a warm friend of John Mitchel. This was Miss Mary Pegram. Miss Pegram, now Mrs. General Anderson, has been kind enough to write down for me some of her recollections of Mitchel during this time. There are passages in these recollections which give a more vivid picture of certain leading traits in Mitchel's character than has been supplied to me from any other quarter. After some reference to Mitchel's political career, and after testifying to his wonderfully wide acquaintance with literature, ancient and modern, Mrs. Anderson proceeds :—

"Of Mr. Mitchel as a man, I can speak without reserve. I had abundant opportunities of seeing him in all the relations of private life, and a kinder husband, a tenderer father, a warmer, truer friend I have never known. It was delightful to see how all the sterner features of his character seemed to be completely effaced in his intercourse with his family and friends. Towards women his manner—while free from the slightest tincture of gallantry or frivolity— was courteous and deferential to a degree seldom seen in modern society. Nothing seemed to be a trouble to him that he could do for them. His unselfishness—always his most marked characteristic—seemed to find its freest scope in his intercourse with women, and with the weak and suffering. How often have I known him to devote hours of his time—sorely needed as it was for the pressing details of his work—to the invalid soldier, to the wounded, to the bereaved. When his own heart was almost broken by the deaths in battle of his two sons, whom he had given to the Confederate cause, he never stopped to bewail his afflictions, but with the ambulance corps in the field, or in the hospitals at home, did all he could to soothe or relieve the suffering. . . . It always seemed to me an ironical destiny that had thrust Mr. Mitchel into politics, and I had the audacity to express this opinion to him. He seemed to me better fitted for anything else. His scholarly tastes, vigorous command of words, keen power of analysis, and racy style seemed to indicate clearly his aptitude for a literary career. . . . Of English writers, he could not give an unprejudiced opinion. He rarely spoke or wrote of them without some tinge of political feeling; and he always protested against classing his favourite Scotch or Irish writers under the generic term *British.* I remember asking him one day what was his interpretation of the word 'idle' in Tennyson's famous little song, 'Tears, idle Tears.' The question had been brought up the evening before at President Davis's in a little impromptu gathering at which I was present; and there had been differences of opinion among us as to the exact meaning and proper emphasis of the word. Mr. Mitchel said, in answer to my question, 'I can scarcely be expected to give an exegetical criticism on Tennyson in a morning call.' But, taking the book, he read aloud, 'Tears, idle tears, etc., tears from the depth of some divine despair.' Then, turning to me with an expression of comic perplexity on his face and in his full, musical tone, he said, 'Will you please tell *me* what he means by *divine despair?*' It is needless to say the exegesis did not go any further. Laughter and a vexed remonstrance on my part ended the discussion; although he confessed to an admiration for Tennyson's poem, 'Œnone.'

"Mr. Mitchel was utterly free from self-consciousness, and hence was always self-possessed, and at ease in any company. He never posed as a martyr, never made any appeals to sympathy, never spoke of his personal trials if he had any. Yet his countenance, when in repose, had the marks of deep mental suffering. . . . His sense of the ludicrous, and his insight into the weaknesses of human nature often caused him much amusement; but it was only to the few who knew him best that this was ever revealed. I was always struck with his extreme amiability, the genial tolerance of his judgments in social matters, the broad charity of his opinions regarding individuals. With his talent for satire, his power of caustic expression, and the many embittering experiences of his life, this reticence and self-repression were the outcome of a thoroughbred refinement of feeling. No one was more regardful than Mr. Mitchel of all the courtesies of life. Utterly unconventional in thought and manner, he yet instinctively and unconsciously acted up to all the nicer requirements of the social code. . . . He never forgot or slighted a friend ; and he never failed, so far as my observation went, to arouse in his friends the most devoted and admiring attachment. His goodness of heart was evinced in everything he said and did in all the intercourse of private life. He had on one occasion, during the war, to break the news of a much-loved brother's death to the sister of the young man. Mr. Mitchel often spoke of it afterwards as the most painful duty he had ever known ; and nothing could have been tenderer or more soothing than his manner to the afflicted sufferer. . . . Among the many foreigners filling the ranks of the Confederate army, and therefore made welcome in all social circles, there were some French and English men of high position in their own countries. With the former, Mr. Mitchel was always on the most cordial terms ; and I remember the mutual pleasure of himself and Prince Polignac (called General in our army) when, both calling on the same evening, I introduced them to each other. They became warm friends, and met after the war in Paris, where, Mr. Mitchel told me, they drank some very fine old Bourbon whiskey together, furnished by the prince—in compliment, of course, to the dynasty to which the Polignacs had been attached.

"A meeting of a very different nature occurred by chance one evening in my parlour. Several Englishmen—officers and journal correspondents—were paying me an informal visit, and a few ladies—mostly young—were also present, when Mr. John Mitchel was announced,—a *rencontre* that I had been constantly dreading, and which, until then, had not happened. I felt quite flustered for a moment, but was soon relieved by the perfect conduct of Mr. Mitchel under the embarrassing ordeal. Bowing formally to the gentlemen, and exchanging friendly greetings with the ladies—all of whom he knew—he seated himself near a group of them, and entered into bright talk, apparently utterly unconscious of anything at all unpleasant. The Englishmen, on the contrary, were very ill at ease, and it required all of the tact and light talk I could command to keep them occupied with me, while my friends on the opposite side of the room seemed to be having the liveliest and most delightful chat. I heard one of the young ladies —the bright and beautiful Hetty Cary—telling Mr. Mitchel of a Confederate officer who was married a few days before in his old, shabby uniform (all that he had, poor fellow!); and Miss Cary pretended to be very indignant at such a solecism. Mr. Mitchel entered warmly into her view of the offence, and asked, ' Would a marriage be considered valid under such circumstances ? '

"When Mr. Mitchel's visit was over, all of the ladies present uttered a chorus of praise of his charming qualities, and were soon engaged in a fierce discussion with the English officers, who said nothing uncomplimentary of Mr. Mitchel personally, but, of course, denounced his efforts in Ireland. But his fair champions defended him with energy, if not eloquence, and silenced, if they did not convince, the adversary.

"Mrs. Jefferson Davis—herself one of the most brilliant

of talkers—delighted in Mr. Mitchel's conversation, and always welcomed him as a guest."

Mrs. Anderson then makes some reference to the circumstances attending Mitchel's death, and concludes :—

" It seemed to me a telling and beautiful finale to a noble—even if a mistaken—career. Better for him, perhaps, than renewed strife and struggle, which must have been inevitable had he taken his seat in Parliament. Speaking with Mr. A. M. Sullivan, and afterwards with Mr. Justin McCarthy in London on the paragraph the latter had written (in his ' History ') about the Irish rebellion and Mr. Mitchel's part in it, I ventured to protest against the opinion expressed therein that Mr. Mitchel's life ' after '48 ' had been ' an anti-climax.' His work in America, his ever-increasing fame, his election to Parliament, after exile and contumely—all contradicted that assertion. And while, from an English point of view, he will, of course, always be regarded as a rebel and perhaps a felon, no unprejudiced mind can fail to admire the courage, fortitude, and brilliant talents of the man and hero, John Mitchel."

The statement by Mr. Justin McCarthy here referred to occurs in the same chapter of the " History of Our Own Times " as the remarks about the method of Mitchel's escape, which have been quoted in a former chapter of this book. Mrs. Anderson's answer is perfectly just. To no one who has a true perception of what was great in Mitchel's character can his American career appear in the light of an anti-climax. His greatest quality, perhaps, was his absolute and unswerving sacrifice of self and self-interest to principle. And at no time in his career—not even when he stood in the dock at Green Street—was this quality more strikingly manifested than when he upheld the cause of slavery against Beecher, or denounced the methods of Fenianism in the *Irish Citizen.*

The statement in Mrs. Anderson's reminiscence to the effect that Mitchel could not give an unprejudiced opinion of English writers is too sweeping. Witness several notices of Ruskin's writings which appeared in the *Citizen* and the *Southern Citizen*. Still, I will admit that he often did allow political feeling to influence his judgment of English writers.

Another Richmond lady with whom Mitchel was intimate during the war time was Mrs. Burton Harrison, at that time Miss Constance Cary. From this lady also I have received an interesting "reminiscence." I extract the following passages :—

" He was always ready to respond to the suggestions of humour struggling against adverse circumstances, and to present droll methods of bridging difficulties. More vivid in memory, however, are our talks with him about literature, his knowledge of which, past and current, seemed to my youthful and ambitious spirit something quite fabulous. The three literary magnates in Richmond in those days were Mr. John R. Thompson, the gentle and genial poet, who was also State librarian ; Mr. John M. Daniel, editor-in-chief of the *Examiner ;* and Mr. Mitchel, his associate. The *Examiner* was a clever, acrid sheet, keeping up to the last an invincible determination to sustain the flag of Walker's Dictionary against that of the northern authority, Webster. Its bitter, brilliant philippics against the weakness of authorities on both sides of the war-line (printed latterly on paper of a bilious hue), made a brave show of the final *k* in such words as eccentrick and dyspeptick, and of the neglected *u* in favour, flavour, etc. Mr. Daniel was a very unpopular man, a sort of a social sphinx, and Mr. Mitchel was regarded as the humanizing element of the partnership, the one hope of sufferers who essayed through him to subdue the roar of that autocratic lion. I distinctly recall the feeling of surprise I experienced upon first identifying the mild-mannered, courteous gentleman, with blue eyes and clear-cut features, who was pointed out to me as 'the famous John Mitchel.' . . . My principal remembrance of his talk was that it related largely to his children, to whom he was tenderly devoted; but when I asked him questions about books and authors, or challenged his individual tastes, he would bring into the conversation such a felicity of expression, quickness of repartee, and purity in the use of English undefiled, joined to an amount of solid information as to quite astonish me. When at last, in fear and trembling, I carried him a copy of verses (written under the stress of feeling after the battle of Seven Pines), fully prepared to be demolished by some courtly satire garbed in criticism, what was my relief to have them not only received by a kindly hand, but elevated to the immediate glory of print, next day, in the fastidious columns of the *Examiner.*"

There was some scarcity and privation in Richmond, though not so much as commonly supposed at the time. Prices were high. It took a surprisingly large quantity of the rose-coloured paper money of the Confederacy to buy a good dinner. "You can always buy one egg for one dollar," says Mitchel, in his "Journal." I don't know whether this is intended to be accepted as an accurate statement of the then price of eggs at Richmond; but I suppose we are safe in concluding that, like most other articles of food, they were pretty dear.

In the late spring General Grant opened the campaign of 1864. He crossed the Rapidan, and on the 5th and 6th of May the terrible battle of the Wilderness was fought. It was a most bloody struggle; and especially on the Federal side the loss of life was horrible. Yet Grant held his ground. During and after this battle, Mitchel was on

active duty with the Ambulance Corps. They had their
head-quarters at a place called Ginney's Station, on the
Richmond and Fredericksburg Railroad, and for some time
after the battle of the Wilderness, their energies were taxed
to the uttermost. When not on duty with the Ambulance
Corps, most of his time was spent at the *Examiner*
office or in Mr. Daniel's library, where many of Mitchel's
articles were written. I have already quoted one passage
in which he speaks of Daniel. I may supplement that
with the following :—

Daniel is very peculiar and somewhat eccentric in all his habits
and ways of thinking ; and he and I *generally* think much alike,
but even where we do not altogether coincide, he does not attempt
to interfere with me. Indeed, he knows very well that if he did
so, I would suddenly cease to write for the *Examiner*. He is a
bachelor and a woman-hater—for good reasons that he has ; is
very familiar with life amongst the higher classes of Turin and
Genoa, and intimately knew Cavour, who never once (as Daniel
declares) told the truth where a lie would serve him as well, which
I believe, for he was a disciple of Palmerston.

And of the articles which he wrote for the *Examiner*,
he says :—

Such articles ! *Mon Dieu !* I point out diligently and conscientiously what is the condition of a nation which suffers itself
to be conquered ; draw pictures of disarmings, and disfranchise-
ments, and civil disabilities, such as we have experienced in Ireland,
and endeavour to keep our good Confederate people up to the
fighting point. Then I have most freely criticised Mr. Davis for
his failure to practice retaliation sternly ; and described the strategy
of Grant, consisting in the simple arithmetical problem before
mentioned, which will beat us, however, at last, simple as it is, if
the North will only stand to it.

On the 24th of May, some three weeks after the battle
of the Wilderness, I find a letter from Mitchel to his son
John. John, being at Charleston, saw his father very

seldom ; while James, the second son, being with Lee near to Richmond, was able to visit his family every now and then.   It was, I assume, owing to this that letters to John are much more numerous than letters to James.   And indeed, the letters to John are mainly taken up with accounts of how James was getting on.   The letter just referred to is as follows :—

. . . James is all safe up to this day ; has been all through the very thickest of the fighting along with Gordon, who never spares himself or anybody else.   And, as usual, James gets high credit, but no promotion ; for although Gordon is to be promoted to be major-general, it seems the whole staff of Johnson's division (now broken up) is assigned to Gordon's division, so Gordon has a Major Hunter for his adjutant-general, and James remains with the old brigade, now commanded by Evans.   All these arrangements, however, are but temporary, during the campaign.   Johnson will be exchanged and will get a division, and will get back his old staff, and then Gordon will be able to get James appointed to be his adjutant-general and a major.   I think General Gordon wishes to do this so soon as he can.

In the mean time the fighting goes on.   Our committee is now at Hanover Junction, from whence I came down yesterday on a two days' leave.   James also came down with me, to return again in the evening in time for the battle expected to come off to-day. Grant is resolutely pressing forward towards Richmond.   He is fully resolved this time to make the spoon or spoil the horn.   I think he is going to be beaten horribly ; and your old commander, Beauregard, is penning up the other enemy in a bend of the James river.   It is a very critical moment for Richmond and for the Confederacy.

The prediction in this letter as to Grant's being about to be "beaten horribly" was not fulfilled.   It is no doubt true that in the series of battles fought during the summer campaign of 1864, the loss of life on the Federal side was something horrible ; yet, from the time Grant assumed the command until the close of the war, there was no repetition of Fredericksburg or Chancellorsville. These mere partial checks and attacks were repelled with fearful loss of life; but all the while Grant was slowly gaining ground. And, whatever ground he gained, he held on to with bulldog tenacity. No doubt, having regard to the great superiority of the Federals in numbers and in war material, it is absurd to claim for Grant, as some of his admirers have claimed, that his campaigns against Lee in 1864 and 1865 entitle him to rank as a military genius with Hannibal and Napoleon. But, on the other hand, we must always remember that these campaigns were, so far as Lee was concerned, strictly defensive ones. General Lee was not the man to make a mistake or to leave an opening. We may be quite sure that his vigilance was unceasing, and that his positions were as well chosen and as strong as consummate generalship could make them. Under these circumstances, to attack successfully, even with a much superior force, was by no means an easy task. General Grant's view seems to have been that the best way of ending the war decisively was to hammer away at any cost, so as to make the resources of the North tell, and to wear out the South. His admirers can at least claim this credit for him, that when at last the end came, it was indeed the end. The exhaustion of the South was so absolute as to preclude all idea of her renewing the struggle.

During all this summer of 1864, Grant doggedly held on to his policy of "hammering." Again and again he tried to turn Lee's right flank, and again and again, when foiled in this attempt, he made furious attacks upon the Confederate positions. In this process the two armies described what Mitchel calls "a bloody arc of a circle." They swung round north-east and east of Richmond until Grant's left reached a point on the James river to the

south of the Confederate capital.   James Mitchel was in all
of this fighting, until Early, in whose division he was, was
detached and sent to the valley to oppose Hunter, and
afterwards Sheridan.   During most of this summer, John
Mitchel was on duty outside of the city with the
Ambulance Committee.   In his " Journal " he gives us a
vivid picture of one evening they spent in the woods close
to Lee's position, during which evening Grant made one of
his most desperate attacks.   It was a lovely summer
evening.   General Lee rode along the front of the lines on
his grey charger, "looking content and placid, as the
impenetrable, solid countenance of the man always did."
He stopped a few minutes at the place where Mitchel and
his friends were encamped, and chatted with the gentlemen
of the Ambulance Committee.   The general passed on ;
evening fell, and the members of the Ambulance Corps
were lying on the grass smoking and chatting with some of
the officers ; when suddenly

burst forth a perfect storm of musketry.   The sound, from its first
opening, was one continued, sustained crash.   Our visitors instantly
jumped on their horses and galloped to the front, wherever their
several commands were posted.   For fully half an hour the
musketry was sustained on either side ; and in that time several
distinct and very determined assaults were made on our position.
At last the fire slackened ; and we could hear ringing through the
woods that unmistakable Confederate yell, which told us the
enemy were repulsed, and that our men were following up their
advantage.   Grant lost that night, in killed and wounded, fourteen
thousand men ; we lost three thousand ; and Grant held himself
to be the gainer.   Gordon's brigade made a flank attack on this
occasion, and James Mitchel had his horse shot.   We lost many
valuable officers ; and my friend, Ned McCarthy, captain of the
Richmond Howitzers, was shot at his guns.

Of the work of the Ambulance Committee during this
summer, I find a further description in a hasty note to

Mrs. Mitchel, written in pencil on a slip of rough paper. The only heading is " Orange Court House, Sunday," but I find, by an indorsement, that the note was received some time during the summer of 1864 :—

> MY DEAR JENNY,
>
> I telegraphed to you yesterday. So far as I have yet learned, James is all right. His brigade was engaged in the thick of the battle, and suffered a good deal. I have heard from men who saw James in the fight and *after it*, unwounded. That was Friday evening. There was more fighting yesterday, in which Ewell's corps was again engaged ; the result favourable to us. I will probably hear further news of James to-day. If so, I will telegraph to you. That brigade is at least twenty-five miles from this. We are here in the midst of a scene of horror and anguish and filth, receiving the wounded and putting them on board the trains. Half of us up and working all night, all of us busily engaged all day. I cannot yet guess when we may get away and go home. We sleep on the ground, under tents. One of our committee is going down to-day, and I avail myself of his offer to bring a letter.

In the month of June, Mitchel heard some good news of his son John—the last good news he was destined to hear of that son. General Beauregard had put John in command of Fort Sumter, the most important of the Charleston defences. It was a marked honour, as John's rank in the army hardly warranted so important a command.

Shortly after this good news reached, there is a long letter to William Mitchel. The writer was evidently in good spirits, and proud of his son. I extract some passages :—

> I owe all of you much more than letters for the very great kindness you all, at Tullycairne, at Dromalane, and at London, showed to my poor *refugees*. You have heard of their melancholy landing upon Confederate ground, but though the country is poor now it is not inhospitable, and we are able, thanks in part to you, to exist from day to day, hoping for better times. We do not go

to sleep for want of excitement. Life is at high pressure here; for the last two weeks an enormous army of the most enraged and desperate enemies has been tearing all round, making furious rushes occasionally to get in upon us, and the roar of their big guns makes our windows jar. Yet nothing can be quieter or more regular than the aspect of the town—the markets supplied as usual, every railroad leading to Richmond (except one, that to York river) carrying its trains outward and inward with punctuality. James has paid us two visits since the approach of the army to Richmond. Last time he came was about a week ago. He and a brother officer hurried to town, dined with us, and rode off to camp again in the evening; but early the next morning the whole division was hurried off on a march of two hundred miles, to Lynchburg. James has been very fortunate in these late battles, always in the thick of them, and always with a general (Gordon) who does not spare himself or anybody else, yet he has not been touched; had two horses shot indeed, one of them killed on the spot. These last two or three days there has been furious fighting about Petersburg. Grant's whole army trying to take that place (twenty miles off), since they cannot get into Richmond. Beauregard and Lee are both there, however, though with an army very much inferior in numbers to Grant's. It will astonish people one day to learn what were the real numbers of our Confederate armies. John is in command of Fort Sumter, with seven companies of artillery; it is a command higher than his grade in the service, and I suppose that he must soon be promoted. The boys, however, have shown no eagerness for promotion, and I am glad of it. If promotion comes to them, it will have been well-earned, as I know that both of them have done their duty faithfully, and are as competent officers as any in the service. All this is a very great satisfaction to me, and therefore I cannot help telling you of it. The two boys are extremely different in character, but both very good; and poor Willy, who fell at Gettysburg, was best of all. I have a little book of entomological memoranda and drawings, that he kept in his knapsack, and one of his comrades sent it to me afterwards.

I believe you never were in Richmond, and have no idea of the city. It is very handsome, and the streets are so shaded by rows of large trees as to be perfect bowers at this season.

Then follows a detailed description of the city of Richmond.   After which he proceeds :—

There is, of course, a great deal of sadness, for every family almost has lost its flower, and bands playing some dead march pass often through these bowery streets, escorting some officer to the cemetery.   But no sadness shows itself; above all, no cowardice. No doubt there are people whose hearts quake within them as they hear the roll of artillery, but public opinion requires an outward cheerfulness and courage.   This people has arrived at such a point of passionate daring and defiance that cowards must pretend to be brave, and traitors in their hearts (for such there are) must act like patriots.   I confess that I delight in the spectacle of a people roused in this way to a full display of all its manhood, feeling itself indeed isolated from all other people, and without a friend in the world, but planting itself firmly on its own ground, stripped for battle, and defying fate.   I write in the Richmond newspapers; I wish I could send you some.   I have written also what I think you would read with pleasure, a kind of rigmarole account of our trip through Dauphiné, etc., in a weekly periodical. It is not finished yet ; I have only got to St. Nazaire near the Isère.   The publication is now suspended because all the printers of that concern are out in the trenches.   Some day or other you and John Martin will be amused to see how much I have remembered and how much invented.

Under date of July the 2nd, I find a letter to John giving an account of some inquiries Mitchel had made at the war office regarding John's expected promotion ; also giving an account of James's progress, and requesting John to write a little oftener.   This letter can only have reached Captain Mitchel a few days before his death.   I copy from Mitchel's " Journal " his account of how the news reached him of his son's death.   The entry is dated July 20, 1864 :—

In the evening of this day, as Daniel and myself—our work being done—sat together talking in the *Examiner* office, a clerk came in and handed me a telegram.   It came from Major-General Sam. Jones, who had succeeded Beauregard in command of the

Department of South Carolina. When I saw whence it came, a kind of mist floated before my eyes; and for a moment or two I could not read. Here it is :—

Charleston, July 20.

Mr. John Mitchel,

It is my painful duty to announce to you that your gallant and accomplished son fell mortally wounded by the fragment of a shell, about one p.m. to-day, whilst in the faithful performance of his duty as commanding officer of Fort Sumter. The shot that has removed him has deprived the country of one of its most valuable defenders.

Sam. Jones, Major-General.

Daniel saw me read this. He stretched out his hand without a word, and I gave him the despatch. He glanced at it, took up his hat, and went home. I went home too; but not without walking two miles round. When I came into our parlour, my wife and two daughters were sitting there.

Besides the original of the telegram above given, there have come to my hands several letters from officers in Fort Sumter giving the details of young John Mitchel's death. The wound did not prove immediately fatal. He lingered for some hours, and was even able to speak a little. I need not here dwell upon the sad details. From amongst the letters that have come to my hands, I select one—from General Beauregard himself—as showing the esteem in which young Mitchel was held by his superior officers. It is written from Petersburg, Va., and is dated August 6, 1864 :—

Dear Sir,

I trust the condition of affairs here will be my excuse for not having addressed you sooner, relative to the irreparable loss you sustained lately in the death of your gallant son, Captain John Mitchel. He served under my orders during the most trying periods of the siege of Charleston, at Fort Sumter, Battery Simpkins, and on Morris Island. He displayed such coolness, energy, and intelligence, that I selected him from many aspirants, ambitious of the honour, to replace Colonel Elliot in the command of Fort Sumter, whenever circumstances compelled that gallant officer to absent himself from that important post.

In your bereavement you should derive consolation from the thought that your son fell at his post gloriously battling for the independence of his country, carrying with him the regret of his friends, and the respect of his enemies.

I remain, with respect, your most obedient servant,

G. T. BEAUREGARD.

It would seem, from the details given in letters from his companions in the fort, that the immediate cause of young Mitchel's death was the entirely fearless manner in which he exposed himself to danger. In the midst of the bombardment, he was standing upon the rampart of the fort examining the damage done by the bursting of a shell, when another shell exploded near him, and he was struck down.

Some fourteen years after his death, the comrades of Captain Mitchel had a handsome monument erected over his grave. It stands in Magnolia Cemetery, near Charleston, where his remains were laid.

There was now only one son left in the Mitchel family. James Mitchel, as we have seen, had fought all through the war in the main army ; had been wounded, and had horses shot under him. Whether it was that the government of the Confederacy thought that the parents of James Mitchel had already suffered enough, and lost enough in the southern cause, or whatever else may have been the reason, I do not know ; but within two months after the death of Captain John Mitchel, an order was issued from the war department removing James Mitchel to a post in Richmond. John Mitchel himself went from Richmond to the army to carry this order to his son. A very striking passage in the " Journal " is that in which Mitchel describes his journey through the Shenandoah Valley, which had then been recently devastated by Sheridan's famous raid. On receipt of this order, James Mitchel came to Richmond, and from that time until the close of the war, he remained on duty at the Confederate capital on the staff of General Kemper, afterwards governor of the State of Virginia.

The fall of 1864 and the following winter passed away. Both armies were close to Richmond, and every now and then there was fighting. Still, life in Richmond continued to be much the same as before :—

Our Confederates are still full of confidence, still investing their money in Confederate securities, still relying upon Lee and his army. Our life here in Richmond varies but little from day to day ; though to many individual families there bursts in from time to time some desolating news, a husband, or son, or brother slain on the lines at Petersburg, or in the fair valley of the Shenandoah. Congress is in session at the capitol ; and my old friend, Swan, of Tennessee, is a member, and lives in our house. Attendance on the debates of either house is an occasional resource for the idle.

The Mr. Swan here mentioned was Mr. Mitchel's former partner in the publication of the *Southern Citizen.*

In the spring of 1865, the end came. General Lee's army was at Petersburg, south-east of Richmond. His position was a strong one, and he still showed a bold front to the enemy. But at other points, the tide was setting strongly against the Confederacy. Sheridan had completed his devastation of the Shenandoah Valley. Sherman had made his famous "march to the sea." One of the imme-diate consequences of this exploit was the evacuation of Charleston ; and Fort Sumter, where Mitchel's son had fallen, was now in the hands of the Federals. Yet still, by force of old habit, many of the Richmond people relied upon Lee and his army.

During the months of February and March, 1865, there

was frequent skirmishing along the lines at Petersburg. At last, seeing that Sherman had been so successful in "breaking the shell of the Confederacy," Grant concluded that the time had come to end the matter.   On the 1st of April the final struggle began.   For two days General Lee was able to hold his ground ; but on the third day Sheridan succeeded in dislodging the force opposed to him, and Lee's position became no longer tenable.   It was Sunday, the 3rd of April, and President Davis was at church when the telegram containing the fatal news was handed to him. General Lee requested that Richmond should be at once evacuated, and that the seat of government should be removed to Danville, on the southern frontier of Virginia. After a hasty consultation, it was decided to do as General Lee advised.   Mitchel determined to go to Danville with the government.   He wished to "keep within the Confederate lines so long as they had any lines at all."   The corps to which James Mitchel was now attached had orders to retreat in the same direction.   As they left Richmond, the flames were already bursting from some of the government stores.   They had to walk fourteen miles to strike the Danville railroad, as the cars no longer ran any nearer to Richmond :—

We walked rapidly the remainder of the night, sometimes crossing a road crowded with trains of commissaries' and quartermasters' waggons; and before sunrise we had sat down to rest and eat a crust and morsel of bacon, when suddenly, in the direction of the city, there burst forth a most tremendous thunder of artillery. Can the Yankee villains be bombarding the defenceless city ! we exclaimed. Again and again the heavy volleys rolled along. It was the explosion of our own ironclad ships in the river, with all their loaded shells. By this time there was a dull red glare upon the eastern sky, which was not the dawn of the spring morning. We knew then that the city was burning.

The burning of Richmond was an accident, not a

deliberate proceeding on the part of the Confederate authorities. There were considerable military stores in Richmond. These stores were set fire to with the object of preventing their falling into the hands of the victors. The fire spread, and the greater part of the business portion of Richmond was burnt. The house in which Mitchel's family were staying had a very narrow escape. The house opposite to it was on fire several times. At last, on the evening of the 4th of April, the city was occupied by the Federal troops. They at once took measures to extinguish the fires and to restore order. For the time being all danger was over.

Mitchel stayed at Danville something more than a week. There he and those with him heard the news of Lee's surrender and of Lincoln's assassination. Of the latter event, Mitchel very truly remarks that it was a most unfortunate occurrence for the Confederacy. Not that he had any great admiration for Lincoln. But he reprobated as strongly as any one could the crime of Lincoln's murder, and he foresaw that an attempt would be made by the exteme party in the North to fix the responsibility for this crime upon the southern leaders.

There is no need for me to here rehearse the story of events which form a part of American history, save in so far as these events may properly enter into the life of Mitchel. With the surrender of Lee, the war was practically over. About the middle of April, Mitchel left Danville, and went to stay with a friend in Halifax County, Mr. Cowardin, proprietor of the Richmond *Dispatch*. The office of the *Dispatch* and everything in it had been burnt up in the Richmond fire; and Mr. Cowardin was now on a farm in the country, waiting for better times. There were three or four ex-Confederate officers also living with Mr. Cowardin; and during Mitchel's short stay there, they were several times reminded by visits from Union troops of the fact that they were living in a conquered country.

Early in May, Mitchel returned to Richmond. James Mitchel, and a few other officers, were with him. They were shocked at the spectacle which met their gaze when they came in sight of Richmond. I extract part of Mitchel's description of how the city looked :—

Richmond presented, from the river, a gaunt and ghastly sight. The shattered ribs of two of our ironclad steamers, sunk near the shore, were partly visible, rising above the brown eddying current of the James. Arrived on the bank, we saw every building burnt, and most of them fallen, so as to block up streets. We set forth to pursue the line of one street, which seemed the most direct way up the hill ; became confused amongst the ruins, and had to stop and take an observation of distant buildings still standing to make sure of the street we were walking upon. It was Pearl Street, formerly one of the busiest and best built streets in the town, consisting of fine wholesale warehouses. They had all been built upon massive granite piers, and with granite lintels over doors and windows ; but granite is a stone that cracks and splinters in very intense heat ; piers and lintels break up, and then down comes the house. We passed the line of Cary Street, all in hideous ruin, upward and downward.

But the house in which Mitchel had lived was intact, save for the destruction of every pane of glass in the house, and a few scars made by shells which had been exploded in the burning of a neighbouring ammunition factory. His family had escaped unhurt, and were as well as when he had left them.

"So," says Mitchel, in the "Journal," "this act in the drama of my life is over ; and we sit down to dinner, with what appetites we may, all together, and review the position."

The position was not a very cheerful one. Two of his sons had been sacrificed in the war ; and the number of his children was now just half what it had been less than three years before, when he sailed from France to join the Confederacy. His means of supporting the famly that remained to him were, for the present, *nil.* Certain friends in New York, whose names they never discovered, had sent them several hundred dollars in Federal money; "knowing," says Mitchel, "that our Confederate rose-tinted money had withered, for indeed the green is far above the red now." Something had to be done, and that quickly. Moreover, the sights and scenes of Richmond were not such as to tempt one to stay there long. To a mind so keenly sensitive as his, sights such as that described in the following passage must have been extremely painful :—

It is sad to see our disbanded Confederate officers—their cause lost, their State down in the dust, their four years' of the best of life thrown away—wandering listlessly in these desolate streets ; the very clothes they wear, being gray and of military cut, are forbidden by general orders ; and as they have worn none other for four years, and have no money to buy new dress, they are liable to arrest on going out of doors. To do justice to "our friend the enemy," there was but little harshness exercised against these forlorn fellows. Some of them quietly accepted positions in mercantile houses ; many others went to friends in the country, and betook themselves to the hoeing of corn and tobacco ; but many others could not get any positions, and had no friends in the country.

Finding that there was nothing for him to do in Richmond, and not caring to stay there idle, Mitchel, towards the end of May, started for New York. For the present, he left his family in Richmond in the house they had lived in during all this exciting time.

CHAPTER VI.

NEW YORK—FORTRESS MONROE—PARIS.

1865, 1866.

How Mitchel fared in New York, when he came there from Richmond, what subjects mainly occupied his thoughts at this time, and what work he went to, can best be told by giving extracts from a letter written by him to his sister Margaret a few days after his arrival at New York. The letter is dated June 3, 1865 :—

The war being over, and the Confederacy, which has cost me dear, being at an end, I have emerged from the prison of the blockade and from the ruins of Richmond, and am once more in New York, where I have just accepted the editorship of the *Daily News*, a staunch southern newspaper, which has opposed the war from the beginning. Jenny and the girls, together with James, are at Richmond still, where, luckily, our house was not burnt down, though it was somewhat torn by shells. They are pretty comfortably situated, though, and may remain where they are for some weeks, until I can make arrangements here. We are all accepting the new position of affairs, and making ourselves at home in it as well as we can.

And now, dear Margaret, I am almost afraid to ask after my friends, and especially my dear mother. It is so long since I heard anything, and at last accounts she was in very poor health. I hope you are well, and that no dreadful gaps have been made in any of your households. Pray write to me at once.

We have had a terrible time of it; not from any personal privations of comfort, which the Confederates did not undergo to any such extent as the outside world supposes, but from the agitation and excitement, and latterly the misery of seeing our cause go down irretrievably, and the best people of the South reduced under the sway of Yankees. The whole southern country is ruined and almost beggared. There is a bitter and mean and cowardly spirit of revenge possessing these northern people. Mr. Davis is a prisoner awaiting trial for treason. They will not be satisfied without having Lee in the same predicament, and God knows how many others. I fear, if they once erect a gallows, it will have many victims. As for myself, I am not sure that I am safe, and when I came on here, several of the more violent newspapers called for my arrest, etc. If I had had the means of living and supporting my family in a foreign country, I would have certainly returned to France. As it is, I must stand my ground and take the risks. I don't know yet what poor James will do with himself. He is deeply distressed and humiliated at the cause in which he has himself suffered so much and lost his two brothers having failed after all, and he talks of trying to quit the country. However, I rather think be will find New York his best place. It is the freest, and, at present, the most southern city on the continent. . . .

Now, will you write to me at once? Tell me where all the family are, and all about my mother and sisters, and what is William about, and how is he? And how fares it with Matilda's family and with your own? I will be eagerly waiting an answer.

The fears expressed in this letter as to his mother were but too well founded. Mrs. Mitchel had died shortly before the close of the war, while her son was still shut up in Richmond. The news reached John Mitchel subsequently, during his imprisonment in Fortress Monroe. I have already, at the commencement of this life, said something of Mrs. Mitchel's character. Few mothers have the good fortune to be loved and looked up to by all their children to the extent that Mrs. Mitchel was. By those of her children who were still living with her, her death was most severely felt. But even to those who, like John Mitchel, had families of their own and were living away from her, the news of her death was a great affliction. Indeed, love for his mother was in John Mitchel's case so strong as to form a leading feature in his character. During all the time she lived in New York, one of his greatest pleasures was to come once or twice a year from Tennessee, or wherever he chanced to be living, and spend a few days at her house. His private letters show with what eagerness he looked forward to these visits. Mrs. Mitchel, like her son, had a character and a will of her own. They sometimes differed in their views of things, and on either side the view was sure to be pretty strongly expressed. But they never quarrelled ; and whenever John Mitchel was in his mother's presence, his manner was always peculiarly affectionate and respectful.

Mitchel was now once more a newspaper editor. His writing for the *Daily News* very soon led to his arrest and imprisonment in Fortress Monroe. It would therefore be very desirable to tell the reader as precisely as possible what it was that he did write. I have not before me the copies of the *Daily News* during the brief period of his editorship. I can, therefore, only give the reader his own summary of the doctrine he began to teach in the *Daily News*. Here it is :—

Of course I set myself at once to tell the truth concerning the southern cause, to explode and expose the villainy of affecting to consider Jefferson Davis as a criminal and our Confederacy as a penitentiary offence ; and generally to denounce Mr. Johnson's " My Policy." I did endeavour, in very good faith, and without language needlessly provocative, to show that, as the South acknowledged and accepted her defeat in a great war, as she was absolutely powerless to renew it, and indeed no way inclined to renew it, the time was come for the victorious party to heal the breach.

    *   *   *   *   *   *   *

I continued to write the chief leading articles for this *Daily News* for just two weeks—the proprietor, Mr. B. Wood, liberally and *boldly* allowing me to write and print just what I liked ; and the other New York papers, especially the *Daily Times* and the *Evening Post,* continually raging and roaring against me—citing, as written by *me,* all the most violent and abusive articles they could find in Richmond newspapers during the war, but generally citing what I had never written, and earnestly calling upon their govern- ment to stop the intolerable nuisance.

General Dix was at that time military commandant of the district in which New York was situated. Some two or three days after Mitchel assumed charge of the *Daily News,* a message came to him from General Dix, in an indirect way ; that is to say, the message was conveyed by an officer on the staff of the general to a person known to be an intimate friend of Mitchel's. It was to this effect : General Dix did not wish to interfere with him ; had rather not ; but Mitchel had better take care. To this com- munication Mitchel replied, more straightforwardly than prudently, that Dix might go to the devil, or words to that effect, and went on writing as before. Again, on the 12th of June, another warning reached him. A gentleman called at the office of the *Daily News* and told Mitchel that a military order for his arrest had actually been made out. This fact, the gentleman said, he had on the very highest authority. Mitchel thanked his visitor, but was still incredulous ; for, as he said, he could not believe that military commanders, in time of peace, could feel themselves authorized to arrest a civilian attending to his lawful business and against whom there was no charge of any kind.

It turned out, however, that this friendly visitor was well informed. There was then, and had been for several days previously, an order for John Mitchel's arrest, made out and signed by General Grant ; and in pursuance of this order of the commander-in-chief, there was another order by General Dix directing the arrest, and designating the place of imprisonment as Fortress Monroe. Mitchel went on writing, as was his habit, with more vehemence the more he was threatened. Just two days after the second warning the order was executed. I take his own account of the arrest :—

At last, on the morning of the 14th of June, I went down as usual from my boarding-house, in West Twelfth Street, to the *Daily News* office. Everything was going on smoothly, and I was just about to write to my own folks to come on to New York, where I was myself established. I was seated in the editor's room at the desk, and busy over a manuscript, when the door opened and an artillery officer appeared, backed by a number of others, two in uniform and three in plain clothes. I rose. "You are my prisoner," said the officer. "By whose order?" "No matter; come along." Three or four men gathered round me, and I was hustled out, through the long outer office. A carriage stood, not *at* the door, but three doors off. I was conducted to this carriage ; the officer and another man (a detective, I believe) entered along with me ; a sergeant took his seat on the box with the driver. Blinds were drawn down, and we started at a very rapid pace.

From the office Mitchel was conveyed direct to the wharf, where a steamer lay with steam up. Two guards, with fixed bayonets, stood at the gangway. The officer who had arrested Mitchel escorted him on board, and in half a minute more the vessel was moving away from the wharf. As they steamed down the bay, the officers sat in the cabin with Mitchel. He tried to find out from them where they were going. This question they declined to answer. Then he asked what was the charge against him. As to that, they assured him they were entirely ignorant. The voyage was delayed by stress of weather ; and it was not until the morning of the 17th that they reached their

destination.   Then Mitchel learned that he was to have
the honour of being imprisoned in the same fortress with
President Davis.   The steamer cast anchor in the Chesa-
peake, off Fortress Monroe.   During the voyage, Mitchel
made some reflections on the peculiarities of his position,
which reflections he afterwards wrote down in his " Journal."
For example, the following :—

I suppose that I am the only person who has ever been a
prisoner-of-state to the British and the American Government one
after the other.   It is true, the English Government took care to
have a special Act of Parliament passed for my incarceration ; but
our Yankees disdain in these days to make any pretence of law at
all—they simply seize upon those who are inconvenient and suppress
the delinquents.   And why, or how am I more inconvenient or
distasteful to these Federal folks than anybody else is ?   Strange,
I was also highly inconvenient and distasteful to the British
Government !   And these two governments, we are told, are the
very highest expression and grandest hope of the civilization of
the nineteenth century.   Here is the very point, I suspect.   I
despise the civilization of the nineteenth century, and its two
highest expressions and grandest hopes, most especially—so the
said century sees nothing that can be done with me, except to tie
me up.   It seems that I make myself so excessively offensive to
these two governments that, right or wrong, law or no law, they
must suppress *me* at any rate.   The English get what they call a
"law" made for the express purpose ; the Americans do the thing
without even that pretext.   They are both in the wrong ; but then,
if I am able to put them in the wrong, they are able to put me
into dungeons.   And when I am locked in they have me just
where they want me ; and they hold the key of the position.

To many persons, both in England and America, the
facts commented on in this passage will be conclusive as
against Mitchel.   It was said at the time, and will no
doubt be always said, by a certain class of people, that
Mitchel's leading idea was to break the law, and defy the
government of whatever country he might chance to find

himself in ; that he was a rebel and a law-breaker by instinct, and was always in opposition to the constituted authorities by a law of his nature.   On the other hand, it is to be remembered that there were others before John Mitchel who found it as hard as he did to get along peacably with the powers that be, and whom, nevertheless, the judgment of succeeding ages has not condemned— notably Socrates, and a greater than Socrates.   Indeed, in all ages, one test of goodness and greatness has been a readiness to oppose the powers that be at the risk of life or liberty when the said powers go wrong, a thing which unfortunately they sometimes do.

As soon as he left the steamer, Mitchel was at once conducted to the fortress, closely guarded.   Arrived there, he was shown to a small vaulted room, lighted by a case-mate porthole.   In one corner was an iron bedstead ; in another a little deal table.   The officer informed Mitchel that this was to be his abode.   Mitchel then asked whether he could go out for fresh air at any time ; whether he could see Mr. Davis or Mr. Clay ; whether he might have books to read.   To all these questions the answer was—no.   He then asked if he would be allowed tobacco.   This the officer promised to procure for him ; but, as we shall see, the promise was not kept.

The officer then retired.   Shortly afterwards the door was again unbarred, and a corporal entered.   He carried in his hand a lump of bread and a piece of cold pork, and these he placed, just as they were, upon the dirty table, without any such superfluous luxuries as plates or knives or forks.   Mr. Davis, a few days previously, had been served with his first rations in like manner, had resented the insult by throwing the rations in the corporal's face, and had thereupon been at once put in irons.   Mitchel thought it likely that the object of the present proceeding was to entrap him into some similar act of violence. He therefore commanded his temper, and only said, " Thank you, sir ; if I had a knife and fork and a plate, I could dine now." The only answer was a repetition of the announcement, "There's your rations," in a loud and insolent tone of voice. Mitchel said no more, and the corporal walked away. In the course of the evening, General Miles, the commander of the fortress, came to see his new prisoner. He was civil, but not communicative. Mitchel asked why, having been neither accused nor tried he should at the start be treated as a felon. To this the general's brief answer was, " I execute my orders." Being asked as to tobacco, he repeated the promise already given, that tobacco, not being forbidden, would be furnished. This promise was afterwards several times repeated by other officers, but it was not till Mitchel had been a month in prison that he was furnished with a little paper of tobacco.

For two months after Mitchel's arrest the course of treatment was such as above described. During this time the prisoner was allowed no exercise and no books ; and the food was of such a kind and served in such a manner as to be all but uneatable to a man accustomed to the decencies of civilized life. As might be expected, the treatment very soon produced a marked effect upon Mitchel's health. Want of food and want of healthful exercise for mind or body made him very unwell. He could no longer sleep at nights. At first he tried to take exercise by walking up and down his little room. But soon, through weakness, he was no longer able to do even this to any considerable extent. No wonder that, as he tells us, the twenty-four hours grew intolerably long. During this weary time, Mitchel had several more brief interviews with General Miles. The manner of this official was such as to impress Mitchel with the idea that he did not very much relish the orders he had to execute. And this surmise was in fact correct. The details of Mitchel's treatment were minutely regulated by orders from the War Department.

One incident which occurred during this period is touching, and I am tempted to give it at length as I find it in the " Journal " :—

One night I lay on the bed, wide awake, but very quiet. The lamp had been lighted in my cell, as usual, and the sentry was pacing up and down the room with bayonet fixed ; another pacing in like manner through the outer guard-room. I observed that the soldier was a fine-looking fellow, and very unlike the Pennsylvania Germans who compose almost the whole of the regiment garrisoning this fort. He had a free and swinging kind of step, and a martial-looking head. Surely, I thought, I have seen you before somewhere—you or some of your kindred. Presently I observed that, in pacing backwards and forwards, he drew nearer and nearer to where I was lying. I seemed not to notice him. At last he came quite close, and leant down over me. "May I spake to you, sir?" he whispered. "Take care, my good fellow, you will be observed." "*He's* all right!"—looking over his shoulder to the man who was walking outside the grating. "Well, what is it?" "I wanted to tell you," he said, still whispering, "that my name's Mike Sullivan, from Fethard, in the County Tipperary, and there's but one company of Irish in all this big regiment, three thousand strong; and we feel badly about you and the way you're used here. Thim two other gentlemen that came before you came, said they were sick and sent for the doctor, and ever since they're on hospital tratement. Now, its easy to see you're sick ; call for the doctor to-morrow, and you'll soon have a change. In the mane time," continued Mike, "I know these divils brought you away from home without letting you get a change of clothes or any little convaniences that you're used to ; and so, as I was to be on guard to-night, I just took the liberty to go to the store, and to buy you a comb and a toothbrush, and—and here they are " (pulling a little parcel out of his

pocket, and actually blushing, as if with shame at his kind action).
"Sure enough, it's little we can do for you, and if we tried to
bring you in any clothes, its hauled up we'd be. God bless you,
anyhow!" I think, that in my feeble state at that time, the tears
came into my eyes as I thanked Mike Sullivan. "And," said he,
again glancing over his shoulder, "one of our men sent you this
orange"—producing one—"he thought it might taste good to you
afther that nasty stuff they bring you to ate." He raised himself
up, as if to resume his walk, but again stooped down. "Take
care, Mike; take care! these people will be watching you." "To
the divil I pitch them all," he said, profanely. "I only wanted
to say this much more to you, sir; I know they won't let you
write a line to your wife. Now I'll try and get on guard here
some other night soon; I can exchange with another man for
that; and I'll bring you in a scrap of paper and a pencil, and
you'll write, and I'll mail it for you to Richmond." Now, here
was a true prince, from the foot of Slieve-na-Mhan. What Mike
did was not much; but it was done to his own imminent risk, and
in a manner at once kindly and careless, rough and delicate.
He never was on guard again, however; he was what he called
"spotted" that night.

In reply to the civil inquiries of General Miles, several
times repeated, Mitchel resolutely refused to make any
complaint. At last, however, on the 10th of August, the
doctor was brought to see him. Doctor Craven found his
patient sitting on the edge of the bed scarcely able to stand.
The doctor made very strong representations as to the
state of Mitchel's health. He certified to the War Department that he could not live long unless he were supplied
with better food and allowed to exercise out of doors. He
also recommended that the prisoner should be allowed the
use of books.

On the 14th of August, exactly two months after
Mitchel's arrest, an order arrived from the War Department
modifying very materially the directions as to his treatment.
On that day, General Miles informed his prisoner that he

would be allowed an hour's exercise each day in the open air, under guard. He was also to be allowed books and newspapers. A catalogue of the fortress library (for the fortress had a library) would be furnished to him, and he could choose his books. In the matter of food, also, a sweeping change was made. From this time forward the food was all that could be expected, at least in a prison. The meals were good and cleanly served, and the prisoner had his choice of tea or coffee, both excellent.

A few days after the change of treatment, as Mitchel was taking his daily exercise, he met Mr. Davis. Both prisoners were guarded, and conversation was forbidden. But as they passed they shook hands. General Miles turned away, and allowed a few commonplace greetings to pass between the prisoners. The ex-president was looking the worse for the treatment he had suffered.

Several times after this he passed both Mr. Davis and Mr. Clay in their morning walks, but had no further conversation with either beyond a passing salutation.

Under date September 1, 1865, I find a letter from Mitchel to his wife, written from Fortress Monroe. After speaking of family matters, he proceeds :—

Tell me all about my two dear little daughters. When you last wrote, Isabelle was still in Cumberland County, but I suppose she is returned to you before this.

Do not believe one single word that you have ever seen in newspapers relating to me since the day of my arrest—not so much as one word. For my part, I was not allowed to see a newspaper for two months after my arrival here; but can well imagine their ingenious inventions. ·I have been wonderfully well in health until lately, when the asthma has come upon me rather badly. I expected this if I were kept confined so long as three months. I fought it off as long as possible, but at last it has fairly floored me. At present my fare is very good, and a very worthy doctor visits me. He has procured me an improvement in my table. I am also allowed to walk twice a day upon the ramparts of the fort, and books are given me out of the fortress library. I received the parcel of tobacco which James sent me, and which is very good; also the little parcel of clothing he brought me when he came down, and asked admission to see me.

This, I think, is all the news I have to tell. I don't in the least know what the charge against me is, or whether there is any. Mr. Clay lives in the casemate next door to me but one. I sometimes meet him in our walk upon the ramparts; we are both attended by guards, and can only ask each other, "How are you?" He seems pretty well. I also meet Mr. Davis sometimes, but he, I think, is failing in his health.

From the time of the change for the better in Mitchel's treatment to the time of his release, there elapsed just two months and a half, making the total period of his imprisonment four months and a half. Of his life during these latter two months and a half there is not much to tell. His health rallied considerably under the influence of the improved treatment. But he never—to the day of his death—completely recovered the effects of his first two months in Fortress Monroe. He read a good deal, especially books on historical and military subjects. Frequently he had conversations with General Miles, who all through was disposed to be friendly. At last, towards the end of October, General Miles spoke of the probability of an early release. Here is the conversation :—

"Who are these Fenians?" General Miles asked me.

"Why, what of the Fenians?"

"Why, it appears that they have been exerting themselves with the Government on your behalf, and that they are supposed to have considerable influence, as representing a large force of Irish voters."

"Very likely. I am not one of them, but I know all about them, and heartily approve of their main object, which is to help their countrymen in Ireland some day to shake off the British domination. What have they been doing now?"

"Several attempts have been made lately," said the general, "to influence the president to release you. An extensively signed memorial has been brought on from New York by a friend of yours,* who has had an interview with the president; but, besides ·this, these Fenians, who are holding a convention or congress or something of that sort in Philadelphia, have been urging the same matter upon the attention of Government, and, in short, it seems to be generally understood that you are not to be much longer here."

"It will be hard to part, general; but I shall always remember the hospitalities of Fortress Monroe."

The general was accurate in his statement. The American Irish had been actively exerting themselves to bring about Mitchel's release; and they were able to bring to bear sufficient pressure to ensure the granting of their request. There was some further delay; but, at last, on the 29th of October, the order came. It was an unconditional release—no terms of any kind being imposed.

The circumstances attending the release are told in the "Journal":—

Next morning (the 30th), an officer came to my room; told me he had authority to allow me to see Mr. Davis and Mr. Clay for a few moments, each in his own cell; that he should leave me alone a little while with Mr. Clay; but that I could only see Mr. Davis through the grating of his door, and in presence of him, the officer; and that our conversation was to be limited to health, weather, and good-bye. The programme was duly carried out. I found Mr. Clay suffering extremely, wasted to a shadow, and very despondent. I promised to write to his wife, though, indeed, I can say but little to comfort that poor lady. Then I had my interview with our ex-president, who also looked very ill.

Coming back to my room, the officer produced a scrap of paper and a pen and ink, and asked me for my autograph, attaching to it some little sentiment, if I would be so good. I wrote: "The thieves have bound the true men," and signed my name. I was then conducted to the great gate, which was open.

* Mr. Richard O'Gorman.

Soon I was sitting all alone upon the gravelly sea beach, with the bright water rippling at my feet.

On the day of his release from Fortress Monroe, John Mitchel wanted just four days of being fifty years of age. Up to the time of this imprisonment, I can find no trace in his writings of any decline of mental vigour. But from this time forward he was not the same man. It is true he conducted a newspaper, subsequently to this time, for several years in New York ; and the editorial writing in this paper is very decidedly superior to the average of such writing. Still, though it would be exceptionally good for the average newspaper editor, it is not good for John Mitchel. As a rule, we miss the vigour which characterizes Mitchel's writings in his earlier journals. Those who knew him most intimately always affirmed that he was shattered both mentally and physically by his treatment at Fortress Monroe, and that from the injury there done to him he never afterwards recovered.

Upon his release from Fortress Monroe, Mitchel went direct to Richmond. He was anxious to see what had become of his family. He found them all well. On the evening of his arrival quite a number of visitors called to see him—many of them ex-Confederate officers and members of the old Ambulance Committee. He stayed only a few days at Richmond, and then proceeded straight to New York. His object was to consult some New York lawyers in whom he had confidence as to his chances of obtaining redress by legal process for his arrest and imprisonment. The law of the case was plain enough. The city of New York not being under martial law, to arrest a civilian upon the mere order of a military officer, and forthwith to carry him off out of reach of the writ of Habeas Corpus, was, of course, an absolutely illegal proceeding. But in times of war, or of extreme popular excitement, it often happens that men in authority can do illegal acts without much risk of being made amenable ; that is, provided the illegality be a popular one. This was precisely what had happened in Mitchel's case. One of the lawyers whom he consulted put the case very plainly. His answer was in substance: "There is no law now in this land ; and if there were law for others, there would be none for *you.* If you should now again disquiet the Government by any legal claims, you would simply be arrested again, and then you would probably never live to see the end of your captivity." The lawyer then went on to suggest, as a friend, what would be the wisest course for Mitchel to pursue. His advice was that Mitchel should go to Europe, and remain away a year or so, hoping that in the mean time there would be a reaction in American sentiment—a suggestion which Mitchel thought well worth considering.

Shortly after his arrival in New York, an offer was made to him which put it in his power to go to Paris for a year or so, and at the same time to provide for his family during his absence. While he was shut up in the Con- federacy, he had heard little of the progress of the Fenian organization. What little he had heard had not led him to look on the organization as likely to do much good. But now things looked different. During the war the organization had spread rapidly, especially in the army. There were now thousands of veteran soldiers members of the organization. Large funds had been collected, and preparations were being openly made for an expedition to Ireland. So far the American Government showed no disposition to interfere with these preparations. The feeling in the North was still bitterly hostile to England ; and it was part of the policy of the American Government to abstain, up to a certain point, from all interference with the

Fenians. Then the accounts given by Stephens and others of the state of the organization in Ireland were such as to lead even cool-headed men to suppose that, if a force of several thousand veteran soldiers were but landed in Ireland, a formidable army might be at once collected.

In what little I have to say regarding John Mitchel's relations with the Fenian Brotherhood, I speak under correction. There must have been quite a number of letters written by Mitchel to leading Fenians which I have never seen. Passages in his own "Journal," letters to him from Stephens and O'Mahony, copies which he kept of certain letters to Stephens and O'Mahony, and the letters on Fenianism subsequently published by him in the *Irish Citizen*—these are the materials upon which I have formed my judgment.

For many of the Fenians—rank and file as well as leaders—John Mitchel had warm admiration and respect. But—save for one short period—he never had any faith in the power of the Fenians to effect the end they put before themselves. Secret organization and secret conspiracy were the essence of Fenianism, and these very things he had always regarded as sure to do more harm than good in Irish politics. The "brief period" just referred to was the period which ensued upon Mitchel's release from Fortress Monroe. Just then the prospects of the Fenians were, for the reasons above explained, exceptionally good. A war between England and America was in the air. For a time it seemed to Mitchel possible that the Fenians might effect some good. It was while he held this belief that he accepted the office hereinafter mentioned. He never would join in any public appeal for money ; and even the office which he did accept, he only held until it became clear to him that the hopes he had formed regarding the Fenians were illusory.

The office I refer to was that of financial agent for the brotherhood in Paris. It happened that, at the time of Mitchel's release, the Fenian Directory were in need of a perfectly trustworthy agent in Paris through whom to make remittances to Ireland. They knew, of course, that Mitchel was perfectly trustworthy, and, as Irishmen, they admired him, and were willing to do him a service, and, if possible, to win him to their views. They offered him the post of their financial agent in Paris with a salary. He at once accepted the offer, and joined the organization. He went to Richmond for a day or two to see his family, and to settle them before he started. Then back to New York; and on the 10th of November, less than a fortnight after his release from Fortress Monroe, he sailed from New York on board one of the French line of steamships for Brest and Havre.

Nothing particular occurred on the passage, except some quarrelling between northern and southern American passengers. The northerns were triumphant, and somewhat insulting in their language. The southerns answered pretty hotly. They did not quite come to blows, but several times came very near to that point. On the 22nd of November the ship reached Havre, and on the following day Mitchel went on to Paris. A day or two after his arrival, he makes the following entry in his " Journal ":—

I have found lodgings in the Rue Richer, quite close to the Rue du Faubourg Poissonnière; have negotiated my bills for Fenian funds through John Monroe, American banker, Rue de la Paix, and have at once been placed in communication with agents and messengers of the Irish Revolutionists, who naturally wish to grasp at once all the money they can get hold of—and indeed what can the poor fellows do without plenty of money?

Just here it is necessary for me to consider what and how much I am at liberty to tell of all these machinations, and on what and how much I must observe silence.

A long letter of instructions from John O'Mahony followed him to Paris. I am not clear that I am justfied in quoting from this letter, even after the time which has since elapsed. But I may say generally that it gives Mitchel minute directions as to the management and disbursement of funds sent to him, and instructs him as to the methods by which he may safely get into communication with Stephens in Dublin. The sums remitted through Mitchel were very considerable.

There was also a notion that Mitchel might be able to do something towards interesting the French Government in the Fenian attempts. O'Mahony's letter has this passage :—

Your diplomatic relations with the French Government, or any other public or private parties on the European continent that may be found useful to the Fenian movement, are left to your own judgment and discretion.

This part of the mission came to nothing. Mitchel was soon convinced that nothing was to be hoped for from the French Government.

The winter of 1865–66 was a severe one in Paris ; and Mitchel was still weak and suffering from the effects of his imprisonment. Shortly after his arrival he had visits from certain agents of Mr. Stephens, and the arrangements necessary to enable him to discharge his duties as financial agent were soon completed. He tells us that he discharged these duties with care, but without very much interest. For he had not been long in Paris before he began to suspect that the hopes he had entertained regarding the work of the Fenians in Ireland were groundless. In Paris he was able to communicate rapidly with friends in Ireland. He wrote to several of those friends in whom he most confided, asking whether the people of Ireland were so thoroughly organized and so ready for revolt as had been represented to him on the other side of the Atlantic. The replies he received were not encouraging. They convinced him that the state of things in Ireland had been very materially misrepresented to the Irish in America ; and, further, that the people in Ireland had been entirely deluded touching the amount of help that was to be looked for from America. Brave, simple, credulous men came to Mitchel, sent from Dublin or Liverpool. They would enter in great excitement, and tell wonderful stories of the masses of men that were coming from America, and how General Sheridan was coming to lead them. To dash such hopes was a painful task.

In addition to all this, the news reached Mitchel, not long after his arrival, that the Fenian Brotherhood in America had split into two sections. Each of these sections claimed to be the original and genuine brotherhood, and each abused the other with vigour. The conviction was being forced on him that the elements of a successful revolution did not exist in the Fenian organization. He continued for some time longer to act as agent for the transmission of funds to Ireland, and, so long as he held the office, he was careful to perform its duties with the utmost exactitude. He mentions in his " Journal " that, during the winter of 1865–66, he had repeated letters from Mr. Stephens, who was then hiding in Dublin, after his escape from Richmond Bridewell. These letters were written by Stephens himself, but were sent over by special messengers. Several of them have come to my hands. There is one long letter, dated January 9, 1866. Stephens gives Mitchel a minute account of the system of organization in Ireland. He refers to the split in America, and denounces the " Canada faction." Answering some objections of Mitchel's, he says :—

Our strength exceeds two hundred thousand sworn men in Ireland alone. Mind, there is no possibility of deceiving me on this head, and few will deem me capable of wilful exaggeration. Of these two hundred thousand, at least fifty thousand are thoroughly trained men, a fair proportion being veterans. Of the enemy's garrison, we have nearly one-third. We count fully a third of them in Dublin. Rely on these figures, and then say if we can do nothing till France or America goes to war with England.

Stephen's letter concludes by pressing Mitchel for an opinion upon the question as to whether they ought to rise at once or wait for further aid from America. I do not find any copy of the answer to this letter; but I find a copy of a long letter to O'Mahony, written early in March. I extract the following passages :—

I need not tell you, dear O'M——, how bitterly I have been grieved by the shameful break-up of the F. B. Its worst effect was not the cutting-off of money supplies; it was the deconsideration of our cause in America, which sentiment of the Americans was what encouraged the enemy to make this swoop upon all the Irish American citizens they could find in Ireland. I make no doubt that Russell had consulted Adams before doing it, and that Adams told him to go ahead—they were but Irish, after all. It is very well for Mr. K—— and others to express indignation—which, indeed, they have a right to feel—at this open abandonment of the rights of naturalized citizens who had " fought for the flag," and all that. But it is what ought to have been expected. . . . The movement in Ireland is, I suppose, entirely stopped, and any combined and intelligent insurrection quite impossible. I am not in possession of Stephens's mind upon this matter.

He speaks then of Stephens's letter above referred to. He says that he declined to give Stephens the advice there asked for, and states his reasons for so declining. He assumes that the recent action of the British Government has " made any respectable fight impossible ;" but he holds that—

This prompt action of the English Government was precisely what they ought to have expected ; what they ought to have been prepared for ; what they ought to have anticipated by striking two months ago, if they were to strike at all.

I do not understand all this, as at present advised. But I wish to say to you that if the movement, so far as immediate action is concerned, be really ruined, and if the I. R. (after so many fine men have been destroyed) is to settle back to its normal state of a chronic conspiracy, I have doubts about the propriety of remaining as a financial agent in Paris. For the next three months, of course, I will remain at my post, and carry out any instructions and dispositions with regard to funds that I may be entrusted with by F. B. That will give both you and me time to convince ourselves of the real history and present situation of affairs in Ireland.

Mitchel had not been long in Paris before he went to visit Mrs. Byrne and his other old friends there. Colonel Byrne was now dead, and his widow was engaged in publishing his memoirs. When the book was ready, the old lady presented a copy of it to Mitchel, and the present was highly valued. Yet, notwithstanding occasional visits to friends, Mitchel was lonely enough. He gives us this summary of how his time was spent: " A weekly letter to the New York *News* (the paper he had edited before his arrest), some study in the great libraries, and visits to certain acquaintances and friends, whom I had known during former residences in Paris, filled up my lonely time."

About the close of the year 1865, he had visitors who, while they remained, made the time pass pleasantly enough. One evening he came home to his lodging about eight o'clock. On opening the door of his room, he was surprised to find the fire already lighted, and candles on the table. Two ladies and a gentleman were in the room. He was near-sighted, and, in the bright light, he at first did not recognize his visitors. He did not long remain in doubt.

His two sisters—Mary and Henrietta—and his brother William had come over to see him without notice. They had matters enough to talk about ; and while these visitors remained there was no loneliness.

After his brother and sisters left, which was early in January, 1866, Mitchel had another visitor. This time it was John Martin who came to see him. They smoked and talked as of old, and before John Martin left, it was agreed that, if possible, he should come again before Mitchel left Paris, and bring Father Kenyon with him. A few days after John Martin's departure, I find the following letter from Mitchel to his sister Margaret. It is dated January 31, 1866 :—

Your letter to me, as well as Matilda's and two or three others, have been weighing upon my conscience for some time. And now that William, Mary, and Henrietta are gone, and John Martin also (who only left Paris two or three days ago), and that I have no excuse for laziness, I am going to make a clean sweep of my correspondence to-day. . . . The girls were telling me all about your children, some of whom I have seen in photographs which Minnie has. How I would like to make a trip into Ireland to see them all. But I can't do that. I would "feel mean," as the Americans say. Besides, I would be arrested as a Fenian, and clapped in gaol ; and I have had enough of that. Certainly I am tolerably familiarized by this time with the gaols *des Deux Mondes.* The Anglo-Saxon race and the nineteenth century seem to have no use for me, except to chain me up. There are prisons in France, but as yet I have only seen the outside of them. It does not seem to have occurred to this emperor—what seems so obvious to Englishmen and Yankees—that it is in the inside I would be the right man in the right place.

This is rigmarole ; but I have so little else to say. I am living at the top of a high house. Whoever comes to visit me has one hundred and five steps of stairs to mount. But when he is arrived here he finds quite a neat little apartment, which, however, I am going to quit the 25th of February, because it is too dear for me, and go to my old quarters, 24, Rue Lacépède, which is cheap and nasty in comparison. I should not say nasty, because, in fact, everything is clean enough; but with the word "cheap" naturally associates itself the word "nasty." I am as lonely as Robinson Crusoe in this great city. Though I know some people, and might, if I chose, know more, and though I am naturally sociable, yet I am solitary, and spend most of my evenings smoking and reading by my little wood fire. You cannot imagine how I long for my little household, or the half of it which remains to me. They are all perfectly good. Not one of my children ever gave me one moment's pain; and I am sure I don't know how that has happened, for it is but little good I have ever taught them.

On the same date as the above, there is also a letter to Mitchel's Irish friend, Miss Thompson, from which I extract the following :—

You need not tell me, because I know it well, that you sympathize with our poor Fenians. Some of the chief men amongst them are now going through the mill which the British Government keeps to grind us. But the thing is not over. On this point I cannot speak very freely, and, besides, I begin to have some misgivings about the chief executive of the Irish Republic. You will remember that I never had an exalted opinion of that gentleman, yet the ability and energy he has shown in organizing, the astonishing trust and confidence that he possesses amongst the masses of Irish, both in Ireland and in America, joined to the formidable increase of power given to the organization by the closing up of the American war, have led me not only to take an interest in what was going on, but to give the organization such service as I can without going over for the present to Ireland. In America I would not stay, for reasons which it would be long to tell you. There is no law now in that "land of the free and home of the brave"—at least, no law for me. . . . We have suffered heavily indeed, one way and another, by that Confederate business, and although it was a good cause, I must admit that I grudge it what it has cost us—the lives of our two sons in defence of a country which, after all, was not their own. By last letters from Richmond, about a fortnight ago, I learn that they are all well, and that matters are going reasonably well with them.

Mr. Martin's " League " is, I fear, a poor affair. The "National Association," of which Mr. Dillon is a member, is much more imposing in numbers, but is not half so straightforward a movement as the League. Yet the late speech of J. B. Dillon is manly, and shows that the fire of '48 is not yet quite extinguished under the snows that now whiten his head. In neither of those movements, however, can I bring myself to take much interest. And, in truth, if they have any power or come to any good, it will be all owing to the Fenians.

A few days after these letters (February 2), there is a letter from Mitchel to his wife, from which I take the following passages :—

John Martin was in town about three weeks. He left the other day, and must now be at home. He was quite well, and desired all sorts of kind remembrances to you. . . . Remember, I am a lonely wretch, and very little can give me pleasure except to hear about my own folk. I have been twice to a theatre since I came, and both times quitted it before the piece was finished. Books are still some resource, and I sometimes sit an evening with the worthy Bayers.

James, in a letter to me, seemed to wish me in some way to vindicate the cause of the South and of the southern army, by writing about them. This would be but unwelcome reading for the readers of the *Daily News*. . . . There is another thing— very few people, either in the northern states or in Europe, care about the South now that it is down, or take any interest in its vindication. This disposition to forget the Confederacy is very visible to me in France, and, in short, it is human nature to sympathize with success, and to admit that success is right, and defeat is wrong. Writings intended to do justice now to the South, to the history of the struggle, or the present rights of citizenship and law, would fall upon cold ears ; just as national and patriotic writings about Ireland are read by nobody but Irishmen. Notwithstanding all this, I do and shall do whatever may be done with any chance of good effect. But let James not trouble himself about those matters. He has done all that *he* was called upon to do ; and now don't let him make a martyr of himself. I have been a martyr now for eighteen years, and it is quite a bad trade. I had rather be a farmer.

Kiss over and over again for me my two dear little daughters. My poor children—it is they who are the real martyrs.

About a month after these letters were written, Mitchel left his lodging in the Rue Richer, and returned to his old quarters at the *pension* in the Rue Lacépède. The reader will remember the description of Madame Bonnerie's establishment given in one of Mitchel's letters during his first visit to Paris. Both at the Rue Richer, and afterwards at the Rue Lacépède, he was a good deal annoyed by the attentions of spies set to watch him by the English authorities. About a week after he moved to the Rue Lacépède, three men came and took up their quarters in a wine-shop nearly opposite to the gateway of the *pension*. Some of the dwellers at Madame Bonnerie's, who had nothing else particular to do, watched the movements of these gentlemen. It was soon obvious that they had come there to study the proceedings of Mr. Mitchel. Whenever he went out, one of the trio was sure to follow him. If Mitchel entered an omnibus, his pursuer would mount on top; and so on. At last two of the boarders—one an Englishman, another a Frenchman—spoke to Mitchel on the subject. They asked him if he had noticed the three *mouchards* who had come to live across the street, and told him how closely he was watched. Mitchel thanked them for the information, and questioned the *concierge* as to whether she also had noticed the *mouchards*. She said she had ; and she further told him that several times in his absence one of the spies had come to the gate, and asked her questions regarding Mr. Mitchel's movements—what he did when at home, and what sort of persons came to see him. She was sure they were not agents of the French police. She had several reasons for this opinion, the principal one being that these *mouchards* were too clumsy in their operations for agents of the French police. Mitchel directed the *concierge*, the next time the spies inquired after him, to show them straight up to his room, if he were at home. There were several young men in the house with whom Mitchel was very popular (he was so with most young men who came to know him well), and they were with difficulty restrained by the entreaties of Madame Bonnerie from crossing over to the wine-shop and taking the law into their own hands. A few days after Mitchel had given his instructions to the *concierge*, he and his young friends were smoking in the garden after *dejeuner*. One of the party mentioned that one of the spies over the way had been seen that very morning talking to the *concierge*. Mitchel at once asked young Bonnerie to accompany him, and the rest to stay where they were. Accompanied by Bonnerie, he went first to see the *concierge*. She told him it was quite true ; that the *mouchards* had been there that morning, and had asked some questions about M. Mitchel. She had told them that M. Mitchel was at home, and would be very glad to see them ; and she had pointed them the way to M. Mitchel's room. They had muttered something about coming another time, and had gone away. The sequel is best told in Mitchel's own words :—

" Are they anywhere near at this moment ? " I asked. " Certainly, monsieur, *sans doute*. Give yourself the trouble to come with me to the *porte cochère*—the large gateway. There they are, monsieur," she said ; "two of them "—pointing to two men who were leaning against the doorposts of the wine-shop, with cigars in their mouths. I went straight over, young Bonnerie keeping close by me. I stopped at the door and took a survey of the two ruffians ; they returned my look with perfect *nonchalance*. Then I walked close up to the first fellow, and asked him what he wanted with *me*. He took his cigar slowly out of his mouth, and said he had not the distinguished honour of knowing me—there was some mistake. "Well," I answered, "you and your comrade here, and another man, have paid very particular attention to me and to my movements; you and they have come many times to the *concierge* of that house over there, where I live, inquiring after my movements." The scoundrel raised his eyelids, and shrugged his shoulders. "*Mais, monsieur*, I don't comprehend you, not the least in the world." By this time a considerable crowd, perhaps fifty or sixty people, from the neighbouring houses, had gathered around. My young companion, Bonnerie, was becoming very much excited; so were the people who surrounded us, for the Parisians do not love spies. I said to the man: "But these people around understand me; and now take care of yourself. If you ever enter that gateway again, under any pretence"—pointing to our *porte cochère*—"you will be flung out into the street. I do not answer for your miserable lives." I had to drag away young Bonnerie by force; he wished to take summary vengeance on the spot. I said to him, but in a tone to be heard by the people around, "One does not quarrel with *mouchards*." In a quarter of an hour after this scene the scoundrels had disappeared from the street called de Lacépède, and I never after saw or heard of any trace of them.

But although this move had the effect of getting rid of the spies for the time being, Mitchel was not yet quite satisfied. He was anxious to find out something more definite about them, and in particular to ascertain, if possible, who had employed them to watch him in this way. He first visited the commissary of police for the quarter of Paris in which he lived. To this official Mitchel related the circumstances of the espionage to which he had been subjected, stated his reasons for believing that the men were not agents of the Paris police, and asked the commissary whether he knew anything about them. To all this the commissary answered that Mitchel was right in assuming that the men were not in his employ, but that, for aught he knew, they might be employed by the French Government. "But," he added "in that case they would have

their instructions from M. le Préfet de Police.   They may,
however, for aught I know, be agents of the English or of the
American Government; and you are aware, monsieur, that
you are obnoxious to them both."   Mitchel could not help
being a little startled at the degree of knowledge possessed
by this subordinate officer of the Paris police regarding his
antecedents.   He left the office of the commissary without
further conversation, resolving to make further inquiries at
the office of the prefect of police.   The prefect of police at
this time was a M. Pietri, who was also private secretary to
the emperor.   A few days after his interview with the
commissary, Mitchel called by appointment on M. Pietri,
and was very courteously received.   To him Mitchel again
told his story.   The prefect listened with close attention,
and made no remark until Mitchel had concluded.   Then
he said: "You are right; these men are not my people,
and have no instructions from me.   You have been resident
several times in Paris, and you have never given to our
police the slightest pretext to look after you or your
movements.   You may be quite sure that you will not
only be quite free from all annoyance from the French
authorities, but that you will be protected from annoyance
by the agents of other governments."   Mitchel then suggested the possibility of the men being employed by Lord
Cowley, the English ambassador.   On this point the
prefect declined to give any opinion, and merely reiterated
his promise that the men should give no further annoyance.
Again I give the sequel, as told by Mitchel himself :—

I thanked the minister, and was about to go away, when he
asked me to reseat myself.   Then, after a minute's thought, he
said, "As you are here, Mr. Mitchel, I had better say to you at
once that it has been confidently asserted to us—*on assure*—that
your present errand in Paris is to purchase arms and equipments
for the political revolutionists or conspirators called *Fenians*, with

a view of organizing an insurrection against a government with which the empire is at peace, and not only at peace, but in alliance." " May one ask, Excellency, who it is that affirms such a thing? Is it, *par hasard*, my Lord Cowley?" "I have not the honour," he replied, "to know his lordship." "Well, then, M. le Préfet, I need scarcely give myself the trouble to deny that I am engaged in the purchase and shipment of arms for a revolution, because if I had been doing business of that nature you would certainly have all the details of my operations before you in that large book upon the table." He smiled. " *C'est possible, monsieur.*" Then he added, "You are aware, monsieur, that our France is a very hospitable country." "Yes, I have always found it so." "But," he said, "it would not be right for you, nor for us to permit you, to avail yourself of the protection of our laws for the purpose of embarrassing our relations with a friendly country." "Oh, I know, sir ; I have never once sought to make any trouble of that kind. I am aware of the exigencies of the *entente cordiale.*" He nodded. "And I can wait my time." He nodded again. In the mean time he assured me that I should have no further trouble from the English detectives. So I took my leave, the prefect very politely escorting me to the door ; and I returned home, with the intention of applying next to Lord Cowley.

Whether or not Mitchel carried out his intention of applying to Lord Cowley I do not know. The promise of M. Pietri was faithfully kept ; and during the remainder of his stay at Paris, Mitchel suffered no further annoyance from English spies.

All through the spring months of 1866 he continued to lead a somewhat lonely life in Paris. Under date March 15, 1866, I find a letter to Mrs. John Dillon, which gives (along with other matters) some little account of the sort of life he was then leading. He begins by referring to the marriage of his son James, then about to take place ; and of this he says :—

As to his marrying and having children (which, of course, makes a grandfather of me), making me feel old, as you say—*hélas !* I feel old enough already to have great grandchildren. I am the Wandering Jew, I am the Count St. Germain, and also Methuselah. It seems to me, however, that I do not grow old in disposition, in fact, I hate old people, and love to be with the young and bright. John O'Hagan, is he married, or only going to be married? Has he actually made the plunge head foremost into the abyss of that *Grand Peut-être?* or is he only bracing himself for the awful leap? In either case nobody wishes John better luck than I do. How happens it, that though I have lived so long in America, and have met many very good people there, I can never think of any Americans as touching me very closely; between them and me is a gulf fixed, and I am essentially, unalterably, *intus et in cute,* an European. Perhaps it is because when I went to America I was too old to transplant; perhaps it is merely because nobody (even if he has not changed his country) can attach the idea of cordial and genial *abandon* to friendships formed late in life—only to the associations of youth—glorious, immortal youth.

I am living here like an anchorite, in a great measure, though there are some pleasant houses to which I go when I am in the humour. I have at present my old chamber, Rue Lacépède, commanding a view very rarely seen from a Paris window. I look down on the Jardin des Plantes, but from a great height, and far beyond that garden I can see about one-third of Paris, and the whole valley of the Seine beyond Choisy-le-roi, and also the superb *donjon* of Vincennes, and Pere-la-Chaise. . . .

Though J. B. Dillon has not written to me, I believe I must write to him. In fact, I want certain information from him about Irish affairs, which have passed during the time of our blockade. On issuing from Fortress Monroe, I found myself about four years in arrear of you denizens of the actual world, and I have by no means yet come up with you. Panting Time toils after you in vain. The world does go at such a devil of a pace—I wish it would stop.

I have no idea how long I may remain here. That depends partly upon certain public affairs. In any event, I cannot go home to Virginia while that state is under military law. There would be no living for me there. In fact, there is no room for me at this moment in "the land of the free and the home of the brave." The Bird of Freedom would claw my eyes out.

And in a letter dated some ten days later, addressed to the husband of the last correspondent, I find the following:—

You write me politics, and tell me I do not believe in the "future of humanity," and that this is the reason why I am not a Yankeè. Poor humanity! If it depends for its future upon the Yankees, it is going to have a damned bad time. Yes, I believe in the future of humanity, and that its future will be just like its past, that is, pretty mean.

There are several letters to his daughters during this time. The following passage is taken from a letter to his daughter Minnie :—

The day before yesterday I visited Mont Parnasse, and placed there a laurustinus in flower, growing in a pot. John Martin had sent me by post that morning a sprig of shamrock, which I also deposited. Poor daughter! I sometimes wish I was under the same stone. But there is no immediate chance of that. My health is perfect ; no asthma—no nothing.

About the middle of May he gives this further account of himself in a letter to his sister Matilda :—

As for me, I am supporting my exile as well as I can ; but that is not saying much. In fact, I hate this place ; but, no doubt, I would hate any other place still more. It is true that I am pretty well accustomed to exiles and imprisonments, and all sorts of martyrdoms. But it seems to me that one does not love that sort of thing the more for having been familiar with it. I visit a little in the evenings, especially the worthy Bayers ; also the Connollys, and one or two southern American families, in which we abuse the Yankees with great sincerity. Then I smoke and drink—more than enough—and write with something like regularity to the New York *Daily News ;* but this last is a job I detest, according to that singular disposition of the human creature, whereby he generally hates the only work which he can really do.

About the end of March, Mr. Stephens arrived in Paris. He had been living in Dublin since his escape from Richmond prison. According to Mitchel's account, he travelled from Dublin to the North of Ireland, then across to Scotland, and then through the length of England, without any disguise whatever. Stephens's arrival made some little sensation in Paris. Every one was familiar with the story of his escape. Photographers waited on him to solicit sittings, and the weekly papers had likenesses of the C.O.I.R. Mitchel introduced Stephens to several leading journalists—M. Marie-Martin, of the *Constitutionnel*, M. Malespine, of the *Opinion Nationale*, and others. Stephens stayed in Paris about a month, and then went to New York. His arrival there did not have the effect of healing the split. Stephens was put in command of the section from which Mitchel received his instructions; but this only seemed to have the effect of making the hostility between the two sections more bitter than ever. Finally, Mitchel resolved to resign his position of financial agent. On the 22nd of June he wrote Stephens a letter, a copy of which I find amongst Mitchel's papers :—

If any money is now on its way to me from New York, of course I will take care to have it forwarded to its destination; but after this reaches you, I beg that you will not have any more sent through me. This is the less necessary, as E. O'L—— is here, and tells me he is to continue here as long as you desire it. Take this letter, therefore, as announcing my resignation of the position of agent in Paris. I need assign no reason further than that I have now lost all hope of being enabled to communicate with the French Government, and that I do not think it right to continue, with a considerable salary, to merely receive and pay over sums of money, which can be as well attended to without me.

I think, at the same time, that your organization, both in Ireland and in America, ought to be kept up, and will soon be more important than ever. England is certainly going to be involved in the war; but, unfortunately, it will be on the same side with France. Still, a good opportunity may arise; and then I trust it may be found that the organization in Ireland is as strong as you think it is.

The rest of the letter is concerned with financial matters. The war here referred to was either the war between the German powers and Denmark, or that between Prussia and Austria, which immediately followed.

In the early summer of 1866 Mitchel went for a trip into Normandy. This was his vacation. He visited several of the old Norman towns ; but his principal object was to see Falaise, with its wonderful castle—the birthplace of the Conqueror of England. He was much interested by the old castle—one of the finest in France ; and in the market-place of Falaise he stopped to admire an equestrian statue in bronze of " the glorious bastard, pointing Englandwards." But for the details of this brief tour, I must, as on former occasions of a similar kind, refer the reader to the " Journal Continuation."

Immediately before this trip to Normandy, he had moved into new lodgings—186, Rue Rivoli. From these new quarters he writes to his sister Mary early in June :—

I have quitted Rue Lacépède altogether, and have a little room here, looking into a court—very quiet, and very convenient. I will certainly stay here so long as I may be in Paris. But how long or how short that may be, I know not. . . .

No letter yet from Richmond announcing that the wedding has taken place, though I suppose it has by this time. As to myself, I am quite well, as usual. Am writing very regularly for the New York *Daily News*. Have given up the sort of agency I had for the Fenians, but have assigned no reason, and do not wish to assign any. . . .

I am glad to hear some news of the Dillons. J. B. must have a handsome opinion by this time of his parliamentary policy. I wish he would drop it. A seat in that concern is certainly no honour to him ; and inasmuch as he is not a place-hunter, or a thief, it will be no profit either.

The marriage here referred to was the marriage of his son James, which took place some time in the month of

May, 1866. Notwithstanding the intention expressed in this letter, Mitchel did not, in fact, remain long at the Rue Rivoli. He found that the sewerage arrangements there were very bad. After being made very ill by foul air, he once more moved back to his old quarters in the Rue Lacépède.

The war between Prussia and Austria, in the summer of 1866, took up much of his attention for a time. But the war was soon over ; and besides, it did not at any time seem likely that England would be involved. A European war, in which England was not concerned, was for Mitchel the tragedy of *Hamlet* with the part of Hamlet left out.

Early in September, John Martin and Father Kenyon came to Paris to see Mitchel. Once more, and for the last time in their lives, the three friends, John Mitchel, John Martin, and John Kenyon, were all together. Mitchel lingers over the visit in the " Journal." He had a presentiment that it was the last time the three would be together. They had many things to talk about, and they often sat up together late into the night. Indeed, on one or two occasions, Father John absolutely declined to go to bed at all. In Mitchel's account of this time, he tells us of a visit which he and Father Kenyon paid to the Irish College. Mitchel and his friend were on their way homeward one day when Father Kenyon suddenly said, " I am going to call on Dr. Lynch, the President of the Irish College. Come along with me." Mitchel had always heard of Dr. Lynch as a very prudent and cautious man, one who would probably regard him (John Mitchel) as a revolutionary and dangerous character. He therefore tried to excuse himself. But Father John, as was usually the case with him, would hear of no excuse. Mitchel had to go. The door of the college was opened for them by a big Tipperary man, who " spoke French like an angel," and who " smiled cordially " as soon as he learned who the visitors were. Dr. Lynch received them with the utmost courtesy. He chatted for some time, and then showed them over the college. But it was as they were leaving that the scene occurred on account of which mainly I repeat the story here. As they passed through the hall, the professors and students were crowded together on either side, and cheer after cheer went up as Mitchel walked through—"such cheers as that quiet quarter had not often heard, ringing through the peaceful region of Ste. Geneviève, and causing the *sergents de ville* in distant streets to prick up their ears." Upon this incident, Mitchel has some comments to make :—

The scene was, under all the circumstances, a strange and touching one. Most of these fine young fellows had been yet unborn when I left my country in 1848 ; they could have known me only by the tradition of their various counties, and by such publications of mine as they might meet with. It strikes me that if they cheer *me* so warmly, they cannot be very earnestly loyal to the British empire ; and next year, or the year after, most of these will be curates in towns and country parishes all over Ireland. It is the young blood that flows each year through the veins of the Church, and the blood thereof is the life thereof. What is his Eminence Cardinal Cullen going to do about it ? How will he ever make the young priests, educated in this Irish College, good, faithful West Britons ? And Maynooth, I hear, is no better, that is, no worse ! Will he excommunicate them and damn all their souls ?

If I have recounted the very honourable, personal compliment to myself, it is not from vanity (though proud I was) ; it is to draw this moral : that Cardinal Cullen will have a tough job in carrying out his contract with the enemy of his country.

As Father John and I passed out together, and along the short *Rue des Irlandais*, tears sprang in his eyes, and for a minute he was silent. Then, " God bless the boys ! " he said ; " God bless the boys, anyhow ; *they're* always right."

Within twenty years from the time this scene took

place, events have occurred in Ireland which go far to justify the prediction here made.

On the 8th of August there is a letter from Mitchel to his wife :—

MY DEAR JENNY,

. . . About ten days ago, I visited General Beauregard. Next day he returned my visit, and sat with me for some time. He was just about starting for Vichy, a watering-place in the centre of France, where he is recommended to go for his health, which, he says, has been a good deal shattered—and, in fact, he looks old. I had also a visit one day from a young Cabell of (I think) Buckingham County, in Virginia, who, after serving the whole four years of the war, has come abroad to put himself to an engineering school, in order to have some way of earning a livelihood. He says he knows the Moseley family well. Seems a fine young man ; dined with me in a restaurant, and I learned from him as well as from General Beauregard, very much of what is going on over there. I also get the *Daily News* (that is, the semi-weekly edition), and can trace the progress of events. It is a progress backwards. I can see no prospect of a speedy end being put to martial law in Virginia ; and till that happens, I cannot resolve to try and live over there. They would not let me write in Virginia at all—not so much as put pen to paper upon any subject. So that if I went to that side of the water at all, I should have to stay in New York. Even there I might be taken up again, if I wrote anything, for I think there are going to be rough times there.

In the following month of September, he writes to his brother William :—

This is to inform you that Father Kenyon, John Martin, and I, are happily met, after vicissitudes. I am back in my old quarters here, and here also are installed those two. I was glad to get away from the place in the Rue Rivoli, where I was poisoned— in the most literal sense poisoned—by foul air, and where I had like to die, but for a capital constitution I have. I find poor Father Kenyon sadly altered in every way. My present intention is to leave this, and go to America before the end of October ;

but I will write to you before that, if I don't see you.   The death
of John Dillon is a real and bitter sorrow to me.   There were few
men of his type in the world.   He was all wrong, about almost
everything.   Nevertheless, he was better than most folk who are
all right.   He was very much attached to you, and, I suppose,
you to him.   I am sorry I wrote as I did in last Saturday's *Nation*
about his project (for his it was) of the Bright banquet.   But it
was a bad project, and is an intolerable idea—that is, to me.

Mr. John B. Dillon, referred to in the above, had died
only a few days before the letter was written.   He and
Mitchel had differed considerably on matters political, both
during the Young Ireland times and more recently.   But
their differences had never interfered with their friendship.
Mitchel's letters show that there were few men for whom
he had a greater regard and respect than John Dillon.

Towards the end of September, Father Kenyon and
John Martin returned to Ireland, and Mitchel was again
left alone.   He now began to prepare for returning to
America.   He had been nearly a year away, and he was
naturally anxious to rejoin his family.   It was clear to
him that he could not manage to bring them over to live
in France ; and the only alternative was to go back to
them in America.   On the 16th of October, there is a letter
to his brother William, in which I find this passage :—

I am going soon to America, but don't know what day yet.
We had an astonishing life of it while Father Kenyon was here
for a fortnight.   The worst of it was, he would hardly ever go to
bed.   As to the fine account he gives you of my health and spirits,
you must know I deliberately deceived the poor old fellow about
all that.   I knew I would never see him again, and tried to make
his visit pleasant.   I am neither in very good health nor in good
spirits at all.   How can I, with such prospects before me and my
children ?   What may become of me, indeed, matters little, but I
am wretched about them.

Towards the middle of October, he was ready to leave.

It was his last visit to France ; and he had a kind of presentiment that it would be so. With this feeling, he perhaps lingered a little longer than he otherwise would have done, paying farewell visits to friends. Here is his account of his last days in France :—

There is charming autumnal weather now in France, which I enjoy in an unquiet kind of way. *Profitons de nos derniers beaux jours.* I go to pay my last visits to certain friends, French and Irish ; to the family of Bramet at Choisy; to the Bayers in Paris, and the ladies kiss me on both cheeks and send kind messages to my family ; to the good Père Hogan at the Seminary of St. Sulpice; to M. Marie-Martin and his wife, at whose pleasant house I have often visited ; to my friends the Leonards, now returned from their sea-bathing, and to the worthy and admirable Mr. Doherty, aged, white-haired, yet still young in heart; also to the grave of my daughter Henrietta in the cemetery of Mont Parnasse, whither I carry a *laurieriin* (what we call laurustinus) in a large pot, and place it on the tombstone, and " Adieu !"

He took his passage on the *Pereire*, of the French Transatlantic line, and made his arrangements so as to join the ship at Brest, instead of at Havre, as on former occasions. He was anxious to see something of Bretagne, and, in particular, of Brest. He thought of Wolfe Tone and of the expedition that was to start from Brest harbour. The journey through Bretagne is described at some length in the " Journal." He arrived at Brest late at night, and the next morning had a few hours to walk about the town before going on board. When he went on board the *Pereire*, the captain at once recognized him ; he was the same captain who had commanded the ship *l'Europe*, in which Mitchel had come over the previous year. Mitchel had his last glimpse of France that October evening :—

I looked back until the last blue lines of the French coast faded into the evening mist. Perhaps it is the last time I shall ever see that fair and pleasant land. Yet who knows ? If this unnatural and poisonous *entente cordiale* happily come to an end in my time, I will certainly come again; and then I may have the chance of steaming out of the *Goulet* of Brest for another destination.   Anyhow, *Vive la France!*

Nothing further worthy of notice occurred until Mitchel once more, and for the fourth time in his life, landed at New York.

CHAPTER VII.

CLOSING YEARS AND DEATH.

1866—1875.

WITH the landing at New York, mentioned at the close of
the last chapter, the "Jail Journal Continuation" comes to
an end. Of the last eight and a half years of his life,
Mitchel has left us no account; and the materials for
writing the narrative of his life during this period are very
scanty. He wrote but few private letters during these
years. I shall, therefore, be obliged to tell the story of
John Mitchel's closing years very briefly. This is the less
to be regretted, firstly because, for the greater part of this
time, Mitchel's life was very uneventful; and secondly,
because, as already intimated, he never recovered, mentally
or physically, from the effects of his imprisonment in
Fortress Monroe. He never was the same man again.
No doubt there is a great deal of good writing in the *Irish
Citizen;* and the "History of Ireland" and "Letters in
Answer to Froude" show a literary faculty that would be
remarkable in any ordinary man. But for John Mitchel
these writings are rather below than above the average.
His best writing, both literary and political, was done
before he reached his fiftieth year.

Of Mitchel's changed appearance, after his release from
Fortress Monroe, I have received the following description
from a member of his family : " On first seeing him after

his release a great change was apparent. His figure, formerly so erect and even military in its carriage, was stooped a little, and the shoulders raised in a way that suggested a weak chest. He would have intervals of comparative ease and health, and then he would be gay and cheerful, and enter into all our pleasures ; but such moments were short-lived, and for the greater part of the remainder of his life, he was very delicate."

The voyage to France and back did him good, and for some few months after his return to America his health was better than it had been since his release. On landing in America, he went straight to Richmond, where his family were still living. He found them all well. His son James had been married during his absence in France to Miss Elizabeth Moseley, of Virginia.

In the late autumn of 1866, Mitchel entered into an arrangement with a New York publishing firm—the Sadleirs —by which he undertook to write a continuation of MacGeoghegan's "History of Ireland." In pursuance of this undertaking, he wrote his "History of Ireland from the Treaty of Limerick." He undertook to have the book ready within a year, and he afterwards regretted having thus limited himself. He had not time to make the book as good as he believed he could have made it. The book was finished and published in the autumn of 1867. During the year he was engaged upon this book, Mitchel continued to live at Richmond.

John Mitchel's "History of Ireland" is well known to many Irish readers. It is now the standard work upon that period of Irish history which it covers. I do not feel called on to criticise the book here ; but there is one feature in it which I may notice. In reading the history, I was much struck with the faculty which Mitchel there displays of adapting his style to the particular kind of composition in which he may for the time being be engaged.   The style of the *United Irishman* and the " Jail Journal " is certainly a very powerful style, but it is not exactly the style best adapted to historical writing.   But in the " History of Ireland," we find a style most admirably adapted to the work it has to do.   There are passages in this book which, if Mitchel had been an English instead of an Irish historian, would certainly have found a place in English "readers" as models of the historical style.

I have already referred to the split which took place in the Fenian organization shortly after Mitchel's last journey to France.   In the spring of 1867, while Mitchel was still living at Richmond, the two "wings" agreed upon a basis of reunion.   One leading term in the stipulation was that the presidency of the reunited brotherhood should be offered to and accepted by Mitchel.   Accordingly, on February 19, 1867, he received from a prominent leader of one of the " wings " the following telegram : " Saw Roberts.   All will unite under you.   Leaders of both branches ready to give way.   Wrote yesterday.   Answer."

To this telegram Mitchel at once replied by letter.   I find a copy of the letter preserved among his papers, and it is dated the same day as the telegram :—

DEAR SIR,
            I once more decline, for the reasons already explained to you, to participate in the Fenian movement as at present organized or rather disorganized.   I disbelieve in the existence of any fighting in Ireland, and in the possibility of making any fight there, while England continues at peace.   This has been my opinion for many years.   I have never yet joined in any appeal to my countrymen in America to contribute their money towards any such premature and impossible attempt.   It is but wasting their means, and, what is worse, it is wasting and using up their patriotic enthusiasm and destroying their trust in the faith of man.

I do not wish either your branch of the organization, or that of Mr. Roberts, to use my name in any manner whatsoever.

The refusal here expressed is precise enough ; but it does not seem to have been accepted as conclusive. On the 28th of the same month of February, I find that the following telegram was sent to Mitchel : " The National Convention of the Fenian Brotherhood of America, now in session in New York, have unanimously resolved to tender you the position of Chief Executive Officer of that Organization. The Convention awaits your reply. Answer immediately."

The telegram is signed by the president of the convention and another. I do not find any copy of the answer to this amongst Mitchel's papers. But I presume the answer was to the same effect as in the case of the former telegram. Certainly, he did not accept the post.

About a year after the above offer was made, Mitchel addressed to his friend John Martin two letters on Fenianism, in which he explained the grounds of his refusal. In these letters he gives a brief account of the position of the Fenian movement in America, and of the split which had taken place in the organization. He then proceeds :—

In this condition of affairs, you are aware that negotiations for *union* were held, with a very sincere desire, I believe, on the part of those two " presidents," to effect that combination, and withdraw themselves from under the heavy responsibility that weighed upon them. A " basis of union " was drawn up ; and the two " presidents," pursuant to that preliminary arrangement, came and offered to *me* the presidency of the joint and united brotherhood. Why to me ? I have had nothing to do with them or their organization for two years ; and very little before that time. I was not responsible for any of their doings or misdoings. I had not approved of any one of their enterprises, either on the side of Canada or on the side of Ireland. Whenever I had ventured to offer them any advice or give them any warning, it had been uniformly disregarded.

He next proceeds to give a rather amusing account of the position he would have found himself in had he accepted the offer of the Fenian leaders. He would have been constantly hindered in everything he tried to do by the " constitution " and the " senate," and so forth :—

" Constitutional " questions would have raged around me ; and a new division would have broken out immediately. Then, the instrument they call a constitution is in itself ridiculous ; and I, being acutely sensitive to ridicule, would feel ashamed of occupying a position in which I should be expected to carry on the sham of a provisional government, and to commission " generals " for an imaginary army. All this, even if it were not illegal, is still ludicrous. So I would have begun by abolishing that " constitution," by dismissing all secretaries of state, disbanding all " paid organizers," cancelling all pretended " commissions " to officers, exhorting the circles everywhere to keep their money within their own power until there should arise an opportunity to use it with effect, and exhorting the people to attach their military companies to the militia service of their respective states,—*and to wait.*

The objections taken to the Fenian plans and principles in these letters come mainly under two heads—(1) He argues that it was quite futile for the Irish to attempt, as proposed by the Fenians, to fight England while England was at peace ; and (2) he argues that the whole plan of the Fenian organization, and the *imperium in imperio* which they proposed to create in the United States, was inconsistent with their duties as American citizens. Many good and earnest Irishmen were deeply offended with Mitchel for preaching such doctrine. In his later years he used to tell how, shortly after these letters appeared, he was accosted in the streets of some western city by a man whom he had never seen before. The stranger spoke of all the conspiring that had been done, and of all the efforts and sacrifices that had been made by the Fenians in behalf of Ireland. "And now, sir," he added, "you tell us that we have been making d——d fools of ourselves all the time." "Well, sir," replied Mitchel, "you know very well that you have." "It may be so," answered the other, "but you are not the man that should say it." Mitchel, who had an exceptionally keen sense of the ludicrous, used to laugh in telling this story. Still, there was an element of reason in the objection. The idea at bottom of it was that Mitchel's teachings in reference to Fenianism and the impracticability of fighting England while at peace were inconsistent with the doctrine which he had himself preached in Ireland in 1848. I am not particularly concerned to repel this charge of inconsistency, since, as already stated, I do not regard it as any reproach to say of a man that he has modified his opinions with experience. Still, that need not prevent us from examining very briefly in how far the charge is true. I have already tried to show that Mitchel's scheme of policy in 1848, as stated by him at the opening of that year, did not contemplate an immediate "rising" or war with England. No doubt Mitchel was to some extent, though not so much as several others of the Young Irelanders, carried away by the excitement of the French Revolution, and after that event the tone of the *United Irishman* became more warlike. It is impossible to doubt that Mitchel saw clearly enough that the ultimate result of his policy, if generally acted on, must be war ; and that his system of offering a general passive resistance to so-called law, and "here and there, whenever occasion offered, trying the steel," was mainly advocated by him as a means of working the people up to the fighting spirit and accustoming them to stand fire. But when all this has been allowed, it still remains to inquire whether there was not any essential difference between the Irish situation in 1848 and the Irish situation in 1867. In the view which Mitchel took, there was one important difference ; and in this one respect he certainly had somewhat modified his opinion with experience. In 1848, he had hopes, and strong hopes, of bringing the northern Protestants round to the national side. He was one of them himself. He had lived among them ; and he knew their good points as well as their bad points. One main object which he set before himself in his writings for the *United Irishman* was to bring the northern Protestants round to the national side. His well-known dictum, " The Pope may be Antichrist, but, Orangemen of the North, he serves no ejectments in Ulster," is only one specimen of a kind of exhortation by which Mitchel sought to wean the minds of the Protestant democracy of the North from that blind bigotry for which they had been conspicuous, and to win them to nationality. Nor was this exhortation entirely without effect. During the few months which immediately preceded Mitchel's transportation, he had many letters from Protestant farmers which justified him in believing that he was making some way. But whatever may have been the impression which he produced upon the northern Protestants, it proved transient. The subsequent course of events made it clear to Mitchel that there was no hope of bringing them round to the national side. There was still in them a sufficient force of unreasoning bigotry to make it possible for their masters to play upon them at will. The Fenian movement was distinguished from the Young Ireland movement, amongst other differences, by this—it included only the Catholic masses, and made no effort to win over the Protestant section of the population. Mitchel hoped at one time that Ireland, united, might be able to shake off the grip of England without foreign aid, or, at least, like America, to keep up the struggle until foreign aid came.   But he never believed and never taught that the Catholic population of Ireland could hope, without foreign aid, to fight the Protestant section of the population and England at the same time.   And there was another essential difference between the two movements.   Mitchel, as we have seen, had always been an opponent of secret conspiracy in Ireland.   Fenianism was a secret conspiracy ; and with most of its secrets, as Mitchel clearly foresaw would prove to be the case, the Government of England was intimately acquainted.   In this respect, at all events, Mitchel's teaching in 1867 was entirely consistent with what he had taught in 1848.

As regards the second point insisted upon in the letters to Martin—that Fenianism in Amercia was an *imperium in imperio*, and inconsistent with the duties of its members as American citizens—Mitchel was only repeating what he had taught since his first coming to the United States. The first lecture which John Mitchel ever delivered in America was delivered at Boston, on December 28, 1853. The subject was "The Duties of Adopted Citizens." I extract the following passages :—

The citizen, as a citizen, belongs absolutely and exclusively to the State ; that is to say, to the community which protects him, which gives him civic privileges, rights, and powers, which guarantees to him the secure exercise of them by its laws, which guards the sacredness of home, and the quiet enjoyment of the fruits of his industry ; that community has a clear title to his sole and undivided allegiance.   To the interests, the exigencies, the honour and dignity of that community, his best exertions, his very life and fortune stand in pledge.   And it makes no difference whatever whether he be a native-born citizen, a citizen fully naturalized, or one who is claiming and waiting for the privileges of naturalization.   In any of all these cases, it would be simply treason towards the commonwealth if he should pay more regard to the national claims or necessities, to the rights or to the wrongs of any other land—even the land where his mother bore him and where his father's bones are laid—than to those of the new country whose nationality he has voluntarily chosen to take upon him.

This is a principle which ought to be clearly understood, explicitly avowed, and universally established. If any refugee, then, from any European country, goes into an American court, declares his intention of becoming an American citizen, and so clothes himself with the character of American nationality, only that he may use that nationality, and the security and freedom of action which it gives him, to serve the interests of any other community on earth, otherwise than any native citizen might lawfully do, he simply commits a fraud upon the American people.

The beliefs expressed in this passage were still Mitchel's beliefs in 1867 ; and he did not shrink from applying them to the case of Fenianism because the doing so was painful to himself, and was sure to give bitter offence to many men whose good opinion he valued.

Early in October, 1867, an event of importance occurred in the Mitchel family. The nature of this event can be gathered from the following letter written by Mitchel to his sister, Mrs. Irvine, on the 3rd of October in that year :—

Minnie was married to-day to Colonel Page. Ceremony performed by his father. The affair was very quiet, early this morning in St. Paul's Church. No cards.

So there, in a few words, you have the bare facts. Page, I suppose you know, is a young lawyer with nothing but his profession. . . .

Next thing I have to tell you is that we are going to remove to New York, where I am about to re-establish my weekly paper— title, *The Irish Citizen.* James and I are going on at once ; but, as we are under rent here till the 1st of December, I will not disturb the rest of the family till then. I have been in New York myself, making my preliminary arrangements, and only came here for the wedding, and am going back to-night. I will send the paper to your address when it comes out. . . .

We are all well, Isabel growing very tall ; and if we can only get money enough to live upon, we shall do.

Mr. Page had been a colonel in the Confederate service. He had turned to the practice of the law when the war was over.   He met Miss Mitchel in Richmond.

Immediately after his daughter's marriage, Mitchel left for New York to establish his paper.   The names of his two former papers in America had been the *Citizen* and the *Southern Citizen*.   This time it was to be the *Irish Citizen*.   As soon as he got the paper fairly started, he took a house in Fordham, a suburb of New York.   Here he was joined by his family towards the close of 1867. They all lived together in the house at Fordham for a year and a half—John Mitchel and his wife and daughter, James Mitchel and his wife, and Colonel and Mrs. Page.   John Mitchel enjoyed this time greatly.   There were pretty grounds and a small patch of garden attached to the house.   Mitchel liked to work in this garden when he had any time to spare.   But he did not often have time to spare.   The work of his newspaper gave him quite enough to do in the then feeble state of his health.   He did not go much into society during these later years.   The interchange of quiet visits among some very intimate friends was all he was able for.

Under date of December 4, 1867, I find a letter to Mrs. John Dillon.   This is the first letter which Mitchel wrote to Mrs. Dillon since the death of her husband in the autumn of 1866.   He naturally refers to that event :—

The arrival of your kind letter, or letters (one to Minnie and one to me), has stirred me up to do what for a long time I have been intending to do—write to you.   Dear lady, what could I say ?   I was in France.   I had just received the two little photographs which you were kind enough to send me, when suddenly the news came to me of John Dillon's death.   What could I say? A few days before I had been writing in a disparaging sense of a movement in which he was much interested —the Bright banquet. Of course, I hated myself for having uttered a word that could grate upon his ear. But I suppose that in fact he never knew that I had done it. I hope not. I have known in my time many good men, but one nobler, more generous-hearted, more pure and gallant than John Dillon I never knew— never hope to know.

In the spring of the following year, he wrote a letter to Mrs. A. M. Sullivan, of Dublin, in which he gives an interesting account of his life at Fordham. Part of this letter has since been published in the *Irish Monthly*. I take the following passage :—

We are now living at Fordham, a village about eight miles from New York, in a very pretty country, which is just putting on its spring robes, and is going to be an Elysium all summer. But we have passed through the most savage winter ever experienced here, and have survived it. We have, living all together in one house at Fordham, my son James and his Virginia wife, my daughter Minnie and her Virginia husband, my own wife and youngest daughter, Isabel—not forgetting myself. All join in sending greetings to you, and some of them can do this feelingly, having gone through something analagous, *only more so.*

During all this time, Mitchel was hard at work on the *Irish Citizen.* The *Irish Citizen* was the last paper he published. I have already expressed the opinion that this paper was not equal in vigour of writing to the previous papers edited by him ; but the editorial matter was, of course, written in a style that was far above the average of newspaper writing, and every now and then we come upon a piece of writing that reminds us of the *United Irishman.* The first number of the paper appeared on October 19, 1867 ; the last number on July 27, 1872. In American politics the paper was strongly Democratic. The policy pursued by President Grant and his advisers towards the South was the subject of constant criticism and attack. In Irish politics the line taken was the same that Mitchel had always taken since 1848. He had no faith in any good coming from the Home Rule agitation then going on in Ireland under the leadership of Mr. Butt. As was usual with him, he spoke out what he thought on the subject, without stopping to ask whether his plain speaking would be acceptable to his friends.

The literary work of the paper was done partly by Mitchel himself, and partly by a gentleman who wrote under the *nom de plume* of Major Muskerry. Mitchel's *nom de plume* in the *Irish Citizen* was Professor Cornelius O'Shaughnessy. The reviews and notices of books were mainly written by Mitchel. There are some long and elaborate reviews, as, for example, the review of Prendergast's " Cromwellian Settlement of Ireland " in the first and second numbers. But, as a rule, the notices of books in the *Irish Citizen* are much shorter than in Mitchel's previous papers. I extract the following notice of a book on " Our Lady of Lourdes," not because of any special literary merit in the passage, but because I believe that the subject is one upon which many of Mitchel's countrymen and countrywomen will be interested to learn his views :—

Among the mountains of the Higher Pyrenees, where the seven valleys of the Lavedan come together, each bringing down its bright stream to form the Gave, stands the small town or village of Lourdes. Some twelve years ago few persons dwelling at a distance even knew of the existence of the village ; but now the town, with its rocks of Massabielle, forms the object of a vast and constant pilgrim procession ; the railroad line which serves that Pyrenean country has made a detour in its course to accommodate the multitudes ; strangers of every European nation, and of many parts of America, are to be found thronging the villages and the country round, all making pilgrimage to the spot where the Blessed Virgin is said to have appeared daily to the innocent little girl

Bernadette. All the miraculous incidents connected with that place of pilgrimage have taken place since 1858—celestial apparitions, miraculous cures, and conversions; and now a magnificent church crowns the rock, the grotto where the child was spoken to by her unearthly visitant is enclosed and rendered more accessible with its healing spring; and on the arrival of a train, especially in summer, processions are formed in the court of the railway station—girls in white, old men, matrons with children in their arms; and they move in solemn march, with banners and chanting, to the scene of the miracle. And this, in the latter half of the nineteenth century! Yes, even so; and better might it be for the said century if these things did not seem to it so incredible and grotesque. It believes in Lottie Fowler the clairvoyante, or in some seventh daughter of a seventh daughter, and finds nothing revolting in *their* visions and miracles! Be this as it may, the full and circumstantial narrative of the favoured childhood of Bernadette, with the testimony of such as have vouched for cures and the like, is surely worth considering. Independently of the visions and wonderful cures, which every reader is welcome to believe or disbelieve, the book is curiously interesting for its picture of the life and ways of the simple people of those French valleys, into which, we trust, King William's Goth will never penetrate.

The concluding sentence has reference to the events then happening in France. The notice was written during the siege of Paris.

I believe it was in the *Irish Citizen* that Mitchel published his original translation of the pope's *non possumus*. He describes the anxiety and efforts of Victor Emmanuel to induce Pius IX. to accept the situation and abdicate his claim to temporal sovereignty. To all which overtures, says Mitchel, the grand old pope has only one answer—*non possumus*, which is ecclesiastical Latin for, "I'll see you d——d first."

Shortly after the starting of the *Irish Citizen*, appeared the letters to John Martin, to which I have already referred some pages back. These "Letters on Fenianism" seriously injured the circulation of the *Irish Citizen*. Mitchel knew very well when he wrote the letters that they would have this effect. But that consideration weighed little with him. In the *Irish Citizen*, as in every other paper he ever published, he wrote what he believed to be right and true, without stopping to ask what might be the consequence of such writing upon his own prospects.

In the September of 1868, John Mitchel became a grandfather. His daughter, Mrs. Page, had a son, called after his grandfather, John Mitchel Page. When the child was old enough to run about and talk a little, he became a great favourite with his grandfather. For the remainder of his life, John Mitchel's greatest pleasure was to play with this child. He was very particular about his desk and papers ; would allow no one in the house to interfere with them. To this rule the little grandson soon became an exception. He would ransack the desk with absolute impunity, looking for bananas, which his grandfather would hide in order that he might have the pleasure of watching the little fellow look for them. His youngest daughter, Isabel, was also a great pet with him. He would enter into all her plans and pleasures and plays with the keenest enjoyment. Afterwards, when she grew up to be a tall young lady, he seemed as if he could never quite realize the fact. To the day of his death she was to him his " dear little daughter." Isabel, like her eldest sister, was a Catholic.

After living for about a year and a half at Fordham, Mitchel found that the constant going in and out of town was too much for him. He took a house on Carleton Avenue, Brooklyn. He lived in Brooklyn for the rest of his life, except about a year and a half spent in New York, and some few months spent at the seaside or in visiting Ireland. The move to Brooklyn took place about the middle of 1869.

In the autumn of 1869, John Mitchel had visitors whose coming was a great pleasure to him. Shortly previous to this time his sister Henrietta had been married to his life-long friend, John Martin. In the fall of 1869, Mr. and Mrs. Martin visited America. They spent the greater part of the winter of 1869 at Mitchel's house in Brooklyn. This visit seemed to cheer and enliven him wonderfully. He was as much attached to Martin as ever, although they had come to differ widely regarding Irish politics. Mr. Martin had re-entered public life in Ireland. At first he went upon the old lines of the days before '48, and advocated the repeal of the union. But subsequently he joined the movement for " Home Rule " led by Isaac Butt.

Mitchel and Martin had the same interminable talks and smokes as of old. They disputed over Irish politics ; could hardly ever agree ; abused one another, and loved one another as much as ever.

It was during this visit of John Martin's that Mitchel first showed any inclination for playing whist. In his active, busy days he had never cared for card-playing, though several of his relatives and of his friends—notably Father Kenyon—were very fond of whist. He began by playing to please John Martin, who liked the game. Eventually he came to like it himself. For the remainder of his life a quiet game of whist in the evenings seemed restful to him, and a relief from the labour of writing.

Some time during this winter of 1869–70, there was a great meeting at the Cooper Institute in New York, in aid of the families of Allen, Larkin, and O'Brien, who, as every Irishman knows, were hanged at Manchester. Both Mitchel and Martin were present, and spoke on this occasion. They also made trips together to Boston and to Philadelphia during the same winter. At both cities demonstrations were organized in their honour.

At last, in the spring of 1870, the visit of Mr. and Mrs. Martin came to an end. On the 20th of April, John Mitchel writes to his brother William :—

As to John Martin and Henty, their visit is drawing to a close, and after taking their berths on the 23rd, they have been with difficulty induced to postpone their departure for one week. So on the 30th they go. My health has prevented me from doing much to promote the movement and hilarity of the occasion, and I would fear there was a certain dulness in it but for the *remuant* spirit of Henty and the eagerness of her many friends to entertain and amuse the pair. So you imagine I might go to Ireland and live quietly. Live on *what*, my boy ? Could I start another *United Irishman* now under the new coercion law ? And wouldn't I look, on the whole, rather like that penitent and broken-winged pigeon of La Fontaine, coming back to his nest ? No, that would not do, even supposing that the enemy would let me live anywhere within your four seas. I must go on to wear my harness here, though it *galls*, as you may possibly have surmised, from my occa- sional sourness and savageness in writing my odious articles. . . . For myself, I am better ; as well perhaps as I can expect to be now at the age of fifty-five; and after the various sorts of trials I have gone through ; not very active now on my feet, which is hard on me certainly, who have always taken and needed so much exercise. We are just going to make a May moving, away from Carleton Avenue to Lafayette ditto. Our dear Minnie and her department of the household are to go up town in New York, which vexes us.

The " May moving " took place early in that month, Colonel and Mrs. Page going to live in New York. The rest of the Mitchel family removed to Lafayette Avenue, Brooklyn, where they lived until the spring of 1872.

From the new home on Lafayette Avenue, he writes to his sister Margaret (Mrs. Irvine) in the summer of 1870 :—

The multitude and magnitude of my epistolary debts prevent me sometimes from trying to pay them. Indeed, I never would write to anybody at all if I could help it. People in the house do write, and then letters come in reply, and I read them, and thus sponge upon the resources and earnings of others. . . . For ourselves, we have nothing new. You know we are living now far apart from Minnie, and we miss her extremely; but, on the whole, the change is for the better, and the system works well. Tell Henty this. I am hammering away at the *Irish Citizen,* and agitating myself much about the Franco-German war. I wonder what H. Irvine's predilections are. As for John Martin, he is for France all the time. We have passed a very hot summer here, the thermometer here, high up in Brooklyn, in the highest part of the city, hanging on a north wall, where the sun never comes, and in a street shaded by high trees, marking some days 96°, but often 88° to 90°. . . . There is great abundance of grapes and of the finest peaches, quite cheap. In fact, peaches form a very large part of the supply of food here in the season, and oysters in *their* season—and what more would people have?

Your son John has entered college, has he not? I hope he will do better there than his uncle ever did. I was very careless about preparation—saw always how easily premiums were to be won, and actually never won one. After I had taken my degree, I regretted that I had not taken just one prize, and regretted it too late. . . . Now, is there anything I have not mentioned? Yes, I am pretty well myself, better than I was last year or in the spring, and can walk better and farther. Jenny is quite well, as usual, and James and his wife. Will you give my warmest regards to Hill and all the household, to Matilda and her household, to William, Mary, John Martin, and Henty?

After all, I find it so easy to write a scrap of a letter when the pen is once dipped in the ink, that I think I will write some more soon. *Il n'y a que le premier pas qui coûte*—as the saint said, after walking half a mile with his head in his teeth. It had been cut off, you understand. Tell John Martin that our good old friend, Mr. Doherty, continues to send me newspapers from Paris. He is very ancient and very white-haired now, yet he writes a very distinct hand.

Adieu, dear Margaret; and don't ever infer from my silence that I forget my own folk, or am indifferent about them or anything that concerns them.

In another letter to the same correspondent, written

more than a year later, he returns to the subject of his nephew and Trinity College :—

I hear sometimes about you and yours, and how your son, my namesake, was about to encounter an examination at T.C.D. That, I hope, has come off all right.   John Irvine will improve on the precedents which his uncle left him in that institution *juxta Dublin ;* for his said uncle, while on the one hand he never was actually cautioned, on the other hand got no honours.

My poor Minnie is all alone beyond the mountains, six hundred miles from here, in a little town upon a river which runs Mississippi-ward.   Yesterday we had a letter from her, with likeness of her famous little boy, who is certainly a first-rate buffer.   I have travelled a good deal this winter, but not in her direction ; and, in fact, the town of Charleston is further off than the mere distance would seem to indicate.   For there is still a small part of the way to be made by stage-coaches over such roads as exist only in the United States.

We are all here much as usual ; living pretty quietly, although every night Brooklyn is the scene of at least one ghastly murder, not to speak of New York.   But then, you see, there are so many people still alive that the dead ones are scarcely missed.

It is Sunday evening.   Jenny and Isabel have come in after hearing a lady preach in the pulpit of a very large church, near this house, a magnificent Gothic building of the highest ecclesiological and architectonical pretensions, but belonging to a species of religionists called " Dutch Reformed "—Christians, I suspect, of some sort.   None of our people had ever been in the church before, or had ever heard a woman preach before.   They are quite pleased.

It gave me great pleasure to hear that my good friend, William Glenny, is well, and leading a pleasant and easy life.   He is one of the few friends I have over in Ireland, outside of our own kindred, whom I would like to see once more.

During these years—1870 and 1871—he kept, as he says himself, "hammering away at the *Irish Citizen."*   But each successive year the difficulty of continuous mental exertion became greater.

His daughter Minnie, with her husband, left New York and went to live in West Virginia in 1871. She took her little son with her. John Mitchel sadly missed the company of his grandchild. He wrote frequently to his daughter; and asked constantly for accounts of the " buffer "—his pet name for the child. His letters to his daughter are characterized by a mixture of playfulness and affection. The following passage, taken from a letter written towards the close of 1871, may serve as a specimen :—

. . . The Russian grand duke is here to-day. Wet day; so the procession cannot take place. I suppose it stands for to-morrow. All the nice people in New York are greatly agitated about this; and I am sure, if you were here, you would put on a chignon and a pannier, and get yourself escorted to some place from whence you could see the sweet fellow. Isabel would like to do that, but I am stern and inexorable. We don't belong, you know, to *l'écume;* and this prince has been completely taken possession of by a committee of the nicest people.

I write this, as you perceive by the printed heading, in the office of our printers, as I wait for proofs. But I won't post it until to-morrow. Don't mind, dear Minnie, if you find me slow and irregular in correspondence. I hear of you through your letters to others. Otherwise I would persecute you with letters myself.

In the month of May, 1872, he gave up his house in Lafayette Avenue, and took a cottage at the seaside for the summer. The place he selected was on Long Island, and was called Port Washington. Mrs. Page and her little son spent two or three months of this summer at the cottage at Port Washington ; and John Mitchel was very glad to have his daughter and his grandson back with him again. It was shortly after this move to the sea that he resolved to discontinue the *Irish Citizen.* For some time past the difficulty of doing the work needed for carrying on the paper had become greater and greater, chiefly for which reason the paper was discontinued in the summer of 1872. The last number appeared on July 27, 1872. It contained a notice that the paper would be discontinued for the present. It also contained two literary papers. The first was entitled, "Filia Dolorosa; the last of the Dauphines;" the second, "The Three False Dauphins."

The months which succeeded the discontinuance of the *Irish Citizen* were months of complete rest for John Mitchel. The cottage by the sea was within pleasant driving distance of the summer residences of several of his most valued friends; among others, Mr. Richard O'Gorman and Christian S. Sloane, the latter a gentleman whose friendship he had enjoyed from the time of his first arrival in New York. His health improved while at the seaside; and to those around him he seemed happier and in better health during the fall of 1872 than he had been for several years before.

During this sojourn at the sea, there came another grandchild, this time a girl, the daughter of Mitchel's son James. This little child was also a great pet with her grandfather while she lived.

In the month of November, they left the seaside and took apartments on West Fifty-sixth Street, in New York. The improvement in his health proved to be but transient. After the removal to New York, his health became much the same as it had been before his sojourn at the sea.

I infer from Mitchel's correspondence that it must have been during the summer or fall of 1872 that Mr. Froude made his lecturing tour in the United States. Mr. Froude seems to have felt rather outraged by the idea that the Irish, when driven out of their own country by England, should find a home in the United States. In a course of lectures which he delivered in the eastern states, he laboured hard to excite a prejudice against the Irish. These lectures had the cleverness, plausibility, and charm of style which are familiar to the reader of Mr. Froude's historical works.* It was feared by the Irish and their friends that the lectures and the book might produce something of the effect desired by the lecturer. Mitchel was requested by the proprietors of the *Irish-American* newspaper to answer Froude. During the winter of 1872–73 he wrote for the *Irish-American* a series of papers, in which he dealt pretty fully with Froude's slanders. His heart was in the work, and there is a great deal of his old fire in the writing. The letters were afterwards published in book form under the title of " The Crusade of the Period." This was the last of John Mitchel's books. I take the following passage as a specimen of the style. It commences with a quotation from Mr. Froude :—

"They (the Normans) were born rulers of men, and were forced by the same necessity which has brought the decrepit kingdoms of Asia under the authority of England and Russia, to take the management, eight centuries ago, of the anarchic nations of Western Europe."

It was hard on the Norman people ! For these poor devoted rulers of men were forced " by the same necessity" to do much forgery, perjury, and murder, to carry out their missioned task. Neither will our rulers of men altogether give us up when we escape from under their clutch. Their care and sympathy follow us round the world. Here, for example, the Irish-Americans, who have been living on good enough terms with native American and other citizens, and who have been doing much honest work here, making themselves independent, marrying and giving in marriage, procreating a good breed, which is to have its full share in the labour and the thought and the honourable effort of every kind upon this continent in the future—these Irish-Americans find themselves followed, even here, from time to time, by agents and

---

* Immediately after his return from America, Froude published his " English in Ireland."

emissaries of those blessed governors of men, whose task is to lower us in the eyes of our fellow-citizens, and to make them understand that we are not fit to be trusted as citizens of this or any other country. These English have taken direction of our people once for all, and cannot without a pang give up the management of us. Though we take the wings of the morning and flee to the uttermost ends of the earth, even there will their hand lead us and their right hand guide us! Even here we find at every turn a vigilant English "ruler of men" cooling our friends, heating our enemies, carefully warning our neighbours that we are false, treacherous, cowardly, and cruel ; that we never knew what to do with our own country, when we had one, and will surely do what in us lies to ruin America, as we ruined Ireland.

So far as concerns the argument of the letters and the mastery of Irish history which they display, I must refer the reader to the book itself. In the fifth chapter he will find Mitchel's answer to a certain well-known passage in " The English in Ireland." I mean the passage in which Froude charges that the Irish, having been endowed by Providence with as lovely a land as the sun ever shone on, " had pared its forests to the stump until it shivered in damp and desolation." Mitchel shows very conclusively (1) that it was not the Irish, but the English settlers and undertakers who " pared the forest to the stump ; " and (2) that Froude (assuming him to be familiar with the authorities he refers to) must have been perfectly well aware of the true state of the facts. Indeed, even to the casual reader, it must seem strange that the native Irish, having preserved their forests from time immemorial, should be suddenly seized with a desire to " pare them to the stump," just at the very time when the land of Ireland was passing into the hands of English and Scotch adventurers.

On the New Year's Day of 1873, Mitchel writes to John Martin from his home on West Fifty-sixth Street :—

MY DEAR JOHN MARTIN,

Happy new year and many of them to you and to Henty. It needs the beginning of a new year, or some other remarkable date, to stir me up to the point of writing a letter. Yet I have here in my desk a part of a letter which I had commenced to you two months ago, only one page of it written; and this has been lying open in the said desk staring me in the face every time I sat down to it, and reproaching me for not yet having finished it. I mean the letter. As I have no newspaper now, my species of circular, addressed to all my friends, has ceased to be current, and certainly I ought to remember that, and remind you all of my existence by other means. From William I had a pleasant letter lately, and also one from Matilda not long ago, and "I feel bad" about it, as we say in this great country. As for the household news, about moving of residence, about health, and the like, I know that you get intelligence from time to time, so that I have little or nothing really to tell. We are housed this winter in more comfortable quarters, I think, than we ever had in New York or Brooklyn. The French plan of building large houses to accommodate many families, with a hall door on each lobby, is becoming usual here; and in one of these we have a regular *appartement*, everything within our own door, including a good kitchen, spacious bath-room, the whole heated by steam-heaters, which we find very satisfactory. And we have an "elevator" or dumb waiter for bringing up all parcels. In short, housekeeping is here reduced to its minimum of botheration and of uncleanness.

Well, I suppose you know all this already. As for me, I am tolerably well; quite as well or better than when you were in Brooklyn. You have also got over your late delicacy, so that both you and I may live through the year which begins this morning.

I left instructions for the *Irish-American* to be forwarded to you from the office on account of the articles I am contributing to it touching Froude—a name odious to me. I am now a penny-a-liner, working at some such tariff as that, and writing is more and more irksome to me, unless I am well paid. Who, for example, is to pay me for these lines I am writing now? It seems to me also that I am falling gradually into the habit of using long words and roundabout expressions so common with the gentlemen of my craft. If I am to speak of boys, I say juveniles; if of cows, bovines; if dogs, canines. If a thing happened, I say an incident transpired—for every letter *counts*.

I was very sorry indeed, as we all were, to hear of your severe and tedious sickness, aggravated, as I surmise, by disappointment and disgust about public affairs. My dear John, I feared for you that disappointment and disgust. You will console yourself with the consciousness that you have been honestly striving to do what you thought your duty. About this I will not worry myself nor worry you any more.

We get now and then an Irish newspaper from you, so I can see your handwriting; but I don't read the printed part much. I know generally what is going on in Ireland.

That scoundrel Froude has made a failure here, except in the matter of money profit. There, I suspect, his "mission" has been a success. I never saw the man, and don't know where he is now; but possibly he is organizing Orange Lodges, a highly suitable business for him. We hear from Minnie sometimes; had a letter yesterday with the latest *bons mots* of her remarkable son. They have been blocked up by winter weather down there in West Virginia, and it takes nearly a fortnight to bring us a letter.

A few weeks after this letter there is another to his sister, Mrs Dickson. I extract the following passages :—

You miss the *Citizen*. I am glad to hear it. I wish my fellow-creatures to miss the *Citizen*. I have stopped it out of spite to mankind. But still, as that weekly circular is no longer issued, I perceive the obligation it leaves upon me to recall myself to the memory of my folks in some other way. I have been and am now writing for the *Irish-American* a series of articles on Froude's book and lectures, which you appear to have heard of but not to have seen. Well, they are to be printed in a book, and I will send half a dozen copies to Newry, of which you will take one. I don't know whether you will like it much, for it is written with vindictive spite.

No, James has not yet commenced any new business or occupation; but he must soon. It is not so easy for an ex-Confederate now to get on well in this country. Not that people really think anything the worse of a man on that account; but it is thought nice, or, at least, is found profitable in the truly loyal part of the population, to affect disapproval and to form and cherish a sort of public opinion which is in favour of keeping the rebels out in the cold.   Our personal friends here are the Sloanes, O'Gormans, Braniques, Purroys, Serranos, Miss Christy, and the courtly Miss Maxwells, and our own cousins, the Hasletts of Brooklyn.   These last two families are at a distance of eight or ten miles from us, with an arm of the sea to cross; so we do not see them as often as we wish and as I hope they wish. . . .

On the whole, however, I do hate this city and this country, and would like nothing so well as the chance of spending the remainder of my days amongst my own people.   But *que voulez-vous ?*   I suppose, if I were in Ireland, I would be no less discontented with all their Home Rule bother, and I would soon get myself into new troubles.   It is my mission to get into troubles with every government and in every country.   I only wonder that I never saw the inside of a French gaol.   No doubt, if I had lived there long enough, and if I could express myself as clearly in French as I can in English, I should have had that experience to add to my others.   As it is, I believe I am the only person living who has been made a prisoner of state by two governments one after another.   As for my attempt to hold General Dix responsible for his lawless outrage upon me, I have no more chance of succeeding in it than of getting a verdict against St. Peter.

Dear Matilda, I wish I were at Tullycairne, and could stroll down to the Lagan and wade a little.   You tell us of the death of my good friend, Thomas Crawford, a man for whom I believe I had more real affection than for any of my County Down friends and acquaintances.   I say County Down, for there was a Tipperary man whom I did love still better.   My recollection of Thomas Crawford, and of his stately and once beautiful wife, is one of the pleasant memories of my old young days.

The "Tipperary man" here referred to was Father John Kenyon. He says, "there *was*," etc., because Father Kenyon was then dead. He had died at Templederry in the spring of 1869.

During this winter of 1872–73, Mitchel also contributed

certain articles to Appleton's Cyclopædia, at the request of the publishers. The subjects he selected to write on were the "Brehon Laws," and "Languages and Literature of the Celts." He was offered other articles, but did not feel able to undertake them.

In the spring of 1872 the Mitchels moved from West Fifty-sixth Street to Lexington Avenue. Here they lived for about a year—until the spring of 1874. During this year Mitchel's health continued to fail rapidly, and he became much feebler. In the summer of 1873, domestic griefs came. His son James lost his wife, and within a week after her death the little daughter, who had been such a pet with her grandfather, followed her mother to the grave. Mitchel felt keenly for his son, and the affliction told upon his health.

In the fall of 1873, he was invited by the *New York Herald* to write a series of articles on the policy of the Administration in the South, and especially in New Orleans. He declined to do it. As he grew feebler in health and less able for work, it seemed as though his interest in political matters outside of Ireland grew fainter, and his thoughts tended more and more strongly towards the subject which had always been the chief one with him. During these closing years he took an intense and eager interest in the course of events in Ireland. But his old energy and power of work had deserted him. It was with the utmost effort that he was able to do such literary and lecturing work as had to be done in order to procure the necessary funds. In the month of September, 1873, he writes to his brother William :—

The worst of it is, I have been greatly debilitated, partly by sickness, all this summer, and have been actually unable to do what you call my usual literary work. . . . Now you have the whole of it, because you ask it. The weary summer is now nearly over, and the season of work and of better health (as I trust) is beginning. You know how generally the summer of this country suspends work and prostrates energy. I revive somewhat already, and suppose that I shall hammer on, at something, deliver perhaps some stupid lectures, and finish the literary tasks that I have set myself, and so possibly tide over. You may think it strange, and may even reproach me that I have kept my troubles to myself, but I do usually try to " consume my own smoke." Even now I would not say a word to you about it all but for your own earnest demand.

Dr. Johnson has passed two evenings since his return from Europe. He describes your condition as improved from what it was, and he is vastly impressed by Hill Irvine's big mill. Also he passed several immortal evenings, with suppers of the gods, in London, and on the whole saw, in his two months or so, more places, institutions, personages, and cities of articulate-speaking men than any tourist I ever heard of. He was especially delighted with John Martin and Henrietta, and is, in a mild way, a Home Ruler. If the Irish would only unite! he exclaims. Here we are tolerably well, except myself, and I fear I must add except Isabel, who is not in her usual health all this summer. She is better, however, and is out to-day " flying around," in the phrase of this great country. Well, now I have told you nearly all my dismal news, and, whatever may befall me, make sure that I am your affectionate brother and friend.

And two months later there is another letter to the same correspondent :—

As to my worldly affairs, I perceive that I am found out. Others as well as you have discovered me, and I need not tell you how humiliating to me is this " testimonial " movement. . . . All well here. Our best and dearest Minnie is with us, together with her first son, and is now the comfortable and proud mother of another of the same. His father is not in New York, but is expected in a few days. In truth, I have no trouble in this world except impecuniosity. Actually there is no other. I have good friends. My sons and daughters, what are left of them, are capital. . . . I am meditating a tremendous letter to John Martin.

The cruellest privation I experience from want of unlimited funds is, that I cannot afford to go over to Clonmel and offer myself for the representation of Tipperary.

The "testimonial movement," to which Mr. Mitchel here refers, was a movement set on foot by some friends and admirers of his in Ireland. It was considered that he had so far "merited well of his country" as to make it the duty of Irishmen to see that he suffered no pecuniary inconvenience by reason of his failing health and inability to work. A sum of about $10,000 was collected in a short time and presented to him.

During these later years, he could easily have earned all the money he needed by lecturing, had his health permitted. He had numbers of invitations every winter. After he gave up the *Citizen*, he lectured a little now and then. In the winter of 1873–74 he visited St. Louis, Milwaukee, Detroit, and Chicago, lecturing at each of these cities. I find a letter from St. Louis, written by Mitchel to his wife a few days before the Christmas of 1873 :—

All is over here. Two lectures and a great banquet of Knights of St. Patrick, with military parade, etc. Everything passed off well. . . .

I found the travel of two nights and days without stopping a very fatiguing piece of work, and certainly arrived here in wretched condition. Yet, strange to say, on Sunday morning I rose fresh and strong, and have continued to improve ever since. I am now, in fact, a good deal better and stronger than when I left home. I am to quit this on Friday, and to spend this Christmas Day at the house of Mr. Tansey, president of the knights. Tell James I have met all his friends here, and I find that he has many warm ones.

He specially enjoyed visiting St. Louis and Chicago. There were a number of young Irish-Americans in both of those cities whom he liked, and who liked him.

During the same winter he accepted an invitation to

lecture at Washington. The lecture was already announced, when he was taken very ill. One afternoon he was struck down quite suddenly. The disease was what is known in America as a congestive chill. He remained very ill for several weeks, and his life was in serious danger. He had two of these chills, and he never quite recovered from the effects of them.

During this illness his daughter Minnie and her little son were staying in the house. She had come on from Louisville, Kentucky, where she was then living, shortly before her father was taken ill. While his illness was at its worst, he could not bear strange voices anywhere near him. His daughter once asked him if he would not wish her to move with her little son to a room further off from his, so that he might be more free from disturbance. He at once answered, " No, no ; your voices are like the voices of nature to me, and never disturb me." When he began to get better, he would often call the little boy to his bedside to talk to him.

He recovered slowly, and when the spring came he was able to be out again. It was in this spring of 1874 that he moved back to Brooklyn from New York. He took a house on Clinton Avenue, and this continued to be his home until his death. I say his home, because his family resided there ; he himself was absent for part of the time during his visits to Ireland. In these frequent changes of residence during his later years, we see the working of that spirit of restlesness which always pursued him from the time he was banished from the one country which he always regarded as his true and natural home. While the move to Brooklyn was in progress, he went to stay with his friend Dr. William Carroll, of Philadelphia, so as to be out of the noise and confusion of the moving. A little later he paid short visits to Richmond and Washington.

During these years he always had a map of Ireland hanging on the wall near his desk. He would often stand before this map, sometimes for half an hour at a time, " twirling his lock," and going over it from top to bottom and side to side. The longing to see Ireland once more seemed to grow stronger with him as he felt himself growing physically weaker. Ever since his severe illness of the winter, he had thought of paying a visit to his friends in Ireland. There was some difference of opinion amongst his friends as to whether it would be safe for him to do so. Many thought he would be sure to be arrested ; but Mitchel himself was confident that, so long as he did not interfere in politics, he would not be molested. In the summer of 1874, he decided to go.

He started in July, and took with him his daughter Isabel. They were accompanied by Dr. Carroll, of Philadelphia, a valued friend of Mitchel's. Dr. Carroll's medical skill made his companionship very useful, if not necessary, to Mitchel in his then state of health.

He had not seen Ireland for twenty-six years. When he first caught sight of the Irish coast he was powerfully affected. He landed at Queenstown, and spent a few days at Cork. While in the southern city, he stayed at the pleasant house of Mr. George Barry, in Sunday's Well, who, with his hospitable wife, treated him with the utmost kindness and tender solicitude. He was visited by several old friends. Amongst these, one whose visit gave him much pleasure was a sister of Mr. John Martin's, then living with her husband in Cork. In a letter to her brother, this lady gives an account of her visit. The letter is dated July 27, 1874 :—

" I have just seen John Mitchel. He and I gazed at each other for a moment or two without recognition ; but I had my friend perfect—the old man—the moment he spoke.

He was so glad to see me, and so kind. He is splendid still; there is any amount of life in him. It is said that he is broken down by the journey; but he is vastly better of it, and has no look of sickness or delicacy. . . . He does not want any bonfires or speeches. M—— said, 'That is right; I am glad you are learning common sense.' Then we talked about M—— being connected with the godless college; and Mitchel said, 'And quite right, for, as you have just remarked on my want of common sense, I am bound to state that you never had any religion that would hurt anybody." And he looked out of the window to admire both her Majesty's college and her Majesty's gaol. But he 'does not want any connection with either of them.' I cannot express to you the vast pleasure it was to M—— and to me to see him, and the feeling of proud satisfaction that we both had that he looked on us as friends, and received us so kindly."

From Cork Mitchel went direct to the North to visit his relations there. He stayed first with his sister Margaret (Mrs. Irvine), at Dromalane, close to Newry, where his father had lived. Every hill and valley and stream in the country round Newry was familiar to him; and as he was driven round to places where he had wandered on foot as a schoolboy, his eyes would brighten with the light of memory. Of all the various countries and scenes he had visited since his exile, none seemed to him fit to compare to the country around the little town in which he had spent his boyhood. The following account of the impression he made upon his friends during this visit has been supplied to me by a near relative :—

"The next time I saw him was on his short visit to Ireland in 1874. He was much broken. He had, in fact, never recovered from the effect of the severe imprisonment of eight years before. He was still, indeed, erect and light of foot; but he could no longer endure prolonged exertion either of mind or body. A symptom of declining vigour was that he, who never could abide cards, now liked his game of whist, and, I may add, played it badly. Nevertheless, this visit gave him intense pleasure, although few of his old friends were left, and his old enemy, asthma, seized the opportunity to attack him again. I shall never forget the expression of sorrow on his face when we had bid him good-bye on the deck of the *Idaho* at Queenstown, and he was searching near-sightedly and vainly for us among the crowd on the deck of the tender in the full belief that he would never see us or Ireland more."

From Newry he went to visit his sister Matilda, at Tullycairne, near Dromore. Thence to Belfast, where he spent a few days at the house of some old friends. From Belfast he went back to Newry, and again spent a few days at Dromalane. During this second visit to Newry he, for the first time, wrote his wife some account of his proceedings. The letter is dated September 3, 1874 :—

This is the first moment since I left Brooklyn that I put pen to paper—have not even answered a single letter, though I received many from old friends and members of Parliament, etc. I knew well enough that Isabel was keeping you informed about our movements, and about the people we met since our arrival in Cork. So I have little to tell. Yesterday the two Dillons came here to visit me—us, I should say—very fine young men.

To-day I go down to dine with Maxwell Simpson, at Warrenpoint—a gentleman's party. Monday, we go on to Dublin. Mary goes with us ; and we calculate on staying there two weeks. After that, my mission in Ireland will have been accomplished—finished. And nothing that I know of will then prevent a speedy return to America, probably by way of Cork, which would spare us the wild British Channel. But I am not yet sure that during that fortnight in Dublin something might not arise that would require me to prolong my stay in Ireland. . . . In short, I do not choose, under present circumstances, to put in my oar into the puddle of Irish politics.   No duty calls me, and I have no pretext, no recognized position at all ; so that good taste and a sense of plain propriety, restrain me from saying a word for the public.   If, by some accident, an opening should be made for me, to stand for the representation of some county or borough, then, indeed, I would " sail in," and you might well pray for me.   In such a contingency, which is, however, unlikely, I would probably telegraph for James to come over, as I might have need of him.   Don't let him stir, however, unless I expressly ask him ; because, if he did start un-advisedly, he would very probably meet me in mid-ocean.

On the same day he also wrote to Mr. P. J. Smyth. Mr. Smyth, the reader will remember, had taken the main part in aiding Mitchel's escape from Van Diemen's Land. He was now living in Ireland, and had made himself con-spicuous by opposing the Home Rule scheme of Mr. Butt, and advocating "Simple Repeal."   To him Mitchel writes :—

This is the first moment since I left Brooklyn that I put pen to paper.   A few minutes ago, I wrote my first letter to my wife since I left Brooklyn, though, as to that, my daughter Isabel, whom you remember as " Rixy," has kept our people duly informed of all our movements since our arrival in Cork.   We are going to Dublin on Monday next to stay two weeks in lodgings, declining invitations, especially a very pressing invitation from A. M. Sullivan to stay at his house.   I will be the guest of no " Home Ruler " in Dublin—not even with John Martin.   In fact, I am savage against that helpless, driftless concern called " Home Rule," and nearly as vicious against your "Simple Repeal."   But if I were under any obligation (which I am not) to put in my oar at all into the puddle of Irish politics, I would rather—as I have told John Martin—pull in your boat than in his and Butt's.   About all this I hope to have an early opportunity of talking with you face to face.   It is one of the things I have looked forward to with pleasure in my visit to Ireland.

A few days after these letters were written, he went to Dublin.   He took lodgings in Holles Street, and stayed in Dublin several weeks.   Mr. and Mrs. John Martin and

Miss Mary Mitchel were in Dublin during this time. Of Mitchel's old friends of '48 and previous years, many were dead. Of those who were still left, many called on him. He enjoyed these visits much. There were also drives to various objects of interest in and around Dublin ; for his daughter Isabel had never been in Ireland before, and had to be shown everything there was to see. As a rule, Mitchel declined invitations to dine out, on account of the weak state of his health. But a few such invitations he accepted. He used afterwards to speak of a pleasant dinner at Lady Wilde's ("Speranza" of the *Nation*) at which he and his daughter were present, and where they met Father Thomas Burke, the celebrated Dominican.

From Dublin Mitchel went to Killarney. He had with him his daughter, his brother, his sister Mary, and several other relatives. From Killarney the party returned to Cork, where Mitchel spent a few days at Mr. Ronayne's house. Then he embarked for America on the *Idaho*, the same ship on which he had come.

He arrived in Brooklyn in October, about three months from the time of his leaving for Ireland. He had suffered a good deal from asthma during part of the time in Ireland ; but the pleasure of seeing old friends and old places joined with the voyages by sea, had done him good. When he returned home, he seemed to his wife and family to be in better health than when he left. But the improvement did not last long. He was very delicate during the winter of 1874–75 ; suffered much from cough and loss of appetite. While he was in Ireland the previous autumn, he had been asked whether he would stand for one of the counties if a vacancy occurred. He answered that he would, provided it were distinctly understood that he would under no circumstances consent to enter the English House of Commons. He left an election address to be published

in the Dublin *Nation* in case a vacancy should occur, and
that he should be nominated.   He promised that he would
hold himself ready at any moment to return to Ireland in
case he was selected by a constituency.   It was early in
February, 1875, that the summons came.   About a month
previously he had arranged for a lecturing tour.   At the
end of the year 1874, he writes to his daughter Minnie, then
living at Louisville :—

I am bound for a *traik*, going to Montreal, in Canada, for the
5th of January ; then to Chicago, Milwaukee (where I shall see
the health officer) ; then to St. Louis ; and by the 25th of January
I expect to see you all at *Louisville*.   John will point me out all
the peculiarities of the Ohio steamboats, and the peculiar construction of the pump handles.

I am writing to Mr. McAteer, who can set people to work to
organize a lecture for me on or about that day.   You and Roger
and John Page are to have complimentary tickets, and in fact
that lecture is to be John's benefit.

Owing to a sharp attack of illness which prostrated
Mitchel for several weeks, the projected tour did not come
off, and he was still at Brooklyn when the cablegram came
announcing the vacancy in Tipperary.   On the 6th of
February, he writes from Brooklyn, to his daughter Minnie.
The tone of this letter is unusually affectionate.   He seems
to have had a presentiment that he was never to see his
daughter again.   I give the letter in full, as I find it :—

MY DEAR AND DARLING LITTLE DAUGHTER MINNIE.

Instead of seeing you all at Louisville, as I had
hoped, behold I sail to-day at three o'clock for Cork, being summoned by an ocean telegram (which I last year undertook to
attend to), to go and stand for Tipperary County, now vacant.
What is more strange still, James goes with me.   He would not
let me start without him, although it involves the abandonment
of his position in the Photo-Litog., not very eminent or lucrative
position, indeed, but something.

You will be sure to hear how things fare with me. It is quite possible that James and I may return within three months.

Your mother and Isabel will be two lonely birds for that time. It is a great disappointment to me to have missed the chance of visiting your household in Kentucky. But, *que voulez-vous ?* We cannot always (especially poor people) arrange everything just to suit us.

Best regards to Roger, and to that *enfant terrible*, John Page. If you should write to me, address to *Nation* Office, Dublin, Ireland.

And so, darling Minnie, adieu.

At three o'clock on the evening of February 6, 1875, John Mitchel sailed for Ireland for the last time. He never returned to America. He was accompanied this time by his son James. When the cablegram came calling him to Ireland, Mrs. Mitchel desired to go with him ; and she was the more anxious to do this because of the extremely feeble state of his health. But he thought that, in such work as he had before him in Ireland, James would be more useful to him. So Mrs. Mitchel stayed behind with her daughter Isabel. She afterwards regretted very much that she had not gone with her husband. It seemed hard that after following him all round the world, and standing by his side through all his fortunes, good and bad, she should be far away from him when the end came.

The vacancy in Tipperary came about in this way. About a year previous to the period we have now reached— that is, at the beginning of 1874—there had been an election in Tipperary, at which Colonel White and Mr. Wilfred O'Callaghan were the Liberal candidates. Mitchel was then put in nomination ; but the supporters of White and O'Callaghan had recourse to the device of warning the people, just before the election came off, that it was useless to vote for Mitchel ; that votes for him would be votes thrown away—would not, in fact, be even counted. As there was not time to remove the impression created, the trick was successful, and Mitchel was defeated by a large majority.   Early in 1875, from some cause or other—ill-health, I believe—Colonel White resigned his seat.   Mitchel's friends at once decided to start him again, and cabled for him to come over.   The first public intimation of the intention to start Mitchel as a candidate was contained in a letter written by John Martin to Mr. C. J. Kickham, and published in the Irish papers at the beginning of February, 1875.   In this letter Mr. Martin wrote :—

"I am authorized to state that John Mitchel is a candidate on this occasion, and that he will immediately come to Ireland and present himself before the electors of Tipperary.   I am myself a member of the Home Rule party, elected by the constituency of Meath as an advocate of the Home Rule scheme and policy, convinced of the goodness and wisdom of that scheme and policy, and glad that the great mass of the Nationalists of Ireland have given their adhesion to that scheme and policy.   I am loyal to my party, and sincerely attached to the Home Rule doctrine.   On the other hand, Mr. Mitchel, in his lecture delivered at New York in December last, while declaring that he considers it impracticable by any peaceful movement to induce England to consent to a just and honourable settlement of her national quarrel with Ireland, judges the Home Rule movement in particular and the policy of the Home Rule party in a spirit that seems to me neither impartial nor friendly.   Nevertheless, it is my earnest wish and hope that John Mitchel may be chosen by the Tipperary electors for their parliamentary representative.   No living Irishman better deserves the highest political honour that his country can bestow.   Let Tipperary elect John Mitchel unquestioned, unpledged, and trust to him to do what he may deem right and best for the cause of Tipperary

and of Ireland. Whatever course of conduct he may adopt
as an Irish parliamentary representative, the national dignity
of our country will not suffer in his hands ; and, in my
judgment, the Home Rule movement will not suffer, but
will prosper and advance all the more."

Immediately after writing this letter, Mr. Martin sent
to the papers for publication a copy of the address which
Mitchel had left behind him on the occasion of his visit to
Ireland in the previous year. It was as follows :—

I solicit the high honour of being elected as your representative.

I am in favour of Home Rule—that is, the sovereign independence of Ireland.

I shall seek the total overthrow of the Established Church,
universal tenant-right, and abolition of ejectments ; free education
—that is, denominational education for those who like it, secular
education for those who like that, with the express organic pro-
vision of law, that no person shall be taxed for the education of
other persons' children.

I am in favour of the immediate liberation of those prisoners
of state whom the English Government keeps in prison as
" Fenians."

Lastly, as well as firstly, I am for *Home Rule.*

Electors of Tipperary ! many of you, as I hope, know me by
name and reputation. If you believe that all the strength and
energy now left in me would be faithfully, and perhaps usefully,
dedicated to the service of our native country, then give me your
suffrages, and believe that the honour of Tipperary will not suffer
in my hands.

I shall immediately present myself to you in person, and ask
Tipperary to confer upon me the highest honour that I can even
conceive awarded to mortal man—that of being the representative
of the premier county.

It was just three days after the first publication of
this address that the author of it sailed from New York.
Nothing worthy of note occurred on the voyage. At two
o'clock on the morning of the 17th of February John

Mitchel landed at Queenstown. He was met on the steamer by a few friends and members of his committee, who greeted him as member for Tipperary.

The nomination for Tipperary had taken place on the 16th of February. John Mitchel, described as "of 505, Clinton Avenue, Brooklyn, United States of America," was the only candidate nominated, and he was accordingly declared duly elected. On the evening of the day upon which the election took place, Mr. Disraeli, the then Prime Minister of England, rose in his place in the House of Commons, and gave notice that upon the 18th of February he would move a resolution to the following effect :—

"That John Mitchel, returned as member for the county of Tipperary, having been adjudged guilty of felony, and sentenced to transportation for fourteen years, and not having endured the punishment to which he was adjudged or received a pardon under the Great Seal, has become and continues to be incapable of being elected or returned as a member of this House ; that Mr. Speaker do issue his warrant to the Clerk of the Crown in Ireland to make out a new writ for the election of a representative in the present parliament for the said county in the room of John Mitchel, adjudged and sentenced as aforesaid."

At the same time certain papers regarding Mitchel's conviction and escape from Van Diemen's Land were moved for by one of the Government officials. There was a debate, in which Mr. A. M. Sullivan and Mr. John Martin both took part ; but, as a matter of course, the papers asked for were granted by an overwhelming majority.

The news of the Government proceedings were communicated to Mitchel at the same time as the news of his election. He took it all very quietly, and did not seem particularly surprised at either piece of news. He was very much exhausted when he landed, but he was anxious,

at the earliest possible moment, to redeem his promise of
presenting himself in person before the electors. After a
rest of only a few hours in Cork, he started for Tipperary
at half-past twelve o'clock. He was accompanied by his
sister, Mrs. John Martin, Mr. P. J. Smyth, M.P., Mr. C. G.
Doran, Mr. George Barry, Mr. John Dillon, and other
friends. At all the principal stations along the way crowds
had assembled, and there was much cheering as the train
passed through. At the Limerick junction, an immense
concourse of people were assembled, with bands and banners
to escort the new member from the junction into the town
of Tipperary. At Tipperary, John Mitchel made what
may fairly be called his last public speech. Some hours
later he spoke a few words to the people at Clonmel ; and
some ten days later he again spoke a few words at Cork to
the audience who had come to hear him lecture. But,
practically speaking, it was at Tipperary that he made his
last public speech. He was extremely weak—hardly able
to stand up while he spoke. But the spirit within was still
unconquered. I give the speech—interruptions and all—
as I find it in the newspapers of the day :—

Men of Tipperary, it is true that I have come over more than
three thousand miles of this globe's surface to the people of
Tipperary to get returned by them to Parliament (loud cheers).
It was nothing to come three thousand miles to receive such an
honour as I have received this day, and especially such a distinguished honour as I received yesterday (cheers). I would
have come from the North Pole for it (cheers and laughter). It
makes it the more impressive upon me that I have not even the
honour to be a Tipperary man. I have the honour to belong to
Down, but I suppose Down is as Irish as Tipperary (cheers). At
any rate I am an Irishman (loud cheering).

A voice—The first Irishman living.

Mr. Mitchel—I am an Irishman, and I think you all seem to
acknowledge that (cheers and laughter). My friend, Mr. Doran,

has alluded to some steps he thinks the Government are about to take—that is, the British Government over in London (laughter). There is a man over there in London who writes novels (laughter), and he is of opinion that he knows better who Tipperary should elect than you do—that is his opinion (great laughter).

A voice—He lies.

Mr. Mitchel—Now, if Tipperary is to submit to the dictation of this novel-writer, why, the next thing will be Cork, and then he will go to Limerick, and will make them all select for their representatives such men as he shall approve of.

A voice—Limerick is not rotten, sir.

Mr. Mitchel—No, I think not. Men of Tipperary, some years ago the British Government selected me as a fit subject to carry a felon's chain, and to bear the penalties of felony at the antipodes. And now, when I have returned here, you, the people of Tipperary, have thought me the very person worthy of being your representative at her Majesty's counsels, to offer her Majesty's ministers and advisers the best and all my information and talents to help them to govern a free country (laughter). I am now going to help the English, the Scotch, and the Welsh to govern their own countries as well as to govern this country. It seems they cannot do it without us (laughter); and I have only this much further to say to you—you have had little experience of me yet. You have only heard or read of me. Well, there is one thing I wish to state to you, and it is—that as long as I have the honour of representing you I will not sell you (cheers). I will not trade upon you in any shape or form. The efforts and sacrifices the people of Tipperary have made in putting me in the very proud position I hold to-day—these efforts and sacrifices I will not trade or traffic upon (loud cheers). I will not be found haunting the doors of ministers, pressing them to give little offices and places to my constituents, or the relations of my constituents (cheers). I am not going to say to his lordship, the Premier, or the Secretary of State, "Now, in my district of so-and-so there is a very eminent and influential constituent; he has a little estate, and it will gratify him to be made a J.P; or he has a cousin or brother-in-law who would like a good office—inspector of police, say" (laughter). "Now," I should continue, "you will gratify me and maintain me in my county, barony, or parish, and we will

maintain you and your administration " (cheers).   That is a fair
bargain.   Now, I suppose a great many of you know that is the
sort of bargain and traffic made every day in London (hisses).
I hope the days of that base trade are nearly at an end.   I think
there is a better class of representatives now going over to London
than we used to have (cheers).   I did not say, recollect, that I
am ever going to London at all.   I didn't promise to go to London.
I have not pledged myself to that effect ; but whether I go to
London or stop here at home, I think Tipperary may be very
sure I will never bring disgrace upon her (enthusiastic cheering).

From Tipperary, Mitchel and his party went on to
Clonmel.   Here he was again received with the wildest
enthusiasm.   He tried to speak again, but was only able
to say a few words.   He remained in Clonmel that night,
and the next morning he was very prostrate.   By the
advice of his friends, he decided to relinquish for the present
his intention of visiting all the principal towns of Tipperary.
He returned to Cork on Thursday, February 18, and went
to stay with his friend Mr. George Barry at Sunday's
Well.   His intention was to rest for a few days, and then
to return to Tipperary and see more of his constituents.
This intention, however, he was never destined to carry
into effect.

On the evening of Mitchel's return to Cork, occurred
the debate on the Prime Minister's resolution in the House
of Commons.   Several leading English lawyers joined the
Irish Home Rule members in opposing the resolution.
The argument against the resolution went upon two distinct
grounds.   In the first place, it was urged that a statute had
recently been passed handing over all questions regarding
the validity of elections to the judges, and depriving the
House of Commons of all jurisdiction over such questions.
It was now proposed, by a resolution of the House of
Commons, to declare an election void upon certain grounds ;
that is to say, it was proposed, by a resolution of one

branch of the legislature, to repeal, *pro hac vice*, an Act of Parliament. Suppose that a petition were presented under the statute to test the validity of the election before the law courts, and that the judges differed from the House of Commons, what then ? In the second place, it was urged that, inasmuch as the term of Mitchel's sentence had admittedly expired, the question of his disqualification by reason of that sentence was a question of great doubt and difficulty. The House of Commons, even if they had the jurisdiction, ought not to take it upon themselves to decide a difficult legal question, involving a constitutional right of the first importance, after a short and heated debate, and without making even a pretence of deciding the matter upon legal, as distinguished from political grounds. These arguments would undoubtedly have carried weight had the return been from an English instead of from an Irish constituency. But in this case the House of Commons had to deal with an Irish constituency and an Irish court. The one could be coerced, if need be ; the other was pretty sure to prove subservient. The minister had a majority, and, as a matter of course, the resolution passed. The election was declared void, and a new writ was ordered to be issued. The writ issued on the 20th of February. The 4th of March was fixed for the nomination, and the 11th of March for the polling.

Meantime, John Mitchel was staying at Sunday's Well, near Cork, keeping as quiet and taking as much rest as the circumstances would admit of. But he did not gain strength. The prostration he was suffering under was not merely any temporary result of over-exertion or excitement ; it was, in truth, a final prostration of vital energy, a gradual ebbing away of life.

Mitchel's friends in Tipperary decided at once to start him again. Mitchel issued a very brief address, stating his intention to stand as often as he was unseated. The issue was now a simple one. Which had the right to choose the member for Tipperary—the electors of Tipperary or the members of the House of Commons? Tipperary was not disposed to surrender without a struggle.

It was arranged that Mitchel should deliver a lecture in the Theatre Royal, at Cork, on the evening of the 26th of February. When the evening came, the theatre was crowded to the doors, but the lecturer did not appear at the appointed hour. A deputation went out to Mr. George Barry's house at Sunday's Well to seek him. They found Mr. Mitchel very unwell and in a very prostrate state. He made a great effort, and accompanied them to the theatre. In response to repeated calls he spoke a few words to the people, but was quite unable to read his lecture. He requested his friend, Mr. John Dillon, to read the lecture for him ; and, after sitting on the stage for a few minutes, he became so very unwell that he was obliged to leave.

The lecture opened with some general remarks about the election, and the conduct of the Government in reference thereto. He then referred to Mr. Disraeli's charge against him of parole-breaking. In answer to that he simply recalled the circumstances of his escape as told in his "Journal," and the opinions of his companions, especially of Mr. Smith O'Brien, upon the point of honour. He did not condescend to make any further defence. Upon the question of the lesson to be derived from the Tipperary election, he said :—

The first and greatest good which I see in that election is, that it was a magnificent pronouncement in favour of the national right of Ireland, and against the usurpation of the British parliament. The people of Tipperary elected me as the most implacable enemy of the British tyranny.

*　　*　　*　　*　　*　　*　　*

One would suppose that no one in the whole world who read of that election could possibly mistake its meaning. Surely no one takes me for a man well affected to the English Government. In offering myself to the electors of Tipperary I had nothing to go on but my past life, and I take it that the chief fact about my past life which recommended me to the people of Tipperary was that I had made no peace with England.

* * * * * * *

I have one thing more to say now, with regard to the bearing of this election on the Home Rule movement. If there be any virtue at all in that movement—if it be really pregnant with any good at all for Ireland—the Tipperary election will greatly assist that movement; it will strengthen the hands of Home Rulers by demonstrating that behind them there exists a great mass of desperate and irreconcilable disaffection. If British ministers were to yield one iota of the Home Rule demand, they will do so in the fear that their persistent refusal would strengthen and increase that desperate disaffection which the Tipperary election has once more brought prominently before the world. My political mission in regard to the Tipperary election is nearly ended. I wanted to offer to the gallant people of that county one more opportunity of telling the whole world what value they set on the verdicts of packed juries, what respect they have for the decision of the judges whom England hires to do her work in this country.

On the same night upon which this lecture incident occurred, there was another Mitchel debate in the House of Commons. Mr. John Martin moved for papers regarding Mitchel's trial and conviction, with the object of exposing the methods by which the conviction had been obtained. He made a very able speech, and gave that account of the packing of Mitchel's jury which has been already quoted in this life. He was supported by Mr. A. M. Sullivan and by Mr. P. J. Smyth, who confined himself mainly to a vindication of Mitchel against the charge of parole-breaking. When the discussion closed, Mr. Martin, knowing that his motion had no chance of passing, withdrew it.

Mitchel remained in Cork until the 9th of March. During all this time he stayed at Mr. George Barry's house. He was visited by a few friends, but he kept as quiet as possible. His intention still was, so soon as he felt a little stronger, to go amongst his constituents in Tipperary. But he did not recover strength. In fact, as already stated, his strength was ebbing away from him. When it became clear to him that he must abandon his intention of visiting Tipperary, he began to be uneasy, and to express a desire to visit his old home at Newry. It may well be that he suspected the end was near, and that—

> " He still had hopes, his long vexations past,
>   There to return, and die at home at last."

On Tuesday, the 9th of March, he left Cork, accompanied by his sister, Mrs. John Martin, and travelled to Dublin. His intended coming to Dublin was kept a secret, so that there might be no demonstration. He was met at the King's Bridge by Mr. and Mrs. A. M. Sullivan. He drove straight from the terminus to Mr. Sullivan's residence in North Great George's Street. Three or four detectives were on the platform at the station, and two of them mounted a side car and drove after Mr. Mitchel along the quays. During the period of his stay with Mr. Sullivan, the house was closely watched.

He remained at Mr. Sullivan's house until the afternoon of the 11th of March, when he left for Newry, still accompanied by his sister. During this brief stay in Dublin he was visited by quite a number of friends ; and, even in his then exhausted state, he took great pleasure in talking with the survivors of those he had known in Young Ireland days.

The day upon which Mitchel returned to his old home at Newry was the day of the polling in Tipperary. He arrived at Dromalane in the evening, looking very haggard and worn. The sight of the old place and of his brother and sisters seemed to revive him. He sat up and chatted in quite an animated manner until it was time to go to bed After that evening he was never downstairs again.

On the following day, the 12th of March, came a telegram announcing the result in Tipperary. At the last moment the Tories had nominated a candidate against Mitchel. Their choice fell upon Mr. Stephen Moore, a country gentleman in Tipperary. Previous to the polling, notices were posted over the county warning the electors that Mr. Mitchel was disqualified. The object of this was to lay a ground for claiming the seat for Mr. Moore on petition, in accordance with certain decisions then recently rendered by election judges. The gentlemen on Mr. Mitchel's committee worked hard to make up for his unavoidable absence. When the poll was announced, it was found that Mitchel had 3114 votes, and Moore 746. The people had not yet become accustomed to voting by ballot, and nearly 500 of Mitchel's votes were rejected. So that, if every elector who meant to vote for him were counted, his majority was not far from 3000.

This was a sufficiently decisive answer on the part of the Tipperary electors to the resolution of the House of Commons. The next question was, What was the House of Commons going to do about it? If the course of voiding election by resolution was really constitutional and within their power, then why not repeat the process and void the election again? But it was plain that ministers themselves were not over-confident of the legality of the course they had taken. On this second occasion, they did not repeat the resolution experiment. They decided to allow the matter to be tried out in the law courts in the regular way. A petition was presented to the proper court, praying that the election of John Mitchel might be declared void, and the seat given to Mr. Moore.

Meantime, John Mitchel, at Newry, was getting weaker every day. For a day or two after the news of his victory arrived he sat up a little while by the fire in his bedroom every day. He was much gratified on hearing of the majority, which was larger than he had been led to expect. Some three or four days after his arrival in Newry he ceased to even sit up in his bedroom ; and for nearly a week before his death he was confined to bed.

From letters received after the election, he learned that some of his constituents were dissatisfied with his policy of not going to Parliament. The need of justifying his action in that respect, as well as the need of thanking the electors for the honour conferred upon him, induced him to attempt to compose an address. It was on the 17th of March, just three days before his death, that he made this effort. After writing a few sentences himself, he handed the pen to his brother, and dictated the rest, until he came within a sentence or two of the end, when he turned to his brother, and said, "You must finish it for me. I can do no more."

This address is dated Newry, March 17, 1875. It commences by thanking the electors and referring to the largeness of the majority. It then proceeds :—

Then at once arose the question for me—Having been honoured with this high responsibility, what am I do with it ? Not that I laboured under any doubt or perplexity on that subject. I thought that there was no man in Tipperary, or in Ireland, who really supposed that I was going to creep up to the bar of the House of Commons and crave permission to take oaths and my seat, or that I would appear, cap in hand, before Monahan and Keogh and the other election judges, to defend my election against a petition by a Mr. Moore. In short, I concluded that all was already done. All that was possible for the Tipperary franchise or Tipperary freeholders to accomplish was already done.

＊　　＊　　＊　　＊　　＊　　　　＊

Your county has used her franchise in the very best manner possible—that is, in making a desperate protest against the whole system of pretended parliamentary government in Ireland. If, nevertheless, any friend of mine in Tipperary thinks he has reason to be surprised at my manner of meeting the present emergency, or that I have ever, at any time or in any manner, led him or others to suppose that I should act otherwise than I am doing, I can only refer him to my whole past political career, and to all my published writings and speeches, so far as they relate to this subject of Irish representation in the English House of Commons. More particularly, I refer him to the lecture I delivered in New York on my return from Ireland last summer—a lecture which was reprinted in almost all the Irish journals, and which was intended rather as a manifesto to the Irish in Ireland than as an address to the people of New York.

He then proceeds to quote a passage from the lecture here referred to, in which he had expressly stated that, if returned for an Irish constituency, he would never go to the London Parliament.

The address just quoted was the last thing Mitchel ever wrote or dictated. There was no specific disease, and seemingly no suffering; only extreme prostration. His native gaiety remained with him to the end. I have been told by one who was with him at this time that his mood, which was always sweet and pleasant to his familiars, was peculiarly so during these last few days. He did not seem to be uneasy or troubled about his family in America, though he often spoke of them. When the news of the second election in Tipperary reached him, he said, " How pleased Jenny will be to hear all this; how pleased my poor wife will be ! " After he gave up the idea of going amongst the people in Tipperary, he became anxious that his son James should return to his mother. He said that he would return himself as soon as he got a little stronger. James did go back, at his father's request, and it was on landing at New York that he heard of his father's death.

Whether John Mitchel knew he was dying, it is impossible to say. The idea of death certainly did not seem to trouble him. Once he said to his brother, "Am I dying, William—for that would be a serious business for me?" But he did not pursue the subject any further. On the morning of the 20th of March, William Mitchel was sitting at his brother's bedside. They were talking about some matter, and John observed, "I feel better this morning; I think I will rise soon." It was the "lightning before death." Almost immediately after he had said it, he fell into a doze. As William sat by the bedside watching his brother sleep, he noticed a sudden change in his breathing, and a peculiar expression on his features. William, guessing that the end was at hand, summoned the other members of the family. In a few minutes more, John Mitchel had ceased to breathe. There was no pain and no struggle; not even an awakening from sleep. It was impossible to tell the moment at which the end actually came. It was a gradual and imperceptible passing from sleep to sleep's twin-brother —death.

From an account of the closing scene written for me by one of those who stood by the bedside, I take the following sentences: "Unlike many deathbeds, there was nothing one would wish to forget. There was no physical suffering, neither was there mental obscuration, and the charm of his presence was undiminished. His colour was fresh, and his eye bright; his face lost the worn look it had in late years, and I thought it beautiful."

A day or so before his death a cable message was sent to Mrs. Mitchel, saying they thought he was sinking. Mrs. Mitchel had her preparations made, and was just about to start for Ireland, when she received a second message saying that her husband was dead.

Excepting Mitchel's own relations, the only person

present at the death scene was John Dillon, son of the John Dillon whom Mitchel had known in the Young Ireland days, and afterwards in America. Mr. Dillon stood by the bed as John Mitchel drew his last breath.

They buried him in the Unitarian cemetery—called the "Old Meeting-house Green"—in the High Street of Newry. He was placed in the same tomb with his father and mother. There was a monument to his father already there; and beside this there now stands a simple granite monument in memory of John Mitchel, placed there by his widow.

John Martin was amongst those who stood by the grave as the funeral service was read. Mr. William Mitchel, on whose arm he leaned, felt him lean more heavily as the service proceeded. When it was over, he grew faint, and had to be lifted into the carriage. He seemed not to wish to live after he had looked on the dead face of his lifelong friend. Within a week he too died, in the same house in which his friend had died—the old home where, as boys, they had spent so much time together. Of the friendship of these two, I have already spoken.

In connection with the death of John Mitchel, there were two circumstances worthy of special note. Firstly, he died, and came a long way to die, in the old home of his boyhood; and, secondly, he died almost in the hour of victory, a few days only after he had received the highest honour which his countrymen had it in their power to bestow upon him.

There is no need for me here to discuss the question whether or not Mitchel's policy would have been approved by the Tipperary electors. He had told them clearly beforehand that he would not go to Parliament, and they had elected him. And whether they agreed with him or not, they did rightly. He was the greatest Irishman of his generation. Love of Ireland was his leading passion, and to her cause he had devoted his splendid gifts, and sacrificed everything that men hold most precious. England had passed a special law in her Parliament, and had elaborately packed a jury from his bitterest enemies, in order to have him declared a felon. It was fitting that his countrymen should say in the clearest manner what they thought of this proceeding, and what value they set upon the verdict of the packed jury. Before it was too late, and while he was yet alive to appreciate the honour, Tipperary spoke, and spoke in a manner not to be mistaken. She asked no explanations as to opinions of policy. Speaking on behalf of Ireland, the men of Tipperary said to John Mitchel, the convicted felon, "You shall have the highest honour that it is in our power to bestow upon you, and that simply because you, more than any living Irishman, have merited well of your country."

Two days after John Mitchel's death, John Martin wrote to his sister a letter, in which he said much about his dead friend. So far as I have been able to ascertain, this was the last letter John Martin ever wrote. I extract from it the following passages :—

" I was told all the circumstances of the poor fellow's last days, which were a perfect piece of all his life, and the most perfect and beautiful conclusion to it. He was himself, even to the little graces and plays of manner, to the very last. He spoke to William in his natural voice, humour, spirit, ten minutes before he expired. He was manifestly happy, satisfied, free of anxiety, unclouded in spirit or intelligence. He probably did not *know* that he was about to die ; but an instinct of the great change appeared in many things he did and said—a winding-up and settlement of what was proper to be wound up and settled. ' With many sighs and stoppages,' he had written me a brief letter, which I received in London on Thursday night. There was the old gaiety, and the old earnestness of heart. He hoped soon to see me ; he had so very much to say to me. He sent his thanks to certain members of Parliament, to each in person, who had spoken out in the House on the national side in his case. The face, as I looked at it last night, had a wondrous beauty, both of features and expression. This morning it has the beauty still, but it seems to me to be of a graver sort, and not the almost smiling grace that beamed on it last night.

"John Mitchel has died well—at home in Ireland, in his father's house, surrounded by his loving brother and sisters and other friends ; after a nobly consistent life, crowned with the affectionate gratitude of the people he loved and served, triumphant in every respect but material force over his enemies."

There were, of course, numerous notices of Mitchel's death in Irish and American papers. All the leading New York papers had articles descriptive of his life and character. The best of these that has come to my notice is that of the *New York Sun*, written, I believe, by Mr. Dana himself, who was a personal friend of Mitchel's. The following passage contains a good summary of some leading points in his character :—

"John Mitchel was a man of extraordinary and noble qualities. He was honest through and through, but not in any sense of mere pecuniary integrity, but in all his opinions, motives, and impulses. There was no tint of falseness about him. While he hated the English Government with a supreme hatred, his detestation of every form of sham was even greater. He not only spoke the truth at all times, but he spoke the whole truth by a kind of moral necessity. He knew no reserve and no disguise, and, we may even say, no prudence in this regard. Beyond all other men, his sincerity was perfect and his courage fearless. He possessed the highest bravery—the bravery which scorns every compromise, and glories in avowing an unpopular conviction. He was always ready to do battle for his ideas, and the odds he never counted. A crust with truth seemed better to him than untold wealth with a compromise. Yet, while he was always armed and ready for fighting, he did not love fighting in itself, and, except for an idea or a sentiment he would not contend. His heart was as kindly and tender as it was sincere, and in friendship he was as true and faithful as in patriotism."

There were also many resolutions of condolence sent to Mrs. Mitchel from public bodies in Ireland and in America. In Ireland there was no public body entitled to speak on behalf of the nation. But many local bodies met and gave expression to their feelings.

There was another country which Mitchel had loved next to Ireland—though a long way after her—and in whose cause he had lost and suffered much. I speak of the State of Virginia. As soon as the news of John Mitchel's death reached Virginia, the governor of the state summoned a meeting of the leading citizens at Richmond. Resolutions were passed expressing admiration of Mitchel's character and life, and, in particular, gratitude for his services to the South. In transmitting these resolutions to Mrs. Mitchel, Governor Kemper wrote of the meeting: "As a tribute of Virginia's admiration, affection, and sympathy, the assemblage and its proceedings were all your own heart could have desired."

There were also meetings in all the states of the Union, north and south. To one of these, held in Memphis, Tennessee, ex-President Davis sent this telegram: "Unable to be with you, I send my heartfelt sympathy in your proposed tribute to the patriot and devotee of liberty, John

Mitchel. Together we struggled for state rights, for the supremacy of the constitution, for community independence, and, after defeat, were imprisoned together. As my friend I mourn for him, and regret his death as a loss to mankind."

I find also a tribute to Mitchel from another very eminent Confederate—perhaps I ought rather to say the most eminent Confederate. In an interview which took place shortly after the war, General Lee is reported to have spoken of John Mitchel as "a powerful and brilliant writer, a scholar of splendid ability, a gallant gentleman, and a tower of strength to the Confederate cause."

This reference on the part of General Lee to Mitchel's scholarship reminds me that I have not, perhaps, said enough upon that head.

I have mentioned in the early part of this book that Mitchel had a university education, and I have spoken of his classical scholarship. In later life he kept up the practice of reading classical—especially Greek—authors. He never had much taste for mathematics, but he studied them while at college, and came off with credit at his mathematical examinations. I cannot say exactly how far he went. In after years his interest in human life was too keen and his sympathy with human passion too strong to allow of his spending much time over the calculus or the theory of equations. Of modern languages the only one— excepting English—that he could speak with fluency was French. Among his favourite French authors were Rabelais, Molière, Beranger, and De Maistre. He could not abide either Lamartine or Victor Hugo. He was fond of reading French aloud to his family, and would at times show keen enjoyment as he came upon some instance of the bright and clever way in which the French are able to present an idea. He was able to read German and Italian, but could not speak either language with any fluency. He

had not much knowledge of German literature, except
German lyric poetry, of which he had read a good deal,
and which he greatly admired. It would be difficult to
give a list of the English authors he had read. He never
read on a system, and he had nothing about him of the
litterateur. When he studied a book, it was almost always
under the influence of some keen interest. It is to this
habit of mind that I attribute the fact of his not having
done as well at college as was expected of him ; and to
the same habit he probably owed, in a large degree, his
marvellous power of remembering what he read. This
faculty I have already spoken of. It was markedly displayed in regard to the Bible. If any one in his presence
began a text and was unable to finish it, he was nearly
always able to supply the missing words and to give the
reference in the Bible. Shakespeare and Scott he also
read constantly all through life. Indeed, his fondness for
Sir Walter seemed to increase rather than to diminish as
he grew older. These, with Swift, Mangan, and Davis,
were lifelong favourites. Other writers he read more or
less at different times of his life. Carlyle, as we have seen,
influenced him powerfully at one period. In later years he
was very fond of Cobbett's books, especially his " History
of the Reformation in England." In early life he read
eagerly poetry of all kinds ; in later life he read mostly
prose, and, with few exceptions, he cared nothing for
modern poetry. He used to say himself that he was
" thoroughly eupeptic in the matter of books," a phrase
which, I believe, he borrowed from Carlyle. He could
keenly enjoy a good book, and could take all the good
there was to be had out of a bad book. He very seldom
made any display of his book knowledge in conversation,
unless when directly appealed to. On one occasion he
was in a company where some question arose regarding

the prose works of Milton. Mitchel listened and said nothing; but when asked by some one in the company whether he had read Milton's prose writings, he answered promptly, " Yes, all of them."

At one time in his life he took a good deal of interest in metaphysical studies, and, as was his habit when interested, he read all he could find on the subject. But from the time of his removal to Dublin, he seems to have lost his interest in metaphysics. Two authors, however, who, I suppose, may fairly be called metaphysical, he always read and always took pleasure in—Plato and Berkeley. He was very fond, in later life, of reading books of travel. In going through the reviews and notices of books to be found in the papers which he conducted in America, one is struck with the number of books of travel. He was never a student of the natural sciences; but he took an interest in these subjects, and read now and then books by leading writers, as he chanced to come across them. He was familiar with most of the writings of Darwin, and had read several of Spencer's books; but the so-called " System of Philosophy " of which Spencer was the most famous exponent, had no attraction for him ; indeed, he would not admit that it was "philosophy" at all, as he understood the term.

John Mitchel was not a musician in the ordinary sense. He had a good ear, and could whistle an air very correctly. But he did not play on any instrument, and he did not sing. Judging, however, from his delight in some of the more perfectly musical verses of Mangan and Ferguson, he must have had " music in his soul." In his youth he could draw very well, but I believe that he had no regular teaching. The members of his family still possess some landscapes drawn by him in pencil and India ink. He had such a vivid perception and memory of form, that he

could draw tolerably correct landscapes and maps from
memory.

So much for educational accomplishments. As to the
other leading traits in Mitchel's character, a good deal has
already been said in the course of this narrative. What
little more I care to say upon that head will be found in
the following extracts. They are taken from reminiscences
supplied to me by a near relative of his, from whom I have
already quoted more than once :—

" What, more than his intellectual gifts, distinguished
John Mitchel, was an indestructible simplicity of character
that resisted all sophistication, and with this an unfading
freshness, as of perpetual youth. He did not grow old.
His experience, and it was both wide and deep, his sorrows,
and they were many, did never daunt his spirit, or cause
him to abate a jot of that which he demanded of the world.
And what he mainly demanded was that things should be
what they purported to be—a simple demand, yet fraught
with conflict. When Nature wove this particular thread into
the web of his being, she settled it that his life was to be
a tragedy, and such indeed it was. Of mere human frailties
he was as tolerant as any man ; but that anything should
set itself up as being what it was not—whether the said
thing clothed itself in ermine or other official trappings, or
walked at noon-day as cant, poisoning the general air—this
moved him to inappeasable wrath. And conventions he
would have none. His *modus vivendi* with the ' solemnly
constituted impostor' was to smite him hip and thigh ;
hence, not unnaturally, a tacit coalition among all such to
extinguish him if possible.

" Part and parcel of his perennially vivid temper was
the high value he set upon personal freedom, freedom not
merely of the body—that, as we know, he could and did
dispense with at times—but of the mind and spirit ; this

was the breath of his nostrils, which he must breathe or die. Nor would he deprive any human being of what he himself prized so highly.   Let a man be what he might, if only he did not encroach or impose, John Mitchel, as Pericles said of the Athenians, would not, by so much as sour looks, molest him or seek to prevent his living *à sa guise*.   His natural element was one of sweetness, friendliness, gay *camaraderie*.   With women, children, with simple, unpretentious persons, he was gentleness itself.   Censure, how severe soever, he would bear patiently, if it went upon grounds; but if there were any attempt to overbear, his manner changed instantly, and he became stern, almost fierce.   At such times his speech was a cutting instrument, and one of the keenest.   Solemn pretenders he treated at all times with a shocking levity.

"He loved Sir Walter Scott.   Of the 'Lay of the Last Minstrel,' in particular, I have heard him speak with such warmth, that the thought occurred to me, whether we might not look for his prototypes in some respects among those Celto-Teutons, the hot and hardy riders of the Scottish border.   The two strains seemed to be always contending in him.   On the one hand, he loved the individual independence, amounting almost to savage isolation, that the Teuton loves; on the other, there was something in the relation of the Celtic clan to its chief, as seen in *Rob Roy*, that went to his heart of hearts."

What is said in this extract regarding the Scottish borderers may be true; but if I were to seek for John Mitchel's prototypes, I think I should go further back in the world's history.   When I speak of his prototypes, however, I am not quite sure that I use the word which best expresses my meaning.   I mean the men who exhibited in the highest degree the virtues which John Mitchel honoured and practised most.   At one period of his life—when he was much disgusted with the doings of the various sects of Christians he came in contact with— Mitchel was fond of calling himself a pagan. Of course this was intended mainly as a joke ; yet there was an element of truth in it withal. The virtues which attracted Mitchel most strongly, and which were most conspicuous in his own character, were precisely those upon which men set most store in the best days of Greece and Rome. In the preface to this book I quoted a saying from a famous Greek historian. There is another historian of ancient Greece, whom most judges would rank even above Herodotus ; and I do not know that I can better close this life than by referring to a celebrated passage in Thucydides. There is not, perhaps, in all literature a more striking tribute to national greatness than the splendid eulogy of the Athenians which Thucydides attributes to their most bitter foes. In the following sentences, taken from the speech I refer to, it would be easy to change the form of expression so as to make it apply to an individual instead of to a nation ; but I prefer to allow the reader to do this for himself :—

"Their bodies they devote to their country, as though they belonged to other men ; their true self is their mind, which is most truly their own when employed in her service. . . . With them alone to hope is to have, for they lose not a moment in the execution of an idea. This is the lifelong task, full of danger and toil, which they are always imposing upon themselves. . . . To do their duty is their only holiday, and they deem the quiet of inaction to be as disagreeable as the most tiresome work. In a word, if a man should say of them that they were born neither to have peace themselves nor to allow peace to other men, he would speak the simple truth."

" Neither to have peace themselves, nor to allow peace

to other men "—this may not at first sight look like the language of praise. Yet I believe I do ample justice to Mitchel's character and work when I ask the reader to take the sentences I have quoted as applicable to him. So long as human nature continues to be what it is in the majority of men, so long as injustice and cant remain as rife in high places as we know they were twenty centuries ago, and as they are to-day, the mission of the best and noblest will always be "neither to have peace themselves nor to allow peace to other men." But note, *only* of the best and noblest, not of ordinary men ; only of those to whom it is given to distinguish between true peace and false peace, between the peace which it is a sin and the peace which it is a duty to disturb. Some friends of John Mitchel's may regret that he did not possess more of the qualities which help men to succeed in life ; that he was so absolutely uncompromising, that he was not more willing to make concessions to the feelings and even to the prejudices of his fellow-men. But to those whose admiration for him is based upon a true perception of what was great in his character, it will always be a source of pride to remember that no defeat and no discouragement could ever induce him to compromise with injustice. The voice within urged him to wage war against oppression and cant in whatsoever places these might be found, and, at the cost of much suffering to himself and to those he loved, he obeyed the promptings of that voice even to the end.

THE END.

PRINTED BY WILLIAM CLOWES AND SONS, LIMITED, LONDON AND BECCLES.

www.ingramcontent.com/pod-product-compliance
Lightning Source LLC
Chambersburg PA
CBHW020951030726
47496CB00005B/1465